Future Schism

Jeff W. Horton

World Castle Publishing, LLC
Pensacola, Florida
Copyright © Jeff W. Horton 2017
Paperback ISBN: 9798891263918
eBook ISBN: 9781629898186
First Edition World Castle Publishing, LLC, November 6, 2017

PROLOGUE

They called it the Great Schism.

Looking back now, I suppose everyone should have seen it coming. After all, the country had gradually become increasingly polarized over the last century into two diametrically opposed groups, each on the extreme ends of the cultural spectrum.

The ideological beliefs that these two groups embraced shifted and fluctuated somewhat over time, but perhaps the underlying difference that set them apart was as old as humanity itself, and it was part of the larger battle for the hearts and minds of humanity that had waged on since the world began. Maybe the conflict between the two groups grew out of the ancient battle between the light and the darkness, between good and evil, between those who served God and those who did not.

Some believe this conflict first began in the Garden of Eden, when Eve was deceived by the serpent and sin first entered the human heart; that it took root when Cain, the first man born to Adam & Eve, murdered his brother Abel, the second man born to them. In time God established the children of Israel as His chosen people, and taught the world His laws and the difference between right and wrong, and gave humanity the opportunity to serve Him. In due time Jesus Christ, the Son of God, came into the world to ultimately save humanity from sin, to restore humanity's relationship with God, and to reveal even greater truths. Since that time man's rebellion against God would claim many victims, as a succession of Roman Emperors sought out and exterminated Christians throughout the empire. Some emperors, like Nero, had Christians set afire to be used as torches in his garden, while small Christian children were wrapped in

3

sheepskins before being sent to their deaths in the arena with ravenous dogs.

Centuries later, following Constantine's embrace of Christianity and the creation of the Holy Roman Empire, the conflict morphed into something new — science versus religion — with the scientific discoveries of men like Copernicus and Galileo that went against Church teachings, leading many to begin questioning their faith in God and His Church.

The battle intensified in the 19th century with the publication of *Origin of the Species* by Charles Darwin, and the now infamous Scopes trial of 1925, and expanded significantly during and following the cultural revolution of the 1960s. Nowhere, however, was the conflict more evident than the battle to legalize abortion, with science on one side of the issue and religion on the other. The issue was resolved legally with the landmark decision by the U.S. Supreme Court known as Roe vs. Wade, which made abortions legal across the United States.

Thus, the age old conflict soon came to be known as The Culture War, a term which basically gave a label to an ancient dilemma. Inside the United States, it was considered by many to be an ideological war between the progressive movement and those who held to more traditional, or conservative ideals.

By the early 1960s the progressive movement, or "liberals," especially the media, had begun infiltrating all areas of government, especially schools, universities, and the judicial branch, affording them the opportunity to have the greatest impact in the shortest timeframe possible. These inroads enabled them to make tremendous progress in their efforts to spread their influence worldwide. The liberal ideology quickly spread like wildfire on college campuses across America, spurred on by like-minded professors who shared the liberal vision of a society free of God and everything that went along with Him.

The traditional, or "conservative," movement was caught off-guard, and was somewhat ill-prepared to deal with the onslaught, though by the 1990s they had started "digging-in" and began mounting a series of short-lived counter attacks, including

The Christian Coalition, Speaker of the House Newt Gingrich's Contract with America, and later the Tea Party.

By the close of the first decade of the new millennium, a new president, elected with the hope of bringing the nation together, had proven to be one of the most divisive presidents in American history, deepening the divisiveness and distrust already in progress by forcing both sides to harden their positions on issues such as legal immigration versus illegal immigration, free trade versus America first, homosexual rights versus traditional marriage, and unlimited tax and spend versus fiscal responsibility.

Throughout most of the 21st century the divide grew deeper and deeper, until eventually someone decided that, in America at least, it might be best if the two competing ideological groups segregated, essentially splitting the country into two equal parts, with the more liberal citizens migrating toward the west coast and the more conservative citizens migrating toward the east coast. Many reasoned that the United States had, after all, been divided nearly 50/50 for over a century anyway; this step only made it official.

On January 21, 2076, a large gathering of activists in San Francisco, California, led by Governor Jose Leto, suddenly declared that the entire liberal movement, now calling itself the People's Liberal Socialist Democratic State, was seceding from the United States and forming its own government. The secession was, of course, considered an act of rebellion, leaving the rest of the country no choice but to respond, leading to the start of the Second Civil War of the United States.

Soon after it began, however, it soon became clear that the outcome of the second war would be considerably different than the first. The PLSDS was losing terribly and was on the verge of annihilation; with the PLSDS too stubborn or too foolhardy to surrender despite abundant devastation and massive casualties, the leadership in Washington, DC eventually decided to end the war in hopes that one day, the two halves would eventually become whole again. The move was widely celebrated, since most people understood that had the war continued much longer, the devastation and death resulting from even a nuke-free war would not have left enough of the PLSDS to rejoin the rest of the country. So, the war ended in a cease fire, and concluded with an eventual peace treaty, which was signed on a Christmas Eve nearly three years after the war began, on December 24, 2079.

The war had taken a very heavy toll, however, and not just on the United States. By the year 2079 global economies had become intricately intertwined and linked, so much so that even countries who had the foresight to see what was coming *before* the secession of the PLSDS had been unable to untangle themselves in time to avert disaster. With the economic and financial infrastructure of the world's largest economy, the United States, in complete collapse and disarray following the Great Schism, country after country soon found themselves following suit. Economy after economy crashed, until the entire global market had collapsed to the point that it would be several decades before it was ever to recover to the point that any meaningful trading could take place again. It was a global disaster of biblical proportions, which left governments, who might otherwise have sought to capitalize on the misfortunes of the United States, so busy trying to hold their own countries together that it offered them little time to cause trouble.

With the PLSDS having left and taken half the country with it, the more conservative citizens of what remained of the United States, coming to grips with the new state of affairs, decided to make a fresh start of it as well, changing the name of what remained of their country to the Free Market Republic of Conservatism.

On that dark day for the world, and what was to become a very sad day for America, after nearly three-hundred years as a nation, the country that rose to become the most powerful nation the world has ever known, the United States of America, was suddenly no more. From then on there would be not one civilization between Canada and Mexico, but *two*, the People's Liberal Socialist Democratic State, commonly referred to as The Blue Zone, and the Free Market Republic of Conservatism, commonly referred to as The Red Zone.

A single nation, once divided by ideology, had split into two distinct provinces now ruled by the respective ideology of each. It was a social experiment that would have ramifications for billions of people the world over for generations to come.

Future Schism Timeline

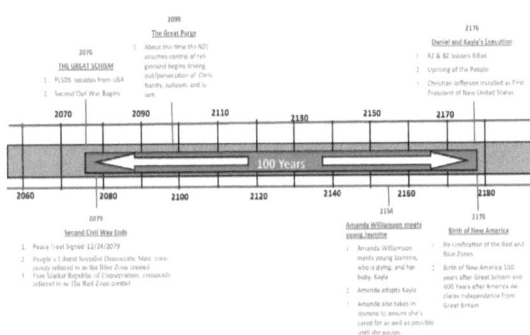

CHAPTER 1

July 1, 2126

The butt of the weapon struck my friend on the side of his head, producing a cracking sound that I could easily hear over the crowd. The blow barely missed his temple, a blow that would likely have killed him. I would have considered it a mercy, given what he'd already been through and what lay ahead of him. Undoubtedly the soldier who'd struck him would have been executed on the spot had the reckless blow prematurely killed the man who had been like a brother to me, the leader of the revolution, and my best friend's husband.

From where I stood watching from across the crowded stadium, I could catch glimpses of his face as he made his way toward the platform, surrounded by soldiers from both camps. The pronounced limp and the repeated tumbles to the pavement, along with the swollen eyes and blood flowing from his nose and mouth, made it evident that he'd been severely beaten and tortured, his captors determined to glean all the information they could about the number of remaining resistance fighters, troop movements, and planned attacks prior to his very public execution.

Eventually my friend cleared the crowd and entered the area surrounding the platform where the security and police forces were, and I was offered a much better view of his face. I sighed heavily, relaxed, and took in a deep breath upon catching a glimpse of the now all-too-familiar look of pure determination, and even a slight grin, on his bloodied, tortured face. I shook my head in amazement, wondering how he was able to keep his composure after the way he'd been treated. I supposed he knew they would have eventually extracted everything they wanted to know, given enough time and torture, but there was a sense of urgency for the Red Council to bring an abrupt end to the revolution, and their inability to break him gave him some measure of victory over his enemies, however slight the victory may have been. At last I had come to understand something that had puzzled me since he'd been chosen to lead the resistance; why Daniel? Watching my friend sneer at his enemies to his left as he approached the steps to the platform, it was clear that it was his strength, his raw courage, and faith that had brought them so far, nearly to the point of toppling not just one government, but two. Daniel truly was a man of great strength and courage.

CHAPTER 2
Twenty-Four Years Earlier

October 21, 2102

The two women sat without speaking in the back of the spacious limousine, with the younger of the two women wearing a lavender dress and a gold necklace that would easily have cost the other more than a year's salary. It would not take a discerning eye to conclude the older woman was likely employed by the younger, and in truth, this was the case, for Helen Jacobski was indeed the housekeeper for Amanda Williamson.

It was dark outside, yet a reading light inside the limousine enabled Helen to read from a small paperback while the limousine made its way through the endless stoplights, turns, and stretches of road.

If time passed quickly and easily for Helen, the same could hardly be said for Amanda. Her brow often furrowed as she stared aimlessly out the window, her mind fully engaged with whatever thoughts occupied her mind. The occasional biting of the lip only served to accentuate the anxiety she felt over whatever was about to happen.

"Are you okay, Mrs. Williamson?"

The housekeeper's question broke the silence, and for a moment, distracted Amanda from her concerns.

"Quite, thank you, Helen," she replied, aware her answer was only half true. "At least, I think so."

"If you're having second thoughts, ma'am, I'm certain it won't be any problem at all; I can just tell —"

"No...no, Helen, it's not that. You know how long Paul and

11

I've waited for something like this."

"Yes, ma'am, I do."

"It's just…well, are we doing the right thing?"

"I suppose only you can answer that, Mrs. Williamson."

Amanda smiled back at the older woman, and nodded. She knew Helen was right.

***

Amanda and Helen were sitting across the table from one another, engaged in some idle conversation, when a much younger woman in a black leather jacket, most likely in her late teens, entered the restaurant. She was beautiful, despite having something of an unhealthy demeanor, something Amanda felt certain couldn't have been helped any by the sort of lifestyle she was certain the young woman lived.

The visitor looked around in all directions for several seconds until her eyes finally landed on Helen. Her eyes immediately widened, and an expression of joy mixed with sadness and fear covered her face as she approached the table. The two women stood up to greet her.

"Helen!"

"Jasmine, dear! How are you holding up?"

"About as well as can be expected, I suppose, Helen. The doctors…well, they say I won't have to wait much longer."

"Oh…I'm so sorry, sweetheart, truly I am!"

Jasmine smiled appreciatively before turning to Amanda. "You must be Amanda Williamson."

"I am; it's such a pleasure to meet you, my dear. You must be Jasmine."

"Yeah, that's right." The younger woman studied Amanda for several moments, as if assessing her trustworthiness. After a while, she nodded to herself, as if concluding she liked her. Jasmine then reached up and unzipped her jacket. Nestled inside her jacket was a beautiful baby dressed in a pink outfit. "And *this* is Kayla."

Jasmine carefully took Kayla and held her for several moments, looking into her daughter's emerald-green eyes for some time, before finally looking up at Amanda. Perhaps it was the look of warmth she saw in the woman's face, or maybe it was the tears Jasmine saw forming in the corners of Amanda's eyes. For whatever reason, without saying another word Jasmine smiled and handed Kayla to Amanda, whose stunned expression amused Jasmine.

"What; you wanted to adopt a baby, didn't you?"

Amanda stood there for a while, speechless. "Oh yes, of course. She's just so...beautiful!"

"Yeah, she is, isn't she?"

Amanda stood staring at Jasmine for several seconds, until the girl grew increasingly uncomfortable.

"What?"

"Oh, nothing.

"What?"

"Well...I was just wondering—"

"Why I'm giving her up?"

Amanda furrowed her brow before eventually nodding.

"Because *I'm dying*. I can't trust myself to take care of her anymore."

"I'm...very, very sorry, my dear."

"Don't be; we all die eventually, it's just a matter of time. I didn't know about the cancer until after she was born. When I found out I started looking around to see who might take care of her when I'm gone; her dirt-bag father was nowhere to be found, both of my parents are dead, and I don't have any other relatives around that I can depend on. To be honest, I was scared to death about what was going to happen to my little Kayla...." Tears burst forth on their own accord, no longer willing to be constrained. Amanda rushed over and wrapped her free arm around Jasmine, who continued. "So, when I was telling Helen about my situation, and she told me about you and your husband, that you'd been unable to adopt because you're such a traditional couple, we thought you'd be the perfect couple to adopt Kayla."

"Listen, Jasmine, I think you're a very brave, young woman. If you're willing, I'd very much like for you to come live with us, and with Kayla."

Jasmine gently pulled away from Amanda so she could look her in the eyes. "Are you saying you'd like to adopt me too?"

Amanda smiled warmly at Jasmine. She also turned for a moment and looked at Helen, who to her surprise had tears streaming down her face.

"Yes, Jasmine, I suppose I am. What do you say...will you come live with us?"

Jasmine looked at Amanda, at Kayla, then at Helen, who nodded at her with great encouragement. Jasmine turned and looked back at Kayla, and after gently rubbing her head, looked back at Amanda. "Yeah, thanks; I think I'd like that very much."

CHAPTER 3
Six Years Earlier

August 15, 2120

Daniel Washington stared out of the window and into the darkness of Sector 48, watching the rain fall. His eyes darted here and there, from the lights of a nearby building to the flashing lights of air traffic, his hair still dripping water on the floor from where he'd stepped out of the shower minutes earlier.

Like everyone else in the sector he'd spent a full day at school each day, followed by a half-day of work, and now, at the end of the week, he was exhausted and feeling it. Life was hard for most in the Free Market Republic of Conservatism, or what those who grew up there commonly called The Red Zone, or RZ. It wasn't something anyone talked about; no one had to. Sometimes, on days like today, as he continued staring out into the rain, Daniel would wonder what kind of incredible, wonderful life he might have had if he'd only been born inside the New Zion Church or the Corporate Synod instead of the Production Class. He'd heard stories about the tall, gleaming cathedrals in New Zion City, and the glittering commercial towers in Synod City. How wonderful it must have been to live and raise a family there!

Aside from The NZC and Synod, Daniel had also heard stories of what life was like inside the Executive and Intelligentsia classes, two more strata of society in the Red Zone. Considered by everyone to be far superior to the physical laborers in the Production Class, members of the Executive and Intelligentsia classes were granted privileges far beyond those held by families like his. His class was, after all, at the bottom of the barrel, even inside the management tier where Daniel's family was positioned. Brother Thomas, their local NZC priest, was keen to remind Daniel that he'd been born into the Production Class to serve the greater good, and that he should be grateful to the benevolent, life-giving universe for the opportunity to suffer the heat, the physical labor, and the occasional unhealthy air.

Some, however, thought life in the Red Zone was perfect, a utopia of sorts. The Blue Zone rebels, who were somewhat begrudgingly permitted to live in Sector 48, often shared stories of life in the Blue Zone. According to the rebels, life was far worse there, with widespread shortages of food and supplies, and a growing death rate among the general populace. Unless you were in the Gentry, or one of the other socially protected classes, access to employment, like food, was rare. To the Blue Zone rebels, life in Sector 48 was paradise.

Like nearly everyone else who lived in Sector 48, Daniel and his family were members of the blue-collar Production Class. Like most other families who lived there, they were also devout members of the New Zion Church, or the NZC as it was commonly called. His father, Harold, was a mid-level manager over a group of production laborers at Zion Industries, and his mother was a low-level teacher at Synod City Modular School.

As a member of a lower-class, very little news of what was happening in other sectors ever made it into 48. It was one of the things Daniel had always hated about his station in life, the way the Corporate Synod kept his class in the dark about nearly everything of any importance. Except for the occasional resistance broadcast, only the most mundane and trivial events ever made it into the corporate news broadcasts. They may not have been called prisoners, but they certainly were treated as if they were.

The problem in Sector 48, and if the rebel broadcasts could be believed the rest of the Red Zone as well, wasn't that the RZ lacked food or jobs. It was the lack of freedom, the punishing rigor of the work, the growing travel restrictions both within and between the regions, and the lack of representation in the Corporate Synod, that together had served to disenfranchise more and more people and create greater unrest. Citizens of the Red Zone were now little more than prisoners in their own homes, and they were getting angrier about it by the day.

To make matters worse, hopelessness and despair also ran rampant throughout the RZ, especially among the Production Class, given that the chances of ever improving one's place in society was near zero. Word got out that the genetic mods given to nearly everyone in the Production Class did nothing to enhance their cognitive abilities, that they were only designed mostly for strength, stamina, and endurance so that workers would be more productive and therefore more profitable for the Synod.

People in 48 grew especially outraged when they learned one particularly disturbing truth about the genetic modifications the Synod had been making to the children for decades; the same upgrades that made the workers more profitable for the Synod also had the unfortunate side-effect of shortening their lives by as much as two decades. Perhaps, had the Corporate Synod tolerated dissent and free expression, they could have worked with the people to change things and correct some of these inequalities and injustices, and events would have unfolded quite differently than they did. The Synod tolerated neither dissent nor free expression, however, especially from anyone in the Production Class.

For Daniel's family, their best shot at escaping the Production Class had come when a man named Reid Willingsworth had somehow met and then married his Aunt Ruth. Reid had come from a wealthy family in Synod City, and he'd been upgraded to Intelligentsia before birth. His Uncle Reid died in a work-related accident before he and Ruth had any children, however, thereby dashing the family's hopes of escaping the perpetual cycle of generational churn in the Production Class. It seemed they were doomed to never leave Sector 48.

Had Daniel's family been wealthy, they might have been able to afford the genetic upgrades to Intelligentsia that would have enhanced his cognitive abilities, thereby virtually guaranteeing him a position in New Zion or Synod City. But they *weren't* wealthy, and he'd never be able to afford the necessary modifications.

Perhaps everything had worked out for the best in the end, however. Rumors had been circulating for some time about side effects related to the genetic upgrades to Intelligentsia that worried him. These side effects, which seemed to have gone mostly un-noticed by the public, were generally associated with the most effective of the cognitive enhancements. In every case he was personally aware of, the person who'd received the upgrade had never been the same person afterwards; in every instance, it seemed as if some part of that man, woman, or child's humanity had been forever lost during the process of modifying their genetic code.

He'd once heard of an applied physics professor at the city university, Professor Kernard, a Superior GEMP (Genetically Modified Person), who'd been thrust out of the prestigious Temple of Divine Business University in New Zion City after being convicted of corporate heresy. He was a brilliant professor, with an understanding of physics unlike anything anyone had ever seen. Professor Kernard was also a very peculiar person, described by students and some faculty as being virtually devoid of human emotion, as if the greatly enhanced mental acuity was accompanied by a corresponding drop in emotional empathy. He'd been described by some people who knew him as both creepy and disturbing.

"Are you okay, son?" Daniel flinched. "Sorry, I didn't mean to startle you."

Daniel turned to face his father, whose kind gaze met his own. "No, that's okay, Dad. I'm fine; I was just thinking about next week."

"I'm so proud of you, Danny. I just can't say it enough, son. You'll be the first in our family to make it out of the factory. Just think son, you're going to college; as smart as you are, my boy, you may even make it into the Intelligentsia Class one day!"

"That's just it, Dad...I don't *want* to leave here. I'd rather work in the factory than leave our family."

"No! Don't you *dare* say that again; *ever!*" The look of deep concern on his father's face left Daniel speechless. "You can't stay here, son; promise me you won't! Staying here is an early death sentence for you, Danny. You'd just be working yourself into an early grave like the rest of us…it's no way to live, son. I've always wanted a lot more for you and the others…I just never knew what I could do to help any of you." He stood up straight and cupped his big, calloused hands around his son's head, just before a lone tear began streaming down his cheek. "But you; you can make a difference, Danny…you're special, son. This world we live in, it's wrong, corrupt; the world's turned upside down. I don't know how or why, but I believe you're meant to do something about it; to change things for the better."

"But Dad, if I leave I probably won't get a chance to ever see you again, at least not in person, because of the travel restrictions."

His father turned and paused for a moment, taking the opportunity to let out a long, heavy sigh. "I know, son, I know." He reached out and pulled Daniel toward him, embracing him in the kind of long and endearing hug that only a father who dearly loves his son can give. "You know, son," he said at length, "my father once told me that during the Great Schism, one word was often shared with the public as to why the Red Zone should separate from the Blue Zone. Care to guess what it was?"

"I don't know, Dad."

"Freedom. It was believed that separating from the Blue Zone would give each zone greater freedom to live the way the citizens of each respective zone wanted."

"Did it?"

"Well, for a while, yes, but it didn't last. It now seems that the Great Schism made a lot of things worse, much worse, for our people. I can't say for sure, but if what I hear about the BZ rebels is true, it seems it hasn't worked out well for them either. Perhaps the folks in the BZ had it wrong; maybe they needed us after all, and maybe we needed them."

"What does this have to do with me, Dad? I love you guys, and I'm just afraid that if I leave Sector 48 I'll never see you again!" Tears welled up in Daniel's eyes as he stood facing his father.

19

"My point is this, Daniel. One day things *are* going to get better, and when they do, it will happen because of people like *you*, son. You're a good, man, Daniel…you are. *Never* forget that. And you're also strong, and smart. I'll tell you something else, son; good men that are strong and smart, *they can change the world.*"

CHAPTER 4

The warm feeling from the rays of the sun as they penetrated her skin caused Kayla to fall into a drowsy, semi-conscious sleep. She'd already swam twenty laps and was exhausted from the effort, so it didn't take much for her to fall out. Nor did it take much for her to be jolted back to being wide-awake when something ice-cold suddenly touched and then covered her back, causing her to gasp for breath before jolting upright so quickly she nearly forgot the top to her bathing suit…nearly. She turned to find me standing over her, grinning from ear-to-ear.

"Christian! Look what you almost made me do!"

"Yes, I know," I replied with a sly smile. "It would have been a real tragedy."

"Ooohhh…you're incorrigible sometimes, Chris, really! What would you have done had my father been here?" she asked me.

"He's not, I checked," I answered with a laugh. "I'm sorry to disturb your basking in the sun the way I did, but you were turning as red as a lobster, and at the rate you were going…well, let's just say I didn't want you to spend tonight and the next few days suffering. I thought I should warn you; it is, after all, what a friend should do, is it not?"

I looked down at her and found she was now smiling at me. "Yes, I suppose it is," she answered with a giggle, while she finished reconnecting her bathing suit. When she had finished she ran over to me and jumped into my arms. "It's so good to see you again, Christian. Where have you been for the past month?"

"Traveling. Didn't I tell you?"

"Yes, you said you'd be gone for short while, but you said

21

nothing about it being for a whole month! You're my best friend, Chris, you're supposed to tell me everything!"

I dropped my head, ashamed that I'd withheld from Kayla the length of time I'd be away. She missed me, as I knew she would, just as I had missed her. We'd been friends for a very long time, and we were close. "I'm sorry, Kayla. I should have said something."

She leaned in slightly and looked into my eyes. "It's okay, Christian. I was just *soooo* worried about you."

That's when it happened, one of those moments in life you wish you could take back and do over. Thinking both of us had the same thing in mind, I leaned in close to her to kiss her. She jerked back in response.

"Whoa, stop, what's this? Hold on now, Chris, we talked about this after we split the last time, right? We decided — we *both* decided — that we'd be better off as friends. I mean, we *agreed*, right? As I recall we tried the whole dating thing, but we both thought it felt wrong, right? I mean, you've got to tell me, Chris, if I'm wrong about this. I thought we felt the same way."

"Yeah...no, we do. We talked about this. Of course you're right, Kayla...I'm sorry. Sometimes I...well, I guess old habits die hard."

"You're not having second thoughts about our arrangement, are you?"

I had to stop and consider that for a moment. With a slender athletic-build, long, dark, flowing auburn hair, and fiery-green eyes, Kayla was drop dead gorgeous to be sure, and she *was* a lot of fun to be with. But the truth was, there just weren't any sparks or romantic chemistry between us whatsoever, no matter how much we both wanted there to be. We did care deeply for one another, however...far too much to allow ourselves to be the cause of the other's unhappiness. If the only way the other person could find happiness was with someone else, we would not only give our blessing, we would bend over backwards to help them find it.

"No, I guess I'm not, Kayla. Sometimes I *think* maybe I am,

22

but then I think back to how it was with us...we tried it, several times, and it was obviously just never going to work. It's sad though, because you really are hot, and I love being with you!"

"Well, so are you, Chris, and every girl I know thinks so too!"

"Really?"

Kayla nodded. "Okay then, so where were you all this time?"

"I was on a 'Compassionate Doctors' trip with my father to the Oregon province. There is a community there that's suffered through a recent epidemic of cholera. Apparently, the water supply was tainted and tens of thousands of people were sick. My father said the Gentry was growing concerned about it spreading into the California province, so they sent him to Oregon."

"Wow, no wonder you were gone so long. So how did it go?"

"It's unbelievable, Kayla. The medical care there is horrible, practically non-existent. It's so bad that the only doctor at the facility in the city we went to had been prioritizing the children by life expectancy, then from youngest to oldest; isn't that awful? Oh, hey, listen, I've got to go somewhere for a bit, but there's something I'd like to show you. Would you mind some company later this afternoon?"

"Not at all, that sounds great. I'd love to see you again, silly; there's so much to talk about, and we've not had a chance to catch up any!"

"Great; then I'll be back in a few hours. And, um, Kayla, I've someone I'd like you to meet," I replied, smiling from ear to ear as I walked out the door.

"Really? Sounds intriguing!"

***

I allowed my mind to wander as I drove back to Kayla's home later that same day. Her family's massive estate would have been considered lavish at any time in history, but considering that this was post-Schism Blue Zone, it was rare indeed. Only the most prominent families in the BZ owned such properties.

Kayla had mentioned to me on several occasions over the years—when she was feeling contemplative, and she was quite certain we were alone and not under any type of surveillance—

that her parents felt significant guilt over their substantial wealth, especially considering the devastating poverty that now raged throughout the zone. Given the delicate, intricate attitudes toward the poor and toward each other, she said her parents had told her that they had to be extremely cautious, however, and keep such feelings well-hidden. The elite inside the Gentry jealously guarded their privileged place in society, and were determined to preserve their own security and way of life no matter what it might cost someone else. They would kill or arrest them, seize her family's estate, and then take it for themselves long before they'd ever allow the precious resources of such a powerful gentry to fall into the hands of the common people.

I'd known Kayla since we were in primary indoctrination together, so I'd come to know her and her parents well. I knew them to be good people, which sometimes led me to wonder why, with all their wealth and their kind demeanor, they didn't do more to help the less fortunate, regardless of what others in the Gentry might do to them. I suppose at the time I expected they should give everything they owned to others. Only later did I come to understand what a mistake that would have been. Such an act of generosity would have been quickly depleted, and the situation made even more dire. It was time to face the fact that the system was broken and not working. The system had to be fixed, and that could only come about through political change, either by working inside the system to change it, or by toppling it and creating a new one.

Traffic had been light as it often was these days, so it had taken me no more than fifteen minutes to make the short drive to her family's estate from my family's more modest home on the outer edges of the city. I smiled as I approached the first pair of guards stationed at the outer gate into the estate, which sat between two tall, massive stone walls. While magnificent, they were clearly as powerful and effective as they were beautiful. Tall, luscious palm trees lined the outside of the wall.

"Good afternoon, Sam," I said to the older man, as I extended my arm out the shielded opening for the guards at the entrance to scan. He'd seen me come and go for years, of course, but he knew he could lose his job for not following protocol to the letter. Not to mention that the Gentry Enforcers would have his head on a platter were he ever to ignore protocol and they found out he'd done so. Sam followed procedure and scanned my arm.

"Good afternoon, sir. Here to see Miss Kayla this fine day?"

"You bet."

"And who's this little lady?"

"She's a very special friend of mine. Her name is also Sam."

"Well then, her name should be easy for me to remember. Hello Sam, it's nice to meet you! Shall I register her as your guest, sir?"

"Please do."

"Very good. Last name, please?"

"Woodward."

"Okay, very good. Well then, head right on in, sir. It was very nice to meet you, Sam. I hope you *both* have a very pleasant day."

"You too, Sam," I answered. "Thanks."

I drove in through the gates and made my way down the long road toward the next gate, with the large, beautiful mansion waiting some distance beyond it.

"Wow, that's *butiful!*" The squeal of excitement that came from the seat beside me caused me to smile as we neared the second gate.

"Yes, it certainly is," I replied, as the car pulled up to the gate. Another security guard approached the car, this one much taller and larger, with a hard and penetrating stare that always unnerved me. His name was Jarrod Cain. It was said that he'd been deployed on the front lines during some of the fiercest battles of the Great Los Angeles Riot, where he'd come to be feared by friend and foe alike.

"Good afternoon, Mr. Jefferson."

"Good afternoon."

"One moment please, Mr. Jefferson. I need to call it in. We've been on a higher level of alert than normal since the latest wave of riots began spreading throughout the region. It won't take but just a moment, sir."

"No worries; I understand."

Jarrod nodded and walked back to the small station inside of the booth. He sat down on a stool facing a small console, pushed a button on his special glasses, and began speaking.

"Scan vehicle."

A small globe-shaped drone rose from inside the booth and hovered silently until it was positioned directly in front of the vehicle. It then emitted a green beam of light that focused on the front passenger areas of the vehicle. Images of the two passengers appeared above the console, while streams of data split out in two tables on the console itself. Moments later, the data and images disappeared and the words ALL CLEAR flashed on the screen.

"Okay, Mr. Jefferson, you're cleared to proceed inside the mansion. Thank you for your patience, and have a nice day."

"Thanks, Jarrod, you too."

We continued down the same road until at last we arrived at the front of the palatial mansion. I stopped the car out front and a man in a red and black uniform soon appeared with a ticket in hand. My passenger and I climbed out of my car, and after taking the ticket, watched as the man drove the car towards the estate's underground parking garage. We climbed the first three steps from the driveway, walked several yards, and then climbed a few more before finally arriving at the door. Before knocking or wringing the bell, the door suddenly opened brightly in front of as if on its own accord, and Jerome, the butler, stood smiling.

"Ah, hello again, Master Jefferson, it's good to see you again, sir."

"Hello again, Jerome, thank you."

"And who might *this* be?" he asked, smiling warmly towards my companion.

"This is my new friend, Samantha. I've brought her here to meet Kayla."

"Oh, my, she will be most delighted…I'm certain of it, Mister Jefferson. Oh, please, come in. She is expecting you, of course."

We'd only taken five or six steps inside the entrance of

the massive home when Kayla appeared as if out of nowhere, throwing her arms around me as if she'd not seen me in years. She finally released her hold on my neck long enough to turn and see the little girl standing behind her, staring back with her dark-brown hair and fierce blue eyes.

"Chris…have you already ditched me for another girl, even if she is as pretty as this one?" Kayla walked over to the little girl, who stood facing her with a mixture of fear and awe. "Hello little girl," she said, stooping over to meet her at eye level. "And what is your name?"

"My name is Samantha, but most people call me Sam."

"And how old are you, Sam?" she asked the girl.

"I'm seven years old," she replied, looking over at me for assurance. I just nodded my head and smiled back.

"Well, you certainly are a beautiful, precious little girl, Sam," Kayla told her, smiling excitedly. Kayla then suddenly turned toward the back of the house and called out, "Jerome!"

Jerome appeared a short time later. "Yes, Miss Kayla?"

"I think our little guest here would enjoy a tour of our topiary garden; would you like that, Sam?"

"What is a topee-airy?"

"It's a garden with bushes shaped like all kinds of wonderful animals, like elephants, camels, lions, and giraffes. Do you think you'd enjoy that?"

"Oh, yes!"

"Jerome, would you please escort our little guest on a tour of the garden?

"Certainly, Miss Kayla."

Sam held out her hand to Jerome, who then took it into his own. He looked back with uncertainty at Kayla, who simply smiled in reply and shrugged her shoulders. Within seconds the two had vanished, leaving Kayla free to give me the third degree.

"Okay, Chris, spill; what gives?"

"She's cute as a button, isn't she?" I asked, testing her patience to its limits.

"Christian Jefferson!"

"Okay, okay, I'll tell you…please just don't get cross with me again!" I replied, laughing so hard my right side started to hurt. I gestured for her to sit down on a nearby sofa and I sat next to her. The solemnity of the girl's tale forced an abrupt change in my demeanor that Kayla noticed immediately. "My father and I met Sam on our recent trip to Oregon. Do you recall how desperate I described the situation to be?"

Kayla instantly dropped her head in shame upon recalling the sad affair. "Yes, I remember."

"Well, it turns out that a number of the people there, including several children, were in urgent need of organ transplants to save their lives. One of them was in far worse shape than the rest."

"Let me guess; that child was Sam?"

I nodded solemnly in response. "Sadly, it was. It's a shame, too…she's such a sweet little girl."

"Will you be able to help her, Chris?" she asked me, her eyes filled with concern for a little girl who was still a complete stranger to her.

"That's why we brought her with us. Father called before we left and had her added to the emergency donor list; we understand she's next in line."

"Really? How? She's clearly not Gentry…she's just a little girl from Oregon, a commoner. How was he able to arrange that?"

"Well, as you know, my father is not without a little pull around the capital. It didn't hurt that she's such a precious little girl."

Kayla managed a slight smile, which accompanied the puzzled expression and furrowed brow. "Really? That's all it took?"

"No, I'm just kidding. He does have a lot of pull, and she really is precious, but even together it was nowhere near enough to leapfrog Sam ahead of the Gentry children already in line. Of course, it didn't matter that not one of those children were in any immediate danger, much less in anywhere near as much danger as Sam. Still, all of that together was still nowhere near enough to make any difference to those selfish snobs. No, my father had a little help."

"From who?"

"From *your* father?"

"*My* father? Seriously?"

We were both distracted for a moment as we saw the wispy figure of a little girl run playfully by one of the windows close to where we now sat in the living room, followed by poor Jerome, who was doing his best to keep up with the little girl while giving chase.

"Yeah. I don't know how, or why, but my father called yours and the next thing you know, voila, Sam's at the top of the list. It's a good thing, too."

"Why do you say that?"

I involuntarily swallowed hard at the question. I knew Kayla, and I knew how easy it was for her to grow attached to someone, particularly someone like little Sam, and to a cause like hers. "Because the doctors were doubtful she had more than a month, two at the outside, to live."

"No...no way, Christian. You *must* be mistaken! Look at that little girl outside running and playing; she's so full of life and vigor! They were mistaken."

"There was no mistake, Kayla; my father triple-checked the results himself." I paused to walk over to the window. I looked outside briefly, and upon finding what I was looking for, called over to Kayla. "Come here, Kayla, and take a look out the window."

Kayla hurried over to me and peered outside at where Jerome now stood, bent over Sam, who sat down on the ground in front of him, exhausted and completely out of breath. "It's her *heart*, Kayla. Sam's young, but her heart is unable to pump enough oxygen to the rest of her body. She's been able to get by until now because she's so small, but as she grows—"

"Her heart has a harder and harder time keeping up?"

"Yes, pretty much."

"That poor thing." Kayla opened the window and yelled out to the butler and little girl. "Jerome, please bring Samantha inside so she can rest. Perhaps she'd enjoy some almond ice cream and some wafers."

"Oh yes, please!" Samantha yelled back in reply, jumping up and preparing to race back in, being restrained by a thoughtful and concerned Jerome.

"Please, Miss Samantha, take it slow. The ice cream will still be there when we get inside."

***

So engrossed was Sebastian Ross in the information presented on the datapad sitting on the desk before him, he never noticed the sound of the door to his study opening behind him. He was, therefore, quite surprised when a pair of delicate arms suddenly wrapped themselves around his torso.

"Oh, Daddy, I think it's so wonderful. *You're* so wonderful… thank you!"

Sebastian smiled warmly as he turned away from the desk, thankful for the respite his wonderful daughter's attention offered from the daily politics of his office.

"To what do I owe such wonderful accolades, my darling Kayla?"

"Chris told me all about Sam, Dad, and I think it's wonderful what you did."

Sebastian tightened his lips slightly, but not so much that it caught Kayla's attention. "Yes, well, you know how much I respect Chris's father, Dr. Jefferson, and the work he does. When he called and asked…well, I could hardly refuse him."

Kayla eyed her father with suspicion. "Uh-huh. So, it had nothing to do with a little girl needing your help…a little girl who needed your help the same way I once needed it?"

"Now hold on a minute," her father protested, before Kayla turned and walked towards the door.

"It's okay, Daddy, your secret's safe with me!" she said with a smile, before closing the door.

A smile appeared on the face of Sebastian Ross, and he shook his head as he watched the door close behind her. The smile soon faded, however, replaced by a look of concern, and then of fear.

CHAPTER 5

Daniel was running late for his first class on the first day of his junior year at Free Market University. He quickly ran for the first seat available, which happened to be in the first row of desks which clustered around the professor's lectern in a semi-circle. The arrangement was clearly designed to enhance and maximize the student-professor interaction, which most students and faculty alike considered to be a useless relic of the bygone days of university instruction, especially considering the advanced tech mandated for all university programs by the Corporate Directorate. Despite the widespread use of virtual classrooms following the Great Schism, some professors remained old-school, preferring to teach their students in a physical, face-to-face environment. Few campus buildings at FMU still contained physical classrooms or lecture halls, however, since everything could be done in a virtual setting at a fraction of the cost. Labs were, of course, still prevalent across university campuses, and remained one of the preeminent reasons for maintaining campus infrastructures…along with establishing social interactions and relationships, of course.

"I hope you brought a pencil and some paper; he'll expect it."

Daniel turned around to find the source of the strange comment. "What?"

"Professor Kellogg…he'll expect you to have a pencil and paper, and not just your Smox," he told Daniel, referring to the smart box, AI computers required of all college students, and most high school students as well.

"You're kidding," Daniel replied, displaying a genuine expression of disgust for his fellow captive's benefit. "I'm Daniel," he told him, extending his hand toward him as he did so.

"Simon Bender," the student replied with a boyish grin. It wasn't unlike the sheepish look worn on the faces of so many of the Corporate Directorate's "true believers." But while he looked like one of the directorate's many drones on the surface, Daniel immediately sensed there was something different about Simon Bender, as if there was something lurking beneath that boyish grin, something deep and profound. Everyone grew quiet as the door opened. Professor Kellogg appeared, entered the room, and came forward to speak to the class.

"Good morning, ladies and gentlemen," he began. "I'm Dr. Jason Kellogg; you can just call me 'Professor' if you'd like. In case you didn't know this, you're in Corporate Religion 300, Advanced Studies of Business Theology." A light wave of laughter passed through the classroom. Kellogg turned toward his desk with his back to the class for a moment, before turning around with a pencil in his hand, which he held up high enough that everyone could see.

"So, let's see how bright you all are; who can tell me what this small utensil is that I'm holding in my hand?" This time a blanket of silence fell over the room. It wasn't long until a somewhat perturbed Kellogg turned his attention to Daniel. "Can *you* tell me what this is, Mr...err...?"

"Washington...*Daniel* Washington, sir."

"*Daniel* Washington, son?" he asked him, a look of surprise on his face. "Isn't '*Daniel*' still on the list of names banned by the corporate theocracy?"

"Yes sir, it is; but it is sometimes allowed when chosen for secular reasons, like naming a child after a parent or a close relative. In my case, my father signed a form swearing I was named after my grandfather, and that he does not follow the old God of the Jews or Christians, or the Way of the Nazarene."

Professor Kellogg spent several long, agonizing seconds looking him over from head to toe, as if examining whether Daniel was worthy to even breathe the same air he was.

"It's not going to be a problem, sir," Daniel told Kellogg. "I promise."

The rather spindly professor stared at him until Daniel began feeling extremely self-conscious. Finally, Kellogg replied, "See that it isn't."

"Yes, sir."

Daniel looked away for a moment, expecting Kellogg's gaze to be gone by the time he looked back, but when he turned back around, the professor had not moved an inch.

"I'm waiting, Mr. Washington."

"Sir?"

"You never answered my question; what is this object I'm holding?"

"Oh, sorry, Professor. It's a pencil; an ancient writing instrument used for writing or sometimes drawing on paper, or wood products. It was used for writing during much of the twentieth century, especially when revisions were expected. It was supplanted toward the end of the twentieth and the beginning of the twenty-first century by increasingly inexpensive computers or computer-related products."

Kellogg made no indication whether he approved of the answer or not; instead, he simply turned away from Daniel and returned to his lecturing.

"Now then, let's get started. We'll be starting off the semester discussing how and why our forefathers rejected the ancient religions. These ancient, hate-filled religions were filled with stories of fire and brimstone meant to scare people into belief, or wonderful fairytales promising a perfect afterlife. These ancient religions that worshipped the old God, or the Way of the Nazarene, or both, were dissolved a few decades after those embracing legalizing illegal drugs, legalizing same-sex marriages, abortions, and the like left to join the Blue Zone during the Great Schism. I'm talking, of course, about the Great Purge. The Great Purge came about following a time when religious conflict in the Red Zone was out of control, and there was disorder everywhere. Fortunately, the New Zion Church, which had been established to bring order to religion in the Red Zone, took control and cleansed the zone of the radical, dangerous religions that caused so much pain and suffering. Now, of course, the old religions have been completely banned, and the New Zion Church is the one and only church we may attend."

***

Daniel placed his tray under the dispenser. After making his choices and pressing the appropriate selections on the menus, the food cubes dropped from the dispenser and onto his plate. He placed his plate into the reintegration chamber and withdrew it with a full plate of food, including a chopped steak, potatoes, and carrots.

"Nice choice; mind if I join you?" He recognized the voice but couldn't place it. He turned to find Simon Bender staring down at him.

"Please do," he replied, before returning to his meal.

Simon looked around at the empty seats. "Hmm, looks like neither of us have made a lot of friends since we've been here."

"That obvious, is it?"

"Heh, heh; yeah, you could say that."

Simon sat down and the two young men ate their lunches in relative silence, until he finally spoke.

"So, Daniel, I heard that your family is Production Class; is that true?"

Daniel's face grew flush with anger. "Yeah, so…what of it? What's the matter? Do you suddenly find my company distasteful?"

"Hey, hey, ho, man, take it easy, I'm sorry; I meant no offense, I promise. In fact, I detest the whole class system we have. It's not fair, it's corrupt, and I believe it should go."

Daniel stopped and studied Simon for a moment. "Are you serious? Why would you say that?"

"Because it's what I believe. We're *forced* to undergo genetic engineering, we're *forced* to practice a 'religion' we don't believe in, and we're *told* what we can and cannot read or watch for entertainment. Our country is broken, Daniel, can't you see it?"

"Yeah, I suppose so."

34

"Take you, for example."

"Me?"

"Yes, you. You were born into the Production Class. Because of the mere circumstance of your birth you were condemned to live out your life the same way your father had done, and his father before him."

"But I'm not."

"Exactly, you're not. But why aren't you working next to your father at this very moment instead of attending an elite university? Is it because you worked harder than everyone else and your effort was rewarded as a result?"

"Yeah, I know, Simon; it's because I happened to be born this way. It doesn't seem fair, does it?"

"It's not that it's 'just not fair,' Daniel…it's flat out *wrong*. Too much power in too few hands; it's been proven time and time again throughout history to be a terrible idea."

"I agree with you, Simon, and I concede your points. There's nothing we can do about it, however; we're just a couple of college students."

"Yes, and Albert Einstein was just a patent clerk, Abe Lincoln was nothing but a lawyer from the backwoods of Kentucky, and King David was only a shepherd boy from a small town in the middle of nowhere."

"King David?"

Simon looked at Daniel with a blank expression for a few seconds, until the blank look turned into a look of sadness and despair.

"Yes, King David. He was a very important king in ancient Israel, a king who walked very close with Yahweh, the Lord God, the God of my people."

"Simon, shhh!" Daniel looked around hurriedly to see if anyone had overheard them. If they had, no one gave any indication of it. "Simon, you must be more careful! You know that worship of the Jewish or Christian God is *forbidden*!"

"How could I? They never let any of us forget!"

"You sound like one of those radicals from the resistance,

Simon."

"Maybe that's not such a bad thing," the other man replied, staring out the window.

"Wow; you *must* be joking. Why would you say that? Those people are insane; they're anarchists."

"They may be anarchists, Daniel, but they're *not* insane," Simon replied flatly, sounding irritated.

"How would you know that, Simon? We hear next to nothing about them, except what little we hear about on the news."

Simon offered only silence in reply, busying himself with eating his meal instead. Daniel turned his attention to his own plate of food as well, wondering whether he'd somehow offended his newfound friend. After a few more bites of his potatoes, Daniel decided to probe a little more.

"Say, listen, Simon, I'm sorry if I said anything to offend you. I know some people agree with some of what the resistance stands for. If you—"

"Look, Daniel…I guess I thought you'd be different than the rest of the mindless sycophants we go to school with. I mean, given your background, and what your family has been forced to endure in Sector 48, I was sure that you'd understand, that you of all people would appreciate what the cause is trying to accomplish, and why it's so important. The way your people have been treated, the way they've suffered…this is *not* how it's supposed to be. You *must* know that!"

This time Daniel took time to reflect on what Simon said, and slowly it began to make sense.

"Wait a minute, Simon," he whispered quietly, pausing to look around to ensure he was not overheard, "Are *you* with the resistance?"

CHAPTER 6

"Checkmate!"

The expression of joy on Sam's face made Kayla smile for the first time in weeks.

"But remember," Kayla said to the girl, "you must never tell *anyone* we played this game together today, okay?"

"But why not, Miss Kayla?"

"Because this *place* where we live has some very ugly rules, and one of them is that we're not supposed play games like checkers, since only one person can win. The state sanctions only games where there is always an equal outcome, where everyone wins; understand?"

"Yes," she replied weakly. "No," she soon added.

"That's okay, Sam," Kayla said, while looking with great love into the child's eyes. "Neither do I!"

This time Sam managed a slight laugh. The seven-year-old was tired; she was *always* tired now. Kayla and I agreed that Sam was looking worse with each passing hour. Black circles had taken up permanent residence under her eyes, and nearly all color had fled her face. When Kayla looked up at me again, I could tell by the way her eyes were watering up that she was on the verge of tears.

"Hey, Sam, Kayla and I are going to leave for a bit so you can get some rest, okay?"

"Okay. Thank you for letting me win, Kayla."

"What? Are you kidding? You beat me fair and square, kiddo!"

"Okay." Sam smiled weakly and was already falling asleep

as we walked away.

"How are you holding up, Kayla? You know you don't have to do this; I can take her back home with me, where Dad and I could keep a close eye on her."

"Really? Your father is one of the busiest people I know, Christian; he's almost never home. I grew up hanging out at your place, remember? Besides, what do you mean 'I don't *have* to keep her here with me?' You just try to take that little girl away from me and see what happens!"

One determined glance told me all I needed to know; she loved the little girl.

"Okay, okay," I replied with a smile, which soon turned into a more solemn expression as I looked evenly into her eyes. "Listen, Kayla, it might be better if I took her. You don't have as much experience dealing with this sort of thing as I do. It could be really hard if—"

"Don't say it, Christian; in fact, don't even think it! Nothing is going to happen to this amazing, sweet, wonderful little girl. You heard how she's taken to calling me Miss Kayla? No, I'm not going to let anything happen to her; don't worry."

I looked down and began staring at the floor at hearing this. "Kayla, listen. If something doesn't happen soon it's going to be too—"

"Have you heard anything yet, Chris? This waiting is driving me crazy! I can only imagine what it's doing to her family back home."

"She's an orphan, didn't I tell you?"

"Oh. No, I don't think so." It grew silent in the room for a while, as we both struggled with the inevitable outcome if she wasn't notified of a transplant soon. "Okay, so what of your father; hasn't your father heard anything yet?"

"No, I'm afraid he hasn't. I know he's been trying to find out what the hold-up is, especially since she *was* at the top of the list. Something definitely should have happened by now."

"I'll check with my father, too; maybe he can find out what happened and then do something about it."

***

"Good morning, Minister Ross."

"Good morning, Betty."

Sebastian Ross smiled as he opened the door and walked into his office. Once inside, he sat down in the comfortable black leather executive chair sitting behind the desk. It was Monday morning and, as always, his schedule was full. There was, however, an urgent personal matter that he would have to take care of first, something he'd promised his daughter a week earlier he would handle, and it could not wait. With a wave of his hand in front of his face a virtual console appeared. He pressed the computer-generated button next to his executive assistant's name, and her image soon appeared in the middle of the display.

"Yes, Minister Ross; is there something I can do for you?"

"Yes, Betty, can you please get Joe Miller on the holocom for me? Tell him it's a personal but urgent matter I need to discuss with him as soon as possible. Betty, be sure to add that this matter is extremely time sensitive."

"Yes, Minister Ross, of course."

They'd attended university together as young men and they'd been casual friends there. There had always been a cordial if somewhat distant aspect to their relationship since. As Sebastian rose to become Minister of Public Affairs, Joe Miller had gone on to become an important staff member on Parliament's Committee of Public Health, a committee that worked with members of Sebastian's team. The Committee of Public Health also had oversight of the Medical Board of Regents, the group responsible for determining which patients did and which patients did not receive critical medical services when such services were scarce and where demand exceeded supply, like donated human organs.

"Hello?"

"Good morning, Joe; it's Sebastian." The expression on the man's face didn't change in the least, so that Sebastian was beginning to wonder whether the connection had frozen.

"Minister Ross, good morning!"

"Joe, I know you're a busy man, so I'll get right to the point.

I'm calling about one of the patients on your organ list. I believe her name *was* at the top of the list to receive a new heart, and that was months ago, Joe."

"Oh, yes, of course. What is the name, Minister?"

"Her name is Samantha, Samantha Woodward."

"Oh, I see. Um, Minister, would you like for me to call you once I find something?"

The many years of experience he'd garnered throughout his political career were now screaming at him. "No, I'll wait if it's all the same to you, Joe."

"Very well, suit yourself," came Miller's reply. "It will just take a moment."

There was a palpable look of fear on Miller's face now which, when combined with the color that so quickly drained from his face as if forcibly removed, suggested that he recognized the name, and that the information he provided was almost certainly not going to be what he, Kayla, and Christian were going to want to hear. Sebastian took a deep breath and braced himself. He watched as Joe Miller began fidgeting with increasing intensity, and as the panicked expression on Miller's face grew plainer by the second.

"Um, Minster, I've found the name," he finally offered after several minutes.

"Good; what's her status?"

Miller's look of anxiety was now at an all-time high. "I'm afraid she's listed as number twenty-one now, Minister Ross."

"I'm sorry, Joe, we must have a bad connection. It sounded like you said she was now twenty-first on the list, instead of number one."

"Yes, that's correct, sir."

"What? Would you like to explain how a girl *I personally* arranged to be placed at the top can get bumped back to twenty-one? This little girl is very important to me, Joe, and *she is dying!*"

"I understand, and I'm very, very sorry, Minister; there was nothing I could do!"

"I think you'd better spit it out, while you still have a job.

What's going on, Joe? You'd better tell me, and fast. This little girl is of particular importance to my family."

"I simply don't have the answer, sir. There's no explanation indicated here."

"Then find the answer, Miller. I'll be waiting."

"Of course, Minister. I'll see what I can do." Another round of silence followed while Miller waved his hands incessantly, frantically searching through a virtual filing system. Moments later, he suddenly stopped. "Oh no."

"What is it, Joe, what did you find?"

"I, um, can't explain it, Minister Ross, but it appears that since your initial request was made over a month ago, five suitable human hearts have become available, with three going to various Gentry members, who were in parliament, or their families, one went to a powerful member of the land guild, and the fifth to a member of Central Authority."

"How were they advanced in front of her?"

"Well sir, they were all senior members of the Gentry hierarchy, all of whom were in good standing having made substantial contributions to the Board of Regents or to the Committee of Public Health."

"And were any of them as critical as this little girl?"

"No, Minister; all of them could have waited up to a year for a transplant."

"So they bumped this suffering little girl, this *dying* child, down the list *against* my orders?" Sebastian roared, venting his frustration at the system on the poor man.

"I'm sorry!" Miller whimpered. "It seems no one knew that *you* were involved in this affair, Minister. All evidence of your involvement seems to have been 'misplaced.' I'm so sorry, sir, it's not my fault!"

"Then you'd better do something, Joe; I'm holding you accountable. If that little girl dies, my daughter will have my head on a silver platter. And if that happens, Joe, would you like to guess whose head *I'm* going after?"

"No, sir. We'll find another heart, Minister, I promise!"

"You'd better, Joe, or I'll—"

His warning was suddenly interrupted by Betty. "Please pardon the interruption, Minister Ross."

"Yes Betty, what is it?"

"An urgent call, sir, from your daughter."

"Kayla's calling me here?"

"Shall I put her through, sir?"

"Yes, please do." Sebastian waved his hand and soon found himself staring at Kayla. "Kayla, is everything okay?" He could see by her face that she was distraught.

"What happened, Daddy? What happened to the heart Sam was supposed to get?"

Sebastian grimaced and braced himself before answering his daughter. "It went to some old, fat senior Gentry member who could have waited another year, Kayla. It seems no one here associated my name with Sam's; it seems there were others too, Gentry, who were also in need a transplant. I was assured that heart would go to Sam, baby; I'm so sorry, sweetheart."

"You mean she lost her heart because these selfish politicians jumped the line in front of a precious little girl who needed it far more than they did? There's no heart for her because the system saved some pretentious, wrinkly old fart with the right connection, and sacrificed a precious little girl like Sam, with her entire life ahead of her, just so this wrinkly old man could live another month or two? Are you telling me these rich Gentry bastards are alive because they were rich and Sam was not? She was worth more than the lot of them put together."

"Kayla, *I'm sorry*. We're doing everything we can here. We'll find Sam a heart—"

"Just stop, Dad. Forget about Sam; there's no more need to do anything." The anger that now burned in her eyes revealed a side of his daughter Sebastian had never seen before. It was a strange feeling, as if he were suddenly staring into the eyes of a stranger, or perhaps a wild animal.

"But *why*, Kayla...I'm confused."

"She held on for as long as she could, Daddy," Kayla told

him, her voice cracking, with tears bursting forth and flowing down both cheeks and onto the floor below her. "Little Sam just couldn't wait any longer for a heart, Daddy; she's dead."

CHAPTER 7

Daniel marveled at some of the antique machinery, equipment, and furniture they passed as they walked hurriedly down the myriad of corridors underneath the school. Much of what he'd seen had been covered either with sheets or with cobwebs. He surmised that in all likelihood, most of it had been stored away and forgotten many, many years earlier, perhaps even before the Great Schism, and from the looks of things, no one had been down there since that time.

Before long they came to a small room in the far corner of one of the larger spaces. Simon stopped and, using a key that must be as old as the lock it fit into, opened the door. Inside were a few modern conveniences including food, communications equipment, and several modern computers, all of which seemed woefully out of place among the collection of antiquities from a long lost era.

"Where are we?' Daniel asked as they sat down to catch their breath.

"We're seven levels down in the substructure underneath the university. This level pre-dates the Great Schism by several decades, so no one ever comes down here, unless they're with me."

"What do you mean by that?"

"You were right earlier, Daniel...I *do* work for the resistance. I'm a recruiter for them, working to identify individuals like yourself, who I feel are ideal candidates for recruitment."

Daniel stood staring at Simon for some time, waiting for a punchline that never came. Once it became obvious Simon was quite serious, Daniel's attitude changed.

"Then I'm afraid you're mistaken about me, Simon. I have no interest in joining the resistance. I mean, I do sympathize with what the resistance is trying to do, and I very much appreciate the level of trust you have in bringing me here."

At this Simon reached into a drawer and took out a subdermal injector and laid it on the desk. "I believe once you hear what I have to tell you, it will become clear that it is you, my friend, who are mistaken. As for the trust...well, I do trust you, Daniel, but we can't afford to take such risks. This injector is loaded with a compound that can erase memories for up to a decade."

"A decade? Hey, wait a minute...," Daniel protested as he reached for the door.

"Relax, Daniel, I'm only setting this for two hours. But even at that, I doubt it will be needed once you hear what I have to say."

Daniel took a deep breath, and after leaning over, he placed his face into the palms of his hands and started shaking his head, exasperated.

"Let's just go back to the main level. You should know by now that I want nothing to do with the resistance. I promised my father I'd work hard here and make something of myself. I'm hoping that one day, if I'm able, maybe I'll have an opportunity to reunite with them."

Simon grimaced at that, and when Daniel stood back up, Simon met his gaze with a sympathetic yet firm expression.

"Look Daniel, there's something I really need to tell you; *please* sit back down."

Daniel furrowed his brow, and after letting out a heavy sigh, he sat down in the chair.

"I'm very sorry, Daniel, and I hate that I'm the one having to tell you this; your father is dead."

Daniel sat there for a moment, his facial expression frozen somewhere between shock and denial.

"My father...dead? No, he's still alive, Simon, he has to be. Why would you say something like that? Don't crack jokes about my father!" he bellowed, his voice filled with anger and rage.

Simon sat back and watched in awe at the pent up emotion inside his friend. "Daniel, I promise, it's true."

"But he's still relatively young! He's in great shape, and he never gets sick. I just haven't seen him in a while, which is probably why I don't speak of him more often."

Simon grimaced again before placing each hand on Daniel's shoulders. "He's dead, Daniel, trust me. I learned of it this morning through the resistance via my handler."

"What? No, Simon, they've made a mistake."

"You need to trust me, Daniel; your father's gone, I'm sorry."

"No!" he replied while standing, still angry. "You're just saying that because you want me to join the resistance. He's not dead, the NZC would have told me!"

Simon just stared back at Daniel, dejected and saddened by his friend's response. "Come on, Daniel; really? You should know me better than that by now; I'm your friend, you idiot. Do I want you to join us? Yes, of course I do. Am I willing to lie to you about your father dying? Of course not! I'm actually hurt that you'd even think that."

Daniel stared at Simon for some time until at last, he sat back, took a deep breath, and sighed.

"You're absolutely certain about this?"

"Yes; I trust my source completely. The report stated your father was killed in an industrial accident six months ago," Simon replied.

A light stream of tears had started flowing down his face when Daniel suddenly looked up. "My mother; she's okay?"

Simon paused for a moment before reaching out to place his hand on Daniel's shoulder. "Daniel, I'm afraid there's more bad news."

"More?"

"Yes, I'm afraid so. When your father died, your mother blamed the company. I'm told she raised quite a ruckus about the accident, and brought a lot of unwanted publicity on the company."

"What happened?"

"It would seem that your mother suddenly lost her job, and was subsequently evicted from her home."

"Oh, no, no, no...." Daniel buried his head in his hands and began sobbing. "She lost her job *and* was evicted?"

"Yes. I'm so sorry, Daniel."

"How is any of this even possible, Simon? It makes no sense! Maybe your source was mistaken."

"Trust me, Daniel, there's been no mistake."

"But the Corporate Synod normally *helps* employee families instead of punishing them. They go out of their way to ensure that victim's families are well taken care of following an accidental death; it helps ensure the loyalty and hard work from the rest of the employees at a facility. Why would my father's death be any different?"

"True, you're right about that of course, Daniel. At one time, the Synod *did* take care of families following the death of an employee. But those days are long gone. Based on the intel, the truth about your father's accident was buried and then covered up by the Synod, but it wasn't the only one. Apparently, there's been an increasing number of deaths at Synod production facilities in recent years, and the public is starting to take notice."

"My family's always been actively involved with the local NZC chapter. Surely *they* would speak out on my family's behalf. The NZC would never allow my mother to be evicted, that's crazy!"

"The church was in on the cover up with the Synod. The Synod was desperate to shift blame away from the plant, so they cut a deal with the NZC. As a result, the land and property of victims' families are forfeited by the family and 'donated' to the NZC. That way everyone wins...everyone except for the family, of course."

A lifetime's worth of memories suddenly filled Daniel's mind, even while tears streamed silently down his face until a small pool formed on the floor. After a few minutes, however, his expression hardened, and an uncharacteristic scowl came over his face, causing Simon's eyes to widen.

"Can your contacts get me more details on exactly what happened?" Daniel asked, his voice betraying an intensity and anger Simon had never witnessed in his friend before. "I need to find out what happened to my mother, make certain she's okay."

"I don't know for sure; information doesn't flow so well in and out of Sector 48, as you know. But I'll see what I can do."

"Thanks, Simon."

"No problem. I'm so sorry to be the bearer of such bad news, my friend." Simon waited for a few moments before continuing. "So, what will you do now?"

Daniel looked up with a hard, cold expression on his face. "The Synod has been murdering their employees and then destroying their families, and the NZC has been helping them. What do you *think* I'm going to do? Once I'm certain my mother is safe, I'm going to expose them, and I'm going to make them pay."

"Does that mean you'll join us, Daniel?"

"No," began Daniel, in a fierce and determined reply. "But the resistance is welcome to join *me*."

CHAPTER 8

As I climbed out of the car I glanced up to gaze at the beautiful blue sky above. It was a bright, sunny day, the kind of day that would normally warm the heart and fill it full of cheer. Even as I made my way to the door, I suspected that even such a magnificent morning could do little to ease the pain I knew I'd find inside of the Ross home.

"Good morning, Mr. Jefferson." A holographic image of the butler appeared in the middle of the doorway.

"Good morning, Jerome."

"I'm afraid I'm out running errands at the moment, sir, and Mr. and Mrs. Ross have been out of town for the past two weeks."

"Really? What about Kayla, is she home?"

"Yes, sir, she is. She dismissed the rest of the house and kitchen staff this morning and gave them the weekend off. She's been in bad sorts, Mister Jefferson," he told me. "She disappeared for most of last week; I had no idea what to tell the Rosses when they checked in."

"What did they say when you told them?" he asked the kindly butler.

"They said she's probably been staying with a friend and just forgot to tell anyone."

"You don't believe that though, do you, Jerome?" I asked, able to tell even via holcom that Jerome was highly agitated about something.

"No sir, I don't. She's been deeply troubled ever since that precious child passed away last month. I'm afraid she's just not been herself. I tried to say something to her parents, Mister Jefferson, but it's not my place. I'm afraid I've already gone too far and made them both a bit angry with me."

"I understand, Jerome; you don't have to explain."

"Thank you, sir. Please, Mr. Jefferson, won't you go inside and have a talk with her? She refuses to talk about what happened with me or even her family, but I know that she'll open up to you, sir."

"You really care about her, don't you, Jerome?"

"I've been with the Rosses for over twenty years now, Mister Jefferson; Miss Kayla is like the daughter I never had." The door buzzed before opening as if on its own accord. "Won't you go in, sir? I believe you'll find Miss Kayla in her bedroom."

"Of course, Jerome, and thanks."

"You're certainly welcome, sir. I'll see you both shortly."

The house seemed unnaturally quiet as I walked inside and began making my way upstairs and toward Kayla's room. The house was nearly always abuzz with some sort of activity or another, either by a family member, guest, or the house staff. I began calling out as I neared her bedroom.

"Kayla? Kayla, it's me, Christian; Jerome let me in."

"Christian!" The sound of my name was muffled and faint, but grew much louder as Kayla threw open her bedroom door and hollered it out again. "Christian, I'm so glad you're here!" she exclaimed upon seeing me. She ran toward me with tears in her eyes, nearly knocking me down as she leapt into my arms.

"Kayla, are you okay?" I thought I heard another muffled response, but after considering it for a few seconds, I finally concluded it had been nothing more than her sobbing with her face buried in my chest. "Are you okay, Kayla? Jerome said your parents are out of the country and that you were gone somewhere last week by yourself. What's going on? Where did you go?"

Kayla paused her sobbing long enough to look up at me. "I'm fine," she replied dryly.

"Come on, Kayla, clearly you're not. Listen, it's going to be okay, I promise." I heard her snicker. It was a strange, callous, and inappropriate response, but I decided to ignore it. "Now tell me, what's this all about, Kayla? Is this about Sam?"

50

"Yes...no...well, it was in the beginning," she replied, speaking more clearly now.

"And now?" I asked her bluntly as I led her towards the sofa in the nearby living area.

"Now it's *everything!*"

"What do you mean?"

"Our province, our society...it's *sick*, Chris; do you know what I mean?"

"Um, no; I'm afraid you've lost me Kayla."

"Come on, Christian!" she exclaimed, clearly growing frustrated with me. "Most everyone in the BZ stays stoned out of their minds on government distributed blue pills, and when they're not, they're standing in line to pick up their government checks, where drones, under the orders of our benevolent Gentry Class, download the latest List of Instructions, Necessities, and Controls. LINC...what a joke!"

"Where did you go, Kayla?" I asked, trying to understand what she was talking about.

She looked up at me with an expression I'd never seen on her face before. It was an odd mixture of anger, frustration, fear, and confusion.

"I went here, I went there, I went everywhere!" she exclaimed, throwing both arms up in the air.

"What kind of drugs are you on, anyway?" I asked, absolutely convinced she was stoned out of *her* mind. She looked up as sober as a judge, and her answer surprised me.

"I'm not on any drugs, Christian, just life. When Sam died... it was as if I'd just opened my eyes for the first time. I'd never really thought about it before, probably because like everyone else, I did everything I could to ignore the suffering of others. I'd never really looked around to *see* what was going on around me. Maybe I didn't see how bad things were because my parents protected me from it; maybe I've just pretended for so long that it didn't exist that I actually started to believe it.

"The world's a stinking cesspool, Chris, at least it is here in the Blue Zone. The Gentry is corrupt at all levels, as you and I discovered with Sam. With the People's Guard as their muscle, they're pretty much unstoppable."

"What are you talking about, Kayla? The Gentry's kept the peace ever since the Great Schism!"

Kayla offered a twisted smile as a response. "Yeah, that's what we've always been taught, isn't it? Have you ever been outside of the capital cities, Christian?"

"You know I have, on trips with my father."

"No…that's not what I mean, Chris. I mean, have you ever left a capital city and just driven for miles and miles in any direction?"

I shook my head.

"Well I did; that's where I went last week. I loaded up supplies and just took off. I wanted to see what happened outside of the capital cities. It was awful, Chris," she told me, making a horrific face before becoming agitated and distraught. "It looks like the Dark Ages out there, Christian. It's *wrong*! It's awful the way I saw people living! How could the Gentry stand by while people practically starve out there? Oh, it was horrible, Chris…some of what I witnessed was unspeakable."

"What else did you see out there, Kayla?" I asked her, partly out of concern for her safety, but mostly out of abject curiosity. In truth, though I'd travelled to rural areas with my father from time to time, I'd never really been given a chance to explore any of them beyond what my father and his security team allowed me to see. Needless to say, it scarcely resembled what Kayla was describing to me now.

Kayla began sobbing again. "I saw men, women, and children lying dead in rundown areas, Chris; it was horrible! It looked like they'd been dosing constantly until one day, they passed out and never woke up. Where was the government, Chris? Why hadn't they been buried?

"I saw women and children walking the streets of some of the cities, clothes ragged, all skin and bones. Where is the food, Chris…why are these people starving? Our government is supposed to be taking care of *everyone*, not just the Gentry!"

"They do, Kayla; at least they're supposed to. Free and equal access to food and healthcare for everyone. That's what we were taught, right?"

"Yeah, right," Kayla muttered, more to herself than to me. It was clear a storm was brewing within her.

She stopped and stared at me for several moments, more looking through me than at me. Suddenly her face grew dark and tightened.

"There was something else, Christian, something else that troubled me."

"What?"

"Well, you know how we're so connected that we're able to easily keep up with laws and regulations that directly affect us, as Gentry, right?"

"Sure, of course."

"Well, I happened to drive into a small town about fifty miles from here one day last week. While I was hanging out around the town for the day, I happened to walk by the local CA…you know, the Central Authority office. Anyway, I saw a couple near the front of the line where government workers were passing out credits, along with monthly LINC injections."

"LINC injections; what's that?"

"Oh yeah, you probably wouldn't know if your father hadn't taking you near a CA office. That's how everyone outside of the Gentry class is kept up-to-date on all the many laws and regulations the Gentry pass every month; my father told me about them last year. Well, to make sure everyone gets theirs, the government forces everyone who wants to receive their monthly allotment of credits to get an injection while they're waiting in line. It's supposed to keep everyone up to date."

"Okay, that sounds reasonable enough. What's wrong with that, Kayla?"

"It's a little intrusive if you ask me, that's what!" snapped Kayla. When she noticed my reaction, however, she took a deep breath. "Wow, I'm sorry, Chris."

"No worries, K."

Kayla nodded. "Well, that wasn't what really bothered me, Chris. That couple I mentioned, remember?"

"Yeah, right."

"From what I could tell they'd been arguing about something the entire time they'd been in line; they were driving others around them up the wall. Anyway, they eventually made it to the front of the line, and after receiving their injection, collected their credits."

"Okay, so?"

Kayla suddenly lowered her voice. "It's what happened after, Chris. The couple couldn't have taken more than ten or fifteen steps away from the CA when it happened."

"When what happened, K?"

"They suddenly stopped yelling; in fact, they stopped talking to one another at all. Suddenly their faces were totally without expression, as if their minds had suddenly changed gears completely. They turned from the direction they'd been walking in and walked into this large building with a covered entrance, then walked inside the door that was apparently already open."

"Then what happened?"

"Well you know me, Chris…I had to find out what was going on."

"Yes, Kayla, I know."

"Well, I followed them. Inside the building were hundreds, maybe thousands, of people, all waiting in lines across the entire building."

"Lines for what?"

"For a train, an underground train. Chris, these people were supposed to be receiving their LINC injections. Instead, they were given some kind of programming drug that turned them into mindless drones."

"There must be a logical explanation for all of this, Kayla, come on. So, what happened next?"

"After some mysterious train appeared out of nowhere, they were loaded up with the others like cattle and shipped off."

"Where?"

"I have no idea, but I'm going to find out. Then I'm going to do something about it."

I'd known Kayla Ross for most of my life, so I knew what that meant. About all I could do at that point was take a deep breath, roll my eyes, and let out a long and heavy sigh. Life was about to get interesting.

CHAPTER 9

The streets were all but deserted as Daniel made his way down the street through a forest of enormous buildings, most of which flashed images of either a serene and peaceful nature, a flattering picture of the current Leader of the Red Council, Mikos Romano, or advertisements for one of the many member companies that belonged to the Corporate Synod. He marveled at the beautiful office building that stretched into the sky, the building that served as the headquarters for the Synod's regional leadership. He'd studied it carefully, as he'd cased the building over the past two weeks.

Having grown up in Sector 48, Daniel had little experience with the ways of the city, and even less experience navigating it. The regular trips into the heart of the city had proven invaluable as he tried to familiarize himself with various routes for getting to, and later away from, the building. A full block before reaching the street where the building was, Daniel turned right, dodging in and out from behind buildings and objects, carefully trying to avoid the holocams that would surely alert authorities should he be picked up by one. Daniel pulled the hood of his jacket down to try to cover more of his face. He'd tried to be as careful when he'd gone on similar missions, but it would take only a single mistake, a minor oversight, or overlooking a single camera for him to be identified by the authorities.

A strong vibrating motion emanating from a device inside his jacket pocket prompted Daniel to take cover underneath a nearby transport vehicle. The telltale sound of a drone soon came within range, and Daniel took a deep breath and held it upon hearing it come closer. His heart began racing. The Synod's security drones posed the greatest risk to nearly every mission he'd been on. Should one of them spot him and identify him as a threat, it would all be over. There would be no way to get away from it. Even if he could hit it with a shot from his EMP emitter, it would take less than thirty seconds for another one to arrive on the scene. In addition, it had been rumored that the Synod Security Force, the SSF, had recently begun arming drones with sonic disrupters, designed as offering both a non-lethal and lethal means of disabling a suspect without causing any permanent damage or terminating them. It was a necessary tool for the drones to have when suspects needed to be questioned for information. Most drones still carried the lasers which were, of course, useful only for terminating suspects, and it was an option the Synod used frequently and without hesitation whenever information was not an issue, or when the desire to eliminate a threat overrode the need for intelligence.

The drone hovered over Daniel's position for some time. Soon Daniel's chest began to heave as his lungs started to burn, desperate for oxygen. He summoned every bit of effort he could to not take a refreshing breath to end his agony. Even when his lungs felt as if they would burst, it took only the thought of his family's suffering at the hands of the Synod and the NZC for him to stiffen his resolve so he could hold on for another thirty seconds. Just seconds before his body caved in to its intense need for oxygen, he heard the sound of the drone speeding away. Within a few seconds it was gone and the vibrating warning in his pocket ceased. Desperately fighting the urge to take a long, deep, but also loud gasp of air, he exhaled, and as quietly as he could he sat down and took in a deep and rewarding breath, filling both lungs to capacity. He sat there for another minute, telling himself it was to ensure the drone was long gone, and to drink in as much oxygen as possible before continuing. Daniel quietly whispered a barely audible "Thank you, Simon" as he climbed out from under the vehicle. It had been at his friend's urging that Daniel had begun training to hold his breath for longer and longer periods of time, a practice Simon suggested was becoming more and more common among the Resistance fighters as the Synod had stepped-up its use of drones in battling the Resistance.

As he neared the building's side entrance Daniel glanced down at his watch. Once inside, he'd have less than a minute to get in and get out before SSF troops arrived. His security pin would enable him to get through the door, but the unauthorized entry during NZC indoctrination hours would trigger the silent alarm. It was because everyone would be at the mandatory NZC facilities that he'd chosen this time for the mission.

He took the package from the pouch around his waist, as well as a small device. He pressed a small button several times until a small screen read "02:00:00." It would have to be long enough. Daniel paused to mentally walk through the sequence of events as they would soon unfold. Confident he was ready to proceed, he looked around once more, took a deep breath, and after pressing a button on his watch that triggered a stopwatch function, he reached for the door.

Daniel pulled up his scarf, to cover as much of his face as he could without obstructing his vision, and opened the door. He'd studied the plans in detail, and knew where he had to go. He immediately made for the stairwell, and raced down the stairs until he'd descended two stories to the lowest level. His security pin granted him full access to the building, so when he arrived at the electrical room where the fusion-reactor was stored, he was able to enter. Once inside, he ran to where the fuel cells were stored, took out the device he'd retrieved earlier, and held it next to the metal housing of the fuel cell. The magnet at the base of the device locked on to the metal in the fuel cell housing and held fast. Daniel then pushed the button before glancing down at his watch. The screen read out "0:59" as it counted down.

"Crap!" he exclaimed, surprised that he'd already used up over a minute of his time. He ran back up the stairs in leaps and bounds, glancing back at his watch as he approached the door. This time the watch read "0:15." Daniel glanced around briefly as he exited the building; the Synod's goons had not yet arrived.

He let out a sigh before running at breakneck speed to the corner, and back down the street in the opposite direction. He heard the explosion behind him but, knowing he could not spare even a second to turn around to watch, continued racing to get as far away as possible. He was already three blocks away when there was a loud, secondary blast, followed by a rumble that sounded, and felt, like a massive earthquake, even from over four blocks away. Only then did he glance behind him briefly to see what he could, but his vision was obscured by the buildings surrounding him.

A sound from down the street drew his attention. It was Simon, waiting in a transport. He hurried to the waiting vehicle and found the door open for him when he arrived.

"Get in!" Simon yelled. Daniel was all too happy to comply, and a mere few seconds later, the pair was outside the city. Daniel glanced back, and now that they were slightly elevated above the level of the city, he could see a pile of rubble where the Synod's regional headquarters had been.

"Look at that!" he exclaimed. "Do you think that will get their attention?" he asked his friend.

Simon glanced back in his mirror and saw some what remained of the building.

"Wow! Yeah, Daniel, I think that will get their attention."

Daniel smiled and nodded before retrieving a device. "I'm going to send the message now, Simon."

Simon looked around in all directions, and seeing no activity, he pulled over and stopped the transport. "Fellow citizens of the Red Zone. Today, the People of The Founders struck at the heart of the Corporate Synod and the Red Council. We destroyed their regional headquarters building; we did this because we wanted to get their attention, and because we wanted to get yours.

"Our so-called leaders in the Red Zone have abandoned *everything* the founders of this once-great country intended. I would like to ask that you consider the following words from a document developed and implemented by the brave and noble men we refer to as the Founding Fathers, who founded the United

States of America, the great country from which the Red Zone and the Blue Zone came. These words come from the Preamble of the Constitution of the United States of America, a document written by the Founding Fathers almost four-hundred years ago:

"'We the People of the United States, in Order to form a more perfect Union, establish Justice, insure domestic Tranquility, provide for the common defense, promote the general Welfare, and secure the Blessings of Liberty to ourselves and our Posterity, do ordain and establish this Constitution for the United States of America.'

"Has the Corporate Synod and the NZC established justice? Has the Red Council ensured domestic tranquility? Has it secured the blessings of liberty for you, for your children, and for your children's children? No! Instead, those on the Council have enslaved us! Just consider the poor, innocent children in the Production Class, forced to undergo genetic modifications that enhance productivity and a better bottom line for the company, but an early death for the child. They don't just enslave the Production Class, however...they enslave us all! They force us, everyone, to submit to genetic engineering whether we like it or not. They tell us who and what and how we are supposed to worship. There is no freedom and prosperity in the Red Zone, only slavery.

"We're told that only those in the Intelligentsia Class are worthy to make decisions because they were genetically designed to be the most intelligent among us. Well, I've got news for our overlords; your time of tyranny is over, because I, and the People of the Founders, *will bring you down*. We *will* return the power to the people; this is our sacred duty, this is our destiny. I swear on my life this will happen; this is only the beginning!"

Daniel clicked the button and looked over at Simon.

"I just sent that out across the entire Red Zone over the emergency channel. What did you think?" Daniel furrowed his brow at the expression frozen on his friend's face. His eyes were open wide and his mouth hung down as if a trapdoor supporting his jaw had opened. "What?"

"That was mega hot, Daniel; I can't believe that was you!"

Daniel's face tightened slightly while his eyes narrowed. "Believe it, Simon. And the destruction of that empty building, it was mere child's play. The real key to winning the insurgency against the Red Council is by destroying their means of enforcing their edicts."

"What? Are you saying we have to take out the Synod's military and police, *and* the NZC's Red Guard? Impossible!"

Daniel offered no reply as he inserted a small device into the holocom before pressing another button. He watched as a small indicator light changed from a flashing blue to green. "Okay, it's on the Nexus."

He then pushed another button on the holocom, which caused a virtual display to appear above it in the form of a 3-dimensional hologram. Daniel waved his hands and used his fingers to manipulate the display. In less than five seconds he and Simon watched and listened to the recording he'd made a minute earlier. Daniel smiled before nodding his head in approval. "You're right, Simon, that *was* impressive."

"I told you; you iced it, Daniel!"

"Thanks. But you're wrong, Simon."

"Wrong...about what?" he asked while continuing to drive.

"We *will* take out the Synod's military and police, or at least convince enough of them to join our cause and help us. This will be more than enough to weaken the military and police enough that they fall apart. From what I've been hearing, more and more of the military's been thinking about coming over to us; eventually we'll have the majority. That's when we attack them head-on." He turned to Simon to ensure the maximum effect of his words. "A strong leader must be strategic and not rely purely on brute force. If we tried that, we'd all end up dead. No, we'll use stealth, cunning, and the truth to win over the military, the police, and the people."

"What about the Red Guard" You know they're filled with idealists who've endured years of indoctrination and lies at the hands their masters in the NZC. Despite the way they've been treated, they are 100% loyal to their overlords."

"Then I'm afraid we'll have to destroy the Red Guard entirely, and wipe them off the face of the Earth...."

His words trailed off as Simon continued driving. As they left the city for the more rural areas, Simon glanced over at his friend, and deep in the recesses of his heart, he realized he was slowly coming to fear the monster he'd created.

CHAPTER 10

It had been a long and exhausting day, filled with haggling, maneuvering, and posturing. It seemed no matter how hard he tried or how many hours he put into trying to make a difference, to change things from within the system, he felt only as if he were constantly spinning his wheels. It felt as if the whole zone were sliding further and further over the precipice, and there seemed to be nothing he could to stop it.

Sebastian Ross poured himself a glass of wine, sat down on the sofa, and said the command, "*Holo on.*"

The holoprojector came on and he sipped on his wine as he began watching a Blue Zone News Broadcast already in progress.

"Be well, my brothers and sisters," the man sitting across from Sebastian said, "and good evening from me, Walt Benning, and all of your comrades here at Central Authority News, your BZNN, Blue Zone National News, broadcast.

"We begin our broadcast this evening with some terrible and frightening news. A major terrorist attack took place early this morning in the city of New Portland. The attack took place on a rehabilitation facility just outside the city, which houses several hundred inmates. The inmates were set free by the attacking force, who subsequently stood by quietly and watched as the horde of prisoners scattered in all directions and were soon gone. The prisoners, reported to be among the most dangerous men and women in the state, remain at large.

"The motivation for the attacks and for freeing so many dangerous criminals remains unclear at this time, with the enforcement bureau saying only that this is a top priority for them. The People's Guard was also on the scene investigating this incident, suggesting it could even have captured the attention of the leader himself, though that could not be confirmed by the People's Guard spokesman.

"The terrorist group blamed for this morning's attack is a group calling themselves the Militiamen Freedom Fighters, and it is their third such attack in as many weeks. Last week a caravan carrying food to the town of Richland, which has been suffering a severe food shortage over the last six months, was attacked by the brigands, and all the food rations, intended for the poor, suffering people of Richland, were stolen. Dozens of people died during that attack, leading Richard Smythe, the local commissioner for the People's Guard, to publicly announce that anybody identified as being a member of the terrorist organization, or any citizen accused of aiding or abetting the Militiamen, will be shot on sight, with or without trial, as authorized by our Sovereign Leader.

"These so-called Militiamen are...."

Suddenly the man disappeared and a new figure suddenly sat there, causing Sebastian to jerk back momentarily.

"These *so-called* Militiamen are interrupting your regularly scheduled lying, windbag, sack of propaganda...to bring *you*, the people of the BZ, a little truth; for the *Gentry* we have, of course, some consequences."

The man who'd been announcing the news was suddenly gone, replaced by the strange, solitary figure sitting behind a desk while speaking to the camera. Based on the outline of the shape, the gestures, and the voice, the person was a woman, but with the face covered by a mask, which covered her entire face and head, and with the synthesized voice, she'd be impossible to identify.

"You know something? Times are hard, *really* hard, for normal folks. I'm referring to people—you know, *human beings*—in the BZ. Of course, our beloved 'Leader,' sitting on his backside, is so busy filling his own belly, and his own pockets, that he hasn't got much time for helping regular folks like you and me. But we're kind of hoping maybe there are some left in the BZ who can and will help. Now, we know that many of you watching tonight are

Gentry, and we suspect that if you worked *really* hard at it, some of you might come to discover that deep down inside, *you too* are still human beings, as hard as that might be to believe! You still have compassion for a small child going to bed hungry at night, sympathy for a mother forced to watch her children waste away in front of her from starvation, no matter how hard she works to feed and clothe them.

"I am, therefore, tonight appealing to whatever humanity you have left, to please...help. Stop turning a blind eye to the starving masses all around you, to the abuses heaped upon the poor by the very government charged with protecting them.

"The People's Guard has been lying to you, as has their media arm, the government-run Central Authority News. We've hijacked their broadcast signal for a few minutes in order to open your eyes to what's really going on. Please, listen to what we tell you. We don't know how long we have before they take the signal back from us.

"I swear that the food convoy *was not* headed to the poor people of Richland...that is a complete fabrication. The Militiamen fight *for* the people, *not* against them. The food in that convoy wasn't headed to feed the poor of Richland...oh no. Ha! No, not unless you call those fat, rich bastards attending the lavish Gentry banquet at a large, nearby estate the 'poor of Richland.' No, I'm afraid that the estate owner had simply invited too many guests and required a special shipment of food in order to feed them all. We felt it incumbent upon us, of course, to 'intercept' this shipment, so we could reroute it to several deserving towns nearby, to the poor who *really* needed it. The sad part of our story is that *we* had to act because no one else would. And tonight, children in those towns will go to bed with a full belly, some for the first time in weeks.

"People are dying all over the Blue Zone from starvation, and the problem gets worse by the day. The Gentry take all the food and resources, paying next to nothing, or trading cheap and dangerous drugs in exchange for the food the commoners grow, while commoners starve and go without. The number of deaths due to excessive drug use in the BZ has also grown exponentially in recent years, to the point that on a recent trip to a small town, I found dozens of people — *dozens* — lying on sidewalks or alongside roads, all dead from overdose, starvation, or neglect."

Up to this point the woman had been speaking evenly and matter-of-factly. Sebastian watched as tears began streaming from her eyes and down into the inside of her mask.

"I recently heard a very sad story about a little girl who was bumped off the organ donor list so that a fat, old man, Gentry of course, was able to live for six more months. That precious little girl, however, had the rest of her life ahead of her, maybe *sixty years*.

"This is our world, people, this is *your* world; you've got to wake up and take it back!

"The Gentry and their lackeys haven't done anything to improve the lives of everyday folks like you and me; they've only made things exponentially worse. Food shortages, drugs, and now, something far more sinister and much more dangerous has started happening, thanks to our Gentry friends."

The woman paused and clicked a button on a device she held in her hand. Her image on the screen was suddenly replaced by some outdoor footage, showing a long line of common people. As the camera panned closer to the front of the line, people could be seen administering injections.

"Watch and you'll see what the government, your government, is doing to its own people. As you can see, citizens arrive at the local CA office to pick up their monthly government check and, as the government often does, they're supposedly receiving their monthly LINC downloads. Only watch what happens immediately afterwards."

The woman ceased speaking while the camera zoomed in on the faces of the people. Each person received a check, then an injection. Immediately afterwards, each one, to a person, lost all facial expression, turned from whatever direction they were heading in, and began walking directly toward the large building in the background. In the distance, a train could be seen filling up with people as they were processed through the building.

"This footage was taken in a small, rural town in California. Each citizen receives their monthly credit, then the required injection. Then each one immediately makes his or her way to the large building, where they are processed and, depending on who they are and what they do, either sent home or loaded onto one of these trains. We followed a couple of these trains to their destinations. One of them carried everyone on the train to a large agricultural farm, where they worked very long days in the fields, while the other train carried its unsuspecting citizens to a large factory floor, where they were put to work assembling and testing machinery and equipment used in various machines.

"In both cases these people worked all day every day, seven days a week. They were turned into slaves by the State, people... *slaves!* The State decided it needed more workers, so the State decided who and when it would get them; where's the freedom in that?

"Many years ago, following the Great Schism, the Blue Zone split with the Red Zone because our people were promised more freedom than any civilization on the planet had ever experienced. Each man, woman, and child was promised they could do what they wanted, when they wanted, and how they wanted, and that no one would tell them what to do. The people were promised that food, medical care, and education in our new world would be plentiful, and that it would be provided free of charge, by the state.

"Well then, look where we are now! Our people are starving from lack of food, our people are dying from lack of medical care, and our people are suffering greatly from the lack of an education. The State has failed us people; wake up!

"The so called terrorist attacks you heard about recently were Militiamen Freedom Fighters liberating these two work camps. It took two to three days for these human beings to snap out of whatever the slavers had done to them. This is what *you've* sacrificed, the freedom that *you've* surrendered.

"Now the men, women, and children we've freed know the

truth, and they're angry…oh, are they angry, believe me. We've added hundreds to our number now, and with each camp we liberate from the government slavers the resistance grows. We invite you to help us, to join us, and to help liberate the BZ from the Gentry, so we can be a free people once again. Long live the Militiamen, and freedom for everyone in the BZ!"

Sebastian Ross issued another verbal command. "Holo off!" He then spent the next several minutes sipping on the rest of his wine, contemplating everything he'd just heard, and the future.

***

A wine glass sailed through the air, turning end over end before smashing against the holo-projector. The projection fizzled before going out completely. The man uttered a low growl before lightly squeezing his right earlobe.

"You saw it?"

"Yes, sir."

"So busy sitting on his backside…aarrgghh! The insolence!"

"Yes, sir."

"This is not good, Francis. I want you to find out who that witch is, and I want you to do it tonight, understood?"

"But—"

"Understand?" the man roared.

"Yes, sir."

"Good."

The leader walked over to where a carafe of wine sat and picked up the second of what had been a pair of wine glasses. He poured himself another glass, took a sip, and walked over to the window.

"You can run, little lady, and you can hide behind that mask of yours, but I've got news for you; I'm going to learn who you are, I'm going to find out where you are, and then…I'm going to *end* you."

CHAPTER 11

I took another drink from the glass of tea I'd poured and then turned to face Kayla. I marveled at how much she had changed over the last six months. I remembered the beautiful young woman lying in a lounge chair by the pool every day during the summer, the giddy, carefree girl of my youth. Then I looked up at the face of the strange woman in front of me, and saw a hard, callous woman, a woman devoted to a cause, determined not to stop and rest until she'd finished what she'd started out to do. It was a face I realized I no longer recognized.

Oh, I'd known for some time that it had been more than Sam's death that convinced Kayla to join the resistance. She'd have reacted sooner had she known of all of the pain and suffering happening all around her before that sweet little girl came along, but I'd been wholly unprepared for the depth of her enmity, or the impact Sam's death would have on Kayla.

"Take a picture, Christian, it would last longer."

My eyes must have lingered a little too long on my friend. I looked up to find her smiling at me.

"Yeah, I guess it would at that," I laughed, smiling back at her.

Kayla paused to glance down at her abysmal wardrobe, and began shaking her head soberly. "Though honestly, I can't imagine anyone *wanting* a picture of me, at least not the way I look right now. I mean, I—"

"What are you talking about, Kay? You look great!" We both knew I only half-meant it, but it brought my friend another smile.

"Thank you, Christian; I could always count on you when I needed a kind word."

I was about to engage in some friendly banter with Kayla, the first real conversation we'd had since the recent slew of events that culminated with the freedom of the camps, when a woman suddenly walked in and interrupted. She was a beautiful brunette, and I was immediately smitten. Kayla couldn't help but snicker ever so slightly at my not-so-subtle ogling, and she nodded slightly with her approval.

"Please pardon the interruption, ma'am," the beauty said to Kayla.

"Yes, Vanessa, what is it?"

"We've just gotten word that Stone and his men are closing in; it seems they were able to track the signal back to a hundred-mile radius. We have to leave now if we're going to escape before they close the net."

Kayla looked at Vanessa, then at me. "Say, Chris, would you like to stay with us or would you rather go back home? I'll send someone once we get settled somewhere."

I thought about it for a few moments. "I'll go with you."

"Are you sure, Chris?" she asked, concern written all over her face. "Chris…it's dangerous, and I have no idea how long it will be until we come back this way. It could be tough to get you back home should you want to come back before—"

"Well, the way I see it, I'm your friend, Kayla, and we're in this together. So wherever you go, I go."

"Oh, that's so sweet," Vanessa opined, injecting herself into the discussion. I just smiled back in a dopey, ridiculous manner. I was hopelessly lost in her beautiful, hazel eyes. For a moment I felt as if I might swoon, until I glanced back up at Kayla, who was all business.

"Chris, get out of here while you can. There's no need for you to get mixed up in all of this."

"Really?" I roared back, immediately regretting the tone and volume I'd taken. We were surrounded by resistance fighters who'd flocked to Kayla's side following the brazen camp raids and the subsequent shamecast. I immediately dialed back both the intensity and the tone. Kayla was my best friend, but the others barely knew me, if they even knew who I was. "I'm sorry, Kayla, but first of all you're my best friend, and I'm concerned for your safety. Besides, you're doing the right thing here; the truth is the zone's been on the wrong track for a long time, and you've started waking folks up. I'm with you, Kayla, wherever you and this movement of yours goes."

"Don't worry, Commander Ross, I'll look after him," Vanessa added, taking me by the arm. I didn't mind it at all. In fact, I found the thought of her spending a lot of time with me very appealing. Clearly, Kayla recognized this.

"Okay, Christian, if you're certain about this."

"I am," I replied, turning my attention away from Vanessa long enough to say the words.

"Okay, I guess it's settled. The truth is, I could really use your counsel, Christian. I need it, desperately!"

"Then you will have it, m'lady, as we saunter forth to right the wrongs of the evil empire."

Kayla just laughed before rising to prepare to leave. "Okay, Vanessa, I will leave my most cherished friend in your very capable hands."

I heard Kayla, but I'm not sure Vanessa did, for she'd already whisked me away from Kayla and towards a nearby series of temporary shelters that had been hastily put together sometime earlier.

***

It was late morning sometime the following day, and we were finally nearing completion of the long trip to our new campsite. Vanessa and I rode with Kayla and some of the senior members in a mobile command center. The weather had been fair and extremely temperate, so we rode with the windows cracked. We'd traveled overnight under the cover of darkness and a new moon, so I had little idea where we were, other than that we'd traveled due east all morning, and far from the capital in San Francisco.

Based on what Kayla had told me the night before, a lot would be riding on the resistance's ability to establish a permanent base of operations somewhere far from the capital, where it would be much harder for the Gentry to lead a major assault. Of course, everyone also hoped it would be a long time before the Gentry and their People's Guard ever learned where the base was located.

"We should be there soon," Kayla said to me from across the cabin.

I'd been staring solemnly out the window for some time, but nodded in response to her declaration. Still, there was something heavier weighing on me at the moment.

"Kayla?"

"Yes?"

"I saw something last night that's been troubling me; I thought I should probably say something."

"What did you see?" she asked.

"It was in the wee hours of the morning, so you and most of the others were asleep. Well, you know how I don't sleep much...."

"Yeah, I know, Chris; you're going to have to do something about that one of these days."

"Yeah, I am," I answered, with a slight laugh. "Anyway, at one point very early this morning, we were driving on one of the back roads through the mountains when we passed something, a place which according to my maps, doesn't exist. It was a city, Kayla, a fairly large one from the looks of it, and...well, parts of it looked very, very new."

"I wouldn't worry too much about it, Christian. It was in the middle of the night; you probably just didn't recognize it."

"No. I'm telling you, Kayla, there was something *really* strange about that place; something didn't look right about it. If it hadn't been the middle of the night I might have awakened you and said something about looking the place over."

"How long ago did you see it?" she asked him.

"Oh, no more than a couple of hours ago."

"Okay then. I tell you what, once we get settled down at the new base—we should be there soon—we'll send someone back to investigate. How does that sound?"

"That sounds like a good idea, Kayla, thanks."

I turned back to the window and glanced out at the surrounding countryside.

"Say, that looks like the Rocky Mountains there in the distance. Are we setting up here in Colorado?"

"Oh yeah," Kayla replied, almost giddy. "Oh Chris, we're almost there; this place will blow your mind. It's the perfect base of operations for us!" I was about to ask her what she was talking about when the command center we'd been riding in suddenly came to a halt. "We're here!" she announced.

Kayla made her way to the door. The inside of the cabin exploded with sunlight and blue sky as the door opened wide. Kayla stepped out into the fresh mountain air and I followed, stunned at what I saw.

"Is this what I think it is, Kayla?" I asked her, staring at the answer which towered in front of me.

"If you think that this is Cheyenne Mountain, and that it was once an extremely secure, reinforced military base built into the side of a mountain, then yes, it is what you think it is. This will be perfect base for the resistance, Christian! From here we can launch attack after attack until eventually, we destroy this corrupt, decadent government we have in place now, and re-establish this country as it was once intended. Welcome to N.O.R.A.D."

CHAPTER 12

"Where are we?" Simon asked, fumbling between maps while pausing from time to time to look around, trying in vain to get his bearings from the scarce road signs and the endless trees and fields visible in all directions.

"I don't know, Simon...I don't recognize anything from the map."

"So, we're lost?"

Daniel sighed. "Yeah, I guess we are, but at least we finally lost *them* too."

"For the moment," Simon agreed, looking around to ensure that at last, they were no longer being followed.

Daniel nodded. "Yeah, I guess we must have touched a nerve this time or something; they've never chased us this long or pushed us out this far before. We went much farther west than we've ever gone."

"Well, you did just blow up their regional headquarters, Daniel, and then rubbed salt in the wound of the Red Council... several times, I might add."

"Yeah, I suppose I did," Daniel acknowledged, grinning broadly. "I did indeed, and I expect the impact will be felt by the Synod for quite a while. I expect they'll *continue* coming after us for some time, and they'll be coming hard. We should probably lay low for a while, and regroup with the others once everything's cooled off a little. We'll be back in front of their face before they even know what hit them. Hey, listen, it's probably just me they're after for now. They may not even know about you; you may be able to get away without them even chasing you, if you wanted to take off. I'm going down eventually, Simon, I know that; there's no need for you to go down with me. I'm fine on my own, really."

"Come on, Daniel; I thought you had more respect for me than that. I'm not going to bail after what you did; that's exactly *why* I joined the Resistance, Daniel. Now come on, it hurts when you say something like that, man. It makes me feel like you don't have much of an opinion of me."

"No, no, it's not that at all, Simon. I was just wondering to myself why we should *both* die, that's all."

"Hey, look, no one's going to die, Daniel; we have far too much work to do, got it?"

"Yeah, yeah, okay. So, where should we go? It's going to be next to impossible to get back home right now."

"I agree; we can't go back until things cool off, but we don't need to wait more than a couple of weeks. We'll spend that time preparing for getting safely back home, and then start planning our next moves, perhaps against the NZC this time."

Simon paused for a moment, as if contemplating whether to raise an issue with Daniel. At length, he nodded his head and set his course of action. "Listen, Daniel, I've been thinking. Just how far are you wanting to take this fight? We're talking about going against the military, the police, and the Red Guard here. I know the resistance has been growing, and that we now have people from all three factions, but we're nowhere even close to being able to go up against them head-on."

A furrowed brow settled on Daniel's forehead. "What are you trying to say, Simon? Just spit it out."

"I think maybe we should ease up and give it a rest for a while, Daniel. Maybe we've already done enough to force change within the Synod and the NZC. Just think about it…haven't you already accomplished what you set out to do by getting their attention, and drawing attention to the massive corruption?"

Daniel grew quiet and focused on his driving without responding, reflecting on what Simon had said and the events over the last few months, before offering a reply.

"I can't say for certain how much we've accomplished thus

far, Simon," he began, "but I feel we still have a long way to go. I suppose in the beginning that may have been enough, but it's not any longer. I don't want to just get their attention; I want to stop them. I want what we're doing to change things. Our province, our zone, is way off track, Simon. We are subjugated by a fascist, totalitarian government; we are told how to think, what to believe, and we're forced to undergo genetic manipulation as dictated by the government. Where is the freedom that the United States was founded upon some four-hundred years ago? When the country split during the Great Schism, the Red Zone was intended to become a bastion for religious and economic freedom, while the *Blue Zone* was expected to become the fascist government. I can't speak for the BZ, but the RZ certainly has traveled far down that path. I'll do whatever I must to effect the necessary changes, Simon. We owe it to future generations, to our children, and you want to know something? I think we owe it to ourselves."

"Wow, Daniel, that's a very tall order," Simon answered.

"I know, Simon...I know it is. But we have no choice. Look, if others don't agree with me and don't want to go down this path, that's okay. As far as I'm concerned, however, I'm committed." Daniel paused, and after checking his mirrors looked for and soon found a place on the shoulder of the road where he could pull over safely. "We need to figure out where we are; I'm pulling over." Daniel parked on the shoulder and spent fifteen minutes studying the holographic map, pausing at times to look up around him. "Okay, based on where we started from, and given how long we've traveled, we should be somewhere around here."

Simon looked down at where Daniel was pointing on the map. "Really? We've traveled that far?"

"Well, we drove for hours, Simon, and it *was* due west almost the entire way. I can't get GPS coverage out this far, but I'll be honest with you...I think we may have even crossed the zone."

"*Crossed the zone*...are you kidding? I don't think so, Daniel; I don't think we could possibly have driven that far.

"I don't know. I think that…. Hey, wait a minute. Take a look there…do you see that, Simon?"

Simon turned to look in the direction Daniel had pointed. In the distance there was a sign standing on the side of the road that read, "Colorado Springs — 5 miles."

"We're in Colorado? *No way!*"

"Yeah, well, I guess we are," Daniel replied quietly. "Look there." Once again Simon turned to follow where Daniel pointed. Off in the distance, he could easily make out the snowcapped Rocky Mountains.

"Yeah, okay, so we're in Colorado Springs, Colorado. Where do you want to go now?"

"Let's see if we can find a hotel or something for a few days; just until we can get some rest. Did you happen to see any hotels around? I'm exhausted."

"I saw a small hotel about two miles back."

"Good," Daniel answered. "Look, Simon, we'd better remember where we are and be extremely careful. We're technically in the BZ now, and you know what will happen to us if we're caught here."

"Yeah, I know; it was written into the Great Schism charter that it is the obligation of citizens from both sides to terminate anyone caught crossing the zones without explicit permission from the leadership of both zones."

Daniel sighed. "I think we should probably just clear out of Colorado altogether. Maybe we should turn back and try to find something in Topeka, Wichita, St. Louis, or somewhere in between."

"I agree; it's not worth the risk."

Daniel started the car and was preparing to turn around when a large transport vehicle suddenly pulled in behind them, blocking his path. Daniel quickly assessed the situation, and just as he was preparing to fight his way out, their vehicle was surrounded by transports, assault tanks, and Jeeps, each filled with men armed with assault weapons and a whole lot of attitude.

"Who are you and what do you want?" Daniel asked them

plainly.

"We could ask the same about you," one of them asked as he stepped out of his Jeep and walked over to where Daniel and Simon sat trapped inside of their vehicle, an assault rifle locked and loaded. "In fact, *I am* asking the same thing about you!"

"My friend and I were lost; we pulled over just to try to get our bearings. Maybe you gentlemen could help?"

The leader of the group walked over to Daniel. "My name is Jones, Tom Jones, and these boys are in my band," he said sarcastically.

"Well then, I guess that makes me Ronald, Ronald Reagan, and my sidekick here is George. So again, I ask, where—"

There was a flash and Daniel caught just a glimpse of the butt of Tom Jones's weapon as it sped towards his temple, then everything went black.

CHAPTER 13

The first thing he was aware of was the rhythm of the intense pain in his head, which seemed to emanate from his temple. He gradually remembered being struck by Tom Jones's weapon, and as he opened his eyes, he also reached for the side of his head. It had been bandaged and he found himself lying in a bed, inside what appeared to be some sort of military or police facility. He found Simon lying unconscious in a bed next to him. Simon's head had also been carefully bandaged, and around his hands were magnetic cuffs, which held fast to two metal plates fixed on either side of the bed. Like Simon, Daniel's left wrist was also fixed with a magnetic cuff, though his right hand remained free.

"How are you feeling?" A man stepped out from the shadows. He had a kind face, and must have been around the same age as Daniel and Simon.

"Like I was hit in the head with the butt of a weapon; how are *you*?"

The man smiled. "Considerably better, I'm happy to report. I'm sorry about what happened. We weren't sure who you were and thought you were...well, someone else. I'm Frank, what's your name?"

"Daniel."

Daniel immediately regretted sharing his name before he'd learned who the man was, but it was too late. He wanted to ask if they were from the BZ or the RZ, but he decided it would be better to be cautious about volunteering information until he knew who they were.

"I told your men we were just passing through."

The man smiled again before looking back toward the

darkness from which he'd emerged. Two lights shined brightly into Daniel's face, preventing him from being able to see whoever it was his captor was looking at.

"Just passing through? I think we both know the truth here, Daniel, that you don't belong here at all. Tell me now, why *are* you here? Why did you cross over into the Blue Zone? Was it intentional? Did you leave the Red Zone on purpose? Before you answer, I strongly advise that you answer honestly and completely. You have no enemies here, so there's no reason for you to lie. Unless, of course, you intentionally crossed over into the Blue Zone to cause trouble—"

"No," Daniel quickly replied. "We crossed over purely by accident; we had no idea we were even in Colorado until we saw the signs. We were preparing to turn around and leave when your men stopped us."

"I see." The man turned to someone else in the room. Daniel focused his vision and could make out the shape of someone nodding their head. Frank turned back to Daniel. "So, you admit that you're from the Red Zone?"

"Yes," Daniel replied.

"And you crossed over into the Blue Zone by accident?"

"Yes."

"Have you had any contact whatsoever with anyone inside the Blue Zone prior to this intrusion?"

"Never, no one. Look, we'd driven long and hard for a quite a while; we just didn't realize how far we'd traveled until we saw the signs, and of course the Rocky Mountains in the distance."

Frank leaned in close to Daniel, looking him over, trying to decide whether to believe him or not.

"Careful, sir, he has one hand free," one of the guards pointed out, clearly concerned about Frank's proximity to Daniel.

"It's okay, Ben. I don't think Daniel is a threat; at least not to us. I suspect, however, that maybe he poses a threat to someone in the Red Zone. How about it, Daniel...were you running from someone in the Red Zone? Is that what caused you to grow so reckless as to cross into the Blue Zone? You might as well tell me,

Daniel. I'll find out anyway."

Daniel said nothing. He'd already said too much.

"Why make this more difficult? Tell me what I want to know. Who were you running from, and why?"

Daniel simply stared forward, saying nothing. He had no way of knowing what answering truthfully would mean; it could well mean his own death, which he was prepared for, but they would also kill Simon. Daniel, therefore, said nothing.

"Tell me! Why were they chasing you, Daniel?" Frank paused to give Daniel a chance to answer, but as before, nothing came. "Are you a criminal, Daniel?" Again, Daniel offered no response. "Are you a cold-blooded murderer?" No response. "Did you murder someone? Answer me, damn you!" Frank roared suddenly, growing frustrated.

"That's enough, Frank, thank you." The voice came from the darkness; it was unmistakably feminine, yet strong and authoritative.

Frank glared at Daniel momentarily before turning, nodding, and walking away.

A woman stepped out of the shadows this time, and walked over to Daniel's bedside. She had the appearance of someone who'd spent a lot of time on the move, yet she was beautiful in a way he'd never known. Maybe it was her beauty; she was young and shapely, still in her twenties, yet she possessed a certain stoicism and compassion that led Daniel to suspect she was an "old soul."

The woman looked her captive over, taking time to carefully examine his clothing, his demeanor, and the lines on his face. After walking around the table more than once, she finally stopped at its foot, to afford each of them a better view of the other.

"So…Daniel, is it? My name is Kayla."

Daniel considered saying more, but all that came out in response was, "Hello."

"I've been told that you and your companion claim to be 'lost' in Colorado Springs, after having driven for some time in a straight line due west, crossing the well-marked zone boundary,

I might add. Tell me, Daniel, is that true? Because it doesn't make a lot of sense to me."

This time Daniel's took some time to carefully study his captors. He couldn't help but notice that they were every bit as cautious and nervous about his presence as he was with theirs. Perhaps things weren't quite what they'd initially seemed to be; perhaps they weren't acting on behalf of the Blue Zone government at all.

"Okay, look, I'll make a deal with you; I'm willing to go out on a limb here and tell you everything, but I need your word — not Frank's word, Kayla, *your* word — that you'll do the same for me when I'm done. You will also release us, feed us, and shelter us, and then let us go on our way once we've held up our end of the bargain. Do we have ourselves a deal?"

"Explain to me why I should make a deal at all, Daniel, seeing as how you and your companion are my prisoners."

She'd made a good point, but Daniel now fancied himself an exceptional judge of character; she would agree, he was sure of it.

"You'll make the deal because you need to know the real reason why we're here, because you're curious about what we know and who we're working for, and because your own situation here is so very tenuous that you need all the friends you can get. So tell me, do we have a deal, or was I mistaken and is my visit here destined to be very short regardless?"

The woman had a stern, expressionless look on her face for a long time. After a few minutes, however, she suddenly burst into laughter.

"Wow, okay then. Any man with the chops to come in here and offer me a proposition like that, in my own house and in front of my own men, is a man worth getting to know." She walked closer to the table and looked over at Frank before nodding towards Daniel's restraints and those of his companion, A few minutes later Daniel was sitting in a chair sipping on some hot tea.

"We're on the run, Kayla. Seems we damaged some Red Zone government property, a rather important government building from what I'm told. And then we supposedly told pretty much the entire Red Zone all about it via a holocom broadcast, and told the people how corrupt the Red Council is. Now, for some inexplicable reason, the government seems intent on killing us. We had no intention of crossing the boundary into the Blue Zone, however…as I said, that was an accident. We had soldiers, police, even some Red Guard hot on our tails just hours before we realized where we were. We'd finally lost them an hour or two before finding ourselves in Colorado Springs. We really *were* trying to turn around when your men stopped us. Looking back though, I kind of wish I had crossed over intentionally; it would have been a pretty good escape strategy."

"Tell me, Daniel," his beautiful captor asked, "What is it you're up to over there? Why did you destroy that building, and why does your government consider you such a threat?"

Daniel's air of levity vanished, replaced by a very solemn disposition. "It saddens me to say this, but my people are lost, Kayla. Following the Great Schism, our people set out to forge a land of greater freedom, greater prosperity, and great happiness." Daniel gritted his teeth and furrowed his brow. "What we have now instead is a land ruled by a fascist, totalitarian, tyrannical government, where our people are treated like little more than slaves, where we are told what to believe, where to go, where to live, and where we're forced to undergo genetic manipulation whether we want to or not, based on the needs of the Corporate Synod. Those who defy the NZC by worshipping the Judeo-Christian God or by not worshipping the 'universe,' as the NZC instructs us, are locked away in prison, or condemned to death. When I learned that my father was dead and my family destroyed because of the corruption inside the Synod and the NZC, I finally opened my eyes to what had been going on around me; I decided to do something about it."

Kayla's eyes now sparkled and a warm, endearing smile had settled on her face. Daniel must have startled her by his reaction once he noticed, because she jerked back slightly, causing Daniel to smile. She quickly recovered, however, while retaining a slight smile.

"I'm impressed, Daniel; no, I'm *deeply* touched. You know something, Daniel? It may turn out that you and I have quite a bit in common. We each care deeply about our peoples, and we're both disgusted with what we see happening around us. I think we may have a lot to offer one another, and I'd like to discuss how we might be able to work together…assuming you're interested, of course."

Daniel looked into the young woman's beautiful emerald-green eyes and answered the only way he could. "Yes, of course I'm interested, Kayla; as long as I get an opportunity to get to know *you* better as well."

"I believe *that* can be arranged," she replied with a smile.

For the first time Daniel was beginning to realize that maybe, just maybe, their accidental crossing into the Blue Zone wasn't an accident at all, but destiny.

CHAPTER 14

Daniel opened his eyes and smiled. He decided to turn over slightly just to be sure it was real. He saw Kayla lying in bed next to him, still asleep, and he smiled again, much broader this time, and with an expression filled with love. They'd only known each other for a short time, yet their feelings for one another were intense in a manner that was beyond the ability for words to describe. How ironic, he thought, that neither of them had any idea up until three months ago that the other even existed, yet here they were falling in love. This pleasant train of thought was rudely interrupted by the chiming sound of someone waiting to speak with him.

"Yes, who is it?" he asked.

"Danny, it's me, Simon. I just wanted to let you know that I'm back, and I need to speak with you when you have a minute."

"Simon! Sure, give me a few minutes—" A nudge at his side called his attention to the fact that Kayla was awake and trying to get his attention. She was watching him with a wry, playful expression on her face. "Err…better make that thirty minutes."

***

Daniel walked up to his old friend and embraced him warmly. "Simon, it's so good to see you again; I'm glad you made it back safely. So please, tell me, what were you able to find out?"

Simon returned the embrace, unable to contain his unbridled enthusiasm. "Daniel, it was unbelievable! Once I was able to connect with the resistance, they wouldn't shut up about the level of excitement and enthusiasm your little display of defiance generated throughout the RZ. Membership in the resistance has been growing in leaps and bounds as more and more people

85

have been flocking to the resistance in droves. Destroying the Synod's Regional HQ and your subsequent holocom was just the spark needed to ignite a full-fledge rebellion within the zone. Everyone's looking to *you* now, Daniel, for leadership. Even longtime resistance fighters are hailing you as their new leader. In fact, a small entourage is on its way to you as we speak, and is due to arrive here tomorrow."

"Simon, I—"

"Now we talked about this, Daniel. We agreed that if I connected with other resistance leaders and felt it was the right move, I could invite them here."

"I never agreed to that, Simon."

"But I did." Kayla had quietly entered the room and taken a seat behind Daniel without him even hearing her. *Sneaky.*

"Kayla, you know I was against this. It places you and your team at too great a risk."

"Come on, Daniel. Like you, I'm in the middle of a full-blown resistance fight against my government in the BZ. Do you really think there's anything safe about that? Besides, I really think the more people we have at our side in our respective fights for freedom, the better, don't you think? I mean, if we stick to the plan and pool our resources, we can each help the other gain a victory, right?"

"Yes, Kayla, of course," Daniel offered. "I'm just trying to keep you safe. I couldn't live with myself if something happened to you because me, or because my men led our enemy to your front door."

"Maybe he's got a point, Kayla." Kayla turned to find Christian and Vanessa walking in.

"It's not about keeping me safe, Chris, it's about defeating the Gentry and winning freedom for everyone in the BZ, and everyone in the RZ as well for that matter."

"But why, Commander?" asked Vanessa. "How does entangling ourselves in *their* conflict in the RZ help us win ours in the BZ? Isn't that just asking for trouble?"

"NO!" Kayla was growing hot, causing Christian and

Vanessa both to immediately start backing down. They knew her well enough. "Our respective enemies are far too powerful on their own to defeat in a protracted conflict. Oh, we can win individual battles, the occasional high-profile skirmish, but they have far more and vastly superior resources at their disposal. I'm convinced that if we work together, we *might* actually be able to achieve victory and topple these tyrants."

"You know," Daniel began, slowly, "we might have an opportunity here to achieve something far greater than just freeing our respective peoples from oppressive tyrants. Remember how, at one time before the Great Schism, our two peoples were one, and this was a *single* country...the United States of America? What if...what if after toppling our corrupt governments, we could reunite the two zones and re-establish the United States, or at least try to; what do you think?"

There was silence in the room for quite some time. Everyone had been so focused on the zones that no one had ever considered the possibility of reuniting the country.

Everyone remained silent, leading Daniel to believe his idea had fallen on deaf ears. Suddenly, however, Kayla responded, followed by others.

"I think it sounds like an incredibly noble idea, Daniel; fantastic!"

"Okay," said Simon. "As long as we liberate the Red Zone first, I'm all for it."

"I must admit, I like it," Christian added. "I mean, I've often wondered what it must have been like back then, one large country full of a free and noble people. I've even dreamed about the possibility of it happening again one day, but I've never *dared* hope it might actually happen anytime soon, at least not in my lifetime."

"It sounds awesome to me. I mean...wow, an entire country, a *new* United States," Vanessa chimed in. "I guess it certainly makes more sense now, us getting involved in the RZ resistance, if we're working to reunite the country, doesn't it?"

"Okay then, so we're agreed, Daniel," said Kayla, edging

up close to Daniel while looking intently into his eyes. "Your resistance leaders will come here to meet with you, and to establish you as their leader; agreed?"

"Sure, okay, Kayla. I'm just going to see what I can do to make sure they're not followed coming here."

"I'd expect nothing less, darling," she replied with a smile.

***

They were still cleaning up from dinner when several scouts returned to base, bringing word back to Kayla on their findings. She greeted them on their return, but insisted they eat and rest before delivering their report. It would be another two hours before they would sit down and review their findings with her in her office.

"Good evening, Sergeant Marcel, gentlemen. So please, I'm anxious to hear what you discovered; report."

"It's not good news, I'm afraid, ma'am," Marcel answered. Marcel, a tall, dark-skinned, gruff man with former People's Guard Military training, was not easily shaken. On this occasion, however, Kayla could easily see he was worried. "As you ordered, we went back to the site where you said Mr. Jefferson said he saw something, the city in question, up near Peak's Lake, to investigate anything unusual there, and well, I can't quite explain how or why we saw what we saw."

"Why, what exactly *did* you see, Sergeant Marcel?"

"Well, Commander, it was as if we landed in a foreign country or something. People spoke in a foreign language, and everything was written in some foreign language as well... alongside English, of course. It was everywhere; on the street signs, the signs on buildings, on billboards, even on the sides of commercial vans and trucks."

"How strange."

"Yeah, that's what we thought as well. "

"Any idea what language it was in?" asked Christian, who, along with Daniel, Simon, and Vanessa, had also been invited to the debriefing.

"I couldn't tell for certain, Mr. Jefferson, I'm sorry. It sounded

Asian. I believe it was maybe Chinese, or Korean, but I'm not sure."

"I wonder how a city packed with foreign nationals could possibly have appeared so suddenly and without warning in the middle of Colorado without someone within the Gentry soon learning of it," Christian continued. "Perhaps they invaded overnight and have held the city under siege ever since."

"Maybe they took over the city gradually," Vanessa suggested.

"Or there may be another, even less pleasant possibility," offered Daniel, who had up to this point remained quiet.

"And what is that?" Kayla asked, interested in hearing his perspective.

"Maybe the foreigners entered the city with permission from your government, the Gentry, who was authorized to grant foreign nationals a presence there. Someone in your government *must* have sanctioned this activity for such a large presence of foreign nationals. Perhaps they were even given a large sum of currency in exchange for this presence?" Daniel added.

"Never! The Gentry are patriots; they would never...."

Kayla stopped in mid-sentence, grimaced, and paused to pull her hair back and put it in a ponytail. She made an odd face, as if the words she'd just spoken had left a bitter taste in her mouth. "You know, I was just sitting here thinking back on the outrage and shock I felt when I learned that some wrinkly, bitter old man, a selfish old bastard on the verge of death, just snatched away a donor's heart being held for a young, precious, beautiful, seven-year-old girl named Sam. That conceited old maggot was Gentry, and he had absolutely no qualms about snatching that heart from her, even though he knew — *he knew* — that he had less than a year to live. He sentenced a seven-year-old girl to death without hesitation because in his eyes, she was nothing; she was less than nothing. You know what? That precious child died less than a month later.

"I was a bit hasty, Daniel. On second thought, the Gentry have grown so corrupt in recent years that I *can* believe they would sell even their own country, if it enabled them to line their own pockets with enough wealth."

"Hey, it's even worse in the RZ, Kayla, so don't beat yourself up over it. Over there, the Synod steals ten to twenty years of life from everyone in Sector 48 with genetic mods just so they can get more work out of them. And we have the New Zion Church, a church that is actually anything but a church, whose only function seems to be to make sure that we worship the NZC and the Synod, and to ensure we have nothing to do with the old God. Our people expected to have complete freedom of religion following the Great Schism; instead, we have NO religious freedom. In fact, we can't worship God at all. And we have virtually no rights any more there either; we're all told what do, where to live…it's awful."

Kayla looked up at the taller Daniel with understanding and compassionate eyes. She wanted to kiss him, but it was hugely inappropriate now; she'd make up for it later.

"That's why we fight I guess, isn't it, Danny?"

"Yes, *it is*."

"Okay then," she continued, turning back to Marcel. "What about troop estimates? How much resistance could we expect should we try to retake Peak's Lake?"

The dejected look and downcast eyes was all the answer she needed.

"That bad, huh?"

"Commander, they outnumber us two to one, and that's just in troops alone. They must have at least three times as many people when it comes to their police force."

"I see." Kayla looked up at the despondency in the faces of those all around her and knew she had to do something. "Okay, listen, not to worry. I remember my father telling me something once when I was very young I'd like to share with you. Ironically enough, it was an old Chinese proverb; 'Crisis and opportunity are often two sides of the same coin.'

"Yes, we must do something and we must act quickly, because the longer we wait the worse it's going to be. An opportunity to do something about this situation *will* present itself at the proper time; we must have faith. Until then, let's take a short recess. We'll get back together after lunch to discuss a new list of slave compounds I just received that need liberating; we can start planning raids to rescue many more of our imprisoned brothers and sisters. Okay, get out of here!" she said with a wave of her arms and a smile, encouraging everyone to leave the room. They all complied, of course, except for Daniel.

"You're worried about Peak's Lake, aren't you?" he asked in an almost rhetorical tone.

"I'd be lying if I said I wasn't, Daniel. Something must be done about that city; it must be a priority, and not just for the BZ! Think about it. If another country establishes a strong enough foothold, what's to stop them from expanding, regardless of the wishes of *either* government, the BZ's or the RZ's? I'm afraid if we don't nip this in the bud quickly it will be the end of this country, the entire country. Who knows how many other cities, or the land to build other cities on, have already been sold to other nations by the Gentry? There could be dozens, or hundreds…who knows?"

"Yeah, well, I doubt we can expect the Red Council to do anything, assuming they even know about it. I doubt they'd consider them enough of a threat, at least not yet," replied Daniel.

"I agree; if we're going to stop them we'll be on our own. We simply have no choice though, Daniel; if we don't do something soon, there will be no country to reunite."

"We need to think this thing through now, Kayla. Even if we were somehow able to *take* the city, how would you expect the country that sent the settlers to respond?"

"Granted, it's a risk, potentially a very big one. All we can do is hope that the foreign country doesn't launch a full scale attack once we've expelled the settlers."

Daniel turned to Simon, who had just re-entered the room and sat down in the chair next to Daniel. "Say, um…Simon, didn't you tell me a while back that you once overheard something about our government still having nuclear weapons?"

"Quite a few, actually. One of my professors was related to

a general in the Synod's military division, and he told me the Synod has kept the nuclear arsenal updated over the years…and not just our nuclear arsenal. Apparently, they've kept advancing technologically since the Great Schism; maybe it's got something to do with the genetically engineered eggheads."

"That could explain why neither zone was attacked or invaded following the Great Schism."

"That's what he said the general told him. It seems some of the new weapons they developed were extremely advanced and very powerful, well beyond anything any other country has developed. The Red Council has been keeping all of it under extremely tight security, so that few people in our government even know anything about them. My professor said they probably want to ensure the technology stays with us, and that it's not stolen by foreign governments."

"Yeah, that makes a lot of sense, actually…thanks." Daniel looked off into the distance as his mind pondered the possibilities. "Hmmm, that information could prove to be very useful." Daniel then turned to Kayla. "Okay, so tell me what they have in the BZ in terms of military weapons."

"It doesn't matter, Daniel!" she exclaimed. "*They* must be the ones who gave those foreign bastards the land in the first place. There's no way they're going to do anything!"

"I know, Kayla, I understand. Please, indulge me and just answer the question."

Clearly annoyed and frustrated, Kayla shrugged her shoulders and let out a heavy sigh. "Well, to be honest, I don't really know what we have. Growing up, my father told me a few times that while we were no longer as powerful as we once were militarily, we still had a powerful military and weapons powerful enough to scare our enemies to the point that they'd *never* attack us. I'd assume, therefore, that we still possess nuclear weapons, and probably as many conventional weapons as an average country our size. I'm certain, however, that the BZ's military is not even in the same league as the RZ when it comes to military strength. I'd just feel better knowing that we still have people in the BZ smart enough to build and operate nuclear weapons. It seems the only thing anyone cares about in the BZ these days is getting stoned, getting rich, or getting a little."

Daniel smiled. "Hey, there's nothing wrong with a little making out once in a while, now is there?"

"No, I suppose there isn't," she answered, staring into his eyes intensely for a brief moment before looking away. When she turned back to him, her eyes had started to water. "What are we going to do, Daniel?" she whispered in a low voice while the others were engaged in sidebar conversations. "I've had this dream for the last few years that if we could just tear down the corrupt government in the BZ, then maybe, just maybe, we could build something new, something better, and give the people something to really live for where they can thrive, and where they can be free."

"I know that dream, Kayla. I've had it too."

Kayla smiled and wrapped her arms around him. "Oh, Danny, how do we stop this invasion?"

"I'm working on something, Kayla. I'll let you know if and/or when I have something concrete, okay?"

"What? What is it? You have to tell me, Daniel!"

"Kayla, please; give me a few days, sweetheart. I should know something then, okay?"

Kayla looked at him with uncertainty and disappointment. Soon, however, her demeanor changed and it was evident she trusted him. "Sure, of course, Daniel," she answered, wanting to kiss him passionately but settling for a kiss on the cheek instead.

***

Daniel was in one of the conference rooms with maps sprawled all over the table. After several long discussions with Marcel, he'd continued looking at various ways of trying to take the city from the superior force, but no matter how he tried it, he came up short each time. They'd spent days going over it, putting everything else on hold as they focused on capturing the city. He had a plan, he just didn't have everything he needed to execute it, and he was growing increasingly frustrated as a result.

93

"Excuse me, Daniel. Have a minute?"

Daniel turned and flashed Simon an angry scowl. "No, Simon, I don't have a minute. The longer we delay the more everything seems to slip out of our grasp. I...."

Daniel turned to look at Simon and saw a look on his friend's face that left Daniel feeling sickened and disgusted with himself. He'd been a jerk recently to everyone who mattered. He let out a heavy sigh before collapsing in the closest chair.

"Crap. I'm really sorry, Simon, I didn't mean to snap at you. I've been racking my brain trying to find a way to take back that city, but it's impossible. We simply lack sufficient resources to stand even an outside chance of taking it; at this point we'd be slaughtered."

"Um, Daniel, can I *please* have just a moment of your time?"

"Of course, old friend. What can I do for you?"

"Well, it just so happens that I may have someone that might be able to do something for *all of us*! One sec...." Simon stuck his head out into the hallway, gestured with it, and whispered. Three men dressed in Synod Military Division soldier uniforms walked into the conference room. Simon must have seen the look of alarm written all over Daniel's face as he jumped out of his chair and to his feet, because he raced over to intervene.

"No, no, no, no...it's okay, Daniel; please just relax. These men are friends; they're here because they want to join us, to join the resistance."

"Join the resistance? Okay, then why are they *here*?"

"Because they saw your holo-recording, Daniel; they know what you did, and they like what you had to say. It seems there's a lot of people out there who agreed with you. And...." Simon paused, grimaced, and looked away in an awkward and uncomfortable manner.

"And what, Simon?"

"And we need to get you back to the RZ as soon as possible so you can start recruiting some of those eager to join the movement before they grow fearful, lose courage, and change their minds, Daniel." Simon paused again before continuing. "Look, Danny,

I know you're comfortable here…with her…but if we don't get re-engaged soon, it *will* fizzle."

Daniel hesitated, but only for a moment, as if he'd already considered the notion. "I know, I know…," he replied, allowing his voice to trail off as he began glancing around briefly to see if Kayla was within earshot, since he'd not said anything to her about it. "I've been thinking about it, and you're right, Simon. I've slowly come to realize that it's about time to do some recruitment and get out to meet some folks. I just wasn't sure—"

"I understand, Daniel. I'm sure I'd feel the same way if it was me."

Daniel nodded. "Okay then, so let's have a look at these fine soldiers who want to join the cause; well, we certainly can use more RZ soldiers on our side. I guess you three men left your unit to come and join us then?"

The three men turned to look at Simon with a confused expression on their faces.

"Um, no, Daniel, I don't think you understand. That's just it, they didn't come alone. They have three-hundred men waiting just outside the main entrance, and they have another seven-hundred men back at their local barracks in Kansas. They all want to come over together, Daniel, as a unit, and with you as their leader."

CHAPTER 15

"A thousand men? You've got to be kidding!"

"No sir, we wouldn't do that, sir. A group of us saw your holo-recording, and before we knew it the entire division had seen it. Each and every one of us on the base, down to a man or woman, was deeply moved by what you said, sir. Most of us have increasingly questioned orders we've been given, and we've found the direction in which the Red Council has been taking the RZ to be more and more troubling. It's time to give freedom back to the people, sir. It's what my great-grandfather died for, and my grandfather, and my father, and it's most definitely what *I'm* prepared to die for. We're with you, sir, all of us. I, and the men and women under my command, will fight and die for you."

"I, um…don't know what to say, um…."

"Colonel, sir, Colonel Jack Davis. This here is Major Tom Crane and Captain Mike Sullivan."

"Nice to meet you, Major…Captain."

"Nice to meet you, *General* Washington, sir," quipped Crane, after which all five men burst into laughter.

"Well then, it seems I have some pretty big shoes to fill, haven't I?" Daniel replied, as wittily as he could muster at a moment's notice. "I guess it's just a good thing *my* parents didn't name me George, or I'd be in a real pickle, eh?"

Another round of light-hearted laughter erupted. Everyone felt the elation at having a thousand soldiers come over to the resistance; it truly marked a turning point in the journey of both movements. A thought suddenly came to Daniel, however, which morphed his features into something slightly more stoic and reflective.

"Um, say, Colonel, do you and your men happen to have access to any armored vehicles? You know, like tanks, armored personnel carriers, airships, and maybe some surface-to-air missile systems?"

"Yes, General, we have all that, sir, and considerably more."

"And just to be clear, you can bring all of that with you?"

"Yes, sir, absolutely."

"Good, very good...thank you, Colonel. How soon could you have the rest of your men here, along with that equipment you just mentioned?"

"I'd say I could have them here first thing in the morning, sir, if that's what is needed. Should I go ahead and make the arrangements?"

"Yes, Colonel Davis, please do, but not for tomorrow; how about first thing next week, say Monday morning at 9:00 AM? Tell them to be ready to pull out again sometime after nightfall."

"0-dark-thirty...yes, sir. May I ask what the mission is, sir?"

"Of course. We'll finalize plans in here shortly. Why don't you gentlemen grab yourselves some coffee and something to eat while I gather some more of our people together. We'll meet back here in two hours, agreed?"

"Yes sir, General, of course."

"Good; dismissed."

The title had stuck from that moment on, and though he never in a million years beforehand would have considered himself a military man by any stretch, much less a general, here he was, the leader of the resistance in the Red Zone, and starting to question his sanity at having started down the path which he sincerely doubted would end up with him as president, as had the General Washington of old. He couldn't help but crack a slight smile as he left the conference room on his way to find Kayla and the others.

***

It was still dark, and as far as he could tell everyone was in position about as well as could be expected. The weapons system for taking out the communications equipment had been an unexpected piece of good news. It would work to their favor that they were now blocking all communications outbound and inbound to the city. The fact that the airships and the tanks had a stealth mode had proven to be added bonuses, as they were able to move everything into place much more quickly and without alerting anyone to their presence. The shock and awe, the intimidation that their overwhelming presence alone would provide, would deliver a powerful and dramatic psychological blow to their enemy, helping to greatly minimize bloodshed.

Daniel glanced over his left shoulder at the rising sun, their signal. Glancing over at Kayla and then at Davis, they all nodded, and as the signal went out, everyone began converging on the four checkpoints that guarded the entrances into the city. Two tanks pulled up to each checkpoint, followed by at least five personnel carriers, which carried two-hundred and fifty soldiers each, as well as a number of Kayla's men. Armored transports carried Daniel and Kayla to the main entrance. Christian, Major Crane, and several of Kayla's men went to the second entrance. Simon, Captain Sullivan, and some of his men went to the third entrance, while Vanessa, Colonel Davis, and some of his men ventured toward the fourth and last checkpoint.

Sergeant Marcel climbed out of the lead tank and approached the first guard. A sign, with the words, "Welcome to Peak's Lake" in Chinese and English, stood next to the entrance into the city's main entrance. The guard, upon seeing what waited outside the gate, suddenly looked down as if checking to see if he'd wet himself.

"Do you speak English?" Marcel asked, wasting no time.

"Yes, of course."

"Then I need someone in charge up here immediately. I have two senior representatives, one from each zone; one is from the Free Market Republic of Conservatism, or the Red Zone, and the other from the People's Liberal Socialist Democratic State — the Blue Zone." Marcel waited but the man simply stood there, his jaw agape, staring at the tanks, the soldiers. "*Today*, man; get your superiors here, *now*! Does it look to you like I have all day?"

"No, sir; I'm sorry sir. I'll let my superiors know right away that you're here."

"Good; tell them we're pressed for time."

"Yes, sir; of course."

The man disappeared into a small building for a few minutes, presumably to make the calls to his superiors. It soon became evident that he'd gotten through to the right people, because moments later an older man and a much younger, beautiful woman, accompanied by a hard-nosed, somewhat younger man in a military uniform and a half-dozen guards, approached. It was clear they were trying to appear confident, and even angered and offended, though the constant darting of their eyes to the tanks, the men, and the hardware all around them betrayed the fear and shock they were feeling. While the men likely had anticipated meeting resistance at some point, given that they were in the Blue Zone, and since they had most likely been sold the land they were clearly on, they'd not been expecting any *real* trouble. They'd probably assumed that greed and avarice had opened a way for them to defeat their enemy without conflict and any loss on their side; they were mistaken.

The man in charge stepped forward and bowed, before introducing himself.

"I am Governor Zhang Yong," he stated proudly, as if greeting foreigners visiting him in his own country. "And here," he said, gesturing to the man in uniform, "is General Wang le, the man in charge of our armed forces. Over to my left here is my assistant and advisor, the beautiful Li Min."

Marcel stepped aside as Daniel and Kayla approached. As the Blue Zone representative, Kayla took the lead.

"Good morning, Governor Yong, General, Ms. Min. I'm Kayla Ross. I am now in charge of this area for the Blue Zone. My companion here is General Daniel Washington from the neighboring Red Zone region. He has responsibility for the Red Zone's armed forces based in the region that borders this one."

"Forgive me. Did you say Washington...*Daniel* Washington?"

"I did. Why, does that concern you?"

The governor turned to his companions; both nodded in

affirmation. "We know that name; your reputation precedes you, '*General*.'"

"Uh-oh. Well, that certainly complicates things."

"We heard what happened to the regional headquarters of the Corporate Synod, Mr. Washington. It is said that you accomplished this incredible feat alone; please tell us whether this is true."

Daniel grew angry. "Look around us, *Governor*. Do you see these tanks, these soldiers, these weapons? You have my word they are all 100% authentic. We have more and more men and women coming over to join our cause every day. If you think for one second that you're going to waltz in here now, or sometime after our little revolution is over, you're sadly mistaken, I assure you. We're only going to become stronger, not weaker."

The governor and the others all grew somewhat alarmed. "No, please...forgive me. I did not mean to offend you, General; I believe you misunderstand me."

"Now you listen to me, Governor Yong, because I'm only going to say this once. I'm a true patriot, a man who loves his country...the way it used to be that is, the way the founders intended it, free and strong. I'm giving you until sundown tomorrow for you and your people to evacuate this city, and to begin moving your people to an alternate location for pickup. You have one week to be completely off our soil."

"But we bought and paid your government for this land *and* this city. We now own it!"

"Wrong and wrong, Mr. Yong. First, it was not my government you bought it from, and it wouldn't matter if it had been; it was an *illegal* purchase. Second, you can't just waltz in and buy a country from a bunch of greedy bureaucrats...the land, the country itself, belongs to the people. The corrupt idiots in charge these days have forgotten that; Kayla and I, along with those who have graciously chosen to come along with us on this journey, plan to educate them on the error of their ways."

"I see, and *now* I understand," Yong responded, pacing while gently stroking his lightly bearded chin, before stopping in front of Daniel with an expression that both stunned and puzzled everyone there; he wore a heartfelt and endearing smile, and looked with warmth and understanding into Daniel's eyes. "You can't know this of course, Mr. Washington, but I've been a student of ancient history since I was a very young man. I'm not sure why, really, I only know that the subject's always held great interest and fascination for me. Believe it or not, what has always stood out the most for me, aside from China's own history of course, was the history of your own United States. We have shared many parallels, our two countries; oh, we have had many differences as well, to be sure, but there have also been many similarities.

"China is, of course, a much older country, with a much longer and richer history. Also, when once we were finally free from an endless parade of tyrants, we chose a completely different form of government than your people. But consider the many similarities. We were both British colonies that shirked off our oppressive masters. We both eventually embraced free market economies. And now, we have this in common as well, that we have both sought to throw off the oppressive rule of the very few in the aristocracy. In the case of China, it was the emperor and all of his sycophants. For the former United States, now your Blue Zone and Red Zone, you also seek to overthrow the aristocracy and give power back to the people. Ironic, is it not, Mr. Washington?"

Daniel and Kayla stopped and looked at one another for several moments with quizzical expressions, as if to say, "*What do we do now?*"

"In any event, I would just like to add that I very much *admire* what you, and those with you, are doing in *both* zones. We are kindred spirits, Mr. Washington, and much like your namesake, I suspect you will play a pivotal role in freeing your people from your own tyrants."

Daniel faced Yong with a solemn expression, which seemed contrary to the surprisingly friendly welcome they had received.

"You and your people still have to be gone by sunset

tomorrow, Mr. Yong. This is in no way open to negotiation. That said, perhaps, once this is all over, you'll come back to visit or, perhaps, even to become a New American citizen."

Yong smiled. "Perhaps," he replied.

"Governor Yong!"

Daniel had been waiting for the Chinese general to say something; he'd wondered how long it would take before the blustering began.

"Yes, General Ie; what is it?"

"You cannot agree to this; the terms are completely unacceptable! The president will never agree to this."

Yong subtly shook his head, seemingly intending it more for himself than for anyone else. "I *can* agree to their terms and I *will*, General. Just take some time to look around, General Ie. As I believe that you too have received a formal education in mathematics, just as I have, you can see that in headcount alone we are easily outnumbered. But take into account the heavy artillery, the missiles, the tanks, the gunships, and I suspect the additional air support as well, and I'd say that they can pretty much order us to do just about whatever they want, won't you agree?"

"Well, I err...I don't know. What about the *Party*?"

"Consider what's at stake here, General. You have two regimes, both under siege by their own populaces. I believe you'll agree that the Red Zone's military, clearly the more powerful of the two, armed with nuclear weapons and highly-advanced technological weaponry, are in a state of open rebellion. Do you believe that President Chao will really want to expose the citizens of the Peoples' Republic of China to such a threat? I think not. It was a gamble, comrade, but it was a gamble that has played out. It's time for us to leave." Yong turned to Daniel. "May we contact our superiors to arrange transportation home?"

Daniel turned to Kayla, wanting to give her time to speak as well. "Yes, of course, Governor. Will you be leaving by land or by sea? Either way, we'd like to be there when you depart."

Yong nodded. "I understand. We have a rather large

population, as I'm sure you're aware, but given the constraints you've given us, our leaders will likely send large aircraft capable of carrying large numbers of passengers and cargo. There is an airport nearby with runways large enough to accommodate our large aircraft. If we contact them now we should have no difficulty meeting your demands." Governor Yong extended his hand to Kayla first in a warm gesture of farewell. "Goodbye, Ms. Ross. Perhaps, once this is all over, as Mr. Washington has suggested, we might have an opportunity to sit down once more and get better acquainted, under more *pleasant* circumstances."

"Maybe so, Governor. I believe I'd enjoy that."

"As would I," Yong replied, before bowing and kissing her hand. He then turned to Daniel, but this time with a sterner look in his eyes. "It is most unfortunate, Mr. Washington, that so many bold and courageous men like yourself often burn ever so brightly for such a brief period of time, before going out *much* too soon. A revolution is a *very* dangerous thing, my friend, and people often die during such a time. It is my sincerest hope that you and Ms. Ross *are not* among that number. But if you are, I will pray that you are remembered well."

"Thank you, Governor Yong. Just before I left Sector 48, where my family worked in the Production Class, to leave for college, my father's final words to me were these; live well son, and die free if you can. That's exactly what I intend to do, Mr. Yong, for as long as I can."

"Good words; your father is a wise man." Daniel nodded. "Good luck, Daniel."

"Thanks, Governor Yong; safe journey."

The others turned without addressing Daniel, Kayla, or the others, and Yong now turned to join them. There was much to do, so neither Daniel nor Kayla wanted to detain them any further. They turned as well, and once outside the gate, boarded the transport for the trip back to NORAD.

"Well, that didn't go quite as planned, did it, Danny?"

"Hmmm...what?"

"Hello...are you okay, Daniel? What's going on with you?

You haven't said a word since we left the governor."

"Oh, yeah, I guess I haven't; I'm sorry, Kayla. I guess I've been thinking about something he said."

"About what?"

"You do realize that there's a rather good chance that you and I won't make it out of this thing alive, right? They know our faces, and they know who we are. Our only chance at survival is to hit them with everything we've got from here on out. If we do that, and if we can keep them off-balance, there's a chance we might bring these guys down and actually come out of this thing alive."

"There he is, my Mr. Optimism! Don't worry, Daniel, we're doing the right thing here, I'm certain of it."

"But what if he's right, Kayla?"

Kayla looked around. The others were either napping or staring out the window. She kissed him passionately, allowing their fluids to mingle for some time before breaking it off. "Then, lover-boy, I guess we'd better make sure we make the most of every second we have together."

CHAPTER 16
The Wedding

Kayla was beautiful; more than that, she was radiant. Daniel had asked her to be his wife, and she'd eagerly leapt at the opportunity. Her love for him was increasingly evident in her face, her eyes, her smile, and in every other way possible as their wedding day had drawn closer. It was clear to anyone with eyes that Kayla was at her best when she was around Daniel; he made her happy…really, really, happy.

I suppose I must have had some lingering feelings for her buried somewhere deep down in the recesses of my being, because it hurt me in some small way to think of her having a family and then spending the rest of her life with some other man. I was, however, also very much overjoyed by the fact that the man she'd chosen to spend the rest of her life with was Daniel, and that he brought her such joy and happiness. It had been one of those extremely rare cases of genuine love-at-first-sight between Daniel and Kayla; the two of them had been a perfect fit from the start. It warmed my heart that Kayla had found love, and from what I'd learned of the particularly tough breaks in Daniel's life, it certainly sounded like he deserved some happiness of his own.

We'd all felt the undercurrent that ebbed and flowed in and around the preparations that had preceded the arrival of the big day. The wedding preparations brought with them a sense of normalcy that none of us had felt for quite some time. Preparing for such a celebration of life, love, and happiness served to remind us how all three had been in short supply for such a very long time.

One might expect such a festive occasion to spark feelings

of regret and people second-guessing themselves about putting their lives at risk by joining the resistance, but that never happened, not really. The growing oppression and brutality each of us had witnessed or experienced in the zones in recent years had marked us. The joyous occasion of Kayla and Daniel's wedding only served to remind us of what we'd been missing in the zones because of the festering corruption that had been growing and growing, like a consuming plague or invading darkness before which all happiness and joy fled. If anything, the happy occasion of their nuptials only served to spur everyone forward, impressing upon us all the desperate need for us to win the battle for the heart and soul of our country, even if that came at the cost of our lives. We owed it to those who'd already laid down their lives for us, and owed it to our parents, wives, our children, and our children's children.

"Chris, you okay?"

I'd been daydreaming. "Oh, yeah, I'm good. I was just thinking about you and Daniel, about Vanessa, and about what we might all be doing after all of this is over...assuming we're alive to find out, of course."

"Chris, don't think like that, ever, you understand? We're going to make it out of this thing, or at least most of us will. If something happens and you make it out and I don't, I want you to promise me that you'll keep going and finish what we've started. And I want you to promise me that you'll stay alive; Vanessa's going to need you, and this country's going to need you, whether we win this thing or not." Kayla paused and began looking around frantically. "Oh, no, where is she, Christian? Where's Vanessa, where's my maid of honor? I'm going to fall apart if she's not here in the next couple of minutes!"

"Don't worry, I'll find her."

"Thanks, Chris...you're the best! Oh, and Chris?"

"Yeah?"

"Thank you for walking me down the aisle today. I know my father wanted to be here, but given the circumstances...."

"I'm sure he would have been here if he could have come

106

without endangering you, Kayla," I reminded her.

"Yeah, I know, Chris. I'm just glad I at least had the opportunity to speak with him yesterday over the holocom, even if it was only for a few minutes."

"You *called* him, Kayla? You know they probably traced the call directly back here; you placed everyone at risk!"

Kayla glared at me with the new yet now all too familiar expression of hers, which told me I'd overstepped my bounds... again.

"Kayla...."

Kayla sighed and took a deep breath, a sign that I was really in trouble. "Look, Chris, you're still my best friend aside from Daniel, and I know that we've known each other for our entire lives. But things are *different* now; I've suddenly found myself the commander of a resistance movement, marrying the leader of another, even larger resistance movement, with both intending to topple the governments and then do the same to corrupt systems that have been devastating the way of life for hundreds of millions of people for over half a century now. You and I are going to have to establish some new boundaries in our relationship, at least until this is over."

"I wasn't trying to challenge your authority, Kayla...ha, I never have. I've always known better!" I said, pleading my case as best as I could. "I was merely trying to point out the risk that I know *you know* your call carried with it, however well deserved, and no matter how important it may have been, Kay, to the men, women, and now children that live here with us," I added, hoping to get through.

In all honesty, her reaction surprised me. She looked at me for what seemed like an eternity, then glanced around at the now-empty room before walking over to me with tears streaming down her face.

Kayla threw her arms around me and said, "Oh, Chris, I'm sorry. You're right; oh you were right. I *did* place us at risk. It seemed so important at the time, and at that moment, I felt as if I deserved it, considering how many risks I've already taken for the cause. I just thought, well—"

"Just this once?" I interjected.

"Yeah," she replied, "that just this once it would be okay."

"I understand, Kay, believe me I do."

"But you were right, Chris; I placed everyone here at risk. I should never have taken the chance."

"Well, we really do need some way of scrambling the calls… maybe bouncing them off satellites, something to keep them off our tracks," I suggested.

Kayla turned back to me and said, "Yeah, I know; we'll look into that. But listen, you just go ahead and keep pointing out to me when I'm making mistakes, okay? I need someone doing that for me, because with the exception of Daniel and a few others, no one else will. Can you do that for me?"

"Sure, Kayla, you bet."

"But, Chris?"

"Yes?"

"Always do it in private. In front of the others always remember, I'm the commander of the resistance. In private, however, I'll always be Kayla, your lifelong friend. Deal?"

"Deal," I responded, reaching out to shake hands before changing up and giving her a tight embrace instead. When we finished I looked at her and said, "We'd better get some help in here; your makeup's ruined and you're about to get married." I handed her a mirror, and after taking a quick look she quickly nodded in agreement.

"Yes, please, hurry, see who you can find; it's almost time!"

***

It turned out to be quite an affair, something quite unlike anything anyone had seen in many, many years. Everyone staying at the base had been invited, though the base's largest chapel could have accommodated even more people. Kayla and Daniel had wanted to limit attendance to only their closest friends and acquaintances within the resistance movements, along with a few others who had helped with pulling together the wedding, the reception, and the festivities so quickly. Simon and I vigorously objected, however, stressing how important the event could be for the cause. The uniting of the two resistance leaders — their bond in marriage — would stand as a symbol of the bond between the two resistance movements, and by extension, the reunification of the two zones.

Despite the risk, and with assistance from Sergeant Marcel, Colonel Davis, Major Crane, and Captain Sullivan, we'd even been able to persuade Kayla that a holocom of the wedding being broadcast throughout the zones might go far in helping with morale, not to mention with recruiting efforts. With Kayla won over, they'd eventually persuaded Daniel as well.

Thus, the grand celebration had begun. As Kayla entered and the ancient wedding music began to sound, I could only admire her grace, beauty, and radiance. Although Vanessa and I were now a couple and our relationship had gotten serious, I couldn't help but feel an ever-so-slight pang of longing for what life could have been like with Kayla as her husband. As she stared down the aisle at her husband-to-be, however, and as her face brightened with a broad smile, my longing vanished like a thin mist before the blazing of the morning sun. She and Daniel belonged together; they were soulmates, just as I was now becoming convinced that Vanessa and I belonged together.

I met Kayla and took her arm in mine as we began walking arm-in-arm down the aisle toward her betrothed and the clergyman who would marry them. I reflected for a few moments about how very fortunate we'd been to discover Jonathan O'Conner among our number. Pastor Jonathan O'Conner had been with a group of resistance fighters from the Red Zone, serving as the group's spiritual guide. When the fighters learned about Daniel and decided to join him, the minister had been eager to sign on as well. When Kayla later asked whether he'd be willing to officiate at their wedding, he'd accepted with great enthusiasm.

Kayla later filled me in on some of the minister's background. A holdout from the pre-Schism days, he had been born into a very special community, where he'd been raised, in secret, to become a Christian man of God, just like his father, and his father's father before him. They were a rare find living under such totalitarian rule, yet such communities were still around and some, especially those located in the more rural, isolated communities, located far from the prying eyes and ears of the NZC and the Synod, thrived. Oh sure, there was electronic surveillance even out in the rural areas, but they were much easier to circumvent.

As we neared the altar at the front of the sanctuary, I couldn't help casting one final glance over at Kayla. Her eyes watered but there were no tears; there was a light, or radiance that emanated from them like nothing I'd ever seen. I was amazed at how quickly and at how deeply she'd fallen for Daniel Washington. Yet given the current state of affairs in the world in which we lived, I could also not think of anyone at that moment more worthy of my Kayla. I smiled as I released her arm, nodded at Daniel, and stepped off to the side to join the others, as Kayla and Daniel turned to face one another.

Pastor O'Conner held up his hands to everyone, gesturing for silence, and the chapel grew quiet. He made the sign of the cross, something only a handful of them had ever seen, and the minister began.

"In the name of the Father, and the Son, and the Holy Spirit. Amen.

"Dearly beloved, we are gathered here in the sight of God, and before His Church, to witness the union of this man and this woman in holy matrimony. This is an honorable estate instituted and blessed by God in Paradise before humanity's fall into sin. This estate is not to be entered into recklessly and without great forethought, but reverently, and for the purpose for which it was instituted by God.

"The union of a man and a woman into one heart, one body, and one mind is intended by God for the mutual companionship, help, comfort, and support of one another through times of adversity and times of plenty.

"Now let the man and the woman who would enter into the state of Holy Matrimony state their intentions before God, who has established this holy estate.

110

"Daniel Elijah Washington, will you take this woman to be your wedded wife, to live together in the holy estate of matrimony as God ordained it? Will you care for her as Christ cared for and loved His Church, laying down His life for it? Will you love, honor, and cherish her, forsaking all others, as long as you both shall live?"

Daniel and Kayla had not taken their eyes off one another the entire time. I felt certain that everyone watching must have wondered, as I did, whether they'd heard anything Pastor O'Conner had said, for their gaze into one another's eyes seemed so piercing and so pure as to seem almost unreal.

"Daniel, this is where you answer, 'I will,'" the pastor whispered with a smile.

"Oh yes, I will, I definitely will. I one-hundred percent will take this amazing, wonderful, beautiful woman as my wife, forever."

Pastor O'Conner cleared his throat and offered a faux frown. "A simple, 'I will' would have sufficed, young man, but that will do nicely," he added with another smile.

"And you, Kayla Summer Ross, will you take this man to be your wedded husband, to live together in the holy estate of matrimony as God ordained it? Will you submit to him as the Church submits to Jesus Christ, our Lord? Will you love, honor, and cherish him, forsaking all others, as long as you both may live?"

"Oh, yes. I love you, Daniel Washington, like I've never loved anyone and like I will never love anyone ever again. You're the most beautiful, caring, brave, and pure soul I have ever encountered, and I will absolutely take you as my husband, willingly, thankfully, and enthusiastically, for all eternity, my love!"

The two embraced and kissed passionately in front of everyone, leaving Pastor O'Conner standing awkwardly in front of them. The kindly pastor threw up his arms and shook his head in a playful, mocking manner. "Well, um, may I continue then?"

Kayla pulled away and they both smiled sheepishly before

turning back to the pastor.

"Sorry," Daniel offered.

"Sorry, Pastor O'Conner."

"Now, now, there's nothing to be sorry for...this is *your* wedding. It might be nice, however, to wrap this up so these nice people can move on to the reception, don't you think?" He smiled broadly before picking up his book and continuing.

"Now then, since you have committed yourselves to one another before God and these witnesses, I now therefore pronounce you to be husband and wife, in the name of the Father, the Son, and the Holy Spirit. Congratulations, you two." Turning to Daniel, he then added, "Oh, and Daniel, you may kiss the bride, *again.*"

The music played and everyone jumped to their feet in celebration.

CHAPTER 17

Four months following their wedding, the time finally came for Daniel to leave his new bride and rejoin the war. Word had recently reached them from the RZ of a rising tide of public anger and ferment against the oppression of the NZC and the Corporate Synod. The citizens of the RZ, many of whom had been forced to undergo decades of forced genetic manipulation, endure severe travel restrictions, abandon their religion or do their best to hide it while being forced to join the NZC or risk imprisonment, torture, death, or worse, had finally had enough. It appeared that the kindling, and indeed the logs themselves, had at last been set aflame on the bonfire of revolution.

Daniel's *very* courageous and *very* public act of rebellion against the Red Council, which he'd started when he'd destroyed the Synod's building, and the subsequent holocom he'd broadcast across most of the zone, along with his subsequent acts of defiance, had merely been the match that lit the fires of rebellion. The people of the Red Zone had long been waiting for an opportunity like this, and they were now ready to seize it. Just as a raging wildfire can start with only a small spark, consuming everything in its path, so too were the people of the Red Zone now primed and ready for a revolution.

Daniel was running late as he walked into the conference room, as he could see by the looks on their slightly annoyed faces. The room was filled with people.

"Good morning, everyone," he said, as he took his place at one of the two chairs at the front of the tables. Kayla walked in seconds later and sat down across from him.

"Good morning," she began, not bothering to look around.

She was all business these days. "Our meeting ran a little long this morning, sorry for the delay." There were a few murmurs of various people stating it was okay. Kayla continued. "Well, as I'm sure everyone's heard by now, there's been some very good news coming out of the Red Zone recently. It seems Daniel's started something there that's really catching on. This could be just what we've been waiting for, a sign from the people that they've finally had enough and awakened, that that they're ready to do what it takes to cast off their shackles, to pay in blood the cost to regain their freedom." Kayla turned to Daniel, looking somewhat more annoyed than usual. It appeared to me as if they'd had a disagreement immediately prior to joining us in the meeting.

"Kayla's quite right, of course," he said, with an uncomfortable nod toward his wife. "We've had a number of reports come in recently that activity's really been picking up across the RZ. The people are revolting against the Corporate Synod and the NZC, against the oppressors who betrayed, corrupted, and then enslaved them.

"According to reports, a number of Synod vehicles have been vandalized or destroyed, and several empty buildings have been destroyed as well. A bomb was recently detonated near New Chicago inside an infamous and much-despised genetic enhancement laboratory, which subsequently burnt to the ground. Soon after, an NZC center was burnt completely to the ground. The NZC has been long known for its dark reputation for having thousands, perhaps tens of thousands, of Christians arrested for not rejecting their Christian faith to follow the NZC doctrine. It appears a handful of the senior NZC leadership responsible for those arrests died during that fire. Before any of you shed a tear, keep in mind that those arrested included men, women, and even small children, and that most of those arrested died in that hellhole of a prison.

"Anyway, I'll be leaving for the RZ tomorrow morning, along with a handful of others, to do what I can to help the resistance movement grow, organize, and strategize."

114

"I have a question."

A lone hand was up in the back of the room from someone standing in the corner. Daniel strained to see who it was, and after a few seconds made out the young face of Captain Mike Sullivan.

"Go ahead, Captain Sullivan, what's on your mind?"

"I was just wondering whether you'd heard, sir."

"Heard what?"

"That someone, either members of the resistance or supporters of the cause, are spray-painting our symbol everywhere, all over the RZ."

"Symbol...what symbol?"

"Why, the People of the Founders, of course, sir. The founding father — you know, of the United States — holding a United States flag the way it was just before the Great Schism. It's awesome, sir, and it's everywhere."

"Interesting. What else have you heard, Captain?"

"Only that the string of attacks, along with the uprisings and some recent gatherings, are really starting to make the powers that be nervous."

"Nervous? What do you mean?"

"Martial law, sir. In many of the cities where there have been 'incidents,' they've declared martial law."

"That's good news," Kayla offered.

"No, that's *great* news," Daniel countered.

"How's that, sir?"

"The more they oppress the people, the harder the people will fight back."

***

The building was in a run down, largely abandoned part of town well outside the nearest city, in the heart of the Red Zone not far from the capital. The manufacturing plant had been shut down for a decade, and the power had been cut off at the same time. The lack of electricity and the location served to make it an ideal meeting place so long as their travel to and from the site went unnoticed. As an added precaution, the local resistance leader had constructed a large faraday cage for them to meet inside, to ensure there would be no electronic communications in or out during the meeting. Daniel was duly impressed at the pragmatism and the appropriateness of the precautions.

Around fifty people were gathered together in the room with them, not counting the five or so in the small entourage traveling with Daniel. Once everyone had entered and taken a seat at the large oval table in the center of the room, Daniel stood to speak.

"Good evening. My name is Daniel Washington. Who is in charge here?"

A woman stood up in the back of the room. "I am, sir; Commander Samantha Jones, but everyone just calls me Sam. It's really nice to finally meet you, General."

Daniel was surprised, for while appearing a bit rugged in appearance, the woman was surprisingly attractive. Had he not been so in love with Kayla, and married now, he might have had an interest in getting to know her better. Of course, he too found her beautiful, but looking over at Simon, Daniel could see *he* was even *more* enamored than the others; he was also the first to speak after her introduction.

"Pardon me, Commander, but what happened to Commander Bridges? He was in charge here when I left six months ago."

"And you are?"

"My name is Simon Bender. I've been assigned the rank of colonel. I was recruited into the resistance five years ago while in college."

"I see. Please forgive me, Colonel Bender, but Fred Bridges died four months ago, during a mission. I came in from one of our northeast cells to replace him."

"He was a good man," Simon said, clearly saddened by the news, while at the same time still fascinated by this new commander. "I served under him for my first two years; he was something of a second father to me during a very difficult period."

"So I've heard. It's...um...a pleasure to meet you, Colonel Bender. Maybe, if we both have a moment, we could sit down, have a cup of coffee together, and you could tell me a little about him."

"Certainly, Commander Jones; I would, um…enjoy that very much," Simon replied, blushing at all the smiles and snickers that resonated throughout the gathering. Daniel came to his rescue.

"So, Commander, what can you tell me about the mood of the people here? We've gotten word that there's been growing unrest throughout the RZ, a swelling in the ranks of the resistance, and an uptick in open talk of one day trying to topple the Synod and the NZC. Is any of this true?"

"Oh, yes, sir, General, that, and much more!" Jones walked over to a table and pressed a button. A three-dimensional hologram appeared above the table that changed as she touched an image that appeared on the surface of the table itself. In the hologram, a 3D map suddenly appeared with the capital and two neighboring states displayed. At least twenty or thirty squares appeared across the three states. In seven of those a red circle flashed on and off. "Each of these squares denote an RZ military base, and each flashing red circle inside the box denotes the bases whose forces have sworn allegiance to come over to us.

"Our numbers have grown a hundred-fold over the last few months alone. When news got out about what you and your men did in the Blue Zone, I mean…wow! We were blown away! I mean, you sent the Chinese packing, sir. And then, the idea of broadcasting your wedding, the leader of the Red Zone's POF resistance marrying the leader of the Blue Zone's MFF resistance movement, what a message! You've definitely started something, sir. I guess the big question is, what will you do now?"

"Don't worry, Commander, the general's loyalty is always to the Red Zone first; the needs of the Blue Zone will always take a back seat to the needs of the RZ."

Daniel cast a hard look at Simon before turning to the commander and smiling. "Funny you should ask, Commander. It just so happens I do have an idea or two. First, tell me more about what' going on in the RZ as a whole, not just in your section, that you're aware of."

"Well, sir, as you know the resistance keeps information

compartmentalized, in the event any of us are captured and tortured, well...."

"I understand, please go on."

"Well, I told you some of the good news, about the military units joining us, the vast swelling of public support for the cause, and the growing hunger for freedom. It's not all good news though, sir. The Synod and the NZC has responded with a heavy hand, much as we expected. They've implemented tighter and tighter travel restrictions, increased surveillance, and the prison houses have been growing exponentially. There have been rumors that they've begun executing entire families for merely suspecting them to be in the resistance. Recently they've begun stealing small children in the middle of the night and holding them hostage in order to ensure the cooperation of their parents. There's also another rumor, sir, that they've been testing some type of experimental nanites, surveillance drones of some sort, and injecting them into certain prisoners who they suspect of being in the resistance. The nanites would enable the Synod to eavesdrop on what happens in the immediate vicinity of the test subject. Given under the guise of a vaccine, the individual would never have any idea he or she was putting his resistance cell at risk."

"Have you taken precautions?"

"Yes, General; we've done what we can. We do our best to avoid taking any vaccines, and when we simply can't avoid it, we make certain *we* select who administers it. If all else fails, we simply ask the individual who receives the vaccine to sever ties with the cell until we can find a way to test for the nanites, at which point we'll reach out to them. So far this has only happened to a couple of people."

"Well, it sounds more and more like we need to step things up as much as possible, keep them off-balance, and keep moving forward."

"General?"

"Yes, Commander?"

"Do you really think we can pull this thing off? I mean, do

you really believe we can defeat the NZC and the Corporate Synod? They're so powerful, and we're just simple folks for the most part."

"Tell me, Commander, do you know much about what happened before the Great Schism?"

"Well, sir, you know it's technically forbidden to read or even talk about that, though some folks do. Some of the more educated among us have even read about it in books; they talk about something called the United States and freedom, and elections, and rights."

"Yes, that's right. That country, the United States, was founded by simple folks a lot like us, who had to fight to throw off a repressive, tyrannical government much like we are now."

"Were they successful?"

"Oh yeah; they were successful, all right, and the United States became the greatest country the world has even known."

"Then what happened, General?" someone asked from the crowded room.

Daniel paused for a moment; he'd pondered that same question many nights. He offered the best answer he'd been able to come up with.

"I guess that at some time they just lost their way, concerned and focused on the wrong things at the wrong times, until they *broke* the country; permanently. But we intend to fix the country permanently, with this movement. That's what Kayla, my wife, and I both intend to do. We want to reunite the Red Zone and the Blue Zone into a single, strong, and united country again, and I believe we have a plan to make it happen.

"First, however, I need your help with something."

"Of course, sir…anything."

"I need to find a way to broadcast a recording I've made directly to the people of the Red Zone. Now, I imagine after my last broadcast, they've likely tightened up their security. Do you know anyone who can help with that, Commander?"

"We will find you someone, sir, I promise you."

"Good. You might want to start with someone who used to

work at one of the NZC network broadcast buildings some years ago. I've been told that security is a little lighter there than at the Corporate Synod, though we may have to keep an eye out for the Red Guard."

"Your reports were quite right, General, though perhaps they didn't go quite far enough. It seems with the little trouble you've kicked up, sir, most of the leadership within the NZC is scared and worried about looking out for their own skin. Between all the so-called 'clergymen,' if you want to call those hypocritical, heathen scumbags 'clergymen,' the executive leadership, and the administrative staff, they've consumed not only everyone within the Red Guard, but they've cut deeply into the Synod's police force as well. Seems it was some sort of *quid pro quo* arrangement they had worked out some time ago."

"So, I take it they're relying completely on automated sentries, weaponry, and AI drones to protect secondary facilities like this communications hub?"

"Yes sir."

"That's great news, Commander. Now then, if you could please work with Colonel Bender on getting us access and use of that communications hub as soon as possible, I would very much appreciate it. Any chance you could make that happen by nightfall tomorrow? I really do need to get a message out. But remember, it needs to be heard over as much of the province as possible."

"That won't be a problem, sir; the NZC's always made certain that whenever they have something they want to be heard, they have a means to get it out to everyone, even past the BZ's checkpoints into *their* secure network, if they ever wanted to."

"How long do we have before they shut us down or lock us out?"

"Well, General, no promises here, but if you keep the broadcast under fifteen minutes, my guy should be able to keep them from being able to trace it back to us."

"So, we can use it again…that's *fabulous*, Commander!"

"Please remember, General, I said should."

The meeting concluded and everyone left, except for Daniel and Simon, as Daniel had something he needed to speak to his old friend about afterwards.

"Simon, really? What was that all about? What were you thinking?"

"What's wrong?"

"'The needs of the Blue Zone will always take a back seat to the needs of the Red Zone'? *Really*? Since when?"

"I was just—"

"Simon, I know we've been friends for a long time, but please, don't *ever* do that again."

"What are you talking about, Daniel?"

"We're *not* putting the Red Zone before the Blue Zone, Simon, not ever! We'll be treating both zones with equal importance from now on; this isn't just about the RZ anymore, it's about the entire country."

"What? Come on, Daniel, you've got to be kidding! You and I are...we're *from* the RZ. We have to look out for our own *first*!"

"Simon, please, remember what I said; don't ever do that again."

CHAPTER 18

"Are you certain we'll be able to pick it up from here?"

"Yes, Kayla, I'm as certain as I can be."

Kayla was worried, and she was wondering whether any of those around her had noticed it. She'd never shown fear before, at least not like this. She couldn't avoid looking up from time to time to scan the faces of those around her in the room where they'd set up the main command center. She'd made every effort at subtlety, but she sometimes forgot we'd grown-up together. I knew her better than she knew herself.

"Don't worry about it, Kayla," I said to her quietly, so only she could hear. "Everything's going to be just fine. If anyone notices, they'll just have to get over themselves. He's your husband, after all; you have every right to be concerned."

Her head snapped around and the look on her face betrayed how off-guard my comment had caught her. Always the brave commander, I was so very proud of the woman she'd become over the last few years. I resolved at that moment that I needed to tell her so, and for some reason, one I really didn't understand at the time, I felt the need to do it sooner rather than later.

"Um, Commander, may I have a word please? Alone, ma'am?"

She looked around at the others, uncomfortable at first, but her demeanor quickly shifted into her leadership persona. "Certainly, Captain. How about the War Room? I believe it's available."

I nodded and we made our way down the hallway about twenty yards before opening the door and entering the War Room, which was nothing more than a glorified conference room where we planned attacks against our enemies. We both took a seat across from each other, with Kayla looking slightly uncomfortable.

"Relax, Kay. It's me, remember? Your friend, Chris?"

Kayla let out a heavy sigh and rested her head on the table face down. "Aarrgghh! I know, Chris, I know. I'm sorry. I'm just so—"

"Worried about Daniel? Yeah, I know, it's been written all over your face for the past several days now."

"I know! But I've tried so hard to put on a brave face, to exude calm, to maintain a sense of confidence and trust that he and the others are fine. Oh, but Chris, all I want to do is jump on a GravJet, a MagTrain, even a horse if that's what it takes to find him! Why isn't he answering his holocom? I'd even try one of those things they used before the Great Schism, the ones they later found fried people's brain cells…what were they called again?"

"Weren't they called cell phones?"

"That's it; I'd even try a cell phone if I could talk to him just long enough to know he was okay!"

"Look, Kayla, there's really no need to keep this thing secret from everyone. It's a lot to keep to yourself, and to be honest, I don't think you should."

"Well, I told *you*, didn't I?"

"Yes, well, that's not quite the same now, is it? Listen, I'd be happy to take a couple of men to go and find Daniel, and to give him the good news. I expect he'd cut the mission short and come back sooner."

"I expect you *could* find him, Chris, and I'm sure he would cut his trip short. But that's exactly why we *can't* do that…his work is too important, you *know* that."

"Kayla, we're trying to do the impossible here, to overturn not just one but two governments. But what's all that effort worth if we can't take time to appreciate the things we're fighting for the most, like family?"

I almost had her with that one, because she turned and looked at me for the longest time, clearly pondering my last comment and weighing it against the value of the mission he was on. In the end, however, it was as it always had been, the *mission* that won over her personal wants and needs.

"No, we'll stay the course, Chris. Hopefully we'll get his broadcast soon, and I'll know he's safe and on his way home."

Kayla started to get up to leave until I reached across the table and placed my hand on her arm. The act surprised her and she sat back down.

"What is it, Chris? Is something bothering you?"

"Yes, there is," I answered, partially being playful, partially curious to see how she'd react.

"Then tell me what I can do to help *you*, dear Christian, my closest, and best of friends."

"Ah, now, I thought we promised not to lie to one another, Kayla."

"Okay, okay…aside from *Daniel* then!"

"That's better." We both laughed for a moment. While I knew we could never go back to the people we'd once been, it warmed my heart to see that my friend, the girl I'd come to love as a sister, if not as a lover, was still there. "Kayla, there's something I've wanted to tell you for some time now, and…well, for whatever reason I felt like I needed to say it sooner rather than later,"

"Okay, what is it, Christian?"

"I've been wanting to tell you how proud I am of you. I remember, going back a year or two ago, finding this wonderful, beautiful, carefree young woman in a skimpy bathing suit, tanning by the pool on a hot summer day, while life in the world outside the compound just passed her by as if it never existed. And then I look at how, once you came to recognize the pain and suffering in others, you've made their pain your own, and I see this incredible leader you've become.

"Then, well, you and Daniel found one another, and I see how much in love you two are, and well, I'm just so…." I felt myself getting choked up a little, so strong were my emotions for her, yet still I continued. "I'm just so *very* proud of the woman you've become! I know for a fact that your mother and father would be so incredibly proud of you too, if they could be here with you right now, and if they'd seen everything I've seen. You've put your life on the line so many times to save others when you didn't have to, and it's...well, *inspiring*, if you want to know the truth. I doubt any of us would even be here if it weren't for you. Thank you!"

By now I'd taken both of her hands into mine; tears had filled her eyes and started running down both of her cheeks. I'd like to say that mine were manly and dry, but I'd be lying.

"Chris, I don't know what to say. I—"

A loud knock on the War Room door interrupted the special moment of sentiment between two very close friends.

"Commander?" Vanessa called out.

"Come in, Vanessa."

The door opened and she stood in the doorway for a moment, caught off guard by the display of tears she witnessed. After cautiously surveying the scene with a slightly furrowed brow, followed by a momentary and a slightly disconcerting pause on me, she turned and focused back on Kayla. "Please pardon the interruption, but General Washington's broadcast...it just started coming through, ma'am. We thought you'd want to know immediately."

Without saying a word Kayla leapt to her feet and shot out the door, all before I'd even had a chance to stand up.

***

She reached the command center to find her husband's handsome face plastered across the large, main screen.

"Good evening, fellow citizens of the Red Zone," Daniel began, in a gentle, friendly, almost fatherly tone.

It was at that moment that I suddenly realized how proud I was of Daniel, too. Though I'd only known him for less than two years, he'd worked very hard and had come a very long way as he'd grown into the role he'd seemed destined to fill as leader of the resistance. Daniel wasn't much older than I was in years, yet there was something about him, about his spirit, his very soul perhaps, that felt much older. Maybe he'd had such a hard life

125

that he'd been forced to mature far beyond his years at a very young age, or perhaps it was merely his nature; I never really learned the truth of it. I know only that Daniel was always an honest and extremely courageous man, a leader of people, who gladly faced death every morning if by doing so it offered him, his family, and his people a chance at a better life, and freedom. It came as no surprise to me that people were quick to follow him, for he was a natural born leader if ever there'd been one.

"I must apologize for interrupting your regularly scheduled programming, which presumably is more of the same NZC propaganda, the same nonsense packed with subliminal programming and encoded suggestions, the only purpose of which is to rewire your brain into believing the Red Council has your best interest at heart.

"My name is Daniel Washington, and I am proud to lead the Red Zone resistance movement against the NZC and the Corporate Synod. Together with Kayla Ross, the commander of the resistance movement against the Gentry in the Blue Zone — and by the way, she also happens to be my beautiful wife now — we lead the American resistance, dedicated to the reunification of the two zones and the rebuilding of the New United States of America.

"I'm here tonight so I can speak to you, not as citizens of the Red Zone, but as fellow Americans. That's right, Americans. I know many of you don't even know what Americans are, because the Corporate Synod, together with the NZC, decided what you would and would not be allowed to believe, back when they decided what you would and would not be allowed to think, and to learn, *especially* about your past.

"You see, believe it or not, the land on which we live, which extends from coast to coast, from ocean to ocean, which is now home to the Blue Zone to the west and the Red Zone to the east, was once home to one people...a single nation called the United States of America, or just America for short, a word that was synonymous all over the world with another very important word...*freedom*. That's right, freedom. I know, that word probably has little meaning for most of us because most of us have never had a taste of freedom our entire lives. I know I didn't, at least not until I joined with the resistance and became a wanted man, an outlaw, for wanting freedom and human rights for my own people.

"This once great country, the United States, was founded hundreds of years ago by brave, courageous men who, much like the men and woman in the resistance today, sacrificed everything they had, in many cases even their lives, in the name of freedom, and in order to participate in the birth of a great nation, a country founded on a single principle document, the Constitution of the United States. This magnificent document was the very foundation upon which this country was founded, for it guaranteed freedoms, safeguards, and checks and balances in government that were intended to protect people like you and I, to keep our government from being too easily bent towards corruption. You see, under the Constitution, those who work in government are to make laws actually work *for you*, because they are only there to represent *you*, to do *your* bidding. Now doesn't that sound a little better than what we have today, with the NZC telling us who and what to worship and who to marry and when, and the Corporate Synod forcing the Production Class to undergo genetic modifications that will enhance their productivity at work but will take ten years off their lives?

"Now, I've had the pleasure to read the Constitution from front to back, and on my last holocom to you I read a short snippet of it to you. There will be plenty more to talk about concerning the United States Constitution at some point in the future. But for now, there is *another* document that I'd like to share with you. It is a letter written about the same time as the Constitution, by one of our country's most recognized founding fathers. It declares with some specificity why the United States sought to become a free and independent nation, separate from the rule of another tyrant king, someone like Leader Romano, and England, the country that had founded and ruled it for hundreds of years. The man who wrote this Declaration of Independence was named Thomas

Jefferson, and he wrote this letter nearly four-hundred years ago. I believe you will see, however, how his words to King George, the king of England, could just as easily be directed to Mikos Romano, Leader of the Red Council, today.

'IN CONGRESS, JULY 4, 1776

The unanimous Declaration of the thirteen United States of America

When in the Course of human events it becomes necessary for one people to dissolve the political bands which have connected them with another and to assume among the powers of the earth, the separate and equal station to which the Laws of Nature and of Nature's God entitle them, a decent respect to the opinions of mankind requires that they should declare the causes which impel them to the separation.

We hold these truths to be self-evident, that all men are created equal, that they are endowed by their Creator with certain unalienable Rights, that among these are Life, Liberty and the pursuit of Happiness. — That to secure these rights, Governments are instituted among Men, deriving their just powers from the consent of the governed — That whenever any Form of Government becomes destructive of these ends, it is the Right of the People to alter or to abolish it, and to institute new Government, laying its foundation on such principles and organizing its powers in such form, as to them shall seem most likely to effect their Safety and Happiness. Prudence, indeed, will dictate that Governments long established should not be changed for light and transient causes; and accordingly all experience hath shewn that mankind are more disposed to suffer, while evils are sufferable than to right themselves by abolishing the forms to which they are accustomed. But when a long train of abuses and usurpations, pursuing invariably the same Object evinces a design to reduce them under absolute Despotism, it is their right, it is their duty, to throw off such Government, and to provide new Guards for their future security....'

"I hope you can see, my dear friends, how our circumstances parallel those of our ancient forefathers. We too suffer a long train of abuses and usurpations, and we most certainly serve despots of the highest order. I propose that it is time for us to rise and throw off our despots, that it is our right to abolish this corrupt government, and to institute a new one!

"Men and women once had the freedom to go where they wanted, and to be what they wanted to be in this great country. There was no Corporate Synod forcing them to take gene enhancements so they could work longer hours and die younger, or to develop larger brains while becoming increasingly devoid of human emotions. There was no NZC threatening life in prison or death for anyone worshipping the one true God instead of the benevolent life-giving universe and the limitless potential of human achievement, or the casting of entire families into prisons just so they could steal their property, all under the pretense of them not following strict NZC doctrine. No, they were a great and free people, a shining example of freedom for the entire world to emulate.

"It's true that over time, however, these freedoms were gradually taken for granted, and these great, free people began giving away their freedom piece by piece, the result of the endless bickering that broke out among them in regard to differences in ideology or theology, as each group fought tooth and nail for *their* worldview to be the dominant one. Instead of working out a means where both sides could have something they wanted, they fought constantly, with constant streams of lies flowing from one side, confusing the public and making it increasingly difficult for the other side to govern.

"As some of you may know, this infighting eventually led us to a second civil war between two loosely formed groups, the conservatives and liberals. This war, which the liberals eventually lost but at a great cost to both sides, resulted in what we now call the Great Schism. Instead of forcing the losing side to capitulate as happened following the first civil war, however, our ancestors allowed the liberals to split the country in two, with liberals forming the Blue Zone in the west, while our forefathers stayed here and formed the Red Zone.

"In the beginning our leaders in the Red Zone were successful enough; most everyone attended Church and worshipped the one

God, and our people had moral clarity socially and followed a very conservative policy fiscally. Constitutionalists were satisfied because most power and decisions were, at that time, being made at the local level.

"Everything changed over time, however, as the Corporate Synod grew in power and influence over the RZ, helping and supporting the fledgling New Zion Church, which denied the Christian God and Savior in favor of a more generic spirituality, in which there were no absolutes. These two grew in power and corruption until we arrive at where we are today, with the people being brutally treated and oppressed with little to no say in what happens in our lives or the lives of our families.

"I'd like to share a story with you. This story is about a boy and his family, a family forced to grow up in the ignorance and oppression of the Production Class. This young boy and his family were forbidden to leave Sector 48, as were nearly all other Production Class families living there.

"Now some of you may already know that everyone there, including men, women, and children, were all forced to endure regular gene therapy enhancements, which the Synod declared were designed to keep us healthy, enhance our intellectual capacity, and help us live longer. They were supposed to help those of us who were average and to help lift us up on par with the other classes.

"But the Synod lied to us. These gene treatments weren't designed to *help us* at all. They were, in reality, designed to do one thing and one thing only…enhance profits for the Synod. The genetic alterations enhanced the endurance and physical stamina of the production workers so they could work longer shifts with less breaks, while making them as much as five to ten times as productive. But these improvements in productivity came at a cost; instead of increasing their lifespan, the genetic alterations ended up decreasing the average lifespan by an average of ten to twenty years. After learning about this, did the Synod stop the treatments? No. In fact, I recently learned that they ramped up production upon seeing the high rates of increase in productivity, and began dispensing the therapy at younger and younger ages.

"Now of course, this little boy's family didn't now all of this at the time, so like so many others in the PC they were faithful supporters of the NZC, attending services regularly and financially supporting their local chapter far beyond what they could afford. So, given the unquestioned loyalty to the NZC over many, many years, you would think that when hard times fell on this family, and the father died, that the NZC would be there for this kind, generous family, wouldn't you? Well, they were not! Instead, they joined with the Synod to cover up the truth about the father's death, a cover-up that resulted in early death for the mother and with the children still at home being sold into Synod slave houses where they would work off the family's debts.

"It was only because of a fluke, or perhaps a blessing from the one true God, that the little boy was different from the rest of his family, having been born with an unusually high intellect, which led to his being sent out of Sector 48 and separated from his family for the rest of his life.

"Now I'm sure that by now you've surmised that *I* was that little boy, and you'd be correct. I understandably grew very bitter upon learning what the Synod and the NZC had done to my family, and so I started listening to some of the stories I'd heard since leaving Sector 48; stories of abuse, slavery, imprisonment, executions, and worse. I joined the resistance, and the rest is history.

"Sadly, my story is not unique. Take Mrs. Rodriguez, for example. Her son was publicly whipped, beaten, and thrown into prison, after he was overheard telling a close friend that he was a Christian, and for following the old God. That was twenty-five years ago, and Mrs. Rodriguez still has no idea whether her son is alive or dead, and whenever she tries to find out she is either turned away, or she is threatened, or beaten. Is this justice? Is this freedom? Or is this tyranny?"

"Raymond Banyon was elite even among the Intelligentsia. He worked in advanced aeronautics, and was the poster child for the Synod's Genetic Advancement program, making incredible breakthroughs in science, providing answers to scientific puzzles that have plagued mankind since well before the Great Schism. Some of these breakthroughs you may have heard about, such as the means of creating a manmade wormhole for traveling vast distances in space, and fields of energy that can be used to protect ships in space, or even military craft here on the ground.

"What you may not have heard, however, was that Banyon murdered his family in cold-blood last year just as he was finalizing some formulas for his energy fields. It seems one of his younger children disturbed him in his home office one Saturday afternoon, just wanting to spend more time with his father. The man, however, suddenly exploded in a fit of uncontrolled rage. Sadly, even after the fact, the poor man had absolutely no recollection and no emotional connection with the event whatsoever. In fact, when asked how he felt about the death of his wife, daughter, and two sons, he merely stated that he'd 'probably get more work done now.'

"Synod medical personnel refused to admit that the genetic therapy was to blame, yet it was clearly an exaggerated case of what has been seen among other intelligentsia across the zone. Whereas with the Production Class the therapy steals years away from their lives, for the Intelligentsia Class it robs them of their humanity, stealing away their emotion, until eventually, they're little more than human computers.

"In conclusion, I'm asking…no, I'm begging each and every one of you, whether man or woman, young or old, weak or strong…please, please join our cause. We need you, desperately. This could be the last chance we ever have of reclaiming the country that was founded to be free so very long ago. Join the resistance whenever possible, but if you cannot, then I would simply ask this; resist, resist, resist. Resist the Synod, and resist the NZC, in any and every way you can. Yes, you will be punished, and yes, you may even lose your life. But take a look around; do you honestly believe, deep down, that what you are doing today can truly be called living? Are you truly free? If you answer yes to that question, then you are truly blessed, enjoy your life. If you cannot, why haven't you already joined us? Do you doubt you could make a difference? Not so long ago I didn't believe I could make a difference, yet I single-handedly brought down the Synod's regional headquarters, and I've become a leader in this movement to take back our home.

"Some have asked me whether I fear for my life; the answer, to be perfectly candid, is that I don't know that I'll survive this revolution. But that's not what's important; what *is* important is that this *revolution* survives, and that the *New United States of America* is born.

"Again, I plead with you...with all of you, for your sake, for the sake of your family, for the sake of your people, for your zone, and for your country; come and join us. Help us restore this great nation to what it was intended to be. We intend to rebuild America, but we'll learn from the mistakes our forefathers made and make changes which, with God's help, will keep us from going back down that same road. But we need each and every one of you to make this dream become a reality, and we're waiting....

"And now, a message for our friends on the Red Council. We don't want to be your enemies...we're willing to overlook all but the most egregious crimes against the people. We merely want to fix what's broken, to tear down your totalitarian government—the Red Council—and replace it with a government elected by the people and for the people, a government that will represent them in leadership and will make decisions for them *with their consent.*

"If you can live with that, then we would like to work *with you*; please, let us know, and come join us in reshaping our zone, and our country, into what the founders originally intended, into what *God* originally intended for this country to be.

"If, however, you seek only to hold on to your ill-gotten power and to the status quo, then watch out, we're coming for you. We are the P-O-T-F, The People of the Founders."

The image flashed and disappeared, only to be replaced by a man in an NZC robe, selling his wares to whoever would listen. We clicked off the broadcast, while Kayla and I just looked at one another with blank stares for several seconds, before a wicked smile crept in onto Kayla's face.

"I've just had a fantastic idea, Chris, and I think you're going to like it."

"Okay, so tell me."

The enthusiasm in her eyes was radiant. "Remember the day we liberated Peak's Lake from the Chinese?"

"Of course!"

"Didn't we have some of our people carrying holorecorders?"

CHAPTER 19

Kayla donned her mask, took a deep breath, and after slowly releasing it, gave a thumbs up. Vanessa started the countdown and then gave the signal to begin recording and broadcasting. Kayla began.

"Brothers and sisters of the BZ, good evening.

"I must apologize for the delay since my last broadcast, but there have been a number of recent developments, some frightening and some very exciting; so, I'll get right to them.

"I believe that one of these new developments could, with your help, enable us to regain the freedom we once had, and throw off the shackles of slavery with which the Gentry have imprisoned us. I'm going to make what might sound like an unusual request of you tonight. As I do so, however, I ask that you consider the miserable estate so many of our people now find themselves in within the Blue Zone, with many BZers completely lost in a chemically-induced stupor, slaves to their addiction to state-supplied drugs. Others across the BZ are starving, living from meal to meal, often doing everything they can just to survive the day. Still others, many others, spend their days as literal slaves to the state, victims of a state program that manipulated their LINC injections in order to obtain free labor for key projects.

"I realize that most of our families long ago abandoned belief in any religions, especially belief in the ancient Christian God. Consider the dire straits in which we now find ourselves, circumstances that I believe were brought about largely *because* we turned our backs on God. I am, therefore, now pleading with each one of you to consider the very high cost we've paid for that irresponsible decision, and to consider once more seeking out the

Christian God, the Lord, and asking for His divine blessing on our cause.

"Now some of you may have heard that The Militiamen have joined with the Red Zone's People of the Founder's resistance movement and formed the *American Resistance*, in order to attempt something *very* special, something far beyond the toppling of Leader Peloski's pathetic throne. We plan to reunite the zones into one country again, as it was originally intended, into the *New* United States of America.

"The incredibly courageous men and women who established that new democracy were often referred to as the country's Founding Fathers. The Founding Fathers of the United States of America not only believed in, but fervently worshipped and relied upon the Lord God, and it is my hope that you will consider joining me now in turning to Him to seek His favor in our effort, for the sake of your children, and your children's children. Believe me when I say that if we are to win our freedom and reunite our country, we *will* need God's help, and His blessing.

"There's something else I wanted to share with you, something we found to be very, very disturbing. It was, in fact, an act of high treason on the part of Leader Peloski, for which the penalty is death. The Militiamen made a disturbing discovery some time ago when we came across a city filled with foreigners. I don't mean to suggest a city filled with Blue Zoners *and* foreigners...I mean a city filled with foreigners and just a handful of Blue Zoners scattered around here and there. We learned that the land for this city had been illegally 'purchased' from Leader Peloski by a foreign government, the People's Republic of China. Now think about that; the Leader sold your country, *your* land, the same land *your* ancestors farmed, developed, built on, worked on, and died on, and the Leader *sold it* to the *Chinese*, who brought in *their* people. Who knows how much of the BZ has been carved up and sold to the highest bidder by those we've entrusted to be our leaders?

"Well, no more. It's time we take back our country from that disgusting little man, Peloski. Take it back from these invading foreigners, *and* from those inside the Gentry who support them! With the help of some new 'friends' from the RZ, we've already liberated the first such city we've come across, and we will continue to liberate each and every one we find.

"I'm very excited to share with you, my brothers and sisters of the BZ, the Militiamen's intention to work with our new Red Zone friends, the People of the Founders, to topple the tyrannical governments in both zones, with the goal of reuniting this great country into the powerful and free nation it once was.

"But if this country was once so great, what happened, and why is it such a mess now? They would both be fair questions, and not easily answered. The short answer is that two factions arose in a war of cultures within the great United States, and these two factions constantly bickered about what the country should be like. This eventually led to a second civil war and the split into two zones.

"What's to keep us from making the same mistakes all over again, you might ask? Well, the answer is...*you*. It will be up to you, and me, and our children, to learn from the past and never repeat it. Before we can do anything, however, we must first regain control of our zone from the tyrant currently in power, Leader Peloski, and from the corrupt members of the Gentry. The leader, and the corrupted men and women inside the Gentry, are guilty of enslaving their own people, guilty of selling off your country to the highest bidder with the proceeds going into their pockets, and they are guilty of running the BZ into the ground while destroying lives, separating families, and starving their own people.

"We can achieve freedom, my brothers and sisters, but we can only achieve it by working together! Do you want to be treated like cattle for the rest of your lives? Do you want your children, your grandchildren, and your great-grandchildren to die of starvation, to be turned into mindless slaves by the state, or work as foreigners inside their own country and on their own land?

"We need your help; please, lend us your aid in restoring

freedom and democracy to our country. Join the Militiamen and help us build a brand new tomorrow for you, for your children, and their children. You can help no matter where you are or what you do. Join your chapter of the Militiamen, or find ways to help the cause in other ways. Provide supplies, information, financial backing…every little bit helps. If you're in the People's Guard, we need you! If you're Gentry and want to join us because you've had enough of the suffering, the greed, and you've finally come to realize our cause is just and right, then join us! If you're a housewife who can prepare food and supplies for our Militiamen volunteers, then help us!

"Our numbers have grown significantly over the last few years. Combined with the vast numbers of the RZ's People of the Founders Resistance movement, the American Resistance is definitely a force to be reckoned with.

"Stay strong, my people. And remember to keep on striving for freedom, and remember to keep on praying for victory.

"God bless you all, and goodnight."

***

"What time did he get back in?" Vanessa asked before kissing me, and then joining me for breakfast in the mess hall.

"I don't know, but it was sometime very early this morning. I imagine they were being careful, doing everything they could to avoid leading anyone from the NZC or the Synod back here."

"They're going to find us eventually; you know that, don't you?" she asked me, a look of fear mixed with resignation painted on her young and beautiful face.

"Who?"

"The Gentry, the People's Guard, the Synod, the NZC…does it matter? This place was quite a find, but we've really placed all our eggs in one basket here."

I sat in silence for a while, sipping on my coffee while looking down at the latest intelligence briefs as if I were reading them for a third time.

"I suppose you're right, darling, but we'll have to worry about that later. Right now, we have to worry about what we're going to do when the general wakes up."

"What do you mean?"

I sighed. I'd kept my promise to Kayla and I'd told no one her secret, but things had changed. "There's something I've got to tell General Washington, something I promised Kayla I'd not tell anyone. Given what's happened —"

"*What's* happened, Christian? Is something wrong? What is it you need to tell me? And oh, by the way, have you seen my wife? She wasn't in our quarters all night and no one's seen her."

My heart froze in panic. I was completely unprepared to say anything, to do anything, yet here he was. I couldn't help but fear how he'd react to how I'd let everything get so out of hand in his absence.

"Oh…General, you're back. It was an excellent broadcast, sir, very, very impressive. I can't tell you how you never cease to surprise me with your uncanny insight and courage. You're a born leader, Daniel, one in a million."

"Thanks, Christian…I mean that, really. Now, where in the world has Kayla gotten to, Chris? I know if anyone on this base knows where she is, it's you."

"Daniel, we need to talk."

"What's wrong, Chris…is she hurt?"

"Oh, no, she's fine; well, as far as I know."

"*CHRIS!*"

Just as severe weather blowing in on a strong wind can quickly change a beautiful and cheerful sunny day into a terrifying night of terror, his concern for Kayla had transformed his light and friendly demeanor into that of a fierce, raging lion.

"She's fine, Daniel, don't worry. She took off on a mission a week or so ago, but we haven't had any communications with her since two days after she left."

"Then she's broken protocol; she should have checked in several days ago, you know that. Have you sent anyone after her yet?"

"Not yet."

"Why not?"

"Because she had two-hundred men with her, Daniel."

"What? Two-hundre...." I now had his attention, which was a relief. I knew I needed to slow him down, because if I didn't, what I was about to tell him would have sent him exploding off the rails. "What sort of mission was she on, anyway, that would require that many men?"

"She did a holocom broadcast while you were gone, Daniel. I believe she was inspired by yours. But in truth, she did have a few things she needed to catch everyone up on; it had been quite a while since her last one. She updated everyone on what we found with the Chinese in Peak's Lake, the arrangement with you and the rest of the POF, etc."

"No, no...that makes sense. But where is she now, Chris?"

"Well, sir, after that broadcast we had quite the response... through the proper channels, of course. One of the most significant, however, was that we learned that one of the highest ranking generals in the People's Guard, a General Conrad Miller, was interested in joining with us. He first wanted to meet with Kayla face-to-face, in a neutral setting of her choosing; it was his only requirement. He claimed to have over two thousand men under his command, and he was certain that at least fifteen hundred wanted to come over with him; the other five-hundred or so he was less certain of."

Daniel shook his head as if shaking off dust or soot in disgust. "What about Kayla?"

"That's all I know, General. As I said, we haven't heard from her since, and as you indicated, she missed the initial and subsequent check-ins."

"Okay, thank you, Christian. Just get me the location of the meeting and directions, and I'll see what we can do about getting everyone back. This could get messy, but if anything's happened to her, I will make them pay such a price—"

"Um, General...Daniel?"

Daniel stopped at the door he was about to open to leave, and turned back to face me. "Yes?"

"Please come back over here and sit down, just for another

moment. There's one other thing I needed to tell you. This little detail is kind of important; you might want to sit down for this."

Daniel did as I asked, now more curious and worried than before. "Chris...what's going on?"

"She made me promise not to say anything to anyone about this, *especially to you*. She was afraid you'd overreact, be too overprotective, perhaps even act irrationally. Given our present circumstances, however, I feel I have no choice but tell you; you must know." I took a deep breath and swallowed hard. "Kayla's pregnant, Daniel...she's carrying your child." I stood while he continued staring blankly at me for several moments, until a light suddenly flickered on in his eyes before bursting forth like the sun.

"She's pregnant; I'm going to have a child! I'm going to be a father, Christian! Do you hear that? I'm going to be a father, man!"

I couldn't help but smile back in turn, rejoicing with him, infected by his sudden eruption of enthusiasm and emotion. Despite the seriousness and perhaps even direness of the circumstances, Daniel deserved the moment.

"Yes, you are! Congratulations, Daniel. You and Kayla deserve this, my friend; I mean that from the bottom of my heart."

"Thanks, thank you, Christian."

Daniel ran out of the room yelling for Simon for several seconds, until I heard his yells grow quieter and quieter until they were no more than a whisper. Before long he was slowly walking back into the room towards me.

"I'll begin gathering our best men together." He looked up at me with a perplexed look. "What was she thinking, Chris? You've known her since she was a child; surely she must have said something to you."

"She was gone before I knew it, Daniel. She knew I would have found a way to stop her from going. I knew she was pregnant, and we both knew how dangerous it was. I would have talked sense to her and she would have never left here. That's why she left the way she did."

Daniel stared at the floor as if studying some elaborate map or detail etched into the concrete. "I understand *why* she wanted to go; strategically, it was probably worth the risk for the cause. If, as you say, this general was willing to meet only with her, then she must have felt she had an impossibly hard choice to make; placing our child's life at risk or hundreds of thousands, perhaps millions of other couple's children at risk."

"Daniel...."

"Yes?"

"We should probably get moving as quickly as possible."

"Yes, or course. Find Simon, tell him we'll need some heavy armor, some airships, and at least a thousand men. We have no idea what we'll run into, so we'll need to be prepared."

"Yes, sir."

CHAPTER 20

Six days earlier
(before Daniel's return)

It was still early autumn, yet a frosty, steady wind continually rolled in from the mountain tops, which gusted at times, serving to foreshadow the bite of the bitterly cold and difficult winter to come, a reminder that could be felt by all as they stood outside in the cold mountain air, waiting. Of course, it didn't help matters that the valley they were standing in was over thirteen hundred meters, or forty-three hundred feet, above sea level, with the Wasatch Mountains, the western range of the great Rocky Mountains, to the east and the north of their position.

They had arranged to rendezvous with the general at Camp Williams, a former military base that had once served as a National Guard base in an area just north of Provo, Utah and south of Salt Lake City. Based on what they'd been able to discern in the hours they'd spent looking around while waiting for the general, it appeared the base had closed just prior to the time of the Great Schism.

Kayla looked around at the vastness and isolation of the location and appreciated the general's discretion. If his defection was sincere, and she had every reason to expect it was, he obviously did not want to reveal his defection to the enemy, since doing so would likely end up forcing both the general and Kayla to fight their way all the way back to Colorado Springs, something they would both rather avoid unless absolutely necessary.

The thought of such a violent and sustained conflict unconsciously drew her attention down to her abdomen, which she immediately interpreted to her maternal instinct kicking in. Kayla had already accepted that this would likely be her last mission away from camp until the birth of their child. She'd been willing to risk it the one time, but she would not do so a second, no matter how much they had to gain. Her maternal instincts were getting too strong now. And besides, she was quickly becoming a liability to the others. She grew more fearful by the day that if trouble should come, her people could very well end up getting themselves hurt or killed on her behalf, trying to protect her and her unborn child from injury during battle.

"Commander! They're coming! About twenty clicks out, at your two o'clock."

Kayla quickly shook out the cobwebs and raised her digital specs to her eyes. She gasped at what she saw, and suddenly found herself desperately wishing she had more men.

"Okay, everyone, get ready! It's got to be them. There's a lot of them; they're packing heavy, like they're expecting trouble, moving fast, and they're headed directly for us. I see tanks, transports, and infantry. Now we have every reason to believe they're coming over to our side, but we cannot take any chances. If this goes south for any reason I want you to remember something; you soldiers are the very best we have, and each of you are worth a hundred of them. Remember that."

"You heard the commander, knuckleheads," barked Sergeant Marcel. "Now listen up! This general and his men, *if* they're legit, could make a *big* difference in our struggle to win the BZ. So please, don't get trigger happy on me and start an unnecessary bloodbath, okay? Just stay calm, and follow my lead. These people could turn out to be the best friends you ever had, remember that."

By the time Kayla and Marcel had finished speaking, the general and his men had nearly closed the distance. They'd slowed their pace considerably and deliberately, and were now slowly but steadily advancing. The bulk of the contingent stopped some distance back, while the lead transport advanced alone before stopping no more than twenty yards from where

Kayla and Marcel stood, along with a host of special operators, ready to do anything and everything to protect Kayla.

The transport opened, and seconds later several soldiers jumped out, weapons in hand and pointed toward Marcel and his men, until an older man with gray hair and a slight beard climbed out and began slowly advancing.

"Stop! That's enough now; put down your weapons men. Surely, my friends, we didn't come all this way merely to gun down our new allies; nor I expect, did they come here to do the same to us. As former members of the People's Guard, let's begin this discussion with a demonstration of trust, shall we?"

The weapons lowered as the general continued advancing. Kayla turned to her men and gestured. They also lowered their weapons as she stepped toward the general. She held out her hand in greeting, and the two shook hands in a warm and friendly greeting.

"So, *you* are the mysterious woman behind the mask! It is a great pleasure and privilege to finally meet you, my dear!"

"I'm sorry, you are…?"

"Please forgive my poor manners. I am Major General Felix Cole, Commander of the Third Division, *formerly* of the People's Guard. And you are…?"

"Commander Kayla Ross Washington, leader of the Militiamen Freedom Fighters, and second in command of the American Resistance movement."

"Kayla Ross Washington? So, Kayla Ross is your maiden name?"

"Yes, that's right.

"Your father, is he Sebastian Ross, a member of the High Council?"

"Yes, do you know him?"

"Well, let's just say I know *of* him. You should also know that based on what I know of him, your father would be very proud of what you have accomplished, *if* he knew it was you."

"What? But he's a part of the problem, General, part of the system that's destroyed the BZ and enslaved its people."

"On the contrary; from what I hear, he's been doing everything he can to change things from the inside, my dear. Unfortunately, the rate of decay within the Blue Zone is so rapid and so prevalent, I've given up hope that it *can* be stopped, at least without a revolution.

"It's long been said that one's elders are meant to teach and inspire the younger generation to achieve great things. After watching what you, such a determined and optimistic young person, have been able to accomplish in such a short amount of time...why, I fear you have shamed us, my dear! While we cowered in the corner, convincing each other how nothing could be done to change things, you were out here doing it! I've been very impressed with your ideals and your achievements, Mrs. Washington; so much so, in fact, that you inspired me and my men to come join your effort."

"And we're so very glad you did, General Cole, welcome. Please allow me to introduce you to some of my people. My attentive second here is Sergeant Pierre Marcel."

"It's a pleasure to meet you, Sergeant."

"The pleasure, *and honor*, General, are all mine, sir," Marcel replied with a salute, followed by a friendly handshake.

The general then turned to Kayla with a serious yet kind and warm demeanor. "Commander Washington, I hereby pledge myself, my life, my honor, and my men to your service, and the cause of the resistance, to restore democracy and freedom, and to rebuild the United States of America."

"Thank you, General. We are so very glad to have you with us."

Several more men emerged from the transport and began introducing themselves as well, as word began to spread.

After some time had passed the general approached Kayla. "Commander Washington, there's something I would very much like to discuss with you. Before we leave the area, there is a man very high up within the High Council; a man who occupies a position of power that's higher than even your father. While this man and I agree on a great many things about the current state

146

of the BZ, I'm afraid he doesn't quite yet share my opinion of you and the Militiamen, although he does seem to have an open mind. I thought, perhaps, if he had the chance to meet you... before we leave...."

"Of course, General; I'd be happy to meet with him."

"Thank you, Commander. He's a stubborn man, but I believe we owe it to the movement, ourselves, and most importantly the country, to at least try to convince him to join us. His support *could* help determine whether this is a relatively brief and speedy revolution, or a long, bloody, and drawn out affair with many lives lost."

"I understand, General. I promise to do my best to persuade him. We'll leave at first light. We'll take a small contingent of soldiers with us to meet him and leave the rest here. Does that sound reasonable?"

"Yes, ma'am."

***

Kayla glanced back at her watch for the fiftieth time in the past hour. They'd been waiting for nearly two hours now, and even for someone as important as this man was, two hours was really pushing it for a pregnant woman. She was about to turn to the general when the middle-aged secretary sitting nearby received a call. She touched her ear to answer the call.

"Yes, sir? Yes, sir...I understand." She touched her ear gently once more and turned to the two of them. "Secretary Adams is ready to see you now; please come with me." She led them down a short hallway to a large, ornate hardwood door and knocked firmly.

"Enter!"

The secretary opened the door and introduced them as they walked by her. "General Felix Cole and Miss Kayla Ross Washington, the daughter of Councilman Ross; this is Secretary Henry Adams."

"Ah, so *you* are Sebastian's daughter! Does he know, I wonder? I seriously doubt it. But he has been worried sick about you, my dear. I understand why you left so abruptly, but he certainly does not. Won't you please contact him, my dear? I beg you to contact him as soon as possible. If you like, I can furnish you with a holocom that cannot be traced."

"But why would you do this?" she asked him, still trying to discern where the man stood on her and the resistance.

"Because Sebastian has been a dear friend for a very long time, my dear, and it is not his fault that his adopted daughter decided to lead a resistance movement to topple her province's government."

"Then I will accept the holocom, Mr. Secretary, thank you. In truth, one of the primary reasons I *haven't* contacted him more often was the fear of the call being traced."

"The other thing being, of course, that you were afraid your father would discover that *you* are the young woman behind the mystery mask."

"Well...yes. I see you're a discerning man, Mr. Secretary."

"Please...I'm just an old man who's been around long enough to see how the world, and people, tend to operate. So tell me, why are you here? Do you hope to win me to your cause as well?"

"Mr. Secretary, I recommended —"

"I'd prefer to hear from Miss Ross, or Mrs. Washington, whatever her name is now, if you don't mind, General."

"Of course, sir."

"Our people have been turned into slaves, Mr. Secretary... I've seen it for myself. Our cities and our land are sold to foreign nations...I've seen that for myself as well. Worse yet, our children are starving, they are dying, and families all over the BZ are being torn apart. Surely none of this has escaped your notice, Mr. Secretary. And if you are even half as wise and as caring underneath that gruff exterior as I suspect you are, sir, I have no doubt that you are every bit as concerned for the BZ as I am."

Kayla paused and locked eyes with the formidable politician sitting across from her. His gaze was as steady and as hard as any she'd ever endured, and she'd been around some tough birds over the last few years. She kept waiting for a reaction from the man who'd claimed to be a longtime friend of her father's, but nothing came. He seemed cold and callous, as lifeless and as emotionless as one of the bronze statues she'd seen in the lobby. She was about to give up and break eye contact when the man suddenly broke into a broad smile and began to laugh.

"Well, dollar to doughnuts, if you're not every bit Sebastian's daughter! I'm beginning to think he lied to both of us about the whole adoption thing, dear; it's simply asking too much to believe that you are not the genetic offspring of Sebastian Ross! You're every bit as stubborn, determined, and obstinate as he ever was; while at the same time you are even more honest and compassionate than your father, whom I've always greatly admired. You know, Kayla...may I call you Kayla?" Still dumbfounded by the sudden turn of events, Kayla sat there staring dispassionately *at him*, smiling yet momentarily disassociated and disconnected. "Um, Kayla?"

"Hmm? Oh...sure, yes, Mr. Secretary, of course. Please call me Kayla."

"Your father would be very proud of you, Kayla, if he knew. He *doesn't know*, does he, about your leading the resistance?"

"No, sir."

"Why on earth haven't you told him, dear? You've told General Cole and myself, after all."

"True. I haven't told him out of fear I'd be putting his life in danger."

"I see. You *should* tell him. I'm not saying that I'm going to betray you, mind you, but if others don't already know who you are, they will eventually, and once they know...."

"He will be used as leverage against me, which will put him and my mother at great risk."

"Indeed, Leader Peloski would not have hesitated to use your parents as leverage to destroy you, Kayla, whether they already knew or not...were they not *already* at great risk," the aged man replied, with a grimace and dejected expression that revealed his concern and a look of resignation. "The truth is, my dear, your parents could be taken, or killed, at any moment for reasons that have nothing to do with you."

"What? Why? What are you talking about?" Kayla was stunned at the revelation. She didn't want to believe him; she wanted to believe he was lying to her, deceiving her in order to manipulate her for some reason. Yet, she felt the man was being truthful with her, because he *did* care, about the BZ, about her parents, about changing things.

"You may well be as surprised as I was to learn that your father is already involved in acts of rebellion and sedition that are every bit as dangerous as what you have been doing, Kayla. I'm very concerned for him, and I fear he could meet his end even before you meet yours."

"What do you mean?"

"He's been 'rocking the boat,' so to speak, upsetting quite a few people in the Gentry, Kayla. He's been desperately trying to change the established order of things for decades, from the inside, and he's been making a long list of enemies along the way. He was very subtle in the way he went about things in the beginning, but I fear as he's grown older and seen very little change. While the deterioration within the BZ has continued to accelerate, he's grown increasingly frustrated with each passing day. I'm beginning to grow concerned that he's attracted far too much attention. I don't want to see your father live out his remaining years in a prison cell, or worse yet, be executed."

"Please Mr. Secretary, we can change things and save him; please join me, join the resistance. With a man of your stature, of your place in the government joining us, you'd guarantee our success."

Adams lay back in his chair as if contemplating the thought. "I must confess, Kayla, when Felix told me he'd decided to take that step, I very nearly decided to go with him. You see, the sale of our cities, *our cities*, to a foreign nation, offering them a foothold within our sovereign borders, it was unthinkable! Who would do such a thing? You should know that this was the sovereign leader's idea, as head of the Gentry Party, as a means of raising desperately needed revenue. The BZ is in trouble, Kayla, as you've pointed out. I'm just not convinced that a revolution is the best way out of the mess we're in.

"Leader Peloski *has* made some boneheaded decisions to be certain, but I'm not convinced that what he's done has been acts of malicious intent. If I were, I would act without hesitation and throw my full support behind your movement.

"In truth, I've long thought that perhaps reuniting the two zones and reestablishing the United States might be in the best interests of both zones. But so many lives have been lost, so many sacrifices made, trying to make the two-zone system work. After the Great Schism, there was great optimism among our people that at last, those who wanted freedom from God, and the archaic beliefs, morals, and traditions of the past two thousand years, would have the opportunity to find their 'Utopia.'"

"Strange; I've never thought of the BZ as a Utopia, Mr. Secretary. Have you, sir?"

Adams snickered. "No, neither have I, Kayla. I suppose we may have needed God, and a lot of those 'archaic beliefs, morals, and traditions' a lot more than we ever realized," he replied, looking down and shaking his head sadly. He then looked up and stared evenly into Kayla's eyes. "Listen, Kayla. I greatly admire what you're doing, and I'll do everything I can to support you. The time may soon come for me to publicly declare my support for the resistance, but that day has not yet arrived. Until then, I'll do everything I can, within reason, to assist you, as long as I agree with what you're doing at the time."

Kayla smiled and nodded warmly in Adams's direction. "Thank you, Secretary Adams. I very much appreciate your candor, and your support. I must admit that I was hoping to leave with you publicly committed to our cause, but I respect your reasons for abstaining for now."

"Thank you. Before I forget, please give my best to your new husband...Daniel Washington, is it? I hear he's quite a fellow. Oh, one second...." Adams turned away, touched his ear, and whispered something. A short time later the secretary appeared with a holocom in hand. "Thank you, Margaret." She nodded before leaving the room. Adams handed the device to Kayla.

"Thank you, Mr. Secretary. I'll call my father on the way back."

"Do that; as I said, he's been worried sick. He loves you very much, you know."

"Yes, sir, I do know."

"Good. Okay then, one last piece of business and then I'll have to send you on your way." Adams pressed a button on his desk and a three-dimensional map appeared above his desk, a grid with three small cities blinking on and off.

"What's this, Mr. Secretary?" General Cole asked.

"I'm glad you asked, General. I learned just a few days ago that Peloski sold three more cities over the last month, to three different nations. Each of these countries has had either hostile or questionable relations with us in the past."

"Why haven't you done something, Mr. Secretary?" Kayla blurted out, half in anger, half in exasperation.

"I can't, Kayla, not without directly challenging Leader Peloski. *Any* action I take will end up with me in prison, or dead. This would, of course, render me useless and unable to do anything to help in rebuilding the BZ or in aiding the resistance."

"So, you'd like *us* to do something about it?" Cole asked.

"Exactly. You're part of the resistance now, Felix. What you do is completely outside of my control. Oh, Peloski may kick and scream about it, and he'll scream for your heads, of course, but what else is new?" He looked over at Kayla and leaned in closer to her. "Haven't you wondered why the People's Army hasn't already tracked you down and killed you?"

"We've been careful, well hidden, and well-protected."

"Oh yes, the old NORAD Command Center *was* built to withstand something much more powerful than a Gentry assault, of that I'm well aware. But what would you be able to accomplish if you were pinned down inside that bunker; or worse yet, cut off from it one day?"

Kayla's eyes widened in horror, despite her efforts to play it off.

"Oh, don't worry, my dear, I haven't told anyone, and in all honesty, I doubt Peloski knows anything about it yet. My point, however, is this; Leader Peloski hasn't even *tried* to find you, at least not yet."

"But why not, considering everything we've done?"

"Because the people *love* you, dearest Kayla; no, they *adore* you. You are the modern-day *Robin Hood* to Peloski's *Prince John*. At the moment, he's been content to leave you alone, since you've lifted the people's spirits considerably, despite them still going to bed night after night with their bellies empty."

"I don't care whether he comes after me or not, Secretary Adams, because as soon as I'm able I plan to go after *him*."

Adams sat back in his chair in astonishment, caught momentarily by surprise by the young woman's fiery spirit and determination. "My word, aren't you the fiery one!" Adams then leaned in one last time until he was less than a foot from Kayla's face. "Please be careful, my dear. I have no doubt that very soon you will be crossing a line, at which point Peloski is going to forget all about the people and throw everything he has against you. He is sly, conniving, and most importantly, without any integrity, decency, mercy, or compassion whatsoever. The man is entirely unencumbered by the burden of a conscience. When he comes after you, he will use every means at his disposal, including subterfuge, torture, and murder, to find you and destroy you."

Kayla sat there for a bit, digesting what she'd heard, before responding. "Thank you, Mr. Secretary, for everything."

"Kayla, my dear, you *will* help these poor people and save our cities, won't you?"

"You bet I will, sir. Just give us all the data you have and we'll get ready."

"May the Christian God bless you, Kayla Ross Washington, and safe journey."

Kayla and Cole turned to leave, and just as they were walking out the door Adams hollered after them to Kayla. "Please remember to give my best to your husband, and your newborn child!" Kayla froze and stared at Adams for several seconds; all she received back, however, was yet another warm smile.

CHAPTER 21

"Marge, where are you? By all the stars, what do I have to do to find good help these days? Get in here and bring that blasted report with you when you come; you know, the report that says that pregnant sow and a traitorous general just invaded three cities in the People's Liberal Socialist Democratic State, which I just recently *sold* to three rather dangerously psychotic heads of state."

"I'm so sorry, Sovereign; please forgive me!"

"It's so difficult to find good help these days, Henry," Peloski told the other man, as the skittish woman left the report on the desk in front of him and hurriedly left the room. "I'd hoped to build a permanent alliance with these countries, especially since China pulled out after *that* previous debacle. I'm telling you, Henry, I want that woman found, and I want her *dead*!"

"She's very popular with the people, Sovereign."

The prudish Sovereign Leader Peloski sat back in his chair, leaned back, and considered his friend's point before continuing. "Well, I never said we had to kill her right away. We could just throw her in prison and let her rot; that certainly works for me."

"But no one knows where to find them, Sovereign; they strike and then they vanish into the night. We've been trying for years now to find out who she is and where they are based. Even if we found their base, Sovereign, we know they are well-armed, especially since several regiments have joined them from the Red Zone."

"Ah! That was the case, Secretary Adams, but the tide has turned. It seems the winds of fortune now blow in our direction. We've had two major wins today!"

"Pardon me, Sovereign, but you said, 'that *was* the case.' Do we know where their base is now, sir?"

"Well, not yet, but we soon shall."

"But how?"

"Oh, come now, Henry, must I explain everything to you?"

"Forgive me, Sovereign," Adams replied, bowing his head slightly in deference.

"But of course, my old friend."

The sovereign leader gestured for Adams to come closer, as if he were about to convey a secret amidst a crowd of people, despite the fact that it was only the two of them and the guards posted at the entrances to the room.

"You see, Henry, when those fools decided to attack those three cities they signed their own death warrants. By the time they'd finished with the second city, word had reached me that they were already on their way to the third. Despite not having enough time for our generals to mount a counterattack, we *were* able to dispatch members of my personal guard, a platoon of elite soldiers, to track the enemy to the third city. Although there was not enough time to do anything to stop the attack, they were able to lie in wait and remain undetected until the enemy emerged victorious the following morning, heading, no doubt, back to their base of operations. My men are following them even as we speak, from a safe distance of course, with orders to report back the instant they arrive back at their base. Once we have their location, we will gather every soldier, tank, airship, and bomb we have at our disposal, and we will lay waste to their miserable base and put an end to their meddling. We will put an end to this resistance movement once and for all, and stamp-out the flames of rebellion before they consume us all."

"You said we had two major wins today, Sovereign. If an opportunity to discover the location of the resistance base is the first, what is the second?"

Peloski raised his eyebrows. "Oh yes, of course, I can't believe I'd entire forgotten about that. Henry…thank you!" The sovereign turned to one of the guards. "Bring in the prisoner!"

"Yes, Sovereign," the guard hurriedly replied before disappearing out the door. He reappeared minutes later with a prisoner in tow. Henry quickly stood, shocked by what he saw.

"*Sebastian!*"

"Yes, quite a disappointment, isn't he, Henry? I found it quite difficult to believe he was a traitor myself, when I was first informed about his activities. I did, in fact, refuse to believe it, until I saw the evidence with my own eyes."

"But sir...Sebastian?"

"He's guilty, Henry, *guilty*! He was caught red-handed working to get the rest of the council to oppose me — *oppose me* — on the sale of any more cities to foreign governments. I have worked tirelessly to establish long-term, strategic alliances with powerful allies across the globe to ensure the safety, security, and prosperity of our people for generations to come. I will not see that ruined by a group of snot-nosed children, or by treacherous, treasonous, snake-in-the-grass friends like Sebastian here."

Adams stared in horror at Sebastian's face, which was badly bruised, and how he now walked across the floor with a pronounced limp. Both were merely a down payment on what was to come from his cruel and vindictive overlord; of this Adams had very little doubt.

"My lord," Sebastian began, struggling to catch his breath.

Adams suspected his longtime friend must already have several broken ribs to add to his list of grievances against Peloski. Adams resolved that he, too, would remember this.

Adams suddenly realized how much he was seething inside over the horrendous state his longtime friend was in, and he instantly exerted a conscious effort to gain full control over his faculties. Peloski would be watching him very closely now, well aware of their close friendship, and would be evaluating how Adams weighed his friendship with Ross against Peloski's perceived act of betrayal by the same. Adams understood that his own life would now undoubtedly hang in the balance alongside his friend's. It wasn't that Adams valued his life over the fate of the nation, but rather that he felt he would only be in a position to help stop Peloski's madness if he remained alive for at least a little while longer yet, and the best way to do that would be to remain in Peloski's good graces, at least for now.

"My lord," Ross continued, "surely you *must* be able to see what you're doing to everyone in the Blue Zone, the suffering you've inflicted upon your own people. It's wrong, Sovereign; surely you must be able to see the monster you've turned into!" Ross wasn't being hateful or vindictive in what he said; instead, he seemed to be trying to reason with the mad leader, though no doubt the torture and pain had clouded his judgment, leaving him considerably less tactful than Adams had ever known him to be. "Why would you ever do such a thing?"

One of the guards stepped forward, at the gesture of the sovereign leader, and struck Ross with his fist, knocking him instantly backward several feet and onto the ground, where he landed flat on his back. Adams stared in disbelief as he watched Ross attempt to stand back up until, following another gesture from Peloski, the guard struck him again, once more driving him backwards onto the floor. Ross lay there several seconds with all eyes on him before again starting to rise. This time the sovereign allowed him to stand.

"I just don't understand it, Sebastian; why you would betray your own province like this, your own people? How could you betray *me* like this? I thought we were friends...we *were* friends! I've never done anything to you, or to your family for that matter, that would merit such a horrendous act of betrayal. Don't you realize that not only did you betray me, but that you put your own people in grave peril?"

"We *were* friends, Leader. But no, you're wrong. It wasn't I who placed the people at great risk, it was *you*. It wasn't I who betrayed *you*, my sovereign—my friend—it was you who betrayed *me*, along with everyone else in the Blue Zone. Everyone knows it, Sovereign, they're just too scared to say it.

"You've been selling our birthright, handing over our land— our homes—to foreigners, giving them a foothold in our country! Don't you realize the danger, the dire *threat* these foreigners pose? And you've done far more than just sell our birthright, Leader Peloski; you've forced your own people into slavery, and you've nearly starved the rest. Drug addiction is also rampant, and medical care is virtually non-existent except for the wealthy. Virtually every child is raised in a broken home because families have been torn apart here ever since the Great Schism. Even the Ancient Romans understood the importance of families, Sovereign, and that was twenty-five hundred years ago!

"You've *ruined* the province, Sovereign; the Blue Zone is no longer fit to be anything more than a second-rate banana republic, a third-world country in great distress. You've all but destroyed the dream our ancestors once had, the dream of a free and open society here in the Blue Zone. It is you who—"

"Enough!" Peloski nodded to the guard, who stepped in and struck Sebastian hard enough that a tooth popped out of his mouth and onto the floor, before blood began running down his chin, following the tooth to the floor.

Sebastian spit blood out of his mouth. "I doubt any amount of power, death, or destruction could ever be enough for you, Peloski. You'll continue selling or destroying what's left of the BZ until it's all gone, until someone stops you, or until you're dead. You're sick, demented, and you're nothing but a madman—*a madman*! You're either going to be assassinated, or there's going to be a revolution, Leader Peloski. *Something's* going to happen, and soon!"

"It's no longer your concern, Sebastian, because you'll no longer be alive to see me or anything else, ever again," Peloski scoffed as he turned to the guards. "Take him. He's to be executed first thing in the morning, just after breakfast. Say...make it 9:00 AM sharp. I believe I'd like for his execution to be an example to others, so let's make it a hanging."

"A hanging, sir?" asked the guard, uncertain he'd heard correctly, while Adams could only watch on in horror.

"Are you questioning my orders? Perhaps you'd like to hang beside him, Guard?"

"Oh, no sir!"

"Then see to it. And make it a *public* hanging so everyone can come watch. Put as many men on it as necessary. Get me some gallows built, and see to it that members of the press are there. I want every holocom in the province pointed at him when his neck snaps."

The guard swallowed hard. "Yes, sir, Sovereign Leader Peloski; it will be done as you have ordered, sir."

"See that it is."

As the guards disappeared behind the door with poor Sebastian, Adams approached Peloski. "Forgive me, Sovereign, but I must take my leave. I have a few things to finish up back at the office before I leave to pick up my wife for a dinner party."

"How is…um…?"

"Barbara, Sovereign…she's well, sir, thank you. She does, however, seem to love these dinner parties, and I am a firm believer in keeping my wives happy."

"You have five wives if I recall correctly; isn't that right?"

"An excellent memory, Sovereign. I *did* have five. Two died, however, I divorced one, and the other left me."

"Well then, it's time to find you some more wives, Henry! You know how I frown upon anyone in my administration having less than three domestic partners, be they wives or otherwise. It just doesn't seem healthy."

"Yes, Sovereign. It's just that I'm getting so old now, I just don't know if I can take the strain of managing three wives. I have a hard enough time with just the one you know!" Adams laughed, but the grim expression on Peloski's face remained unchanged. "Yes, Sovereign; I will begin making plans immediately."

"Very good then. Have a pleasant day, Henry, and please… do stay out of trouble."

The last comment, with which Peloski had leaned in ever so slightly toward him, troubled him, but it would not deter him. As he made his way home, Adams already had in mind the warning, and the grim news, which he would have to urgently send to his friends in Colorado Springs. He could only hope that the message would reach Kayla before it was too late for her, and the resistance movement as a whole.

CHAPTER 22

Kayla and Cole rode together in the second vehicle from the front. The vehicle in the lead was filled with Kayla's elite special unit, while the transport immediately behind them was filled with Cole's special forces unit. Next came two personnel transports filled with the wounded, and behind them came the lightly wounded or mostly uninjured soldiers. Pulling up the rear of the column, behind the remaining transports, were tanks, a column of attack-bots, most of which were still fully intact, and a single, solitary transport that carried the fallen, protected with attack-bots on all sides, demonstrating the high-regard the commander and general had for the dead.

"Well, General, we did it," Kayla said, finally breaking the long silence since leaving the last battle site.

"Yes, we did, but we paid a steep price for it."

Kayla glanced over Cole briefly and replied. "If history's proven anything, General, it's that freedom rarely comes cheap."

They were both exhausted, as were all of the men, so several minutes passed in silence. Kayla couldn't be certain, but even the attack-bots looked like they were running out of energy halfway through the capture of the third city, and they had miniaturized nuclear-fusion reactors.

"I've noticed that you seem particularly well-versed in history, Commander, given that it's been outlawed in the BZ for well over a half-century," Cole said at length, breaking the silence.

"Yeah, I suppose I am, General. I was adopted by a wealthy family while still an infant. My parents quietly maintained a rather sizeable library, and insisted that I read every single book in that library, instead of relying solely on the censored and heavily revised material downloaded from LINC."

"Humph."

Kayla smile and turned to Cole. "What?"

"I guess I'm just surprised to learn you're Gentry. You're leading a rebellion to overthrow your own people; you've turned your back on your family, and your friends."

"Yeah, well, I didn't want to, General, but I had little choice. What I saw happening all around me, the gross injustice, the slavery, the cruelty; so many people dying from mass starvation. There was this little girl, General...her name was Sam. She was at the top of the organ donor list, scheduled to receive an organ transplant, a new heart."

"Why was she at the top of the list?"

"Largely because she was so young, and because her life depended on it; she was going to die without it."

"What happened?" asked the general, intrigued by her story.

"Take a guess," she answered wryly.

"She was bumped down the list."

Tears began streaming down Kayla's face. "Not just down the list, General, off the list altogether. She died a short time later because of it. A little girl lost her place on the list to a sick old man, who ended up dying less than a year later of an unrelated illness. The thing is, General, his heart had nothing to do with his illness. Had he not been sick, he could have waited for a new heart for at least a full year, and there would have been plenty of hearts available by then. But no, he just had to have *her* heart, my Sam's heart. *That's* what woke me up, General. That's the reason I'm a leader in the resistance today, because my little friend, a wonderful, beautiful little girl named Samantha, the most amazing and sweetest seven-year-old little girl you could ever hope to meet, a child filled with light and with life, is dead. Her life, her entire future, was snuffed out like a candle because some rich, selfish old man decided Sam's life meant nothing, and denying her the life she'll never get to know was fine, if it meant he got his heart a little bit sooner. That's not just wrong, General, it's evil.

"Our great-great-grandparents may have *thought* they were doing the right thing when they split from the Red Zone and founded the Blue Zone, based on what was then referred to as the 'liberal' ideology, but they were wrong. Our society is hopelessly corrupt and it's been falling apart all around us for decades, General. People aren't living as free and equal citizens in the Blue Zone…most are living as slaves! The economy, jobs, and our provincial healthcare system are all in shambles. Our 'Sovereign Leader' is a joke, nothing more than a petty, ruthless dictator, with the BZ left as nothing more than just another floundering socialist state, instead of the grand democracy it was once a part of. I—"

"*Commander.*"

"Yes, Marcel?"

"Pardon the interruption, but you and the general might want to see this."

Kayla turned in the direction Cole was pointing and found a sizeable column of soldiers, tanks, and other military vehicles coming towards them. They were still quite some distance away, but they were closing rapidly at a fast clip.

Kayla picked up a pair of binoculars and watched the lead vehicle as it drew closer. It wasn't long before she saw something. "I see it, I see it!"

"See what?" asked the general.

"The flag, *our flag*. Well, at least one of them. The lead vehicle is sporting the American Resistance Flag. It's Daniel, it's *him*…it has to be him! But what's he doing here?

***

"So not one of the battles to free the three cities were as bloodless as the one with the Chinese. Maybe I should have brought you with me after all," she remarked, with more than a little bitterness dripping from the end. "I'm sorry, Daniel. It's just that you're such a great leader. I wish I had one-tenth your leadership ability."

"Don't be ridiculous, Kayla," he told her, reclining back on

163

the bed. It was rather comfortable considering they were camped out in the open country inside one of the quick-start field barracks, the latest in Red Zone technology for setting up temporary structures while on the move. "We got lucky with the Chinese. Or as the priest might say, we were 'blessed' to have been able to accomplish what we did the way we did. Remember too that we had overwhelming force; it definitely helped make their decision *considerably* easier," he added with a smile. "That doesn't mean we can expect that every time; in fact, I expect things will get considerably tougher going forward." Kayla nodded, lay back, and took a deep breath, giving Daniel the perfect opportunity to begin stroking her swollen belly. "So, how's Danny Jr. been?"

Kayla smiled and lightly smacked his hand. "You mean Danielle, don't you?"

"Yes, of course; *Danielle*. How's Danielle been?"

"She's been doing well. I believe she's probably going to be an energetic, and possibly slightly domineering, young woman, like her mother, when she grows up," she said, kissing her husband as he leaned forward. "The doc says it shouldn't be long now; another six to eight weeks at the most."

"Wow, I guess that means we'd better get ready then. We should…um…probably give her plenty of space to finish growing until she's born," he said, slightly furrowing his brow as he did so. Kayla had no difficulty taking his meaning, and immediately began shaking her head.

"No, I don't believe that will be necessary, mister. I believe she's got all the room she needs in there. Now why don't you come here and keep the two of us company, while you still can." She stared deeply into her husband's eyes as she did so, sharing the deep feelings she had for him, knowing that she had chosen well when she married him.

"Well, okay then; yes ma'am."

***

There must have been a noise. Whatever the reason, Kayla's eyes suddenly popped open and she found herself staring at the ceiling of their temporary home. She turned over to gently kiss her husband before turning back on her side, the sleeping position she'd found to be the most comfortable so far along in her pregnancy, but she found Daniel was not there. A glance at a nearby clock revealed that the time was 2:00 AM. Assuming he was in the restroom, she climbed out of bed and stood outside the door for several seconds, waiting for the familiar sound of the flush followed by the opening of the door. When no such sound followed, however, she looked closer, and found that the restroom door was ajar, with no Daniel inside.

After making a brief stop herself, she looked around once more inside their residence, now fully awake and alert, the result of her increasing alarm at his sudden and unexpected disappearance so early in the morning in a place where they were still quite vulnerable to attack.

Unable to find Daniel inside, she quickly dressed and stepped left outside the barracks. There as a chill in the air, which caused her to pull her coat a little tighter. She looked around, and other than the posted guards making their rounds, it was quiet. She looked in all directions but Daniel was nowhere to be found. There seemed to be no evidence of any disturbance of any kind, which she knew meant that whatever had happened to Daniel, in all likelihood it had been of his own accord.

Kayla let out a heavy sigh. It was a tough life she'd chosen, taking up the mantle of a resistance fighter, and then a resistance leader. It was tougher still to have fallen in love with and then married another resistance leader. She was beginning to grow increasingly accustomed to the notion that in the end, it would likely not end so well for her and Daniel.

"Is everything all right, Commander? Is there anything I can do for you?"

Kayla jumped, uncharacteristically startled at the sound of the gruff man's voice. "Oh, no, Sergeant Kelly, I'm just fine, thank you. I was just looking for my husband; have you seen him?"

Kelly paused and glanced down at the ground before looking back up at her. "Well, I was under strict orders not to say anything until after he'd been gone for a while, ma'am, but I guess it's been long enough now. The general went out an hour ago, along with a small detail of men, on a mission. I don't have any more information than that, ma'am."

"Any idea how long they were supposed to be gone?" she asked, not bothering to conceal her annoyance.

"No, ma'am, I'm sorry."

"That's quite all right, Sergeant. Any complaints I have I'll take up with the general himself when I see him again." Her attention was suddenly caught by the rays of a full moon peering out from behind some thin clouds that had just parted. Along with the beautiful big white orb, the black sky was filled with an endless number of stars.

"It certainly is beautiful, isn't it, Sergeant?"

"Ma'am?" Finding the object of her admiration, the hardened military man melted slightly. "Yes, ma'am. I must confess, it truly is."

Kayla paused and looked down at her swollen belly, the outline of which was visible even through the coat she wore. She then looked around at the many temporary shelters scattered across the structures, the many vehicles parked all around the camp, and the many guards endlessly making their appointed rounds.

"You know, Sergeant, I wonder sometimes whether this is all worth it. There are so many people risking their lives. What do you think?"

"Me? I'm just an old soldier, Commander, you shouldn't care about what *I* think."

"Nonsense. Please…tell me."

Kelly looked at her, shook his head uncomfortably, and scratched his unshaven chin. "Well ma'am, I'm both a father and a grandfather, and like you, I grew up in the BZ. Now *my* son and my grandson are both still alive, at least as far as I know. But there are many, many folks I've known who have lost sons, daughters, grandsons, granddaughters, or all of the above, over the last decade or so. Things have gone from bad to worse in the BZ, and frankly, before you and the general came along, I was worried there wasn't going to be a BZ much longer. The thought that things might actually get better? To be honest, ma'am, that thought hadn't entered my mind since my wife died twenty-five years ago from a nasty infection she picked up after cutting herself one evening. You and the general, Commander, you've given a lot of folks in the BZ, and I imagine in the RZ as well, hope for a future they'd given up on a long time ago. So, if you're asking me whether trying to stop the Gentry and those folks in the RZ so we can reunite the country is worth risking *my* life, and everyone else's life here tonight, I'd say you'd better believe it is, Commander…you'd better believe it. I'd die several times over if I could to give my family a better life than what I had."

Kayla stood staring at Sergeant Kelly—father, grandfather, widower, and longtime military man—and she finally knew, without a doubt, that everything they were doing, everything they were risking, was indeed the right thing to do.

"Thank you, Sergeant Kelly; you'll never know how much what you just told me has meant to me."

Kelly stood facing her, a blank expression plastered across his face, for such a long time that Kayla grew quite uncomfortable. Suddenly, he began shaking his head, removed his hat, and, facing her, bent one knee to the ground.

"Commander, please don't do that; don't thank me. I'm just an ornery, worn-out old soldier. I've lived a long life, had children, had grandchildren, and if I die tonight I've had a good life and can't complain none. But what you and your husband are doing, what you've *already* done, what you're risking; I simply don't know how to respond. You're both still so young that you've barely lived, yet here you are, ready to give your lives for an old dog like me. You're with child, *yet here you are,* just coming back from rescuing three cities from what amounts to foreign invaders. And well, you're risking your lives, even your unborn child's life, in order to save this country, to save the people who call her home, people who've been too beaten down and too darn scared to stand up and fight for themselves.

"Everyone knows you were stinking rich, and that you could

have everything you ever wanted and lacked for nothing, yet here you are, risking *everything* to help people you don't even know. This is why, Commander, this is why right here, right now, I pledge on my honor and my life that I will protect you, your husband, and your child for the rest of my life. For as long as I draw breath, until the day I no longer do, I am *your man,* Commander." Tears were flowing from the grizzled man's eyes at this point. "No ma'am, please, allow me to say thank *you,* thank *you,* for everything you've done, and please trust me when I say, I will never forget it."

CHAPTER 23

Kayla stood speechless as the man knelt before her, having just pledged himself to her. She was struggling for words when something in the night sky caught her attention. She looked up to see a brilliant blue light flash in the sky, followed by a muffled explosion. A few seconds later the stillness of the early morning hours was disturbed by the sound of exploding mortars, rockets, and weapons. Kelly stood and the two of them stared up into the night.

"Sergeant?"

"I'm not sure, Commander. My bet is that's our man."

"What…Daniel? Then let's go!" Kayla started for the armory, then felt the gentle yet firm grasp of the sergeant's rather large hand wrapped around her arm.

"Now hold on just a moment, Commander. First of all, I'm afraid you're in no condition to go into *any* combat situations, ma'am. With all due respect, just take a look at that belly of yours. Your baby's all set to come into this world any day now; are you really willing to put the little one's life at risk when there are so many men and women here ready to fight, and die if necessary, just to keep the two of you safe? You three hold the future in your hands, ma'am; please don't be so reckless with it. My kid and my grandkids are counting on you."

Kayla stared at him for a moment, looked off in the direction of the gun fire which raged on, and then looked back at him once more before letting out a heavy sigh and dropping her head. About that time, a ranking officer, accompanied by fifty men, came to where they stood and stood at attention. An officer stepped forward toward Kayla.

169

"Commander, I'm Duty Officer Lieutenant Howard. We heard the gunfire. With your permission, I'd like to send a platoon of men to investigate."

"Permission granted, Lieutenant, but be careful. I'm not sure what you'll be up against."

"Yes, ma'am."

"And Lieutenant?"

"Yes, ma'am?"

"Keep your holocom channels open."

"Roger that, ma'am."

Kayla and her sergeant stood watching as the platoon rushed towards the gunfire. Kayla turned toward Kelly, half-feigning annoyance. "Well, aren't you going with them?"

"No, ma'am, I am not."

"And why not?"

"There are a couple of good reasons not to, ma'am. My first duty now is to stay here and protect you and your baby."

"And if I order you to?"

"Well, then I'd have to go and find a squad of men to guard you until my return."

Kayla smiled at the man. "So, Sergeant, you never said what the other reason was."

"Commander?"

"The other reason for not going to check on General Washington; oh, that just sounds so silly, doesn't it? Makes me think of the country's first president crossing the Delaware every time."

"Ma'am?"

"Oh, it's not important. So, what was the other reason not to go?"

"Well, I figure whatever the general is up to, he had a plan— he always does—so he most likely already has the situation well in hand. You remember that blue flash we saw?"

"Yes, I do. What about it?"

"I've been thinking that may be one of those EMP bombs I've heard about. We don't have any in the BZ, but we have heard rumors that the RZ has quite a few of them. They supposedly leave a signature blue glow just like the one we saw."

"And what does an EMP bomb do?"

"It stands for electromagnetic pulse. They're commonly used on the battlefield for taking out enemy electronics."

Kayla furrowed her brow. "What's he up to? And more importantly, why didn't he say anything to me about it?"

***

Kayla glanced down at the CAIS cube on her wrist and spoke the command, "time." The small Cyber-Based Artificial Intelligence System wristband, which served as an advanced computing resource as well as a timepiece, projected the time as 4:00 AM in holographic digits three inches above the cube, just over an hour since the last gunfire had been heard.

"Commander."

Kayla looked up at the sound of Kelly's voice, out of instinct more than anything else, so tired and exhausted was she for the lateness of the hour. But the sight of her husband walking toward her, emerging from some nearby woods surrounded by his men, jolted her awake and filled her heart with relief and joy. She was doubly surprised to find that in addition to the soldiers, they had brought with them quite a few prisoners, soldiers of the Peoples' Guard. She ran toward them as they drew close to the camp.

"Daniel! Are you okay?"

"Oh yes; it was a successful mission. We—"

"General, can we have a word please?"

Daniel looked around. He noticed that everyone seemed to know what she wanted except for him. "Um, sure."

"Please come with me."

"Okay." He turned to his second-in-command. "Nick, take the prisoners. Feed them, offer them as comfortable accommodations as we can afford, but keep them restrained and under a close watch. Remember, we had to fight and kill some of these men tonight—that was a necessary evil—but these men are our brothers; they're soldiers like us, who've just found themselves on the wrong side of history. Who knows? Once they understand

171

what we're trying to do here, they may even decide to join and help us."

"Yes, General" Nick replied, barking orders to the soldiers caring for the prisoners, wounded and healthy alike.

Less than a minute later Daniel and Kayla were alone in their quarters. Kayla walked over to their bed, slowly lay down, rolled over on her side, and after tucking a pillow between her thighs trying to get more comfortable with the large belly, continued.

"What exactly happened out there, Daniel; and why wasn't I informed?" Daniel walked over to his wife and leaned over to kiss her. She wrapped her arms around him and the two embraced, kissed, and embraced again. "Why didn't you tell me what was going on?" she asked him, looking up at him with consternation.

"I'm sorry, sweetheart. You know that we suspected we were being followed back to the base."

"Right."

"Well, we weren't certain, at least not until late last night. We got lucky when some of their men got careless and were overheard by one of our patrols. We weren't sure what, if anything, they'd been able to relay back to Peloski, but we had to make sure they had no further opportunity to relay more."

"The blue glow we saw — it was an EMP?"

"That's right. We used it to knock out their communications gear so they couldn't relay anything back. Then we went in to take them down. It was a light force, so we didn't have much trouble."

"Just do me a favor, will you, Daniel?"

"Of course, my sweet Kayla, light and love of my life; you know there's nothing I can deny you," he replied teasingly.

"Wake me before you leave next time," she said, without smiling. "I'm a resistance leader too, Daniel. You should have included me."

The smile faded from his face when he saw she was serious and, more importantly, she was right. "I'm sorry, Kayla, you're right; I should have found a way to keep you informed. I could have left you a note, left instructions with someone, something.

172

I'm sorry."

Kayla's expression softened, but she still did not smile. "But you're also my husband, Daniel, and I value your life above my own now; please remember that."

"Of course, my love; forgive me." Daniel stroked her long silky hair and the two kissed with deep passion and great feeling.

"I love you, Daniel," she said between amorous kisses.

"And I you, my beautiful Kayla."

Kayla grew quiet and stared up at the roof for some time.

"Kayla, what's wrong? I can hear those wheels turning inside that head of yours."

She turned back to face him, a look of deep consternation etched into her features. "Someone pointed out to me today how you and I are risking an awful lot for the resistance, Daniel, perhaps more than most, given we have a baby on the way. What are we going to do once this baby arrives? How are we going to keep him or her safe?"

"Oh, Kayla...." Daniel embraced his wife, holding her as tightly as he could, given her delicate condition. She was crying and trembled slightly. He'd never seen her worried like this before, and he knew she wasn't so much concerned for Daniel or herself as she was for the child. "I understand your point, sweetheart, but I look at things a little differently. I ask myself, 'How can I allow him or her to grow up in a world like I grew up in?' See, I'd do anything, risking my life many times a day if necessary, to make a better life for our child. I can't abide the possibility of our child growing up in a world of slavery and tyranny like we did."

Kayla looked up at Daniel. Her heart was racing and a cold chill passed through her.

"I'm scared, Daniel; I'm scared we're not going to survive this thing, and I don't want our child to die with us."

"Kayla...what's wrong with you, darling? Why all this talk about death? You're not going to die anytime soon, and neither am I."

"Yeah, well, I'm sure the men you attacked and killed tonight in the enemy camp didn't think they were going to die tonight either."

Daniel paused, took a deep breath, and kneeled over her, resting his chin on the palm of his hand, his elbow supported underneath on the table.

"Okay, you've made your point, honey. So, what do you want to do about it?"

"I want you to help me find someone willing to be godparents, someone who'd be willing to look after and raise our child if something happens to the two of us."

"Okay, done. So, who do you have in mind?"

"Well, I don't actually know yet. Think on it, Daniel, and so will I. Then we'll ask them together, okay?"

CHAPTER 24

Discussions had been growing increasingly heated throughout the course of the afternoon. It had been a week since Kayla's return, and the successful mission to locate and destroy or capture the men sent by Peloski.

Still, it hardly seemed a cause for celebration. Nerves were frayed as everyone learned how close they'd come to being discovered, and it suddenly became all too clear how vulnerable they really were. It was not just the risk to their own lives that had most of them worried, but the risk to the resistance as a movement.

"You must listen to me, Daniel; if we don't establish at least one, preferably two more primary bases out of which to run and coordinate the resistance against both zones, then we are dooming this movement to be nothing more than a footnote in history," General Cole pronounced. "Now I don't know whether we have anything in the BZ capable of taking out this base, since it's designed to withstand even a nuclear blast, but I'm near one-hundred percent certainty that the RZ does. Since the two resistance movements have now merged into one, you'll have *both* militaries gunning for you. A single precision blow launched by the RZ could *end* the resistance, and...." Cole let the end of his sentence trail off instead of completing it.

Daniel, however, was unwilling to let it drop. "Go ahead, General, finish your sentence."

"It's not necessary, sir. I'm sorry—"

"I said *FINISH IT!*" Daniel's eyes were fixed on Cole and as hard as steel, his fury churning like a fierce storm.

"A precision attack could take the life of your unborn child as well."

"Okay, there it is...thank you, General Cole. Now that it's out there, let's talk about that. Yes, Kayla and I both know we're risking the life of our unborn child, as well as the lives of everyone else here with our actions, but that's the life, General; you more than most should understand that. Revolutions *never* come without a cost, as I'm sure you'll agree."

"Yes, sir; of course." Cole was clearly regretting upsetting Daniel, yet the confused expression also suggested he wasn't certain he understood exactly *why* Daniel had grown so angry over the point he was making. Clearly there was more going on than merely his suggestion about opening new bases.

Daniel paused, sighed, took a deep breath, then sighed again.

"Look, General Cole, I know the argument. I've heard it repeatedly for over a year now, but my answer is still the same. We simply do not have enough men to cover additional bases. If we spread out to another base, or especially two more, we'd be easy pickings, can't you see that?"

"But General Washington, if *this* base is ever compromised —"

"Compromised? This base is impregnable, General Cole," offered Major Crane. "It was built to withstand a full-scale nuclear attack. It's provisioned with food and supplies that will still be good decades from now, not to mention the fact that we're growing our own food and even raising some of our own livestock, and we even have our own generators here."

"Yes, that's true, Tom. But unless you think we can successfully run a revolution while trapped in here with no way out, I suggest you re-think that idea."

Colonel Davis had been listening closely, and seemed to understand the need for an alternative site better than others. "You believe they know about the other exits?" he asked, looking first at Cole and then at Daniel.

"We believe that we have to make that assumption, yes," Daniel reluctantly replied. "They would, after all, have had detailed records of the base kept in what used to be Washington, D.C."

Davis smacked his lips. "Right smack in the middle of Synod Central."

"Yep."

Davis nodded in agreement. "You're right, sir, it *is* a dilemma. I can't argue with your reasoning. I feel it's my duty, however, to tell you I agree with General Cole, and that my experience tells me that the hard choice is to spread out to at least another two bases, and then work to expand our numbers. Perhaps you could go out, after your child is born, to focus on helping to grow the resistance. In the meantime, maybe you could do another broadcast?"

Daniel looked over at Kayla, who grimaced slightly and shrugged her shoulders. Then Daniel turned to Captain Mike Sullivan.

"Mike, you've been rather quiet; your thoughts please?"

"Well sir, to be frank, I also agree with General Cole. It *is* a difficult choice, because you're correct that we would be dividing our forces too thin, and that could make all of the difference when either attacking or defending the BZ forces."

"You're worried about the Red Zone."

"I am."

"Because they have weapons where numbers will not matter."

"That's right, sir. And honestly, from what I've seen so far, I'd rather take my chances with the Blue Zone military any day. If we spread out, if the RZ hits us, at least some of us might survive to fight another day."

"Hmmm. Well, I don't like it, gentlemen...I'm telling you right now I don't like it one bit. I—"

Daniel was interrupted when the door burst open and Simon appeared. He was one of Daniel's most trusted advisors, which was why Daniel felt comfortable letting Simon run things while he and the others focused on the matter at hand.

"What is it, Simon? You know what we're discussing in here, so I hope it's important."

"Uh, yeah; I'd say it is, Daniel, it is." Daniel grimaced.

Simon was one of the few people left, other than his wife, who he permitted to call him by his given name. "Something has happened that I believe will have a significant impact on your decision here today."

"What is it, Simon? *What's* happened?"

"I'd rather show you, sir; here, take a look."

Simon walked over to the holographic control panel, waved his hand, touched a button, and a live, three-dimensional, holographic image appeared above the table where they were sitting. The streaming image was originating from somewhere outside of Cheyenne Mountain, that much was certain. Based on what he could tell by examining the interior of the building, he surmised the images were most likely coming from inside one of their larger remote staging facilities, which were always considered expendable if ever suspected of possible compromise. An endless stream of men and women stood in disciplined formation in three large groups inside the hangar, most likely a brigade from the looks of it, with a single man, a colonel, at the head of each group, and a senior officer, most likely a major-general, presiding over the entire division.

"What are they doing there, Simon? What's going on?"

"They're thinking about joining us, sir."

"They're Red Zone?"

"Yes."

"An entire division?"

"Yeah, isn't that something?" Simon asked, grinning and gesturing to the projection.

"Yeah, it is," replied Daniel. "Wow."

General Cole cleared his throat before speaking. "General, if I may sir."

"I know, General Cole, I know. I'm not an idiot."

"Of course, sir, I know; I apologize if I—"

Daniel turned to face Cole, who appeared flustered and somewhat dejected. "No, please, General Cole, it is I who must apologize. It's this damn conflict; when I first got started it was just me—and of course, Simon, Kayla, and the few others in both

Zones — but now — "

"Now it's becoming a revolution with the potential for changing everything, there are a lot of lives on the line, and there's a tremendous amount of pressure?"

"Yeah, I guess that's part of it. That, and then our bringing a child into all of this; I don't know what Kayla and I were thinking...." Daniel made the last remark, then looked sheepishly up at his wife, who stared back with a mixture of anger, fear, hurt, and uncertainty in her eyes.

"I understand, sir," Cole replied. "But if I may be so bold, if this revolution succeeds and we're able to reunite the two zones, this is the legacy you'll leave for your son or daughter, General Washington, and it will be a legacy you can be certain he or she will be extremely proud of when they grow up.

"As to your other concern...well, command carries a heavy burden with it, sir, especially for those who must send men, or women, to their deaths. War is messy, General, it just is. And that's what this is, a war...make no mistake about it; it's a second American Revolution.

"This new division, if indeed they do come over to join us, could well be the key to our winning this war, sir. Now we all realize, General, that one or more of these bases may be destroyed — all of them, in fact, could be destroyed before this is over — but in the end, it *will* be worth it, especially if we are successful in finishing what *you* started, sir."

"Thanks, Felix...I really mean that. Listen, you and I are still getting to know one another, so I'll ask you to be patient with me. I'm told I'm something of an acquired taste, and as Simon over there will attest to, I've been known to occasionally vent steam in the direction of those closest to me. For this again, I must apologize. I have already come to truly value your counsel and experience, and I've already come to depend on you, along with Colonel Davis and the others here, for your military and strategy expertise. And I'm certain I will continue to do so."

"And I will always be at your service, sir, as long as I draw breath. I'm in this until the end...for my son, his children, and his children's children."

Daniel nodded and offered a slight smile of understanding, before turning back to Simon. "Okay, Simon, what's the catch?"

"The catch?"

"Yeah, the catch. You said that they're '*thinking* about joining us.'"

"Oh, right. So, the major-general instructed me to tell you that he had one question that you'd need to answer in a certain way before he'd be willing to commit the lives of over thirteen-thousand men into your hands."

"What question?"

"I don't know, he wouldn't tell me. He would only say that it's a question whose answer would tell him exactly what kind of man *you* are, and whether you are the '*right*' man or not."

"What is that supposed to mean?"

"I don't know, Daniel, but we can ask him. He's waiting—"

Daniel stared at Simon, irritated that he'd stopped mid-sentence, and waited for him to continue. He quickly recognized that something had caught his attention, and the moment he recognized the source of Simon's distraction, Daniel jumped out of his chair. Kayla was doubled over at the end of the table. Daniel rushed to her side and took her by the hand.

"Daniel, it's the baby...it's time. I think my water just broke."

Daniel looked up at Simon, this time as his friend. "Simon, please...."

"Say no more; I'm on it." Simon rushed out of the room for help.

Daniel cast a hurried glance around the room, and on the faces of everyone there he found only concern, along with warm, friendly smiles, and a shared joy at the impending arrival of another human being into the world.

"Are you doing okay?" he asked Kayla, who still sat in the chair but now was leaning back as much as possible.

"I'm fine for now; a little messy I'm afraid, but fine."

"Don't you worry about that now, okay?" he told her, glancing around the room once more until his eyes rested on the holographic image of the entire division of men standing… waiting, waiting for *him*. That's when Daniel turned to me, since he knew Kayla now considered me to be her second-in command.

"Christian, would you please finish up?"

"But sir, they wanted to speak with *you!*"

Just then Simon returned with two men from the infirmary and a wheelchair.

"It's okay, Commander, it's going to be just fine. Please, have a seat and let us worry about everything. We'll take care of everything from here…well, except for having the baby, of course." Kayla managed a laugh and a groan as she climbed into the chair and they began wheeling her out.

"Listen, Chris, it will all be fine," Daniel said to me. "Just work with Simon, work together to explain what happened, and ask him to please remain where he is for now. Tell him I promise to contact him within the next two to three hours so we can talk. But for now, I have to focus on my wife and child. Just have this room ready in two hours, and the general online, and we'll talk then. Thanks, Christian!" And with that, Daniel left the conference room along with his wife.

***

"Congratulations, you two, what a beautiful baby boy! Have you decided on a name yet?" Doctor Hortiz was a renowned civilian doctor from the Red Zone who'd come to the Resistance six months earlier, and now led the medical team at the base. When not saving lives or treating patients, he'd also been actively spearheading the effort to train up new field medics, who would be desperately needed in the battles sure to come.

"I believe we have, Dr. Hortiz," Kayla replied, looking over at her husband for confirmation. "Right, honey?"

"Sure, baby, we'll go with that. It's fine."

"Okay, Doctor; the baby's name will be Sebastian Harold Washington."

"Excellent," Hortiz replied, before jotting down some notes. "Well, it's a good thing you were here, Commander. The baby had a slight complication with his left lung. It's a condition called pneumothorax, or collapsed lung. We were able to take care of it, however, and with today's technology, there will be no long term issues or complications. So how are you doing, Mom?"

"I'm just feeling really tired, Doctor."

"Yeah, well, that's not so unusual; this is your first child, isn't that right?"

"Yes, Doctor."

"Okay then. I'll be discharging you shortly, and you'll be able to go back to your quarters, where you should rest easier. I'd like to have a follow up with both mother and baby in one week, Commander, okay?"

"Yes, Doctor."

"Very good. Okay then, again, congratulations!"

The doctor turned and left the room, giving Kayla and Daniel a few moments to themselves. Daniel snuggled up close to his wife.

"I love you, Kayla Ross Washington," he said, running his hand through her hair as he kissed her, before kissing his son.

***

Daniel studied the man before him and quickly surmised he was a very serious, hardened soldier. Whatever the question, Daniel would have to be open and honest, if he were to have any opportunity to win his support.

"Good afternoon, General Hawkins. I understand that you're considering joining the resistance, but that you had a question to ask me first."

"Let me begin by saying how honored I am to meet you, General Washington. Despite your young age, you have accomplished something I have wanted to do but lacked the courage and the wit to accomplish. No matter the outcome of our conversation, therefore, I would like to extend my heartfelt gratitude, and most sincere appreciation, for everything you've accomplished; well done, sir."

"Why thank you, General. I feel quite honored hearing that from someone like yourself."

"And my congratulations also to you, sir, on the birth of your son; there is no finer moment in a man's life than when his child takes his or her first breath and greets his parents for the first time."

"No, there's not. Thank you again, General."

"Now then, let's get down to business; I'd like to ask my question, if I may."

"Yes, please do," Daniel replied.

"What exactly are you hoping to accomplish with this movement of yours, General Washington, and how far are you willing to go to make it happen?"

"That's technically *two* questions, General," Daniel pointed out with a smile.

"So, it is," Hawkins answered, with a slight smirk of his own.

"Well, I'll answer both questions as honestly and completely as I can, General. As to what I — pardon me, what *we* — are hoping to accomplish, we hope to restore democracy and freedom to the people, to rebuild the United States of America as the founding fathers intended. We'll have to take steps to ensure that what happened with the Great Schism doesn't happen again, of course…at least not anytime soon. But that is, nonetheless, the core objective of the mission. The resistance movements of both zones are united under this objective."

"That's the right answer, sir. And how far are you willing to go?"

"All the way. Kayla and I have asked ourselves this very question many times, and we always answer it the same way. We both got involved in the resistance with a commitment to go all the way, and we're still in it until the end."

"What about your son, if I may ask? Are you prepared to leave him an orphan?"

"You're getting a little personal, General," Daniel warned.

"Forgive me, I mean no offense. But war *is* personal sir, because a lot of men and women will pay the ultimate price."

"We've discussed *that* too, General. We've decided we'd rather leave our son an orphan, *if necessary*, than to raise him with everything remaining as it has been for over half a century.

We have some close friends we hope will be willing to shoulder the heavy burden of raising our children if we should die. So, to answer your question, we are prepared to die in order to make this happen, General, because it must happen, and soon."

Major-General Hawkins paused for a moment, staring back at Daniel from many miles away, yet with him in the same room. He then walked over to a few of his senior officers — the colonels in charge of the brigades, Daniel decided — and spoke with them briefly. After conferring for several moments, Hawkins walked back over.

"General Washington, that's all I needed to hear. I just wanted to make sure my senior officers felt the same."

"And?"

"We're with you, General. Until victory or until death, we're with you, sir."

Shouts and cheers erupted on both sides at the announcement.

"Thank you, General Hawkins. Now get here as soon as you can. I'll send one of *our* senior officers to come meet you where you are and escort you here."

"There's no need, General; you're at the old NORAD base in Cheyenne Mountain, at Colorado Springs, Colorado, are you not?"

"What? How did you know that, General; who gave you that information?"

"Oh, I'd heard rumors; besides, it's where I'd probably hole up if I were building an alliance between the Red and Blue zones. It's one of the most secure bases on the planet, and has been for nearly a century."

"Do you think *they* know?"

"Ha! Those arrogant knuckleheads? I doubt it. But even for them, it's only a matter of time. I hope you're planning on expanding and opening new bases, General Washington, because otherwise, when they do find you—"

"We've already made the decision to do just that, especially now that you'll be joining us."

"Then we'd best get started, sir. We should be there within

two weeks, sir, if that works for you."

"*Two weeks*...that long?"

"Yes, sir. I have an entire division of men with me, after all, so I'll have to move men out gradually, *and* in a manner that is inconspicuous enough that it doesn't attract any unwanted attention."

"Can you do that?"

"Absolutely, given two weeks I can, yes sir. I think you may appreciate what we will be bringing along with us as well, General Washington."

"What do you mean?"

"Well sir, we will be deploying under the guise of conducting intensive, full-scale war games. This means we'll have missile deployment systems, Advanced Robotic Early Deployment Systems, or EREDS, advanced plasma based rail guns, shielded weapons system, and personnel, etc. We'll be bringing lots of goodies that will go a very long way toward helping to level the playing field with the Red Zone, sir; I'm sure you'll be pleased."

"Very good then. I anxiously await your arrival, and I look forward to meeting you in person, General Hawkins. We have some ambitious missions coming up, and I'd very much like to get you involved in the planning and execution of them."

"I appreciate your trust, sir, and I promise you will not be disappointed. I'll see you in two weeks."

"Until then."

As Daniel disconnected, he glanced around the room until his eyes met mine. Once our eyes met, I merely raised my eyebrows and shook my head. Neither of us said anything because neither needed to. If there had ever been a doubt before, there couldn't be now...the resistance movement was real, and it was now a force to be reckoned with.

I watched as Daniel's eyes drifted over toward the door, where no more than a hundred steps down the hallway his wife and newborn son waited for him, and I watched as his eyes linger longer than they should have on that door. When he swung his attention back to me, he was caught off guard to find me still watching, as if I'd caught him in an unguarded moment of private deliberation. I could tell what he was thinking as clearly as if he'd just said it aloud; *were things really going to be the same now that Sebastian had arrived?*

CHAPTER 25

He had long black hair down to his shoulders, penetrating, icy-blue eyes, and was nearly always impeccably dressed in formal or semi-formal attire. Arising out of the Intelligentsia Class, he was at the very top of the best and brightest in his class of graduates. As such, and given his family's majority ownership of one of the larger members of the Corporate Synod, he had sat on the board from day one. Unlike most board members, however, he proved to be an effective and charismatic leader from the very beginning.

The unique, highly-advanced genetic modifications to Niko Alexander's intellect made him a giant among the others. Anyone who dared to challenge him, as he aggressively rose through the ranks at a blinding speed within the Corporate Synod, soon found themselves severely outgunned and outmatched by someone far superior to them in every way; no one ever stood a chance against him. Any enemy, whether internal or external to the Synod, soon found Alexander had correctly anticipated each and every step they'd ever take against him long before they'd acted. He quickly moved to establish his power base within the Synod and on the board, and within two years, he was unanimously elected to lead the Corporate Synod's Board of Leadership.

The new position gave Alexander the authority and the room he needed to maneuver and make back room deals with greedy members of the NZCC leadership, effectively placing them in his back pocket. When important votes came up in the Red Council granting Alexander increasing powers on the Council, the votes went increasingly in his favor until eventually, he had not only the military and police completely under his control, but the Red

Guard as well. The new order enabled Alexander to, in effect, dissolve the Red Council, with the NZCC and the Corporate Synod now reporting directly to him.

With the Red Zone now completely under his control within just five years, Niko Alexander set his sights on the severely weakened Blue Zone. In a swift and surprise move, he executed a plan he'd conceived years earlier; he stationed five divisions of RZ military units, complete with land, air, and in some cases sea-based attack craft, outside all major cities, including the capital in San Francisco.

Unable to defend themselves against such overwhelming force, the Sovereign Leader and the Gentry leadership, fearing for their own lives, immediately surrendered, ceding complete control of all lands and governments to Alexander.

It took another year for Alexander to extend his full control over all parts of the former Blue Zone. Soon the Corporate Synod had businesses up and running all over the former BZ, and were turning serious profits, which Alexander used to further expand and build out his military machine, expanding it, pushing technology to the limits. So quickly did his power grow that only two years later, he officially proclaimed the birth of the American Empire to the world, with him as its emperor, and he announced to the world governments that he would soon be expanding his empire to encompass the entire planet.

Other nations scoffed at first, of course, underestimating Alexander's ambition, ruthlessness, and ability. War inevitably ensued between the empire and another nuclear-capable nation with only conventional munitions being used in the beginning. Once the other nation had suffered enough casualties, however, they launched nuclear weapons against Alexander's American Empire in a last act of defiance and desperation. It was to no avail, however, as Alexander's scientists had long since not only perfected the Satellite Laser-Based Targeting Systems, or SLABATS, for detecting and destroying enemy-launched nuclear warheads, they had also perfected a continental energy defense shield, one capable of projecting high enough that any missile escaping SLABATS would strike the shield before detonation, and be destroyed. Of course, Alexander then launched a full-scale nuclear counterattack, which completely obliterated the attacking country, killing the vast majority of its inhabitants immediately while leaving what few survivors remained to die slowly of radiation poisoning. After witnessing the horrific suffering endured by the first two nuclear-capable nations, and the futility of resisting, all but the most powerful of nations soon capitulated and acquiesced to the conqueror's demands. Only the most powerful nations remained, and they joined forces in an attempt to defeat Alexander. Despite their best efforts, however, he was always one step ahead of them, and they too, soon fell before him.

Back home things were equally bad. Alexander proved to be a tyrant of unprecedented cruelty and evil, who went beyond even the ancient Roman Emperor Caligula in his vanity and demand for worship. He crushed everyone who opposed him, executing most of them in public and on global media for all the world to witness. His word became law, and whole cities were wiped out of existence on a whim or a fancy. The world could only hope that his death would come sooner rather than later.

Then one fateful evening, Alexander was interviewed on a global news broadcast, where he announced to the world that his team of scientists had made yet another technological breakthrough; they'd developed nanites capable of indefinitely extending human life by constantly repairing damaged human cells. He, as emperor, and those *he* deemed worthy, would be beneficiaries of this new technology and would live forever.

It seemed the monster would never die, and the torment would go on forever. Men, women, and children, all dying by the tens of thousands. Mass genocide, at the hands of a brilliant, yet monstrous, brutal, and immortal madman, completely devoid of emotions like love, compassion, and empathy…traits that made man uniquely human.

Then, suddenly, Daniel saw him…Sebastian? Yes, somehow *it was* Sebastian, as a grown man. He was standing on a platform with a hangman's noose around his neck, with television cameras pointing at him. Beside him was a woman and two small children, a little girl and a little boy, no more than seven or eight, all with nooses. A man watched until a white light turned red, upon which he pulled a lever and....

There was a blinding white light. Daniel then discovered he was somewhere else, and he was inexplicably in great pain, as if he'd been severely beaten. He looked down to find that his hands were chained. A sharp stab in his left kidney forced him to lurch forward and then climb up a short series of steps. He looked up at what lay ahead at the top of the stairs, and what he saw, ironically enough, was once again gallows, and a hangman's noose dangling from the end of a rope. This time, however, the noose was empty...empty because it was waiting for *him*. Another jab in the same kidney. *If I wasn't about to die anyway, I'd be worried about losing that kidney.* The thought hadn't occurred to him without a sense of irony. He stepped forward, and after the noose was placed around his neck and tightened, the guard behind him, the same one who'd so enjoyed jabbing him, took one last parting shot. This time the pain was so intense Daniel could find no humor in it, no matter how morbid.

"Okay, you too, get up there and join your lover boy," he heard a voice say from behind and below him. A cold chill sent shockwaves throughout his body to the very core of his being.

"Oh no, not—"

"Hi, lover boy. Did you miss me?"

"Kayla! No, not you too!"

"Would you have it any other way, darling? At least our boy is safe. God willing, they'll never get him because soon after we're gone, the prophecy will be fulfilled and this will all be over. Remember, my love, you've always been my one and only love; you, and only you. I die today for my people, but my heart has always belonged to you."

"Oh Kayla, I—"

Then came the sound of the floor dropping out from under them, the sickening sound of their necks breaking...first hers, followed a split second later by his, and the horrifying sight of her at the end of the rope. Oh, Kayla....

Then, bright red letters against a star filled sky two feet above it; it was 2:00 AM.

Daniel awoke in a cold sweat. He immediately looked to his left and found his wife, his sweet, beautiful Kayla, lying next to him, sleeping peacefully beside him. He then glanced over at the holoclock next to the bed, which projected the time.

The vivid images of the two dreams greatly troubled him, and he struggled with what to do next. He climbed out of bed, dressed, and after finding baby Sebastian sleeping soundly in his crib in the next room, he left their quarters. Daniel must have spent at least an hour walking around, reliving the two dreams in his mind, questioning why they troubled him so, and wondering what to do. Then the answer came to him as if someone had quietly whispered it in his ear. He would find Pastor Jonathan O'Conner; maybe, just maybe, there would be something he could do to help.

Daniel walked back to his quarters, lay down next to his wife, and drifted immediately back to sleep. He had no more dreams that night.

***

A large crowd, a mixture of civilians and soldiers, was leaving the chapel just as Daniel arrived. Most carried datapads; a few even carried actual paper Bibles. Pastor O'Conner had been leading daily Bible study classes in an effort to reacquaint those in the resistance with God, the Bible, and Christianity.

The pastor had just shaken the last hand when he noticed Daniel making his way in the front door as the others were leaving. He seemed pleased to see Daniel.

"Ah, good morning, Daniel! So, to what do I owe this unexpected visit? I must say that it is truly gratifying to see you again, though I've been very disappointed not to see more of you at our Sunday worship services. Not only do I believe it would do you a considerable amount of good to be there yourself, but it might also help to encourage others who have been too afraid to participate for so long because of the great persecution."

"You're right, of course, Pastor O'Conner, I'm sorry; there is no excuse for it. I promise I *will* do better, and I renew my pledge to make it to worship service every Sunday, whenever it's possible for me to be there."

The man of God's eyes raised upward and his eyes opened wide at this news. "Praise the Lord then! That is wonderful news, my boy, wonderful news!" O'Conner eyed him for several seconds as Daniel shifted back and forth rather uncomfortably. "Okay, what is it Daniel? Just spit it out. I'm a man of God…you know that whatever you say will remain between us. I swear it."

Daniel looked up at him and grimaced slightly before resolutely deciding to proceed. "Pastor O'Conner, I had a rather troubling dream last night; or rather, two dreams."

"Dreams, you say? Really?" The pastor spied a nearby pew and gestured for Daniel to take a seat, before joining him. "Please, continue."

Daniel proceeded to relay the details of the first dream, in order as they played out, and then the second. Pastor O'Conner's brow soon furrowed, as it became evident that he too was troubled by the dreams.

"So, Pastor, tell me, please, what do *you* think? Were they simply ordinary dreams, the result, perhaps, of a spicy meal or too much wine before bedtime?"

"I must say, Daniel, that I find myself very troubled by your dreams. Just take a moment and consider that we are, at this moment, at a very unique crossroads in history, not just for the country, but for the world. You are, as God would have it, at the nexus of that crossroads. Please, Daniel, I would like to commune with the Lord in prayer regarding this. Can you come back tomorrow about this same time?"

"Of course, Pastor; I'll be here then."

"Go in peace, my son."

***

His step felt lighter as he approached the chapel early the next morning. Maybe because he'd enjoyed a better night's rest, maybe it was because he'd spent some time with Sebastian just before coming, or perhaps it was because sharing the dream with the pastor had somehow lightened his load. Whatever the reason, he felt a little more chipper than usual as he entered the sanctuary.

He found Pastor O'Conner sitting on the first pew, looking contemplatively up at the cross that hung on the wall facing the congregation.

"Good morning! Any news from On High, Pastor O'Conner?"

"Careful, Daniel; I'd be *very* careful if I were you, and certainly not so flippant."

"I'm sorry, Pastor, forgive me. I meant no harm. It's just that the NZC—"

"This is NOT the NZC, Daniel!"

Daniel stood, stunned, for several moments. No one talked to him in this manner, let alone some pastor or priest. He'd once had some measure of respect for the NZC, at least until he'd learned what they were truly like and how they had corrupted and betrayed the people. But the old Christians…he wasn't quite sure what they were all about yet. Perhaps he *should have* been attending services regularly, to learn more about them if nothing else.

"This time it is *I* who must apologize, Daniel. It is not for a man of God to talk so, especially to one the Lord has chosen as He has you. Please pardon my outburst."

"It's already been forgotten, Pastor; think nothing of it. What do you mean by 'one the Lord has chosen'?"

Pastor O'Conner once again gestured for Daniel to sit down, and once again, he joined him. "Long ago, when God would sometimes appear to the leaders of men in dreams, he would also appear to prophets like Daniel or Joseph, who would then go to said rulers and interpret the meaning of their dreams. Now I don't know the exact manner of the interaction between the Lord and his prophets, but I do know my interaction with the Lord last night during my evening prayers, and it was a little less certain to me than I would have expected. Yet I feel, nevertheless, that we have the answers we are looking for."

"And? Please don't make me wait, Pastor."

"It seems the two dreams relate to the same event, but represent two possible outcomes, based on what you decide to do. They were not just dreams, Daniel, they were part of a prophecy.

"You see Daniel, as I said yesterday, you are the nexus of where we are at the crossroads of history; what you do next will literally decide the fate of the world. But God didn't create us to be puppets, Daniel. He gave us free will, the freedom to make our own decisions. It would seem you have a very important choice to make, Daniel.

"You can, if you so desire, choose your family over the revolution. You can step down as leader of the American resistance, and by so doing, you will save your own life, you will save Kayla's life, and you will live to see your son grow into a man. You will also, however, witness the rise of the man in your dream, Niko Alexander, a vile man of unspeakable evil, who will take over the RZ, then the BZ, and then the world. He will become a monster unlike anything the world has ever seen. Eventually, you will live to witness the execution of your son and his entire family before your very eyes, but even the death of your son and his family will seem like a minor offense, so great and so massive will be the death and the horrors of that time. The Lord has shown you what will happen should you turn your back on the revolution.

"If, however, you continue to lead the revolution, striking them where it hurts, you will cause great damage to both sides, and your popularity with the people will soar to unprecedented levels. This in turn will lead to an alliance between the governments of the two zones, and a betrayal from within your ranks. You will then surrender yourself to the enemy, as will Kayla, and you will both be executed."

"And Sebastian?"

"Your son will live, and so will your dream to reunite the country. Your enemies will be defeated, the two zones will reunite, and the New United States will once again be a free and democratic country."

"And Niko Alexander?"

"Alexander will never emerge from obscurity, and will die in prison after selling state secrets to a foreign government, having never been genetically modified by the Red Council."

"Wow."

"Like I said, Daniel, my interaction was a little less certain than what I would have hoped for, but I believe this is an accurate interpretation of your dreams. I certainly prayed that the Lord would give me such an interpretation."

"Pastor O'Conner, I can't thank you enough."

"Daniel?"

"Yes, Pastor?"

"What will you do? Will you save your family or the world?"

"Is there really even a choice, Pastor O'Conner? Thanks again. And Pastor, I'll keep my promise this time; I'll see you Sunday."

"See you Sunday, Daniel. Don't forget to bring young Sebastian in for baptism soon!"

"I won't, Pastor, I promise. I'll mention it again to Kayla later today; goodbye."

Daniel turned and started to leave, but had taken no more than a few steps before he stopped and stared down at the floor for several minutes, lost in quiet contemplation.

The thoughtful but somewhat befuddled clergyman decided not to interrupt him, content instead to allow him to continue in peaceful solitude. Eventually, however, Daniel raised his head, and the pastor saw for the first time that he was visibly shaken.

"If I might be dead soon, I'd like...no, I *need* to ask what I believe is a very important question, Pastor O'Conner."

"Of course, of course. What is it?"

"Tell me, Pastor, what must I do to appease the One God, to serve Him, so that he will receive me when I die?"

O'Conner smiled and placed a hand on Daniel's shoulder. "Now I know for a certainty that the Almighty *has* touched you, Daniel Washington, and that he *is* working through you to restore this great nation. Come, please, take a seat, and I'll tell you about God's Son. You might remember his name from your wedding vows; his name is Jesus Christ; it's from *His* name that we get the term *Christian*...."

CHAPTER 26

Following his meeting with Pastor O'Conner, Daniel sat down for a meeting with Kayla and several of his senior advisors, and after several days of discussion, three other abandoned military bases were identified as ideal candidates for new sites of operation for the resistance. Daniel assigned a brigade to each base, and distributed resources and staff to each base as needed.

Simon would join Commander Sam Jones at the Alpha site in New Chicago. While complaining about how difficult it would be to part from his friends, he added that he'd part willingly as a sacrifice for the good of the cause. We all knew that sacrifice would be greatly lessened, however, by his strong, physical attraction to Commander Sam Jones, which, fortunately for him, was something she felt for him as well.

Vanessa and I were to open a new base at the Bravo site, an abandoned Fort Leonard Wood Army Base in Waynesville, Missouri, before returning to the NORAD base to assist Daniel. Meanwhile, Colonel Jack Davis, Major Tom Crane, and Captain Mike Sullivan were charged with opening and maintaining the Charlie site, the base located deepest in enemy Red Zone territory at the massive Ft. Bragg Army base in Fayetteville, North Carolina. With their experience serving in the RZ military, it was decided they were best suited to operate out of the abandoned base while going undetected by the RZ. General Hawkins stood a better chance of success there, but Daniel was unable and unwilling to spare him, as he was counting on his skill and experience in planning the next major campaigns against the tyrannical leaders of both zones.

Everything was coming together. Daniel smiled tightly as

he thanked everyone for their sacrifice and commitment to the cause, and said his goodbyes to those leaving to prepare the new base locations, reminding them of the importance of constant communications with NORAD and feeding him and Kayla updates on their activities.

Once everyone had left Daniel turned back to Kayla, and after casting a brief look around to ensure no one else was present, he pulled her close to him and stared deeply into her beautiful green eyes, before kissing her passionately for a long, long time.

"Kayla…my beautiful, brave, fierce, and passionate Kayla," he said at length, having finally come up for air. "How I love you so! No words could ever express just how much my heart aches for you when you're not around, how it leaps like a gazelle upon seeing you after a long separation, or how much I yearn to hear your sweet voice, to smell you, to touch you…Kayla, it's so hard to believe I was ever even *alive* before I met you!" He kissed her again and held her close for some time, stroking her long, auburn hair until Kayla grew alarmed.

"Daniel, what's going on?"

"Kayla, we need to talk, my love."

"Daniel?"

"I need to tell you about a dream I had recently…."

***

"What! What did you just say to me? Our scouts have gone *missing*, you say? But they were some of my finest men. *That's* impossible!"

Peloski was beside himself in anger, and he was letting everyone within earshot know it. The Commander of the People's Guard had just brought news that the scouting party, which had been following Kayla and Daniel back to their base, had missed several scheduled check-ins.

"Yes, Sovereign, Team SSR-771 has not been seen or heard from for five days now. We fear they've been captured or killed, sir."

"We must find a way to deal with these vermin, Commander, to *exterminate* them, and soon. Make no mistake about it, they pose the greatest threat to the People's Liberal Socialist Democratic State since the Great Schism. Their numbers have been growing, and they've become incredibly powerful in a very short time."

"Yes, Sovereign, we will intensify our search. Since joining with the Red Zone traitors, the rebels have gained access to the RZ tech, surveillance and communications gear, advanced weaponry, and soldiers, in addition to a growing number of traitors from the BZ. Still…without the help from the RZ, they'd be much easier to deal with."

Peloski sat on his throne, weighing his options. He had to come up with a plan of action before it was too late; but what? Then something came to him…something the commander had said about the RZ; "without help from the RZ, they'd be much easier to deal with."

"Commander, I want you to reach out to Mikos Romano, Leader of the Red Council in the Red Zone. Those Militiamen vermin wisely chose to partner with their counterparts in the Red Zone, and both are stronger for it. Well, two can play at that game; if this brat of a girl was able to arrange a partnership with the Red Zone, why shouldn't I? Perhaps it's still not too late to turn the tables on the conspirators by beating them at their own game."

***

Mikos Romano, Leader of the Red Council, was furious, and it was yet one more time that Jeremy Renner, his chief-of-staff, regretted being the bearer of bad news.

"An entire division has now defected en masse, taking with them a load of heavy weapons, missiles, and equipment, including tactical nukes, ICBMs, and now some highly-advanced experimental weapons as well? I don't believe this! Could this possibly get any worse?

"Pay attention, Jeremy! I want a list of each and every man *and* woman who defected, along with every single piece of equipment they took with them, including every helmet and uniform. Is that clear?"

"Yes, Mr. Leader; I'll see to it personally."

"Please do, Jeremy. These terrorists must be eliminated expeditiously. Do you hear what they're saying about me out there? I'm not just talking about the dredges in the Production Class, it's coming from the other classes as well! They're calling me vicious, ridiculous names like 'tyrant,' 'dictator,' and 'monster,' and I hear some even refer to me as 'the beast.' Oh, I know they've always said such things about me in private, but *never* in public! They feel emboldened by these rebels, and by these very noticeable defections. We must stop the bleeding!"

The chairman paused for several moments to collect his thoughts. Jeremy said nothing, which he knew was most often the correct choice when Romano was as worked up as he was at that moment.

"Do we have *any* idea where they are, Jeremy?"

"You mean where their base is, sir?"

"Yes."

"Well, sir, we have several sites under surveillance—"

"Then the answer is no. How is that possible, Jeremy? We have *wormhole* technology now, yet we can't find these simpletons' base? Now why exactly is that?"

"We're not exactly sure, Mr. Chairman. They could be using some sort of cloaking technology, like the one we've developed."

"We know how to circumvent that technology, do we not, Jeremy? Find me that base!"

"Yes, Mr. Leader, we will, sir, I promise. We have recently come across information that suggests that they're probably holed up somewhere inside the Blue Zone."

"Really...the Blue Zone? Hmmm. Interesting." The leader moved until he was looking his COS directly in the eyes. "Would you like to know why I think we've had such a difficult time finding them, Jeremy? I think these little would-be revolutionaries have sympathizers, maybe even supporters, within my own government. I think these conspirators have been running interference for them whenever possible. Would you like to know why I think that Jeremy?"

"Um.... Yes, sir?"

"Because with the technology at my disposal, I could tell you what color my mistress painted her fingernails this morning, from the moon!" he roared. Leader Romano's face was now glowing a beet red, and the vein on the side of his head was bulging. It was at such time that men were often executed, or killed outright, so Jeremy said as little as possible, and when he did speak, weighed each word carefully. He had grown to hate his job, and wanted nothing more than to go back to running the company he'd run so successfully for ten years before being called by Romano to be his chief of staff.

"I'm holding you personally responsible for finding them, Jeremy, and I'm giving you full discretion, whatever you need — within reason, of course — to find them. Once we find their base we will launch our nanite seeker missiles if necessary to dismantle their defenses, just before we launch a full-scale assault and completely obliterate it from the face of the earth. It will be a cautionary tale for others to never, never, never challenge me, or my successors. Now, get going and go find them."

"Yes, Mr. Leader, you can count on me."

"I know," Romano replied with a wicked smile. He knew how intelligent, clever, and resourceful Jeremy could be when properly motivated, and he knew how much Jeremy loved his wife and four children. His chief of staff would find them, and soon...especially if, as Romano suspected, Jeremy had in fact been a sympathizer himself. Oh, Romano didn't care that he sympathized with their cause; after all, most people hated him, despised him even, and Romano was okay with that. But he would not allow Jeremy's affinity for their cause to interfere with the continuity and safety of everything he'd built.

"Mr. Leader?" A hologram of his executive assistant Janice, from the neck up, appeared above his desk over the holocom plate.

"Yes, Janice."

"Your next appointment is here, sir. The Eminent Senior Bishop Francis Darwin from the NZC Board of Leadership."

"Ah, yes, how could I forget? Please send him in."

Romano stood and walked toward the door. Before he made it halfway, however, the door opened with Janice and Darwin standing in the doorway. Janice gestured for Darwin to enter, and he met Romano halfway.

"Ah, Your Eminence, so good to see you again!" Romano exclaimed, smiling uncharacteristically, something that caused Janice to shutter slightly before closing the door.

While it could not be said that the two men were friends in the truest sense of the word, they were certainly close acquaintances, and they did share a certain affinity for one another, due in part to having so much in common. With Darwin as head of the NZC and Romano as head of the Red Council, the two were mutually despised throughout most of the Red Zone. Both had control over many lives, and both were responsible for the deaths of many, many men, women, and children, often determined by how much sleep or how much to drink the man had the night before. It was a bond shared by very few in a select brotherhood, one forged through years of blood, death, and power.

"And you, Leader Romano; how grows the empire?"

"Ah, come now, Francis, *republic*, not empire; you know how some of the boys on the board still get when you use words like empire around them."

"Can you believe that some still hold to the tired old notions of democracy and civil liberties? Which...err...brings me to why I am here."

"Oh...I didn't realize you had a specific reason for coming today, Francis. So, this is not just a social visit?"

"No, I'm afraid not, Mikos. I'm quite sure you've seen the most recent broadcast by the group that calls itself the 'People of the Founders.'"

"Oh, them. Must you and I talk about them, too, Francis? I'd just finished going over a plan with my chief of staff to find and exterminate those rats before you arrived."

"Yes, I'm afraid I must. I'm afraid that ever since this Daniel Washington's last speech, the attendance at worship services across the zone has dropped off severely, despite our repeated warnings that everyone's attendance is now being tracked and that records are being sent to the NZC Board of Leadership so that disciplinary action can be taken if needed. Please tell me some progress has been made in tracking down this brigand, and bringing him and his band of merry men to justice."

"A *Robin Hood* analogy, Francis, really? I suppose that makes you the Sheriff of Nottingham and me Prince John?"

"Hmmpff!"

"Oh, come now, Francis, relax!"

"That's easy for you to say, Mikos. Your livelihood doesn't rise or fall with the attendance every weekend; ours does."

"Relax, old friend. As I said, I've already taken steps to ensure this little problem of ours is taken care of in short order. I can't tell you—" Romano was interrupted when the hologram of his assistant once more appeared above his desk.

"Mr. Leader?"

"Janice? What are you doing? You know better than to interrupt me when I'm meeting with His Eminence; this had better be important!"

"I'm told it is of the utmost importance, Mr. Leader. It's Jeremy, sir. He says he needs to see you immediately."

"Unbelievable! Tell him I said this had better be earth-shatteringly good news or he may be the next man whose execution photo hangs in my gallery at home."

"Yes, sir."

"Please pardon the interruption, Francis," Romano said to the bishop. "This must be something extremely urgent. Jeremy knows better; he would never have interrupted us otherwise."

"No, that's fine, Miko; maybe it's good news regarding our mutual problem."

"Well, I wouldn't get my hopes up just yet," Romano replied.

"I don't know, Mr. Leader. I believe there may be reason for Bishop Darwin to get his hopes up. I believe I bring good news, sir, very good news, and it is indeed about our friends, The People of the Founders."

"What is it, Jeremy? What's going on?"

"Well, sir, I have a voice-only call on the line right now from someone claiming to be with the resistance. He claims to be a high-ranking member within the organization, and he claims to be a very close friend and confidant of the leader of the resistance himself, Daniel Washington."

"How I've grown to *despise* that name, and how I will *relish* the day when I watch him die slowly before me. So, you must believe this man; why?"

"Well sir, we get calls like this every day, and they almost always turn out to be of little consequence. They're either designed to waste our resources chasing ghosts, or they're merely low-level players seeking their moment in the sun, but none ever have any substantial, actionable intel upon which we can act.

"Our guy knows things; he knows places, people, dates. He's given us details that no one except the perpetuators could possibly have known. Our guy was definitely there when some of these events went down."

"Okay, so what does he want, and *why* did he contact us?"

"He wants to make a deal with us. He said he has certain terms, favors, and commitments he wants us, or more specifically *you*, to make. But most importantly he needs to know right now that you're interested in negotiating with him, sir, or else he said he'll hang-up and he's gone forever. He's really skittish, sir; I believe he means it."

"Okay, sure. If he's legitimate, hell yeah I'll negotiate with him. But first I need to know what he's prepared to offer us in return for whatever these favors and commitments are."

"He says he's willing to offer up to us Daniel Washington, the leader of the resistance."

CHAPTER 27

"Where's Simon?" Daniel asked, having established that the rest of his key advisors were present for the all-important planning session.

"I don't know, sir," Commander Samantha Jones replied. "He said he had something important to attend to earlier. He was aware of the meeting, so I just assumed he'd be back in time; I'm sorry."

"Don't worry about it, Commander, it's not your fault." Daniel paused for a moment before continuing. "Has Simon been acting...peculiar in any way recently?"

"In what way, sir?"

"Oh, I don't know for sure. Has he been angry, resentful, said anything about the resistance being off-track, anything like that?"

"No, not really, sir. I mean, he snaps sometimes, but I don't really know him well enough to know how unusual it may be for him."

"That's okay, Commander, don't worry about it. I think he's just been under some strain lately...we all have." Daniel reached out for his data pad and glanced at the screen. "Okay, before we get started with planning this mission, I'd like to get an update on the establishment of the new bases. We'll start with Bravo Site to give Simon a few more minutes; Christian and Vanessa?"

I cleared my throat to begin, but Vanessa beat me to it.

"Things have been progressing well, General. Christian and I, and the others who went with us, have been working day and night to get the base ready. We estimate we are at 55% readiness, sir."

"Thank you, Vanessa. Christian...anything to add?"

I looked at Vanessa, who was still smiling slyly at me; boy, was she ever competitive. I could only wonder what she would be like *after* we were married.

"I concur, General."

"Very good. Commander Jones? Why don't you go ahead and get started on Alpha Site; looks like Simon is a no-show."

I listened as the other base commanders rattled off the status at their respective bases, until finally, we reached the part we'd all been looking forward to.

"Okay then, thank you all for your updates. Now then, on to new business. As you all know, we've been looking for a means to bring the Red Council to its knees, to bring it to the point that it would be forced to capitulate and meet our demands for a free, open, and democratic election, which would replace the current government with a democratically elected one. They will, of course, fight us to the very end unless we come up with something they hold so dear, of such importance, that they would be willing to do *anything* to stop it.

"Now then, to go over the specifics, I'd like to ask General Hawkins to outline the plan he's put together. General?"

"Thank you, sir, but you're far too kind. We slaved equally over this plan, sir, so any success will be owed to you as much as anyone else. If it fails, *I* must take the blame."

"Nonsense, General; we rise or we fall together, as it should be."

"Thank you, sir." Hawkins pulled out a data crystal, opened the holochamber, and inserted it into the corresponding socket before beginning his presentation. Three-dimensional images of buildings, schematics, and floorplans appeared above the table that correlated to what he was discussing.

"In order to break the will of the Red Council, we settled on a two-pronged attack, simultaneously attacking the NZC and the Corporate Synod at their most vulnerable spots. These attacks will enable us to gain access to critical areas within the NZC and the Corporate Synod, which, if we were to destroy them, would prove devastating to the Red Council, concurrently crippling

206

both the NZC and the Corporate Synod.

"Now, the hope is that this approach mitigates any need for excessive violence and bloodshed since the Red Council, aware of what General Washington—and myself, I might add—are capable of, will quickly capitulate, rather than see everything they've worked for come crashing down around their ears, with no hope of holding onto any measure of power. At least if they agree to the elections, there is some chance that at least a few of them could remain in a leadership position, somewhere, if as nothing else than local dog catcher."

"You don't really expect them to cave so easily though, do you, Daniel?" asked Kayla, who sat in her seat next to Daniel.

"I truly don't know, Kayla," Daniel answered. "I destroyed one building well before they even knew who I was several years ago, and they know I was responsible for that and a number of demolished Synod and NZC buildings since, so they surely know that—"

"What about all of the fighting and bloodshed that would follow, Daniel? Are you ready for that?"

"Yes," he replied flatly, with a hard look cast back at his wife. "We will make certain that the NZC and the Synod *fully* understand what's at stake when we first discuss this with them. Please continue, General Hawkins."

"Yes, sir. These points of attack will be closely guarded, of course, but given our assets, we should have no problem gaining the access we need to pull this off now. First up will be a high-value, NZC target. We've chosen this target, in part, because it offers the prime opportunity to inflict the maximum amount of damage using the munitions we will be employing. The destruction of this site would have a devastating impact on the NZC financially, and it will forever loosen, maybe even eliminate, their grip on the people of the Red Zone; it could even mean the end of the NZC. I'm talking, of course, about their 'NZC Sacred temple,' where all of their records and nearly all of the NZC's considerable wealth has been centrally stored on a temporary basis, along with all records of their real estate holdings, while they upgrade the security at several of their more secure facilities."

"Tell them about the Corporate Synod, General," asked Daniel, impatient for everyone to hear the rest of the plan.

"For the Corporate Synod, the high-value target will be the Corporate Synod Data Repository, where nearly all of the financial transactions and the vast majority of Synod wealth are stored on data crystals."

"Taking out the repository would cripple the Synod severely, and they know it," Daniel remarked, with a calm and detached tone.

"That's correct, General Washington. You should all most definitely be prepared to face a *substantial* amount of resistance, as they will be heavily armed, very well-trained, and their number will include some of the best fighting men left on the planet."

"Then is trying to take out the repository such a good idea, General?" asked Kayla. "Especially if it means costing us dearly in terms of men and equipment."

"Well...I'm not going to say that we couldn't do it, ma'am, because frankly, I believe we could. Oh, we'd lose quite a few men during the battle, as would they, but I know my men well. I've trained them, and I'd put them against these or any other soldiers anywhere, anytime. I'm sure most of our men would fight equally well. Attacking the repository in an all-out frontal assault, however, is not exactly what I had in mind, ma'am."

"Then please enlighten us, General Hawkins."

Hawkins offered a sly grin. "Yes, ma'am, I was *hoping* someone would ask. As General Sun Tzu stated in The Art of War, 'For to win one hundred victories in one hundred battles is not the acme of skill. To subdue the enemy without fighting is the acme of skill.' It is, therefore, my intention that we accomplish our objective with skill, cunning, and subtlety, rather than brute force. I'll explain more about that in just a minute, with your permission and your indulgence, ma'am."

"Of course; I look forward to it, General."

"Thank you, ma'am. So, to recap, it is my belief that we must successfully take control of these three objectives — the NZC's records, the NZC's wealth, and the Corporate Synod's Data Repository — if we hope to obtain the leverage we need to gain control over the Red Zone.

"Now then, let's focus first on the NZC temple. The records and treasures at the NZC are kept in two very large, but highly-fortified vaults inside the temple. The records are kept in the basement vault, while their substantial wealth is stored in the sub-basement vault. Conveniently for us, the regional facilities, which are much more secure and more heavily fortified, and where everything is normally stored, recently began having their infrastructure upgraded. Since the NZC has accumulated its wealth over the past one-hundred years in the form of deeds, trusts, certificates, stocks, contracts, etc. as well as priceless artwork and ancient artifacts collected over a hundred years, their accumulated wealth is extremely vulnerable to fire, which, of course, works in our favor.

"Now then, we get to our strategy for taking this facility. Since, as I mentioned earlier, we'd like to keep our losses to a minimum, and minimize bloodshed, removing all contents from the vault and holding it ransom to force the council to meet our demands really isn't an option. Even if we did take the entire facility by force and remove the contents we seek, holding onto them would be a challenge over the long-term. We believe we've come upon an easier way.

"With the assistance of some of our inside people, we smuggled in four AZ-77 sunbursts, two onto each floor of the NZC. These are some particularly nasty, extremely high-temperature, long-duration, long-burn explosives. Due to the heavy security, we were only able to get them placed in storage closets near the vaults, not in the vaults themselves. Those closets are located between the elevators and the vaults both here and here, and on the sub-basement level here," he explained, pointing to the rooms on the holographic display that floated above the conference room table.

"Unless we get these 'sunbursts' deep inside the vaults, where they can be detonated if necessary, they're not really going to do us much good?"

"They'll do a lot of damage, and they'd certainly get the Red Guard's attention, but that's correct, err...."

"Lieutenant Commander Christian Jefferson, General," I replied meekly, slightly embarrassed the general was still unfamiliar with my name, yet not completely surprised. He had, after all, been dealing almost exclusively with Daniel, and at times with Kayla or Simon.

"So *that* would be the function of the strike team, Lieutenant Commander," the general continued. "To incapacitate the guards just outside the elevator, any patrols encountered on the way to the vault, and the guards stationed outside the vault, which will enable our inside people to use the codes they stole to open the vault. Then finally our strike team will disable the guards stationed throughout the inside of the massive vault as well. Once the guards are down, our strike teams will get the sunbursts inside the vaults, arm them, get the holocams installed, and then seal up the vaults behind them once they exit, before getting out of that hellhole as quickly as possible. If all four sunbursts are detonated in that building at the same time...well, let's just say that there's not likely to be another spot anywhere on Earth more resembling hell at that moment than the site where that building *used* to be."

"Sounds rather horrific, General Hawkins," I remarked, rather shocked that we were employing such weapons.

"Oh, it is, Lieutenant Commander, and they are, sir, believe me, *they are*. Now I can't speak to either the leadership in the BZ or the NZC, but I know for a fact that the Leader Romano knows full well what these beasts are *and* what they will do to his precious data repository. If those crystals are in the repository and we control two sunbursts that are in the same space as those crystals, he *will* negotiate, I promise you."

"What are the holocams for, General?" asked Kayla.

"We'll need to monitor the inside of the vaults, both inside and out, ma'am. Since we can't leave any people anywhere near those vaults with the sunbursts armed, we must have a way to ensure that no one from the Red Guard or the Synod attempt to deactivate the Starbursts and take away our only leverage."

Kayla nodded.

"Okay, General Hawkins," Daniel began. "We send in a small strike team large enough to ensure the sunbursts make it—with the help from our inside folks, I presume—into the vaults, and then get the holocams set up around the perimeter and inside the vault. Once that's done they get out of there; how am I doing so far?"

"Dead-on, sir," General Hawkins replied.

"Good. Once we have the sunbursts and the holocams inside the vaults, we can monitor for any attempts by the NZC or the Synod to interfere, and after warning them, detonate the sunbursts if they do not comply; does that sound about right?"

"Yes sir, more or less."

"Good. Okay, that covers the NZC. What about the Corporate Synod's Data Repository?"

"Well sir, the rules set forth by the founding members of the Board of Leadership state that the data of record would be stored in data crystals, maintained in the main vault of the Synod Headquarters in New Manhattan. This collection of crystals is by far the most vulnerable of those targets, offering us the sort of leverage we'll need to force their hand when it comes to surrendering to the will of the people.

"To gain access to the crystals we'll have to send a third strike team at the exact same time as the two teams in the NZC temple are deployed. This will enable us to strike without giving them any advance warning that we're coming. Security here is significantly tighter and more robust than at the NZC, but we'll be ready when the time comes.

"Like the temple, we have inside men prepared to get us inside the vault, but like the NZC, the Synod has men stationed both outside and throughout the inside of the vault, so access alone isn't enough without both access and military force. Our strike team will enter at the loading dock, as at the NZC temple, and make their way to the 15th floor, where the vault is located.

They will then dispatch the guards at the elevator, the patrols outside the vault, and finally the guards stationed inside the vault. When finished, they will locate the closet, where they will find the sunbursts waiting for them. They will move them into the vault, arm them, and then exit and seal the vault, before getting out of there as quickly as possible."

"Is that it, General Hawkins?" Daniel asked, clearly expecting to wrap the planning session early, since they'd already been over it many times before, and they were clearly as ready as they were going to be. Before Hawkins could respond, however, the conference room door swung open and Simon entered, stooped over and barely able to stand. His face was bruised and bloodied, and his clothes torn. What appeared to be an injury from weapons fire scorched the lower right side of his abdomen, where laser-fire from a blaster had automatically cauterized the wound as it passed through his body.

"Simon! Someone, please catch him before he falls." Daniel punched a button on the holocom system. "We need a medic in here ASAP, and we need the doctor to prep for a possible surgery...Simon Bender's been shot."

CHAPTER 28

"Take it easy now, Simon," Daniel reminded his friend. "The doctor said you're going to have to take it easy for the next few days. You're just a lucky son-of-a-gun that the blast was a clean shot and passed through without hitting any organs."

"Yeah, I'm *feeling* kinda lucky…," Simon retorted dryly.

"Here, drink this, Simon," Kayla instructed him, after bringing Simon a glass of water.

Simon hadn't noticed me yet, sitting quietly, as I had been, in a chair on the opposite side of the room since before he'd awakened. When Daniel and Kayla turned away from Simon just for a moment, to talk amongst themselves while he finished his water, he glared at them strangely for a time from behind his glass, as if seething with anger, but for what reason I could not initially fathom. After considering it, however, I came to realize it was only his anger over the attack, and the painful and embarrassing beating he'd received. Daniel soon finished his brief discussion with Kayla and turned back to Simon, who'd finished his water.

"Simon, what happened to you?" asked Daniel.

"Well, as you know, I'd planned to attend the planning session today, so I was on my way here when I received word two days ago that I should hurry back to Chicago, that an informant had brought important new information that couldn't wait."

"What information?" asked Daniel.

"I didn't know at the time, because the informant would only speak with me in person. She said only that the information was urgent and that it was important to the resistance. She told our people that she was certain that you and Kayla would want to know."

"Okay, so I guess that's where you've been for the past two days?"

"Yes. I hurried back to Chicago, where I quickly arranged a meeting with the informant to meet in person to go over whatever information she had for me. Someone must have betrayed me, however, because the safe house where we met was attacked just as our time together came to an end. My informant was killed during the attack, and as you can see, I was fortunate to escape with my life."

"How fortunate indeed, Simon," Kayla remarked, decidedly suspicious about his story.

"Kayla! Why must you two constantly be at each other's throats? Simon doesn't trust *you* because he thinks you're pulling us away from the Red Zone; you don't trust *him* because you think he wants to pull us away from the BZ. I swear, it sometimes feels like I have *two* wives instead of one."

"It's okay, Daniel; I can understand why she might have questions about why I would suddenly leave at such an important time. The truth is, I'd asked my informant to investigate a rather troubling rumor I'd heard, so when I heard she wanted to see me and said that it was urgent…well, I knew I had to hurry to meet her." Simon turned now, speaking more to Kayla than to Daniel. "Listen, I'm really sorry I missed the planning session today, but I want to go on the mission; I have to go."

"It's okay, Simon, really," Daniel replied. "You've been badly injured; there's no need for you to go in such a condition."

"I *want* to go, Daniel, please, I'll be fine. The doctor said the blast passed right through, and with the healing accelerant filled with nanites, I should be back to new by the day after tomorrow. Come on, I *have* to go, Daniel…this is why I joined the resistance in the first place."

Daniel hesitated. We all knew Simon was his oldest and dearest friend, after Kayla of course. "I don't—"

"Daniel," Kayla interjected. "Simon's right. He's earned the right to go on this campaign, and as long as the doctor clears him, why not let him?"

"I suppose that's true, Kayla. If the doctor concurs, *and* if he eventually gets around to telling us what this all-important news is that his informant shared with him."

Simon attempted to sit up, but the pain forced him to slump back down. Despite this, his face took on a very sober expression. "You're not going to believe this, Daniel. Leader Romano and Leader Peloski from the Blue Zone, *they're working together* now. They've joined forces in order to bring down the resistance movements in both zones. She also warned me that they know an attack is coming soon."

"How is that *possible*?" screamed Kayla. "We've been meticulous about who we told and how much. Only members of the inner circle even know what we're up to."

"That may be true, Kayla, but we have likely shared enough that the rest of the resistance knows something big is coming, even if they don't know the details."

"Then we must act quickly," replied Kayla. "We have our plan in place; I say we go in as soon as we have everything ready. Hold on." Kayla stepped out and called for Marcel, who soon appeared at her side. She whispered some orders in his ear and then he was gone."

"Is everything okay, Commander?" asked Sergeant Kelly, who, as he'd promised, had hardly left her side since returning to base.

"I'm not sure, Sergeant, but we're going to do everything we can to make sure it turns out okay, I can promise you that."

"General Washington. I understand you wanted to see me?"

"Yes, General Hawkins, thank you for coming so quickly."

"It sounded rather urgent."

"Unfortunately, we believe it is, General Hawkins," Daniel answered somewhat solemnly. "I'm afraid my friend here has brought us some rather unpleasant news."

"Is that so?" he replied, curious, but betraying little concern or emotion. He was a man with impressive control over himself and others, even for a general of his stature, and I very much enjoyed watching him work.

"They've joined forces, General Hawkins. The Red Council has allied itself with the Gentry and the Sovereign Leader in the Blue Zone. To make matters even worse, it appears they know of our plans to launch a major attack soon, so we must act quickly before they have a chance to prepare."

We all sat there at the conference room table where we'd gathered, somber and sullen, stoically resigning ourselves to the bitter turn our revolution had taken. Expecting a rather grim and dire response, we nearly fell out of our seats when the general smiled…a small crack in his stern and chiseled features at first, but soon the smile erupted into full-blown laughter; it was, without question, the first time any of us had heard General Hawkins laugh about anything.

"General Hawkins, are you okay?" Daniel asked gingerly.

The general looked up at Daniel, still wearing a thin smile, and still chuckling slightly.

"I'm fine, sir, thank you. I expect we're all going to be just fine. It sounds to me as if the leadership in both zones have been weakened considerably more than any of us expected."

"General?"

"It's simple, sir. They were bound to join forces sooner or later…it was inevitable. I'm actually a little stunned it didn't happen sooner. The fact that they've allowed this 'alliance' of theirs to leak out so quickly could only mean one thing; they wanted us to know about it because they're hoping to unnerve us. They believe *they need* to unnerve us, General Washington, in hopes that we'll make a mistake, because they're *worried*. This fact alone suggests they believe us to be a much greater threat than we ever suspected; it could even mean we have a shot at succeeding here, sir."

"You must be joking, General Hawkins; surely you are!" exclaimed Kayla. "I know for a certainty that the Gentry in the BZ possesses nuclear fusion warheads, delivery systems, energy shielding, and attack bots; now I know, and I mean *I know*, that the Red Zone has a lot more than that at their disposal."

"Yes, ma'am, they absolutely do, but there are two things you

216

should bear in mind when thinking about the deadlier weapons in their arsenal."

"And what is that, General?"

"First, those weapons were designed to be used on populations or military targets on a different continent than themselves. If they were, for example, to detonate powerful energy weapons anywhere in the RZ or even the BZ, the death tolls would be enormous, and, depending on the type of weapons used, the possible fallout and/or long-term contamination could leave the land uninhabitable for hundreds, perhaps even thousands of years. Not only that, but the effect on the economy might be so devastating it could take a hundred years or more to fully recover from the impact of such destruction to our infrastructure, especially given what we've already suffered since the Great Schism.

"The second thing to bear in mind is this…these are populations these governments want to govern after this is all over…assuming *they* win, of course. If Romano were to launch nukes against us, or even some of the other non-nuclear weapons of mass destruction at their disposal, they risk robbing the people of all hope of survival in the aftermath of such devastation. Now, they may be totalitarian governments, perhaps even tyrannical despots, but even *they* cannot rule over a population whose only choice is to revolt or die. The people would almost certainly be unable and unwilling to continue, and would revolt against the government no matter what the cost in a desperate gamble to change their fate. No, while there are still many options open to the Red Council in terms of how to confront us within their own territory, they are growing increasingly limited, and they know it."

"From everything *we* hear, the people are with us in greater number with each passing day. Their courage grows each time they hear of another of our victories against the Synod and the NZC," I added, wanting to call out what I felt was an important observation.

"Exactly, Commander Jefferson; well said! Yes, that's

another reason we are poised, with the success of this mission, to accomplish our common goal, to reunite this great country, and to purge it of all of the would-be despots and petty dictators who seek to corrupt her."

"You sound like a man quite committed to the cause, General," Kayla added, clearly admiring the great man.

"Madam, I'd gladly lay down my life for this cause on a moment's notice, and I'd do so many times over," Hawkins added, with great depth and sincerity of feeling.

"General Hawkins, I have only one thing to say to you," Daniel chimed in, smiling slightly, yet also furrowing his eyebrows.

"And what may that be, sir?" asked the august general.

"I'm so glad you're on *our* side."

CHAPTER 29

It was still exceedingly dark out during the early, pre-dawn hours before sunrise. Even within the city, in a normally busy, rushed metropolitan area like New Manhattan, the air still had that same, early morning smell and sound that seemed common to most inhabited locations all over the earth. It was a Saturday, so the metropolis was slower to wake up than it would have been only the day before, when the streets would have been abuzz with businessmen and businesswomen getting ready for another workday.

We'd already split up into our two assigned teams…a larger team to tackle the NZC and a smaller one to take the Corporate Synod. I'd been given the opportunity to join either team, and predictably, I'd decided to join Kayla, Daniel, Sergeants Marcel and Kelly, Simon, and some forty others on the assault on the NZC. Meanwhile, a smaller but very capable assault team, led by General Hawkins, waited near the Corporate Synod's repository, prepared to assault the facility in hopes of planting the sunbursts inside the Synod's vault. The only holdup was the delay we had encountered waiting for the guard's next shift change, which was due in less than a half hour. We waited in a warehouse near the NZC temple, not unlike, albeit much larger than, the warehouse the Synod team was holed-up in near the Synod, waiting for the synchronized attack.

I looked over at Simon, who still carried the cameras for both NZC missions.

"Simon?" I was surprised at his expression as he turned to me. His face was pale and sullen, even in the dim light of the warehouse, which was currently in power-saving mode. "Are

219

you okay?"

"Yeah, yeah, I'm fine, Christian, thanks. Just a little nervous, and I'm not feeling too well."

"Maybe you haven't fully recovered."

There was no mistaking the look of alarm on Simon's face at that suggestion. "No, no, I'll be fine, I'm sure. Something I ate last night just didn't agree with me; it has nothing to do with the attack, trust me. I'll be fine."

"Okay, Simon, if you say so. I was just thinking, however, that you might want to go ahead and get the holocams out for the first team, since we'll be splitting up before too long."

"Oh yeah, you're right. Wow, time's really snuck up on me. I'll get them ready now."

I watched as Simon got the holorecorders out and began preparing them so the setup for each would be quick and painless. There wasn't going to be much time when the moment of truth came, and everyone knew it.

"I really admire your dedication to the mission, Simon. The amount of time you've spent setting up each and every holocam used in this mission personally, just to ensure they were done right, and in order to give everyone else time to prepare for other aspects of the battle plan, it must have been a real sacrifice so soon after your attack."

Simon looked up before nodding as he went about his work.

"If it had been *me*," I continued, "I would have been spending some quality time with Commander Jones. I understand that you two have grown rather intimate as of late. I must admit, Simon, she is kind of hot for a soldier. If I were you—"

Simon turned toward me, a scowl of anger on his face. "Hey, now listen here, Christian, that's none of your—"

"Yeah, I know, I know. Sorry about that, Simon. I was getting a little worried about you. You've been acting so different ever since the attack; nice to know you're still in there." I offered a smile and he managed a slight smile in return, before slipping back into whatever state of melancholy he'd been living in recently.

"Is everything okay over here?"

I'd not heard Kayla come up from behind me. We watched together as Simon collected one bag packed full of holocams and carried it over to Marcel, who would be responsible for deploying them in and around the vault on the basement level.

"Well, I *think* so."

"Christian…what's wrong?"

"I'm not sure, but maybe Daniel's noticed something, so I'll ask you. Have you noticed anything unusual about Simon recently?"

"Really, Christian? Come on; he was brutally attacked not too long ago, and now he's on a dangerous mission that could change the world. Who here *is* acting normal?"

"Yeah, but there's been something else going on with him even *before* the attack…I just can't put my finger on it." I shook my head. "I don't know, maybe you're right. I suppose we're all a little jittery, and we all handle it in our own way."

"Exactly. It's just about time to go; are you ready?"

"Yes ma'am," I said with a smile. "Vanessa's promised me a hero's welcome home party when we get back, along with a special 'surprise' of some sort," I said with a wink and a nod. Kayla just smirked and shook her head. "But I have no idea what that could be, do you?"

"Well if you *don't*, Chris, *I'm* certainly not going to be the one to tell you," she said, giving me a playful shove. "Now let's stow the chatter and get moving; we have some tyrants to topple."

"Yes, ma'am."

Simon let out a low whistle, and all eyes turned towards Daniel, who'd stepped up on a crate near a side entrance that would be their exit. Simon stood some ten yards in front of him, holding a holoconference projector, which projected his image to the remote team, and theirs, floating several feet above the projector, to us.

"Okay everyone, check your CAIS. We will synchronize time on my mark…mark.

"We are about to strike at the heart of our enemy and, if

we're successful, render him impotent. Team One is in place, as are Team Two and Team Three. We will proceed as previously discussed, and will meet at the rendezvous point at the specified time. Remember, anyone failing to make the rendezvous point in time, or anyone learning that the rendezvous point is compromised, should proceed directly to Safehouse Alpha, until they are contacted by one of the team leaders. This is it, ladies and gentlemen. We have complete confidence in each and every one of you, and your ability to succeed in your part of this mission. Now let's get this done, let's stay alive, and above all, let's remember, ONE COUNTRY, ONE PEOPLE, AND FREEDOM FOR ALL!"

Daniel turned to Simon. "Okay, are we ready?"

"Yes, sir," he answered, with an unusual hint of bitterness in his voice. Simon reached into a container and carefully removed and unpacked two small projectiles. He then proceeded to hand one to each of two snipers armed with rifles. "Okay, you both know what to do."

"Yes, Colonel," they answered in unison. They then exited the building, carefully concealing themselves along the way behind various structures, vehicles, and trees until they were finally in position.

"Tell me again what these will do," Kayla asked Daniel, who stood nearby, close enough I could overhear them.

"The projectiles will take out the camera, record what they see for ten seconds, then feed that image, in a continuous loop, to the camera from then on."

"Genius."

"Yes, it is," Daniel agreed, watching as the snipers each fired his weapon. The projectiles hurled toward their respective targets at tremendous speed, before doing something I'd never seen projectiles do before…they both slowed down just before impacting with the cameras and then expanded, until they were large enough to cover the apertures. This all happened in split-seconds, of course, and was extremely impressive to watch.

"Okay, we're clear, boss."

"Um, Simon…is everything okay?" Daniel asked his longtime

friend. Simon looked down and smiled before looking back up at Daniel.

"Sure, Daniel, everything's good. Thanks."

"Okay, then Teams One and Two, let's move out. Remember, we're using non-lethal force as much and whenever possible, but we do whatever we have to in order to survive, is that clear?"

"Yes, sir!" everyone exclaimed in unison, but at a low enough roar that it did not echo throughout the downtown area.

The teams hurriedly made their way along the sidewalk down the street from the warehouse to the NZC temple, carefully avoiding all cameras along the way. In less than a minute they were standing outside the temple, with each team on either side of the front entrance. Inside the front doors, two guards sat at the main desk, within arm's-reach of a panel that could, within seconds, bring a lot of hurt and pain down on all of us. That's where I came in.

"Okay, Christian, you're up," Daniel said to me. I looked over to Kayla, who looked worried, but managed a smile.

"No problem, Chief, I was born for this."

Daniel grinned and handed me the device. I then opened the door and walked inside, approaching the guards head-on.

"Excuse me, gentlemen. I realize it's dreadfully early yet, but I'm awfully anxious to meet Reverend DeWinters. We have a 7:00 AM meeting scheduled, you see, and well, I'm a little bit nervous."

I was relieved to see that the men barely moved now and, in fact, slumped back in their seats slightly, after having sat up and tensed upon my first entering. I continued walking forward until I was leaning on the counter in front of them.

"No one will be here for at least another two hours; you can't be here now, sir. I'm afraid you'll have to leave and come back then."

I slowly lowered my right hand, the one still holding the small EMP detonator, and with a slight nudge, pressed it against the front of the counter. It stuck, and a moment later, I felt the magnetic lock engage.

"But I promise I can wait quietly here in the lobby until the Reverend gets here. I—"

The two men, now much more confident in their ability to easily bully me, stood up. "If you don't leave now, sir, then we'll have to *make* you leave."

I smiled, bowed my head slightly, and pressed the button on the detonator just before turning and walking away.

"Okay then, be that way," I said with as much feigned disappointment as I could muster. I was nearly to the door when every console, button, and screen all around them suddenly went dark. The two men looked at each other before looking back up at me.

"Hey you, get back here!"

They started after me, but as I walked out the door, more than fifty men poured in around me, all armed to the teeth with weapons. My biggest regret at that moment was that I'd been unable to see whether either of the guards wet themselves at that moment.

The door opened and the two teams, led by Daniel, the team leader for Team Two, followed by his team and then Kayla, the team leader for Team One, poured into the temple while I turned back at my first opportunity to rejoin Daniel on Team Two.

"Do whatever you want, you'll never get me to talk; I don't care what you do!"

Daniel was already at the guard's station, where one guard sat on the floor, already tied up, mouth taped shut, and unconscious. The other guard, meanwhile, sat in a chair in front of Daniel, who held an infamous Shock Stick in his hand, waving it back and forth in front of the guard. The man was putting on a brave front, but everyone present could see that the man was terrified.

"Tell me your name," Daniel said calmly, yet firmly. I paused to reflect how much this man, Daniel, had changed in the few years since I'd first met him. He'd grown into an exceptional commander; he was truly now a great leader of men.

"It's Bill."

"Hello Bill, I'm Daniel. You know, Bill, there is one thing I've

224

always admired about the Synod. Would you like to know what that is?" The man shrugged, nodding slightly in a failed effort to seem uninterested in what was going on around him.

"Well, I'll tell you anyway," Daniel said, smiling at his men. "It's their ability to create such amazing new technologies. Oh, I try not to think about the amount of drugs and genetic engineering they've pumped into our children in order to precipitate such technological advances, but nevertheless, the advances *are* incredible. Some of the inventions are small and go mostly unnoticed by the general public. Inventions like this one; do you what this is?"

The man looked up, evaluated his captor, and wisely decided he'd better answer. "It's a shock stick."

"Yes; very good!" he mocked. "It is indeed a shock stick; and do you know what they are used for?"

"To render people unconscious."

"Very good! So far, my friend, you are two for two. Let's see if you can get the third one right as well. Maybe, if you get the third one correct, I'll let you go; how does that sound?" This time the man didn't answer, but his eyes brightened up and he perked up. "Good! Do you know how the pain stick works?" Daniel paused and looked around at his men, giving the man a chance to answer. His men were growing impatient, however, and a quick glance at his own chronometer warned him he was running out of time.

"Awww. Sorry, Bill, but time's up. The shock stick renders people unconscious by overloading the pain receptors, generating such an intense wave of pain that a person is instantly rendered unconscious; which is a good thing, considering how much pain a person would suffer were they to remain conscious." Daniel took the pain stick and passed it slowly before Bill's face, allowing the man time for his mind to process what he'd just heard. "So, imagine, Bill, what would happen if someone were to, say, remove the safety feature installed in these shock sticks that ensures the level of electricity emitted is either sufficient to knock someone out, or is turned off entirely. Why, it would enable someone say, such as myself, to lower the intensity to a level that would cause an unimaginable amount of pain to course throughout the person's entire body, while still keeping the level just low enough that the person would stay awake to experience every…single…moment…of…it…."

"Okay, okay…I'll talk. What do you want to know? I'll tell you anything you want to know…anything! They don't pay me enough for this. In fact, I never liked these stuck-up, arrogant—"

"The NZC records, where are they stored?"

"The basement."

Daniel nodded and smiled. The man was telling the truth; he had had enough. "Okay, very good. What about all of this vast NZC wealth I keep hearing about?"

"The next floor down…sub-basement."

That's two for three, I thought.

"How do I get there, those two elevators there?"

"Yes…well, the first elevator only. The second elevator is locked down until 9:00 AM."

Crap.

"How do we *unlock* it?" Daniel asked calmly.

"There's a master override. But it notifies the on-call supervisor. He'll call in when it goes off. I'd have to lie to him and tell him later I was threatened."

"Do you *feel* threatened, Bill?" Daniel asked, waving the shock stick in front of the guard once more.

"Yes, sir, indeed I *do* feel threatened," he replied, wearing a slight smile.

"Okay then, please unlock the second elevator. And Bill?"

"Yes, sir?"

"Thanks."

The guard nodded, now seemingly somewhat less scared than before.

He worked for a few seconds and informed them it was done. The expected phone call followed shortly after, but the guard easily convinced his boss it was routine. Daniel and the rest of us started for the elevator while a couple of the men began tying up

Bill, just before sedating him. Before the drug could do its work, however, Bill called out to Daniel.

"Excuse me, sir. I didn't recognize you at first, at least not until after you'd told me your name, but aren't you that leader of the resistance, the one that's been broadcasting all over the holoweb?"

"Yep, that's me, and that's us. We're working to reunite the two zones, Bill, and rebuild the New United States of America."

"And you're here to bring these SOBs down so you can do that?"

"That we are?"

"Then God bless you, sir; and may God be with you."

"You worship the one God? Bill…you surprise me!"

"I do; there's still more of us around than you might think, Mr. Washington. Please sir, bring them down, bring it all down."

Daniel turned to Kayla, then back to Bill. "We *will* Bill; one way or another, we will. I *promise*."

The guard nodded once more just as he was sedated, and seconds later, he was unconscious."

"Now then, first we go to the sub-basement just like we planned it," Daniel began. "Christian and I will go first, the rest of you will follow ninety-seconds later. We'll take out the guards standing just outside the elevator, so there should be no trouble when Kayla begins leading the rest of you down. Marcus, you're to stand watch outside the main elevators and keep us apprised if there's any trouble.

"Remember, we must run silent, especially in the sub-basement. We can't afford to risk alerting the rest of the guards in the building of our presence until *after* we've planted all of the sunbursts, understood?" Everyone nodded. "Okay then. Christian; are you ready?"

"As ready as ever, boss," I answered. I'd grown to not only respect Daniel, but to really like him as well. He felt almost like a brother in-law, of sorts.

We entered the elevator while the others held it open. Two men bent over, allowing Daniel to stand on their backs as he removed the panel from the elevator's ceiling. He then pulled himself up and through the opening in the ceiling. Seconds later I followed him through, and after cutting a small notch out of the corner of the panel, replaced it. We then took out our electromagnetic harnesses, set the magnetics on top of the frame of the elevator roof, and flipped the switch. The quiet hum of the unit told us it was working, and we would be safe from the rapid race to the basement that was about to begin.

"Why do we need these things?" I asked Daniel.

He looked at me, puzzled, before smiling slightly. "Electromagnetic harness secured," he announced to those below us without responding to my question. "Send us on our way."

"Be safe boys, I love you *both!*" Kayla told us.

For a moment, I felt that odd sensation, the old familiar longing for Kayla to love me as something other than a brother or close friend. But the moment soon passed, much sooner than it ever had before. I'd finally found the love of my life in Vanessa, and I was glad, very glad, that Kayla had found hers in Daniel.

Soon, I also had the answer to my question about the harnesses. Newton's Third Law of Motion; *For every action, there is an equal and opposite reaction.* It hit us fast and it hit us unmercifully hard, and the harness that had hardly seemed necessary only a minute ago was now saving my life. We were descending so rapidly that no matter how tightly we'd held on with our hands, we would have been ripped away and hurled upward before being immediately yanked back down to Earth by gravity, to our unfortunate deaths. As if reading my mind, Daniel managed to look over at me long enough to give me an *I told you so* smile.

Then, as quickly as it had begun, the elevator suddenly slowed. Daniel had already disengaged the clamp, reached into his pocket, and removed a small ball from his pocket before the elevator came to a complete stop. By the time the doors opened, Daniel had slipped his hand through the notch I'd taken out of the panel. He released the ball at such an angle that it bounced toward the elevator doors just after they opened so that the bouncing ball expeditiously exited the elevator. The guards standing outside the elevator were so focused on where they expected to find a person or people standing, that they failed to see a man's hand disappear above the ceiling of the elevator as the tips of his fingers receded from the opening in the ceiling. Nor did they notice the small ball rolling at their feet, now quietly hissing as it emitted a colorless, odorless gas. In less than thirty seconds both men lay passed out on the floor, heavily sedated by the powerful yet quickly-dispersing gas.

Daniel and I waited another thirty seconds and then climbed down out of the elevator, and walked out just as the second elevator arrived with the others to join us.

Kayla and Sergeant Kelly exited the elevator, weapons drawn, prepared for battle. Upon noticing Daniel and I watching them with a glint of humor in our eyes, they smirked, looked at each other, and then at the two guards passed out on the floor.

"So…that was easy," Kayla remarked, before turning and heading down the hallway toward the vault.

CHAPTER 30

"Chris! Chris...wake up. General Washington is about to contact the Red Council."

"What...huh? How long have I been asleep?"

"Less than two hours. Come on, honey, I know you're wiped out, but you don't want to miss this!"

"Huh? Hey, we've stopped." I sat up in bed and opened my eyes to find my beautiful Vanessa looking back at me. "Hiya, gorgeous," I said as I reached out to pull her close and kiss her.

"Okay, okay. Now get going, baby, there's plenty of time for that later," she said with a grin.

I smiled back and nodded. "Yeah, okay, I'm going. Where are they, the communications truck?"

"That's what she said. The commander said he wanted to call them before they blew everything up by accident; then we both lose."

"Yeah, he's got that right. Okay, sweetie, thanks for waking me. Man, I can't wait to get back so we can get back to our unfinished business, and after that I can get some *real sleep*." Vanessa smiled. "Well, let's get going."

Our arrival couldn't have been better timed. Daniel had just sat down in front of the holocom the moment we stepped into the trailer. Kayla motioned for us to be quiet, as a three-dimensional image of a man appeared at one-tenth scale above the projector in front of Daniel. The man was approximately sixty to seventy years of age, and was immaculately dressed, as was befitting the Leader of the Red Council.

"I am Mikos Romano, Leader of the Red Council; so, you must be this General George Washington I hear so much about. Please forgive my manners, but you look rather young and spry for a four-hundred-year-old dead man. How *do* you do it, General; I must know your secret!"

"Well, it's nice to know psychotic tyrants can have a sense of humor, too. I expect you'll need it after you've heard what I have to say. And by the way, the name is *Daniel*, not George."

"Ah, of course. Please forgive me…my mistake. What *is* this all about, Mr. Washington? I am, as you can imagine, a *very* busy man. I only agreed to speak with you because I was curious to learn just what sort of man it was that had led so many of my citizens astray."

"And?"

"Well, to be frank, I really don't see what all the fuss is about. I'm rather disappointed, if you must know."

"I guess it's a good thing that I couldn't give a rat's behind *what* you think of me then, isn't it?"

"What is it you want, Mr. Washington? Or was this just a social call?"

"I thought you should know that earlier this morning, the resistance planted a number of AZ-77 sunbursts, extremely high-temperature, long-duration, long-burn explosives, in the basement and sub-basement vaults of the NZC Temple, and the Synod's Data Repository, and after evacuating the vaults, we sealed them shut. We've also placed holocams at strategic locations inside and outside of each of the vaults, so we will know if anyone attempts to gain access to the vaults in order to disarm the sunbursts. Now let me be clear; any attempt whatsoever to access a vault will result in the immediate detonation of the two sunbursts armed and activated inside the vault, resulting in the complete destruction of anything and everything placed inside."

"Just what do you think—?"

"Shut up. I'm not finished, you arrogant windbag!" Daniel bellowed, filled with rage and indignation. Gone was any inclination to witty banter or pointless verbal sparring; Daniel was down to business now. "We have a list of demands—non-negotiable demands, I might add—that you *will* review, discuss, and then *act* upon, immediately upon receiving them. If our demands are not met, we will destroy the contents of all three vaults without hesitation."

There was a long pause, with Romano saying nothing, only staring back into the holocom, and Daniel's holographic image.

"In all seriousness, what exactly is it that you and your resistance are after, Mr. Washington? What do you want exactly? Do you want us to make changes, to end forced genetic enhancements, travel bans, to reinstitute religious freedoms... what?"

"The reunification of the two zones into the New United States of America, and the restoration of a free and democratic people."

This time the silence was deafening, and the expression on the face of the Leader of the Red Council was absolutely priceless. It remained unchanged for nearly a full minute, as if frozen on the man's face, such was the shock of the revelation.

"You...you can't be serious. That's preposterous; you must be joking."

"No sir, I'm not," Daniel replied calmly.

"Then *you* are mad, sir. You have completely and altogether taken leave of your senses, Washington! I would have thought that a man in your position would know something of our history, despite the illegality of possessing such knowledge."

"You mean about the dissension and the cultural warring that took place in the years preceding the Great Schism?"

"Exactly. This *was* a single country once before. What makes you think it could possibly end up any different this time even if we were somehow, miraculously, able to put Humpty Dumpty back together again?"

"Because, Leader Romano, the people have learned the pain, suffering, and misery that the alternative can bring, and no one, present company excluded, would want that." Romano scoffed. "I'm forwarding our demands to you now; you have two days to review them. We will contact you in exactly forty-eight hours. If you are not ready to meet our demands by then, we will destroy the three vaults. Do you understand?"

"Oh, I believe I understand far better than *you* do, Mr. Washington."

Daniel waved his hand and the image of their enemy vanished. Daniel remained at the table, however, having barely moved since the last words were spoken.

"Daniel, honey, are you okay?" Kayla asked, walking over to her husband, who seemed lost in thought. He didn't answer. "Daniel!"

"What? Oh…I'm sorry, sweetheart."

"What's the matter, Daniel?" I asked, now concerned as well.

"How do you two think that went?"

"Something's wrong, Daniel," Kayla remarked.

"Christian?" Daniel asked, looking at me.

"Yeah, everything sounded right up until the end. I think maybe he'd been hiding something. But then, when you told him what we're trying to do, he got rather flustered."

"It's as if he became so emotional about it that it threw him off his game, allowing his true feelings to come through," Kayla added.

"Yeah, that's pretty much how I saw it as well, and it scares me. '*I understand far better than you do.*' What does that mean?"

***

It took another full day to get back to Colorado Springs, but I still remember how good it felt when we finally arrived back at NORAD. The transports we rode back in had been built for the military, which meant they had been built for efficiency and not for comfort. It probably didn't help, of course, that Daniel had us take back roads home as much as possible, even when driving in stealth mode at night to help avoid detection on the drive back to Colorado Springs. We'd taken plenty of other precautions as well to ensure our primary base wasn't discovered, including ensuring that the vehicles would elude radar and would be invisible to satellite, and our communications back to the Synod had been bounced off so many satellites and we had spoofed so many signals that we felt certain we were safe. Still, this *was* the

Synod and the NZC we were talking about, two of the craftiest organizations on the planet, and they both worked together under the Red Council, so we couldn't be too careful.

The morning of the second day back I met Vanessa for breakfast in the mess hall. We each made our meal selections and took our seats at the table. We'd just started eating when Kayla and Daniel appeared at our table, with baby Sebastian in tow.

"Good morning, lovebirds; would you two mind if our little family intrudes for a few minutes?"

"Nonsense, Commander; you are part of *our* family, too!" Vanessa replied, hugging Kayla as they took seats at the table with us.

"Thank you, Vanessa, and please, when it's just us, call me Kayla; just try to remember the rank when we're with the others. After all, like you said, we're family…or at least we will be if the two of you ever decide to make it official and get married."

Vanessa turned to me and smiled. "Now I *like* the sound of that, Kayla."

"Thanks a lot!" I said to Kayla, laughing. "Before you know it, we're be carrying around one of *those* things too."

"Those *things* are called babies, Chris; come on!" corrected Vanessa, slapping me on the shoulder as she did so. "And you'd *better* like children, Christian, because I want to have a *huge* family!"

"See what you've done to me, Daniel? Thanks a lot, man."

"Hey, anytime. Really, it's not so bad. Little Sebastian here is like this little person who's like, half me and half Kayla, which makes him really special to both of us."

"Awww…*that is so romantic*. Come on, Chris, why can't *you* say things like that?"

"Thanks *again*, Daniel."

"Don't mention it!"

We all burst out laughing. After we'd all had a good laugh, Kayla changed the subject.

"I don't know about you, Daniel, but Sebastian and I need something to eat."

"Go ahead, sweetheart, I'll be with you in just a minute." Daniel then turned to Vanessa. "Say, Vanessa, would you mind giving Kayla a hand for a moment? There's something I need to discuss with Christian. I won't be long."

"No problem."

"Thank you, I really appreciate it." After looking slightly puzzled, Vanessa nodded and gladly shuffled off after Kayla, as Daniel turned toward me. "Chris, there's something I've been wanting to talk with you about."

"Sure Daniel, what is it?"

"Listen...this whole thing with the Council. I'm not sure exactly where things are going, and I, um...well, I uh...something happened awhile back, and it's got me a little worried."

"Listen, Daniel, Kayla and I may have grown up together, but over these last few years, you and I have really become exceptionally good friends in our own right, wouldn't you say? I mean, I've really come to think of you more as the brother I never had."

"Yes, Christian, of course, and I hope you know that I feel the same way. I'd trust you with my life...in fact, I already have on several occasions."

"Then whatever it is that you have to say to me, just come out with it and say it!"

"Okay...you're right."

"It just sounds so crazy, or weird. All right, here goes; I had a vision—well, two visions actually—a few months back. In these visions, I made two different choices in regard to what was, at that time, the future of the resistance. The first decision I made was to turn my back on the revolution so I could spend time with Kayla and raise our son. The second decision was a major attack against the NZC and the Synod repository.

"When I made the first choice and stepped down as leader of the resistance, the movement fizzled. Kayla and I survived to raise our son, but the world around us eventually went to hell in a handbasket at the hands of a madman far worse than Peloski and Romano combined. He turns out to be an extremely dangerous world leader, a narcissistic, psychotic madman with a serious god-complex. Early on in his reign he executes our full-grown son and his family, along with many, many others.

"When I make the second choice, by deciding to continue leading the revolution, Kayla and I are captured and executed, but the movement succeeds after we're gone, the Red Council and the Gentry fall, Sebastian survives, and the reunification effort is successful.

"Which brings us up to date. Since we *did* launch the attack, if the vision unfolds as it did in my dream it means our movement will succeed, but…."

"But you and Kayla will die?"

"Yes."

"What? Come on, Daniel; you can't be serious!"

"I am serious, Christian."

"It was a dream, Daniel, *a dream!*"

"No, it was a vision, Christian. Look, you don't have to believe me. I just have two favors to ask of you in case something does happen to us."

"Of course, Daniel, no problem; what are they?"

"First, please look after Sebastian. Both of us will be gone, as are both of our parents. Sebastian will not have anyone."

"Consider it done, Daniel. Little Sebastian is already family. What's the second?"

"Please see to it that the movement keeps going. With us gone, it could fizzle unless someone else picks up the torch and carries it after us. If the prophecy is true, once we're gone there *will be* an uprising, which will end in the toppling of both regimes, and it will usher in a new era, and the *New* United States of America."

"Consider that done as well. You probably know that I got involved in this initially because of Kayla, and because of a pretty little girl named Sam, but I'm a true believer now. I'll do everything I can to see this country made whole again; *I promise.*"

CHAPTER 31

Early the next morning it was my turn to take a shift at the monitoring station, watching the vaults at the temple and the repository just hours before the deadline, ensuring the Synod did nothing to try to disarm the sunbursts. I stepped into the surveillance room where the monitors were, relieving Sergeant Marcel, who'd taken the watch immediately prior to mine.

"Good morning, Pierre."

"Good morning, sir."

"Anything to report?"

"No sir, not really. In fact, I haven't seen anything on any of the monitors the entire time I was on watch. I started really early, so I normally wouldn't have thought anything of it…."

"Except…?"

"Well, sir, when I took over, the man before me said the same thing. He said that *he'd* seen no activity on the monitor whatsoever, *none*, for the entire time he was on *his* watch, which means that not one person crossed the view of any screen that entire time. For there to be no activity at any site for his entire shift, and then for my entire shift as well; it just seems *highly* unlikely, Commander."

"Maybe the Synod's ordered everyone to stay away."

"I suppose that could be the case, sir, of course. Okay, well, have a good watch, sir."

"Thanks, Sergeant, get yourself some sleep."

"Yes, sir."

Marcel left, but as he did so, I couldn't help but wonder what it meant. Why would there be no activity whatsoever? How was it possible that not even a single person had crossed the path of even one of the holocams they'd setup since the morning they were there? I kept staring at the monitors and staring at them, and I had a growing feeling that something was wrong. Shouldn't there be some sort of activity, something? Then it hit me; *the holocams had been looped!* But I breathed easier upon realizing that was impossible. The cameras inside the vaults were secure... they'd sealed them shut, and they'd been monitoring them ever since. There had been zero opportunity for anyone to access even one of the devices, much less all of them!

I began examining each image closer, magnifying each one as I did so, and scrutinizing each and every square inch of each image. On the third image taken from one of the holocams inside the NZC vault on the basement level, I finally found what I was looking for. A holocom pointing toward the door entering the vault on the basement level had captured a reflection, the reflection of a chronometer on the opposing wall. It took some effort for me to magnify and then re-focus the image, but after several minutes, I finally found what I needed. I immediately rushed to wake Daniel and Kayla.

***

"This sounds bad; what does it mean?" Kayla asked as we rushed to the conference room they'd established as our "War Room."

"It means that there's been something going on that someone else doesn't want us to see," Daniel stated.

"It could only mean one thing," I offered. "The removal and disarmament of the sunbursts from the vaults."

"Okay, let's think this through. If they've removed the sunbursts, then why haven't they said something, gloated about it?" Kayla asked, receiving nothing but blank stares for several moments.

"I'm afraid it means something far worse than just the removal of the sunbursts, everyone. I have some very bad news, General Washington." We all recognized the sound of the voice, and moments later General Hawkins entered the room. He then proceeded to activate the holoprojector. The projector came alive and with a wave of his hand, and an image of NORAD and the area surrounding Cheyenne Mountain filled the room. What we all saw next caused a collective gasp to pass among us. Unbeknownst to all of us in the room, within the last few hours a vast army of men, women, tanks, airships, and at least one regiment of Advanced Robotic Early Deployment Systems, or AREDS, had surrounded us. Oh, we were safe for the moment, given how heavily fortified the base inside Cheyenne Mountain remained, even nearly two centuries after it was first built. We had a number of concerns at this point, however, none of which concerned our safety. How did they find us? How did they find out about the sunbursts? Who was giving them information?

"We have a traitor in our midst," I announced, without thinking first.

"What? No. What are you talking about, Christian? That's impossible," Kayla replied. "We've known that the Red Council and the Gentry both have been gunning for our heads, and that we might have low-level spies in our midst, but that's why we've kept operational details to such a select few individuals. The last thing we need, with a couple of armies surrounding us outside, is for us to start turning on each other and to start doing their dirty work for them. No, there has got to be a logical explanation for all of this. Maybe they've bugged us somehow."

"No, I believe Chris may be right, Kayla," said Daniel. "It's the only explanation that makes sense. The only questions now are *who*, and *why*."

The discussion was interrupted when the door suddenly flung open, with Vanessa standing in the doorway. She was really flustered, so I rushed over to her side. She hugged me briefly before turning back to face Daniel and Kayla.

"I'm so, so sorry, you two; I don't understand what happened! I just him left for a few moments, I swear it."

"What are you doing here, Vanessa? You're supposed to be watching Sebastian!"

By the time Vanessa responded Kayla was already heading for the door on her way out.

"He's gone, Commander," Vanessa answered, with tears now pouring down her face. "Someone *must* have taken him... he could never have gotten out on his own; but who would have done such a thing?"

"Funny you should ask." He walked in just as Kayla was about to leave, blocking her from exiting. "Please, Commander, if you would wait one moment, I believe all of your questions will be answered."

Kayla stood still, facing Simon with an expression of mixed emotions, including fear, uncertainty, and doubt.

"Simon. Where have you been? Do you realize we've been looking everywhere for you? Our baby's missing...I've got to go find him!"

"Kayla, please, just wait."

"Simon, what's going on," Daniel asked, staring curiously at his longtime friend.

"Ah, Daniel, my old school pal, ever the perceptive one. Oh, please forgive me! Who am I to address you so informally? Maybe I should address you as Your Highness, King Washington, Supreme General Washington, sir, or President Washington. There you go, whatever title you or your beloved subjects happen to bestow upon you."

"Simon...are you feeling okay? I don't understand why... what are you going on about? We're *friends*, Simon, we have been for years. You were there when I first destroyed the regional Synod regional HQ. You've been my friend since before any of this began."

"Yeah, that's what I thought too, at least up to a couple of years ago."

By now Kayla was staring hard at Simon, wearing a look of anger mixed with hatred and ferocity like I'd never seen before, in *any* woman's face.

"Do you know where my son is, Simon?" Kayla asked, her eyes narrowed and her head lowered, like a great cat about to pounce on its prey.

"It just so happens I do!" he replied, just before Kayla leapt at him like a fierce tigress, landing on top of him and driving him to the floor with such force and fury it nearly knocked him unconscious. She then commenced to striking him with her firsts, one after another, until Daniel came over and pulled her off him.

"What time is it?" Simon asked, after wiping some of the blood away from his mouth with a napkin sitting on a nearby table.

"It's nearing 09:00 hours," I answered, when no one else did.

"You're about to get a call, Daniel; I recommend you take this one."

"If anything happens to my son, Simon, I swear I'll kill you with my bare hands, friend or not, and I'll kill you slowly." Daniel's blood was boiling hotter than Kayla's by now, exacerbated, no doubt, by the pain of the betrayal itself, on top of whatever danger his infant son was now in. Simon was cowering in fear, clearly scared he would not survive until whatever he had planned for next to occur.

"A call? What are you talking about, Simon; are you mad?" I asked. "No one knows how to—"

Suddenly a message popped up on the 3D display; "Incoming Call."

"Okay then, I stand corrected."

"Daniel!" Kayla was pacing like a jungle cat. But even as angry as he was, Daniel still had enough patience for the both of them. It was one of the traits about him that made him so dangerous to his enemies…his ability to demonstrate patience even when he was angry enough to kill.

"It's okay, Kayla; we just have to be smarter than they are. We'll get him back…trust me, okay?"

"I do trust you, Daniel; okay." Kayla ceased pacing.

"Put it up," Daniel said to me, and I selected the incoming call.

We were stunned to find not one but two familiar faces on the screen; that of Leader Peloski of the Gentry in the Blue one, and Leader Romano of the Red Council in the Red Zone. Romano was the first to speak.

"Good morning, General Washington. I hope you don't object to my inviting Leader Peloski this morning. Since I expect your plan was to break into some facility in the Blue Zone in order to blackmail him once you were done with me, I thought he might appreciate the opportunity to participate in the surrender of the criminals he's been after."

"Surrender?" Daniel replied, "You must be out of your mind, Romano, and the only criminals here are the two of you! So tell me, what of our offer, Romano? Are you prepared to abdicate your position, and to support the reunification of the two zones back into the United States, and the holding of open, fair, elections to elect new leadership? Do this and you may live, and perhaps even keep a portion of the riches you've illegally taken from the people."

"Wow! Your offer…it's so generous, Mr. Washington. Let me get this straight. If I refuse, you plan on detonating the sunbursts in the vaults in the NZC Temple, as well as the Synod Archive?"

"That's correct, and time is running out."

"Okay, okay…you win. Blow them up."

"What?"

"You heard me; blow them up!"

"Um, which one?"

"Any of them, all of them, I don't care…just get on with it. I'm a busy man, Mr. Washington, as I believe I've said before."

"But your priceless treasures, your records, they will all be lost!"

"Do it, Mr. Washington…I dare you!" With the last round of taunting Romano leaned into the holocom, while Peloski grinned.

"Very well, let's begin with the records of the NZC temple on the basement level." Daniel watched the monitors of that level as he began counting down. "5-4-3-2-1-0!" At zero Daniel pushed the button, expecting everything on the monitor to vanish, but nothing happened. He pressed the button again but still nothing happened.

"Ah, perhaps you're having difficulty with your feed from the NZC basement level. One second, General," Romano said, sarcasm dripping from his mouth with every word. "Okay, here, try looking at this one." He then pointed the holocam to a monitor next to him. The image on the screen was identical to the one the resistance members had been watching, with one important difference; there was a lot of activity, with many people walking back and forth on the screen.

"Yes, I suppose we cheated a little. Seems your monitors have only been showing you what we wanted you to see. Our people finished disarming the last of your little toys in time to go home for dinner last night. Oh, they could have been finished by breakfast in a pinch, but seeing as you'd been so kind as to give us an entire forty-eight hours, we figured, why waste them?"

Daniel dropped his head in defeat.

"Oh, come now, it's not that bad. You and your people will be relieved to know that our arrangement is only for you and that delicious tigress of yours. We plan to put you both in a cage together before putting the both of you down for good, like the animals you are. So then, I understand we can expect your surrender momentarily. I suggest you contact us again very soon to let us know you're coming out. If we kill you because you fail to do so, our deal's null and void, and we will tighten the noose around your base until everyone inside is dead. We prefer you alive so we can give you the public execution you so richly deserve. Do we understand each other?"

"We understand."

"Very good. I must confess, 'General Washington,' I expected a bit more from you. That said, I truly am looking forward to meeting you in person."

Romano vanished and the silence that fell over the room was deafening. We all felt such a heavy, heavy load of despair. Then, seemingly all at once, all attention turned to Simon.

"Seize him!"

Marcel and Kelly grabbed Simon and held him firm. Kayla reached him before I did, and when she smacked him, it was so loud the sound was deafening, and the imprint on his face left outlines of her fingers in places.

"I can't utter right now the *unspeakable* things I'll do to you, Simon, if *any* harm *whatsoever* befalls my son. Suffice it to say *you will* know pain in a very personal and intimate way. Now tell me where he is, you disgusting, traitorous, sniveling piece of—"

"Kayla! You're not helping at the moment. Please, just give it a rest and let me talk to him." Kayla glared at Daniel with a ferocity that I'd never seen before, and frankly, found rather disturbing. Daniel, however, didn't seem particularly bothered by it. Clearly they both felt the same thing, but he just had much better command of his faculties than did my childhood friend.

"Okay, Simon. First, let's get Kayla's question out of the way…where is Sebastian, and what have you done to him?"

"He's safe, I promise you both on my life!"

"That's good, old friend, because that's exactly what's at stake here. I've loved you like a brother for a long time, Simon, but after what you've done, after kidnapping our infant child and putting *his* life at risk, putting him in the middle of all of this the way you have, I'll tear you apart with my bare hands without a moment's hesitation if one hair on that boy's head is harmed."

"He's safe, I promise, and he'll stay that way. I only took him to get the two of you away from the base."

"I don't understand, Simon. I may have misjudged your loyalty, but I never imagined for a second that you could be stupid and gullible enough to trust that the Synod will deliver on even one of the promises they've made to you, regardless of how significant they may be. They're going to kill you just for spite, regardless of whatever they may have promised you; surely you must know this."

"Of course I know it, Daniel. I'm no fool."

Daniel sat down in the nearest chair and placed his head in both hands. "Simon, you'd dedicated yourself to the resistance before I even knew it existed. How could you throw it all away like this?"

"I haven't, Daniel, *you* have!"

"*Me?*"

"Yes, you! You've been putting everything at risk from the

moment you first got involved with *her* and the Blue Zone, and then the crazy idea of reunification. Come on, Daniel, you knew you were biting off far more than you or anyone else could ever chew."

"It was never about Kayla, the BZ, or reunification, Simon; it was always about you, and your petty jealousy…admit it! Look, unlike you, I never *wanted* this, any of this. It *just* happened!"

"It wasn't fair, Daniel. *I* brought *you* into the resistance, not the other way around, remember? It wasn't right that you were the one to rise up to lead the Red Zone; you should have been the one who became invisible, not me!"

"Do you have any idea how childish, petty, and crazy you sound right now, Simon? It's not about me and it's not about you…it never has been! It's about *everyone*! It's about our families, our friends, our children, and our neighbors; it's about freedom, Simon."

"It doesn't matter, Daniel. There's no way you ever could have put this country back together again."

"That's not true, Simon. It *was* working…we were close! Now you've doomed *everyone* to generations of tyranny and misery, including everyone in the Red Zone. You've *helped* our enemy, and you've betrayed the very people and cause you once claimed to care so much about! Damn you, Simon; damn you for what you've done to us!"

"But it's not over, Daniel, don't you see?"

"What? What do you *mean* it's not over?"

"It *is* over for you and Kayla, Daniel, and for that I'm sorry. But I couldn't let you ruin the last chance we had to save the Red Zone."

"What are you babbling about now?"

"When they take the two of you, they plan to execute you in public. You see, they have no idea how popular you've become with the people, Daniel, how important you've become to the people. Your harebrained idea of unifying the country may have been doomed from the start, but the whole fairytale wedding between you, as leader of the resistance in the Red Zone, and

Kayla, as leader in the Blue Zone, and then the birth of Sebastian, the symbol of the rebirth of America...well, it was a storybook romance for the ages.

"You excited them and you inspired them, Daniel. When the RZ executes the two of you in public, and leaves the infant boy an orphan to boot...! The people are going to revolt, Daniel...oh, are they ever going to revolt! The pot was already boiling when you and I were in college together, but since then it's been boiling over. Once the public sees what those tyrants have done to you... *watch out!*"

"*Sir.*" It was General Hawkins. He'd been ominously silent during the entire drama, since making everyone aware earlier of the surrounding armies; at least until now. "Sir, I believe this lecherous, traitorous piece of trash may actually have a point. If — and I do say *if*, sir, because I'm not at all certain it's a good idea at all to do so — but *if* you were to surrender, he might be correct about the people being ready to revolt. I've studied revolts throughout history, sir, and I mean going back centuries, even thousands of years back before the Great Schism. There have been unique, pivotal moments in history when a country, a people, was ripe for revolution, and this one has all for the earmarks of just such a revolution."

"Really? What would need to be done to take advantage of such an opportunity, General?"

"The most important thing, General Washington...and please forgive me for being so blunt."

"We've no time for being delicate, General Hawkins. Please, speak freely."

"Yes, sir. The most important thing will be continuity of leadership. With both yourself and the commander gone, you will need to appoint someone to succeed you after you're gone, and you'll need to make such an announcement before you turn yourself over to them, sir. Which means you won't have much time."

"Well then, I believe *you* would be —"

"No sir. Thank you, but no. That ship sailed a long time

246

ago, sir. This is a younger man's game, or at least it's a game for someone with a lot more interest in governing and politics than I have. I'm a military man, sir, a fighting man, a man of combat and strategy. I can fight and I can win your wars, but don't ask me to be the one responsible for declaring them; that responsibility must go to someone worthier than I."

"Very well, thank you for your honesty and your candor, General. In truth, that was the answer I expected." Daniel then turned and stared at me for several moments, and smiled. I began shaking my head almost immediately and continued doing so, even as he turned to Kayla, who nodded approvingly as well. He then turned to Hawkins, who also nodded, as did Marcel, and then Kelly. He went on around the room and found there was a consensus, before turning back to me. "Congratulations, Christian Jefferson, the next leader of the Resistance movement!"

There was a round of applause around the room. I couldn't help but feel a slight chill as Daniel turned toward Kayla with something of a sad and somber expression as he stared longingly into her eyes, and I could tell immediately what he was saying to her without speaking; *if only we'd had more time.*

CHAPTER 32

They'd already said their goodbyes to everyone, including me. There would be little need for supplies or provisions, other than what they'd expect little Sebastian might need for the return trip. They were determined not to allow the safety of their son to rest on Daniel's traitorous friend any more than was absolutely necessary, so he and Kayla had already discussed how they would act to protect him.

As the three prepared to leave, I could tell that Daniel and Kayla could barely stand to be in the same building, much less the same room as Simon now without tearing him to pieces. Perhaps all else could have been forgiven, or at least have been understood at some level, but the kidnapping of their infant son and placing his innocent life at risk just to lure them out had crossed a line that was unforgiveable.

"How is this going to work, Simon?" Daniel was gritting his teeth.

I stood there and watched the interaction, along with a few others, as a precaution in case Simon had something else planned. I had a blaster in my right hand pointed at Simon the entire time, as did the others in the room. I was, however, sincerely worried that one of us might blast a hole in him before we recovered little Sebastian.

"It's simple. I negotiated the entire exchange with Leader Romano. He finally agreed to use a neutral, third party to hold Sebastian until the two of you are delivered. There will also be a group of these men with Leader Romano, to ensure no one attacks the base as long as the two of you are delivered as promised."

"What happens if they attack the base?"

"Then they will kill Romano."

"Really? Who are these men?"

"Mercenaries; they are members of a group known as The Creed. They are known to die rather than violate their sacred creed to honor the pact. In this case, the exchange of you two for the life of Sebastian and everyone else on that base. Since Romano is the only one with the ultimate authority in the Red Council, it had to be him."

"But he refused to be at the same site we're going to."

"Of course. He may be a cold, heartless bastard, but he's no fool. He, too, knows the reputation of the Creed. As long as he holds up his end of the deal, he knows he has nothing to fear."

"We're taking someone with us."

"What? No, that wasn't part of the arrangement," complained Simon.

"Well it's part of *our* arrangement. You see, we don't trust you, Simon. I'll leave it to you to figure out why. The safety of our son comes first to us, and we don't trust you to bring him back safely."

I could see that Simon was nervous at this prospect. He'd not expected anyone would be coming with them, but he knew Daniel well enough to know when he'd made up his mind. "Who will you bring with you?" he asked.

"Christian. We're asking him to raise Sebastian after we're gone."

"No! No way; if you insist on bringing Christian the deal's off. I know he and Kayla grew up together; he's likely to kill me on the way back for betraying her. Choose someone else or you lose your child."

Simon must have jumped back some four or five feet in one backward leap, a jump worthy of an Olympian. It wasn't until I caught the look in Daniel's eyes that I understood why, and at that moment I began to wonder how much longer Simon would be alive, for his end was surely near.

About that time Sergeant Kelly came wandering in, as if looking for someone or something. Seizing on the opportunity,

Simon latched onto him. "How about this man? Bring him along and *he* can ensure Sebastian gets back safely. Deal?"

Daniel looked up at Sergeant Kelly, who carefully looked up to meet his gaze in such a manner that his expression was not visible to Simon. Daniel then looked over to Kayla, who'd witnessed the entire affair. She nodded without any visible expression on her face other than a slight squint, which was almost certainly imperceptible to anyone other than Kelly.

"All right then, agreed," Daniel finally announced, as if somewhat reluctantly.

"But you must promise not to kill me," he said, looking at Daniel and then adding, "Both of you!" as he looked at Kayla.

"Simon, you should know me well enough by now to know that if I were going to kill you, you'd already be dead...though the same can't be said for my wife. She's a mama bear, and you've taken her cub."

"Well just remember, if anything happens to me before we retrieve your son and you're in the hands of The Creed, they will kill your son, and there will be nothing I or anyone else can do to stop it.

"We'll remember," Daniel said reluctantly.

***

"Are you ready?" I asked.

"Yeah, let's do this."

I started the holorecorder and Daniel began. The speech was being recorded, but it was also being broadcast out to both zones, courtesy of the booster stations they'd setup over the past few years, to fully cover both zones.

"My fellow Americans.

"Yes, I use the term *Americans,* because that's precisely what you are. You are not citizens of the Blue Zone or citizens of the Red Zone anymore, and don't let *anyone* ever convince you otherwise. This land was founded as one country, as one nation under God, indivisible, with liberty and justice for all. But I fear I may be accused of plagiarism here, so please allow me to recite the entire Pledge of Allegiance to the Flag, something small children once recited in classrooms all over this great country, before spending their days learning how to read and to write, in the land of the free and the home of the brave.

"It was called the Pledge of Allegiance to the Flag, and it went something like this…'I pledge allegiance to the Flag of the United States of America, and to the Republic for which it stands, one Nation under God, indivisible, with liberty and justice for all.'

"Men and women across this great nation were proud, oh so proud, to be called Americans. America was sometimes referred to as a shining city on a hill, a beacon of hope for the rest of the world, a shining example of freedom and democracy in action, a model for the rest of the world to follow. And follow it they did.

"When each of the respective resistance movements started in the two zones, it was the goal of each one to do something, anything, to try to redress some of the atrocities committed by the tyrannical governments we allowed to rule over us. I say 'allowed' because we did little or nothing to topple these tyrants. Instead of refusing to suffer their abuse any longer by overthrowing them, we allowed them to enslave our children, to take our property, to treat us like animals, to experiment on us, to torture and imprison us, even to kill us.

"As our movements grew, and more and more of you decided you'd had enough and came to join us, our voices grew as did our ability to affect great changes, until eventually, these selfsame tyrants came to see us as real and dangerous threats to their ability to remain in power.

"Our recent effort to topple the Red Council, which very nearly succeeded, was foiled recently, the secret location of our primary base was given over to the enemy, and my infant son was kidnapped and delivered into the hands of our enemy in order to force my cooperation, all due to a devastating act of betrayal within our own ranks. My son's life is now in jeopardy, and the only way my wife Kayla and I can save our son, Sebastian, is to surrender ourselves to the Red Council, thus forfeiting our own lives in the process. What our enemy does not know, however, is that you no longer need us. You can finish what we started yourselves, and take back your country without us!

"There was a prophecy given to us, a prophecy that is playing out exactly as my vision, which I am convinced came from God, said it would. My wife and I *will* die, but afterwards, you, the people, *will* rise up, and *you will* overthrow the tyrants, Romano, Leader of the Red Council, and Peloski, Leader of the Gentry. And *you will* reunite this country, the United States of America, under the leadership of my successor, Christian Jefferson, a most capable, caring, and devoted leader, and a very, very good friend. I want you to know that Christian was *my* choice, he was *Kayla's* choice, *and* he was the choice of the resistance leadership. So I ask you—I beg you—*please*, follow Christian as dutifully and as faithfully as you have me, and see this mission, this great mission of ours, though to the end. Remember what awaits you at the end of this long and difficult journey; *freedom*. Thank you, my brothers and my sisters, for your support, for your kind words and your prayers, and for your love.

"Now, as we come to the end of the road which has, for us, been a long and challenging, but very rewarding, journey, Kayla and I must bid you farewell. I would like to say my final goodbye by concluding this broadcast the way presidents of the United States often did when addressing the nation over a century ago; may God bless you, and may God bless the *New* United States of America."

Thunderous applause erupted throughout the room at first, and then throughout the entire base, as the speech, which had been watched on monitors throughout the facility, ended. The applause went on, seemingly forever, with Kayla and myself leading the way, until finally Daniel was able to get us to wrap it up, despite our intense desire to continue throughout the night. After nearly everyone on the base had congratulated him on the power, emotion, and depth of his speech, Daniel finally made his way over to me.

"What did you think?"

"Not bad," I answered him. I felt for Daniel. Only a handful of us really knew just how deeply Simon's betrayal had hurt him. Simon had almost always been the one Daniel went to following a speech to get a somewhat objective opinion, and I felt quite honored that he felt my opinion was worthy to take his best friend's place. "Actually, Daniel, I thought it was your most powerful, most moving speech ever. I was touched by your openness and your honesty."

It was then that Daniel grabbed me gently by the arm and pulled me aside.

"Christian, we don't have much time. There are a few things, a few very important things, I'd like to go over with you. I know after I'm gone there's nothing I can do, unless I can come back from the dead, to ensure you follow up on this. But you've been a friend of Kayla's for a very long time, and you've been like a brother to me these last few years. I've always found you to be one of the most trustworthy, honorable men I've ever met, so I believe you'll do it."

"Thanks, Daniel, but what's this is all about?"

"Chris, it's about the future. Come with me and let me show you what I've been working on. We don't have much time before we go get Sebastian, but I wanted to go through this with you before we leave. You're going to need this, or something like this, if you end up being as successful in our cause as I believe you will be after we're gone."

"Okay, Daniel, sure. Tell me what's on your mind."

"Not here, not yet; wait." Daniel ushered me away from the others. Simon watched, dying to know what it was we were discussing, but helpless to do anything to find out. I suspected at this point he just wanted to stay alive.

A short time later Daniel had ushered me into a room, where it seemed obvious he'd been spending a considerable amount of time, either alone, or alone with Kayla, by my estimation. There were several holorecorders ranging in size from extremely small — built for concealment — to very large ones, built for recording events from a distance. There were also several holodisks, some labeled and some blank, and several data crystals. He'd been a busy bee, this one.

"Christian, there's a lot to be done, and we're out of time." He grabbed a large duffel bag, picked up some of the mid-range holorecorders and some blank holodisks, and placed them inside. "Please make sure Sergeant Kelly gets these; he'll need these for our handoff to the Creed, and then our exchange for baby Sebastian."

Next, Daniel picked up several of the concealable holocams, along with what appeared to be repeater antennas, designed to boost the signal for long distance broadcasts to satellites and terrestrial stations. "Take these, and get them into the hands of our people inside of the Red Council's personal guard. They're going to need these, for the end...."

"What do you mean by that, Daniel? I'm not sure I follow."

"What do you think the Red Council and the Gentry will do to Kayla and me once they have us, Christian? Do you think they'll simply put us in prison, or execute us quietly in our sleep? No...they're going to make it very painful, and they're going to drag it out for as long as they can. Make sure our people get this recorded on the holocams, and then get everything out for the people to see."

"Daniel, I don't know what to say; I'm so...."

My friend and my leader, a true visionary among men, stood and walked over to me, placing one hand on my shoulder. "It's okay, Christian, really. Don't get me wrong; I would like to have seen my son grow up, to have had more children, and to have loved and held Kayla until we grew old together. But the truth of it is that we all die, eventually; but how many have an opportunity to die while making such an impact on the world, the chance to kick-start the rebirth of the greatest nation the world has ever known? It's not just an honor, Chris, it's a rare privilege, and I go to my death thankful to the Christian God, whom I have come to embrace, to have had the opportunity to serve Him in such a manner."

"Daniel Washington, you are a man of singular character, vision, leadership, and compassion. I will never be able to convey to anyone how much it has meant to me to be so privileged to have not only known you, but to have called you my friend."

"Thank you, Chris; I hope you know how Kayla and I feel about you, which is why we're so comfortable leaving this movement in your very capable hands." He hurriedly glanced around the room until his eyes landed on the data crystals. "Oh yes. These…these are so very important, Christian. Please, I beg you, review what is on these crystals carefully, especially what is on the white crystal. It may well hold the key to ensuring that the wonderful new nation that arises from the ashes of this miserable existence we've endured for so long, does not follow the same path as the one before it."

Daniel then packed everything into the bag, closed it, and set it before me, before raising his eyes until they met mine. For the first time since I'd met him, I saw his eyes had teared up, and he was on the verge of crying.

"I'm tired, Christian; to tell the truth, I'm exhausted. But I'd go until my dying breath to see this country reunited, to see men, women, and children from the west to the east free once more. I would gladly die a thousand deaths to see freedom and democracy return to America.

"Thank you, Chris. Thank you for taking up the mantle and finishing what Kayla and I, and all of the others in the resistance before and since, have worked so hard for. I thank you from the bottom of my heart."

I placed my hand on top of his and said, "And from the bottom of my heart, Daniel, my dear and noble friend, you are very welcome."

CHAPTER 33

Sergeant Kelly felt a wave of nausea pass through him, as he had off and on for most of the trip. It physically sickened him to be in the company of the *thing* sitting next to him. He could only count his blessings that he'd had the presence of mind to suggest that *he* do the driving, so Simon could focus on making sure they made no missteps on their way to meet with the Creed, considering everything that was at stake. Fortunately, his rather lame excuse for wanting to drive had sounded plausible enough that Simon hadn't objected, or perhaps Simon was simply lazy and preferred not to drive anyway. In either case it mattered not to Kelly, as keeping both hands on the steering wheel meant it was much more likely that he'd not kill Simon in a moment of weakness, before getting the chance to retrieve baby Sebastian. Such a careless mishap would mean the child of the two people he respected most in the world would die, as perhaps would the revolution, and many of his friends back at the base would likely lose their lives as well. He would have his chance soon enough, he just had to be patient.

"It's like I was saying, my friend," he told Simon, in as amiable a voice as he could muster. "I've always felt that the commander should have stayed the course with the Blue Zone, even after she met General Washington. They could have still been together while running separate military campaigns, could they not?"

"Yes; thank you, Sergeant! That's what I tried getting through to that knuckleheaded friend of mine for so long, but he never got it!"

Kelly glanced in the mirror at the back seat, where he found Daniel and Kayla doing what they'd been doing for hours; either staring adoringly into one another's eyes, or kissing passionately for minutes at a time. He smiled as a thought crossed his mind that poisoned the beautiful scene he'd just witnessed. *The nerve this traitor has to continue referring to my general as his friend! Surely the man has gone completely insane, and I would be doing him a favor by taking his life.*

"Oh, wait, we're coming up on the road up here in another mile or so. Take the next left and it will take you to the cabin."

We soon arrived at the next road, and upon making the left turn, found ourselves on a dirt road leading into some woods, where we saw two men wearing face masks armed with state-of-the-art pulse rifles standing on either side of the road as we pulled in, a clear indication that we were at the right place. After peering inside momentarily they motioned us forward, and as we pulled forward along the winding road, the cabin came into view. Another half-dozen mercenaries were scattered around the cabin, with several more up on the porch. Clearly they were prepared should we come with anything smaller than a full company of soldiers. The dirt road, the dense woods, the isolated location...someone had been thinking strategically. They'd done about all they could, within reason, to defend against a much more powerful military force by using the terrain as a force-multiplier, perhaps borrowing a few pages from ancient history, when a much smaller defending Greek force was able to hold off a far larger invading Persian army by blocking a small pass in the ancient Battle of Thermopylae.

Sergeant Kelly pulled up to the cabin and stopped the vehicle. He stepped out and opened the door for Kayla, helping her out after doing so.

"Commander, I would have preferred to be accompanying you into battle."

"Oh, but you are, Sergeant, you are; don't you ever forget it. This may not look like it, but it's just a different front of the same war, and we're just about to win this thing. Please remember to record everything, okay?"

"Yes, ma'am."

Kelly then went to open Daniel's door and helped him out, since he, like Kayla, had been handcuffed before leaving the base. "I'm sorry about how this turned out, sir. I really am."

"Kayla was right, Sergeant...don't lose faith. This war is almost over, and we've just about won it."

"Yes, sir."

"And Sergeant, I had some time to think on the trip here. You've got to make sure that both zones see what barbarians their little dictators are, and General Jefferson *must* call the people to arms immediately after this is all over, and launch major offensives against the leadership in both zones simultaneously. Let the people see how weak and vulnerable the leadership truly is, and how powerful the resistance truly is."

"Yes sir; I will give him the message."

"Good. And Sergeant?"

"Yes, sir?"

"There's one other thing I want you to do for me as soon as you leave here. I'd like you to...." Daniel leaned in closely and whispered the rest into Kelly's ear, so only he would hear. The others noticed when Daniel had finished; the big sergeant smiled broadly.

"Yes, sir, gladly; thank you!"

With that Daniel turned and joined Kayla at the foot of the stairs, before walking with her up to the porch and inside the cabin.

Once inside they found a crib in the center if the main room, with baby Sebastian sound asleep.

"What's wrong? Why is he sound asleep in the middle of the day like that?" Kayla demanded of his temporary caregivers.

"It is only some very light sedation, madam, I assure you," one of the men, the leader, informed her, struggling to be as respectful as possible while still honoring the spirit of his mission. "Here, he will wake with some gentle nudging, let me show you —"

"No! I will see for myself," she demanded, furious at the thought of her child being harmed or mistreated. She nudged him slightly with a bottle that had already been prepared for him, and the little boy groaned slightly, opened his eyes, and opened his mouth to receive his dinner.

"See? It is as I said."

Kayla nodded. After looking her son over carefully—his crib and his environment—she nodded approvingly before turning to her captor. He was a big man, at least six feet in height and close to three-hundred pounds in weight, most of which was solid muscle. He had long black hair, which he wore much like an old Japanese samurai topknot, and wore a fur vest.

"My name is Kayla Washington; I would like to thank you for taking such good care of my son while he he's been with you. I'm certain neither of the other two men, the man who ordered him taken, or the one who delivered him to you, would ever have cared for him so well."

"I am Abraham Mustafa. I ordered my men to give your son the very best of care, madam, to treat him as if he were their own son. In truth, the Creed may be mercenaries, but we live by the strictest of codes. Beyond that, however, each man here has the greatest respect for what you and your husband have done for the cause of freedom and justice, and the reunification of this once great country."

"Forgive me for saying so, but you have a strange way of showing it."

"I know; these are…strange times."

"Well, thank you anyway for your support."

"Yes, thank you," Daniel added, shaking his hand as he did so, despite the fate that awaited him very soon. "Your people will see to it that Romano keeps his word and pulls back from our base?"

"Of course, and he will do so immediately."

"But how can you possibly know that, Abraham?" Kayla asked.

"Because my people will kill him on the spot if he does not."

"And Leader Peloski in the Blue Zone; what of *his* men?" Daniel asked.

"The same. We have men with Peloski, and our brothers

there are in communication with our brothers at the NORAD base; they will know what is happening and will kill Peloski in a heartbeat if treachery is found. Do not fear, we've done this many times before, with men much more powerful, and clever, than these two clumsy politicians and would-be tyrants."

Kayla sat in a chair nursing Sebastian, but she still had questions. "You and those here with you will be the ones to escort us to Romano and Peloski?"

"Yes, ma'am."

"When?"

"Tomorrow."

Daniel turned to the big man who was their leader. "Abraham, have you ever thought about fighting for anything bigger than the Creed?"

"Oh, I'd really like to help, sir, believe me I would, but I can't! Even if I set you and your son free, my brothers would kill me and elect a new leader on the spot, if that is what it takes to honor the creed; it is our way."

"I understand, and forgive me, I never meant to suggest that you should break your vows, Abraham. I was merely thinking that once we're gone, which I expect will be very soon, the revolution will *need* men like you...like *all of you*," he added, gesturing to the rest of the Creed men in the room as well, "to help lead the way to freedom. I ask only that you consider this. Would it be considered dishonorable for you to leave the Creed for such a cause?"

"No, I can't see why it would be —"

"Then will you consider it?"

Abraham looked down at the ground for a long time, until finally, he raised his head and looked around the room at the rest of the men in the room; to a man each of them gave him a nod. "It seems we are of one accord, General Washington. Once we have fulfilled the terms of this contract, we *will* seek out the resistance and we *will* join in the revolution. I cannot say how many brothers and sisters will join us, but my voice carries some weight within our membership; most of them are honorable men and women, so it may well be that many will join us."

"That is good news, Abraham, wonderful news. Thank you!"

Abraham came closer to him and sat close to him, studying him as carefully as he could, with no thought or concern for social boundaries or personal space. After this went on for some time, he sat back and continued his conversation with Daniel.

"What kind of man are you, Daniel Washington? You are here with your wife and son, on the eve of what will almost certainly be your last night of life on Earth, the day before what is certain to be excruciating torture and death at the hands of your enemies. Yet you show no fear, no regrets, nothing. Instead, all I hear from you is your concern for the revolution, for the future of this country, for a life for which, after tomorrow, you will have no part."

"Our people, Abraham…our people have suffered for *far* too long under tyranny, oppression, lies, and abuse. We *must* teach our children, and our children's children, the value of sacrifice, of character, of honor, respect, and integrity. These aren't just words, Abraham, *they are life*. Without them, we are nothing more than animals, doing only what we must to survive, and nothing more.

"There was a great American soldier and spy for the Continental Army during the first American Revolutionary War, whose name was Nathan Hale. He said something that Americans and people all over the world have never forgotten over the centuries. Just before he was executed, he uttered these very famous words…. 'I only regret that I have but one life to lose for my country' I must confess that at this moment, I feel much the same way."

Abraham shook his head. "You truly are an extraordinary man, General…truly." Abraham sat in silence for several minutes, pondering what he had heard, before continuing. "Your wife is *also* quite extraordinary, General!" Abraham now turned to Kayla and continued speaking. "You seem to care for nothing except your son, and for the words used by your husband, which leads me to believe that you agree completely with everything he says, and that you are of one heart and one mind on this."

"I assure you we are, Abraham Mustafa, my friend. I suppose it is a bit strange, yet perhaps it is not."

"What do you mean, Commander?"

"My husband and I both have come to embrace the Old God, the God of the Christians, the one worshiped by the whole world before being banned by both zones a lifetime ago."

"Ah, yes. I too have heard my parents and grandparents speak of Him, when I was still very small, before they were butchered before me as a child."

"I'm very sorry.

"It was long ago.... So then, you're saying it was this God that brought the two of you together?"

"Who else? The leader of the Blue Zone resistance and the Red Zone resistance, at the pivotal moment in history when the people were finally ready to revolt, risking their lives to topple their cruel oppressors? Did Daniel tell you about the prophecy?"

"What prophecy?" Simon had been listening while seated by himself in the corner, stunned and afraid by the friendly and extremely warm reception Daniel and Kayla had received at the hands of the Creed brothers.

"Shut up, worm!" bellowed Abraham, "or I will slit your throat and feed you to the dogs outside. Your words have no place here." Simon never said another word, but wisely kept quiet until he left some time later that evening. Abraham turned back to Kayla, while looking to Daniel. "Please continue; what prophecy?"

"My husband had a vision some time ago that he was being given a choice. He would have to decide to either walk away from the resistance, or to lead the revolution to victory. If he chose to walk away from the revolution, then the revolution would end in failure and a monstrous dictator would arise in the Red Zone, who would end up killing tens of millions of people.

"If, on the other hand, he chose to lead the revolution and engage in active resistance against the leadership of the zones, then he and I would die at the hands of our enemies, never having the opportunity to see our newborn son grow into a man. But the revolution would succeed and the New United States would flourish."

By this point nearly all the Creed brothers stood transfixed, mesmerized by the recounting of Daniel's prophecy and what it meant.

"And it has been unfolding just as he saw it in the dream?" Abraham asked, directing the question to Daniel, who simply nodded in affirmation. Then, shaking his head in amazement, Abraham simply added, "Wow."

Kayla looked at Daniel for a moment before turning back to her friendly captor. "Abraham, if I asked you to deliver a message to someone high up in the Blue Zone government, do you think you could arrange it; quietly?"

"I believe so, Commander. Who did you have in mind?"

***

"I will miss you, Sergeant Kelly," Kayla told the grizzled old soldier, while Abraham and some of the other Creed brothers kept Simon occupied in another room.

"As will I," Daniel added. "Never has there been anyone with whom I felt safer leaving my wife than with you, Sergeant Kelly, and for that I will be *eternally* grateful."

Tears started streaming down the man's face, a torrent he could no longer hold back. "Some protector I've been to her. Look where she is, and what will happen tomorrow! I swore an oath to *die* to protect her!" he announced, shaking his head, frustrated, sad, and angry all at the same time.

Kayla stepped close and placed one hand on each of the man's shoulders, looking him directly in the eyes. "Now listen to me, Sergeant Leonard J. Kelly. You've done a magnificent job protecting us. What is happening now must happen—it is meant to happen—and as a result, the entire country will once more know peace and freedom, and an end to tyranny. Many, many lives will be saved through our deaths, Leonard. If we can accomplish so much by our deaths, shouldn't we let it happen, in order that so many others, including our son, and *your* son, and your grandson, may enjoy the sweet taste of democracy?

"If you are so inclined, you can help Christian look after our son after we're gone, at least until after the revolution is over, and we'd be mightily grateful to you for doing so. But once the revolution is over and the country has been reunited, please, search for and find your son and grandson, for you too deserve to enjoy your own taste of freedom before your own days of walking this earth have ended."

Kelly hung his head low for some time before shaking his head and raising his eyes to meet hers. Then suddenly, as if due to an afterthought, he turned to Daniel. "Please sir, forgive me if what I'm about to say crosses any line, sir; I promise I mean no offense."

Daniel smiled. "I'm sure you won't, Sergeant, and I'm sure I will take none."

Kelly nodded before turning back to Kayla. "Ma'am, you are every bit as wise and intelligent as you are beautiful. The general here was a fortunate man indeed to have had the privilege to have known you as well as he did, if only for a brief time."

"Oh, I believe he knows that, Sergeant. To be completely forthcoming, however, I believe it was *I* who was the fortunate one, to have *him* as my husband."

Kayla turned to Daniel; the two embraced, kissed passionately for some time, then embraced again while Kelly turned away, too embarrassed to watch.

"Come here, Sergeant," Kayla asked afterwards, prompting Kelly to turn, face her, and then walk over to her. She embraced him before kissing him on the forehead. "Now go, Sergeant, and thank you for being my faithful protector."

"I...I...you're welcome, ma'am."

Kelly turned and then, having locked eyes with Daniel, with a determined but saddened expression he shook Daniel's hand with great respect. After retrieving baby Sebastian and enough infant supplies to get them to the alpha site, Kelly walked to the door. When the Creed brothers saw the signal, their demeanor changed toward Simon, and they told him to get out before they made good on their earlier threat.

A befuddled Simon left first, followed by Kelly, who stepped out, turned, and took one last look, knowing that it would be the last time he would ever see Kayla or Daniel alive.

***

"Man, I am so glad to get out of there; those Creed brothers are *completely* insane. I can't believe I agreed to use them as intermediaries."

Simon was nervous. Kelly had noticed he talked considerably more, and faster, when he was particularly nervous, or agitated. He glanced back into the back seat and found Sebastian still fast asleep and content from being fed well earlier when Kayla had taken care of it. He suspected she may have had Abraham add a little sedative for the trip back as well; he hoped he was right about that.

"Okay, Sergeant, since you're taking the kid back there's really no need for me to go back to the alpha site. Why don't you just drop me off at that little hotel we passed a few miles from here? I'll arrange transportation out of here until the rest of this thing blows over."

Kelly grinned ever so slightly and nodded. He drove on for another few miles, but slowed down when he came across a large patch of woods.

"I need to stop," he said quietly, as if not particularly caring whether Simon heard or not.

"What? Why?"

"Nature calls."

"Oh. There will be a bathroom at the hotel."

"Can't wait," Kelly answered, pulling the vehicle over near a small path into the woods. "Drank too much."

"Ah, crap; now that you mention it, I need to go too."

Simon watched as Kelly walked down the path about ten yards into the woods and turned to face a random bush. Simon soon joined him, turned to face the opposite direction, and soon nature was flowing. He'd nearly finished his business when he suddenly felt a slight burn on his neck, followed by something liquid spilling down his neck. He turned to tell Kelly about it, but jumped back when he found Kelly standing immediately behind him, holding an old-fashioned, military-style K-Bar knife in his hand, with some kind of liquid dropping from it. About that time several things happened all at once; the searing pain hit him, when he tried to speak all that came out was a gurgle, he realized that the liquid he'd felt was blood—his blood—and he realized he was going to die very, very soon.

"What exactly were you thinking, boy? That you'd kidnap that child, betray the general, the commander, and every other man, woman, and child who has fought, bled, and died in this revolution, and that everyone would then wish you good luck and send you on your way? There was ever only one way this was ever going to end, and you should have had the presence of mind to see it."

Kelly watched as Simon fell to the ground, clasping at his throat, trying to speak, to say something, but Kelly figured he already knew what he was trying to say.

"Listen boy, there's no one going to help you now; shoot, I don't reckon anyone could help you at this point anyway, even if they were so inclined. You've already lost too much blood. Look at it this way…you're getting a much more merciful death than what awaits those two, fine, noble people you sentenced to death tomorrow, so stop feeling sorry for yourself and die like a man. I—"

Kelly had more, a lot more he wanted to say to the man who was single-handedly responsible for causing so much pain and suffering, but it was too late; Simon lay on the ground, silent and still, now sleeping the eternal sleep of the dead.

CHAPTER 34

Daniel felt a sick feeling in the pit of his stomach. He'd done everything he could to prepare for this moment, yet now that it was upon him he felt terror. He knew he was certain to endure extreme suffering before the end came...Romano and Peloski would see to it. The resistance had inflicted heavy damages on their enemy; now it was the enemy's turn to make *them* pay for it.

"Are you ready?" asked Abraham.

"You've confirmed the Red Zone troops have completely left the area?"

"They're gone, sir."

"And the BZ troops?"

"They're already halfway back home, sir; I had men following them the entire way."

"What about the evacuation of the base?"

"Our men tell me everyone's left; it's nothing but a ghost town now, sir."

"Good...good! Okay then, let's go ahead and get this over with."

Daniel turned to Kayla as they climbed out of the vehicle, and in her eyes, he saw the same fear he was feeling. He embraced her and kissed her one last time, doing his best to offer her the comfort he knew she needed at that moment.

"Remember, Kayla, this is for our son, and for his family," he whispered in her ear. She looked at him and managed a weak smile, and he took her hand in his as they began walking up the stairs and into the courthouse, commandeered by the two tyrants for just this purpose.

Before reaching the courtroom, a guard managed to attract

Daniel's attention. The young man had short red hair, and quickly yet subtly lifted his sleeve long enough to reveal to Daniel an unusual tattoo on his left forearm...an American flag, Old Betsy. He then showed him one of the small, concealed holocams, causing Daniel to nod his head, smile ever so slightly, and let out a sigh of relief.

A curious thing happened to Daniel upon entering the courtroom, however, and seeing the pompous asses sitting smugly in their chairs at the large table. The fear he'd been holding onto suddenly vanished, and the terror he'd felt earlier simply fell away as if scales from his eyes. In their place came purpose, resolve, and determination. A casual glance over at Kayla suggested something similar had happened to her as well. Perhaps it was what they'd needed to strengthen their resolve...a strong jolt of reality, a reminder of what they'd been fighting for...a reminder that it was, indeed, worth dying for.

"Well, looky, looky who we have here," began Peloski, who was standing when they entered while Romano had remained seated. "If it isn't that meddlesome Ross brat. So, your terrorist, traitorous acts finally caught up with you, did they? Just like they did your treacherous father? *Good!* It's about time! I look forward to seeing your lifeless body swing from the gallows following a public execution!"

"Father? What are you talking about? What have you done to my father?"

"Oh, I guess you didn't know how he died; how sad. Your traitorous father was hung on the gallows in a public execution... isn't that great? Oh, but don't worry, dear, you'll be with him very soon."

"You killed him? *You* killed my father? But he worked for you; why would you do that, you *stupid animal?*"

"*Because he betrayed me,* that's why, child!" Peloski roared. "Because I execute everyone who betrays me, even treacherous, sniveling little snot-nosed brats like yourself, that's why."

"By the Living God, you're going to be dead, soon, Peloski; you just don't know it. And when you die, where would you suppose someone who has starved, murdered, mutilated, enslaved, and tortured as many people as you have would go, Peloski? To Heaven, where most of those poor, innocent people will probably be? Or hell, where so many others like yourself will be?"

"Sounds like you've gone native, Kayla Ross; too bad. I would much preferred to have broken that young firebrand I heard so much about."

Now it was Romano's turn. Peloski sat down as Romano stood, giving his full attention to Daniel.

"*Mr. Washington*, it looks like there will be no crossing of the Delaware for you," Romano scoffed. "No being the first President of the New United States of whatever, etc. etc. etc. I'm afraid there's not much of anything left in *your* future but pain, suffering, humiliation, and finally, of course, death."

Daniel started laughing. "I'm surprised you ever made it to the Red Council, Romano, much less leading it. I would have expected the Synod and NZC to have chosen someone so much brighter than you to lead the council!"

"What are you getting at, Washington?"

"Your lust for vengeance has blinded you."

"Blinded me; blinded me to what?" asked Romano, growing increasingly flustered.

"Blinded you to the fact that you've already *lost* this revolution," Daniel replied. "You just don't know it yet! Already the *people* realize that your grip is slipping, and, more importantly, they are also finally waking up to the truth."

"And what is this 'truth' you believe these fools are waking up to?"

"They are waking up to the fact that *they* are the true power, Romano, not you or your little trained monkey, Peloski, over there," Kayla replied, answering for Daniel.

"Trained monkey? Did she just say '*trained monkey*?'"

"Oh, right, sorry about that, Peloski. I should have left out 'trained' and just said 'monkey,'" she added, laughing as she did so.

269

"We'll see about that," Peloski replied. "I believe when you experience the suffering, misery, and truly tortuous activity we have planned for the both of you today, prior to your execution tomorrow, you will lose your penchant for insulting humor."

"Great; let's get on with it then! I mean, anything has to be better than listening to the two of you prattle on for an entire day!" quipped Daniel.

"Tell me, Mr. Washington, are you a student of history?"

"Only American history."

"Ah, of course. Me, I'm a student of international history as well, particularly specific aspects of it. Say, for example, various methods of torture used by various cultures around the world over the years. There were some truly despicable means of torture used by 'civilizations' throughout history to either extract information, punish criminals, or sometimes, to strike fear in the hearts of enemies of their subjects. Take, for example, Vlad Dracula, the prince of Wallachia, a small country in Eastern Europe in the fifteenth century. He was also known as Vlad the Impaler for his fondness for impaling human beings on long wooden spikes, on which they would gradually be pulled down toward the earth by gravity. It sometimes took three days for the impaled person to die. You probably won't know what I'm talking about here, but Bram Stoker based the vampire Count Dracula on the prince of the same name.

"Torture took many other forms throughout the centuries, of course. The Romans became rather adept at it, I must say, with crucifixion on wooden crosses and the Roman's brazen elephant, which a human being would be roasted alive inside, among the many they are credited with developing. There was one that became popular in the Middle Ages that involves being hung, then drawn, and then quartered, or pulled apart, by horses. Now that was just the Europeans. Given present company, I shan't even begin to describe how Chinese filled water pitchers with starving rats and forced naked men to sit—"

"No, by all means, Leader Romano, please do," Peloski chimed in, smiling broadly the entire time while staring coldly at Kayla.

"Whichever form of torture you choose for my wife and I, let's just get on with it, maggot!" Daniel yelled out, cursing at Romano. "Anything would be better than listening to one more second of you droning on!"

"Well now, we are much more civilized than that, of course, um...'General' is it? No, my men will see to it that you tell me everything I could ever possibly want to know about your band of merry little men out in 'Sherwood Forest.'"

"And what of Kayla?" Daniel asked grimly, looking up at Romano.

"I expect you realize that will depend largely on how *you* do. Should you cooperate, and should your woman here cooperate —"

"I'm his *wife*, you twit!"

"Of course you are, dear." Romano turned back to Daniel, ignoring Kayla for the most part. "Should you both cooperate, perhaps I can persuade my dear friend Leader Peloski to extend *some* kindness and mercy toward her, which is certainly far more than she deserves. Will you give me your word that you will give me strategic, tactical, and operational details about the resistance? I want plans, targets, names of key resistance leaders, how your leadership and strike teams are organized, locations of all resistance bases, and that's just for starters. Will you surrender that to me?"

"Daniel, no! You can't do it, please don't...not for me!"

"I have to, Kayla," Daniel whispered in her ear. "We've talked about it, planned for it, remember? It will be okay, I promise!"

"I know, baby...I understand," she whispered back, assuring him it was an act on her part. Daniel nodded once he understood.

"So you trust me, right? They were going to find out everything either way. We might as well tell them what they need to know." This time Kayla nodded.

"Good. Now that we have that sorted, Leader Peloski and I need to get some rest. The entertainment begins later tonight, and we are told it will likely go late, very late into the night and right through until morning!" He laughed and snickered at the sick and disturbed joke that he'd found so funny, together with Peloski, whose piggish manners caused him to give no thought to spraying the two of them with freshly swallowed wine.

"Oh, you're a bad man, Leader Romano; you're a man after my own heart," he added with a big smile.

"Now then, let's get started, shall we? We have a busy day tomorrow!" Romano said to Peloski, his arm wrapped around the older man in friendship. The two tyrants, once longtime enemies, now walked out of the room together as if lifelong friends. Revolutions, like politics, sometimes made strange bedfellows.

CHAPTER 35

Based on the grogginess and the short-term memory loss, Daniel concluded they'd been drugged; Romano must have ordered something to be put in the food or the water they gave them. The last thing he could remember was suddenly feeling extraordinarily tired, so tired in fact that he'd laid down on his bed to rest for just a moment before falling asleep.

He lifted his head, which required significant effort, enough that he could see he was lying on a bed, similar to what he'd seen in medical facilities. There was some sort of monitor at the head of the bed that displayed a representation of his body, as well as vital statistics like heart rate and oxygen levels.

He had no recollection whatsoever of how he'd gotten there or when, but whoever brought them there had also removed his shirt and left him dressed only in shorts. With some considerable effort he could raise his head just enough to see Kayla sleeping on a similar bed to his right, stripped down to *her* underclothes as well.

"Ah, good evening, General Washington." He turned and found a tall, bald man wearing glasses and a lab coat, fiddling with some equipment. Beside him, sitting in a chair, was a beautiful yet stern-looking woman in her thirties, who had the look of someone who'd long-since accepted her fate as a cog in the system with little to no control over what was happening around or to her. "As you can see, we've had you and Miss Washington brought here together, so that I can 'help you' to remember the details Leader Romano is looking for. Miss Lana here will be doing the interrogation, recording everything you say and taking notes, and...well, I don't want to have to repeat everything, so let's check on Mrs. Washington, shall we?"

"Don't touch her, I'm warning you…!"

"Oh, don't worry, Mr. Washington, I won't have to touch her…well, not very much. I don't particularly enjoy this aspect of the work I do, though I must confess that I do find aspects of it fascinating. As a scientist, that is."

"Really? Then why don't we trade places; it might be *more* fascinating if you experience it firsthand. I'd bet you'd learn more."

"Oh yes, I expect you're quite right. It's the significantly lowered life expectancy I'd find challenging, I'm afraid."

The man walked over to Kayla, injected her with a nanospray, and seconds later she opened her eyes.

"Ah, Mrs. Washington, so glad you could join us. I'm afraid I'll have to dispense with the formalities, seeing how we're on such a tight schedule."

"When is the execution scheduled for?" David asked bluntly.

"Straight to the point, Mr. Washington, very good; I respect that in a man. So here is what will happen. It is almost 10:00 PM now. We will spend the next ten hours or so in here, in this room in this facility. Leader Romano has directed me to follow a very specific schedule, similar, yet slightly different, for each of you. For you, Daniel…may I call you Daniel?"

"No, only friends or family call me Daniel. Call me General Washington or Mr. Washington."

"Very well, Daniel," the man said with a smirk, causing Daniel to bristle. "My name is Dr. Theodore Seal, and I will oversee your interrogation this evening. I assure you I will strive to make this as painless as possible, but given the parameters I have been given, I regret that you will still suffer unimaginable pain."

"Then don't do it, Dr. Seal; we all have a choice," said Kayla, trying to see if she could reach the man inside the scientist.

"No, Mrs. Washington, I'm afraid we don't, at least not anymore. Even if Leader Romano hadn't informed me that it would either be the two of you or my wife and children who suffered tonight, I'm afraid I made my decision to serve the Red Council long ago.

"Now then, I primarily have two tools I use to move through this process. The first is what I affectionately refer to as the 'Thunderer.'" Seal held up a device that had a large suction-cup-like device on one end, and a long cord coming out of the other end. He then set that down and picked up another, which resembled the nanospray injector he'd used to awaken Kayla, except it too had a long tube coming out of the end and was attached to a tank behind him. "The second I call 'The Little Doctor.'

"Now the Thunderer emits focused, very short-range, but high-intensity sound waves to inflict considerable damage to the recipient's body. It ruptures organs, severs veins and arteries, and even fractures bones, all in thirty-seconds of application. I'll be monitoring your vitals of course, and we will stop application of the Thunderer sooner if necessary. I'm afraid Leader Romano will kill me if you die before the execution tomorrow."

"Well, we can't have that now, can we, Seal?" Daniel quipped.

Seal ignored him and continued. "The Little Doctor, on the other hand, does just the opposite; it dispenses thousands of self-replicating medical nanites — state-of-the-art, I might add — which immediately set about repairing all damaged tissues. I'll inject these at the damaged site fifteen minutes after the initial application of the Thunderer...following the interrogation, of course. It usually takes approximately thirty minutes for the nanites to complete the repairs and restore tissue and bone back to normal. That gives you both about fifteen minutes for your bodies to rest before we start all over again with another round.

"Now comes the bad news. Per Leader Romano's instructions, I'm to instruct the nanites to perform only a ninety-eight percent repair the first round, and I'm to decrease the percentage by two-percent each time, which means by the last round —"

"His body will only be eighty-percent repaired from the injuries caused by the repeated exposures to this 'Thunderer' of yours."

"That sounds about right. Leader Romano wanted the nanites

to leave off repairing at only fifty-percent repair, but as I told the Leader, there was no way I could even remotely guarantee that Daniel would be alive to attend his own execution. In fact, there was a strong case to be made that he would not make it more than halfway through the night. In the end, Leader Romano agreed with me.

"The good news, however, is that I'm allowed to half everything for you, Mrs. Washington, including reducing the application time from thirty seconds to fifteen seconds, and instead of two-percent reductions there will only be one-percent reductions. It may not sound like much, but believe me, it will make a *big* difference to you later."

Daniel hadn't been saying much but he'd been looking around, especially at one of the guards in particular, the one closest to them no more than ten yards away. The one who once again inconspicuously raised his sleeve just enough that Daniel was able to glimpse the flag tattoo, and then take notice when the "guard" subtly gestured toward the hidden camera once more, which had been pointed toward the good Dr. Seal the entire time he'd been describing the impending torture session. Daniel couldn't contain the ironic smile that even in his death, he would be taking a final stab at the Red Council.

"What about after that, Dr. Seal? What happens when you deliver my battered and bloodied body to Romano?"

"Ah, yes, you're asking about your execution since I never answered your earlier question; I apologize about that. Yes, well, once we're done here, I'm to have you taken to the local stadium, where some rather large gallows have been built."

"A hanging; they're going to hang us in public?"

"Um, yes, apparently so," the doctor answered, sounding somewhat ashamed as he finished checking his equipment.

"Awesome! That's fantastic! He has no idea what's happening out there, does he?"

"Do you think it will be enough, Daniel?"

"I do, Kayla, I do. It's the prophecy…it's unfolding just the way it was shown to me. We can both take comfort that Sebastian's going to grow up in a much better place, sweetheart."

"Prophecy?" the doctor asked as he picked up the Thunderer and made his way to Daniel's bedside.

"It's nothing, Doc; let's get this over with."

"Okay, remember now, I'm going to hold this against you for thirty seconds, followed by the fifteen minutes of interrogation by Lana. Then I'll administer Little Doc and you'll start feeling better almost immediately; understand?" Daniel nodded. "Good. Now then, I can place this bite-stick in your mouth if you'd like while I apply the Thunderer—"

"No!" Daniel exclaimed. "That won't be necessary, thank you."

After staring at him a bit quizzically, Seal just shrugged and said, "Okay then, let's get started."

As Seal placed the Thunderer on his abdomen, Daniel cast another glance over at the guard, who, as if reading his mind, gently nodded his head toward Daniel as if to say that everything was okay, he was recording every bit of it to show the world later.

Daniel felt the waves immediately, but it took five seconds for the pain to hit, but hit it did, and hard. Suddenly it felt as if someone were kicking him in the gut as hard as they could; soon after it felt as if his insides were about to explode. The pain suddenly eased slightly, and he became aware of someone screaming beside him. Thinking it was Kayla he turned to her, but the look on her face and the slow recognition of his own voice caused him to realize the screams he'd heard were his own.

The intensity of the pain was beyond anything he'd ever felt. Alarmed by the expression he'd seen on Kayla's face he stopped screaming, determined to not cause her any more suffering than she was already bound to endure. That was when "Miss Lana" appeared with her datapad in hand.

"Mr. Washington, I need you to focus now. Leader Romano told me that if you both cooperated I would be authorized to order Dr. Seal to terminate the sessions tonight, which would at least give the two of you one last night together. Do you understand me, Mr. Washington?"

"I...hear you...how can I.... Aaarrrggghhh." Daniel took a deep breath. "...trust you?"

"What choice do you have, Mr. Washington? Now I'm going to ask you some questions, okay?" Daniel nodded as best as he could.

"Who is in charge of this resistance against the Red Council?"

"I...aarrgghh...I can't...too much...pain...."

"Doctor?"

"But it's only been five minutes."

"Do it; on my authorization."

Seal nodded, grabbed Little Doc, and then injected Daniel. "Like I said earlier, you should begin to feel better almost immediately.

Daniel nodded.

"Mr. Washington?" Miss Lana was persistent.

"I am...uuhhh...I...I'm in charge of the resistance."

"Are you leader of the resistance in the Red Zone, the Blue Zone, or both zones?"

"Both."

"So you are the leader of a combined resistance?"

"I...yes...I am."

"Your base was at the old NORAD center in what used to be Colorado Springs, Colorado?"

"Yes."

"Have they abandoned the base?"

"Yes."

"And where have they gone?"

"I don't know."

"Mr. Washington; where have they gone?"

"I told you, I don't know. I told them to find another base of operations...I told them not to tell me where."

"You knew we would torture you for information."

"Yes."

"Still you surrendered."

"They had my son."

"I see."

"Who is in charge of the resistance now that you're gone? Your wife was second-in-command, correct?"

"Yes."

"So, who's in charge now?"

"It won't matter. None of this will matter, don't you see? Anything I tell you, none of it will matter. He can't see it, he *won't see it.*"

"Who won't see what?"

"Romano; he won't see that it's all over. The people are going to topple the governments of both tyrants, and the New United States of America will rise in their place, a land of political, religious, and economic freedom; a land where every man, woman, and child will be able to be whatever he or she wants to be."

"Wait; you're serious about this?" she asked, stunned by what he was saying.

"What did you think the resistance was all about? You should have seen how quickly men, women, and children flocked to us. Military units, even generals and senior commanders, came to us in droves, often along with their men, and their weapons. We launched an attack in the capital and had seized control of the Synod repository and the NZC records vaults. We could have had them both where we wanted them had it not been for a betrayal by a leader in the resistance, and a man who had been a dear friend of mine."

Lana turned back to Seal. "Did you know about this?"

"I'm just following orders, ma'am. I don't know anything except what I'm told."

"So, you're saying that we're on the verge of an actual, full-blown revolution here? We've heard nothing of it here."

"I am. In fact, we're winning. My death will only hasten our victory, not delay it or stop it. You sound like you could be sympathetic to the cause."

"I...I don't know. The reunification of the United States. Such a thing has never been discussed, not in my lifetime. Just the thought...oh my, what a wonderful notion! I—"

Suddenly the door burst open and a number of soldiers poured in, followed by Leader Romano.

"I'm very disappointed, Lana. You've always been one of my most dependable and effective interrogators. What is it about these two that everyone finds so appealing? They are infectious, like a plague or a cancer; I guess that makes *me* the cure." Romano turned towards the soldier in charge. "Seize her and see to it that she's locked up. Also, have another interrogator sent down here A.S.A.P."

"Yes, sir."

"General Daniel Washington. Just one more night and I'll be rid of you at last; how sweet it will be! We can get on with business as usual, and life will go on as it has for nearly a century."

"It won't; you'll see."

"Yes, yes, so you keep saying, 'General' Washington. Let's see how things look tomorrow afternoon, shall we? Oh, wait, you won't be here then, will you? You won't be here, because you'll be dead!" Romano turned back towards the doctor. "Okay, Dr. Seal, let's get back to it, shall we? I'm afraid our little 'event' with Lana has thrown us off schedule by a few minutes. Now then, I believe Kayla Washington was next, wasn't she?"

"No, don't!" Daniel began, but it was too late, for Kayla had already begun to scream.

CHAPTER 36

The butt of the weapon struck my friend on the side of his head, producing a cracking sound that I could easily hear over the crowd. The blow barely missed his temple, a blow that would likely have killed him had it not missed its mark. I would have considered it a mercy, given what he'd already been through, and what lay ahead of him. Undoubtedly the soldier who'd struck him would have been executed on the spot had the reckless blow prematurely killed the man who had been like a brother to me, the leader of the revolution, and my best friend's husband.

From where I stood watching from across the crowded stadium, I could catch glimpses of his face as he made his way toward the platform, surrounded by soldiers from both camps. The pronounced limp and the repeated tumbles to the pavement, along with the swollen eyes and blood flowing from his nose and mouth, made it evident that he'd been severely beaten and tortured, his captors determined to glean all the information they could about the number of remaining resistance fighters, troop movements, and planned attacks, prior to his very public execution.

Eventually my friend cleared the crowd and entered the area surrounding the platform where the security and police forces were, and I was offered a much better view of his face. I sighed heavily, relaxed, and took in a deep breath upon catching a glimpse of the now all too familiar look of pure determination, and even a slight grin, on his bloodied, tortured face. I shook my head in amazement, wondering how he was able to keep his composure after the way he'd been treated. I supposed he knew they would have eventually extracted everything they wanted to know, given enough time and torture, but there was a sense of urgency for the Red Council to bring an abrupt end to the revolution, and their inability to break him had given him some measure of victory over his enemies, however slight the victory may have been. At last I had come to understand something that had puzzled me since he'd been chosen to lead the resistance; why Daniel? Watching my friend sneer at his enemies to his left as he approached the steps to the platform, it was clear that it was his strength, his raw courage, and faith that had brought them so far, nearly to the point of toppling not just one government, but two. Daniel truly was a man of great strength and courage.

***

A sharp stab in his left kidney forced him to lurch forward and to climb up a short series of steps. He looked up at what lay ahead at the top of the stairs, and what he saw, ironically enough, was once again gallows, and a hangman's noose dangling from the end of a rope. This time, however, it was empty, and it was waiting for him. Another jab in the same kidney. *If I wasn't about to die, I might be worried about losing that kidney.* The thought hadn't occurred to him without a sense of irony. He stepped forward and the noose was placed around his neck and tightened, before the guard behind him, the one who'd so enjoyed sticking him in the kidney, took one last parting shot, again in the same kidney. This time the pain was so intense he was unable to find any humor in it, no matter how morbid.

"Okay, you…get up there and join lover boy," he heard a voice say from behind and below him. A cold chill sent shockwaves throughout his body to the very core of his being.

"Oh no, not—"

"Hi, lover boy. Did you miss me?"

"Kayla! No, not you too! I'd hoped…maybe somehow—"

"Come on now, would you really have it any other way, darling? At least our boy is safe. God willing, they'll never get him because soon after we're gone, the prophecy will be fulfilled and this will all be over. Remember, my love, you've always been my one and only love; you, and only you. I die today for my people, but my heart is, and always has been, *yours.*"

His heart sunk as he watched them lower a noose around Kayla's neck. There had been no hangings that he could recall ever seeing or even hearing about. But he had read some stories about hangings in the old American west, and he knew how ghastly they could be, especially when they failed to snap the vertebrae, leaving the person struggling on the end of the rope, choking to death for five minutes or more before finally dying. While he didn't *want* to die that way, he knew for a certainty that he didn't want his beloved to die that way. He looked over at her and his heart filled with love.

"I love you, Kayla…you own my heart. My *only* regret in this life is that I didn't have more time to spend with you, *and* our son."

"And I love you my sweet, and I'm so glad we met. I—"

That's when they noticed it. What had begun as a low hum had steadily grown increasingly louder and louder amongst the buzz of the mass of humanity within the large stadium. The chant, "Long live Daniel Washington. Long live Kayla Washington. Long live the revolution, and long live America! Long live Daniel Washington. Long live Kayla Washington. Long live the revolution, and long live America!" With each pass the chant grew louder and louder, as more and more people seemed to join in, daring to challenge the Red Council, Peloski, and Romano.

Romano and Peloski, each sitting high above the events in their comfortable seats in a cordoned off area near what had once been the fifty-yard line, suddenly became fidgety, motioning to their personal guards to come closer, and to the surrounding soldiers to form a perimeter around them as the crowd seemed to be growing increasingly hostile. Romano then issued the order to the soldier in charge to proceed with the execution.

On the gallows Daniel suddenly heard a sound, a zipping sound like the sound of bullet whizzing through the air, yet different, and suddenly he felt a new sensation, a gentle pain like a pin prick. He looked down to find a dart sticking in his chest. He glanced over at Kayla and found the same thing. He looked up for the first time and, fighting through the pain, looked out into the throng of people who filled the stadium. His heart filled with joy as he suddenly recognized a number of brothers from the resistance. He nearly laughed when he saw big Abraham near the front of the crowd, clearly unafraid to make himself known; the big man smiled when Daniel's eyes met his.

Then he saw Christian, not far from Abraham, wearing a most somber expression. Daniel was beginning to feel the effects of the dart now, which was doing its job and would soon render them both unconscious, sparing them the final suffering Romano and Peloski had so desperately wanted them to experience. He looked back at Christian, taking a moment to convey his displeasure at his being there. As the new leader of the revolution Christian had risked far too much by coming there, yet Daniel was unable to hold his look of displeasure for long, and his face broke out in a warm smile at seeing his friend one last time.

"Kayla, did you see...?" Daniel looked over at his beloved, but she was already unconscious. He was soon glad, because no sooner had he seen she was under than he suddenly heard the order go out.

"Executioner, prepare to execute the criminals, Daniel Washington and Kayla Ross, both charged for—"

Daniel never heard the rest, for at that moment, everything went black.

***

The exact events that transpired over the two weeks that followed the deaths of General Daniel Washington and Commander Kayla Washington, leaders of the Great Second American Revolution, will forever be lost to history.

Triggered by the deaths of their beloved heroes, something within the people inside the stadium snapped, causing them to go berserk as one. Early reports circulated that the delegation from the Blue Zone was the first to riot, and that the Red Zone delegation joined in immediately afterwards, spreading a rage and fury that swept through the stadium like a forest fire. The angry crowd quickly overwhelmed the security forces within the stadium, including the men protecting Romano and Peloski. By the time backup security forces got there in sufficient numbers to disperse the crowd, they found the dead bodies of Romano and Peloski, each swinging from the very same ropes from which Daniel and Kayla had hung earlier. The bodies of the former revolution leaders, however, were nowhere to be found, having been spirited away by members of the revolution long before reinforcements had arrived.

The holorecordings of the sadistic torture sessions all served to add considerable fuel to the public's outrage and fire to the revolution; the constant screams of agony from the husband and the wife, the gruesome sound of bones snapping and crunching each time under the onslaught of the merciless Thunderer, the touching moments with the couple on the gallows just moments before the execution, and the sound of their necks snapping in the hangman's noose. With little or no strong leadership capable or willing to stand up to the rage of the public, all remaining resistance from governments within both zones quickly crumbled. Two weeks after the public execution and subsequent public rampage at the stadium, the leaders of the revolution, led by Christian Jefferson, were firmly in charge of the entire country. The revolution was over…they'd won. Both tyrants had fallen, and a new day had dawned.

Winning a revolution and rebuilding a nation, however, were two very different things, but it was something for which Daniel Washington, fortunately, had prepared.

CHAPTER 37

"You look fine," Vanessa told me as she came over to where I stood in front of the mirror. "Just try to relax a little, will you? It's over, Chris! Everything you worked for, everything *they* worked for, everything we all worked for, it's over; we won! Romano is dead. Peloski is dead. As if that wasn't enough, Secretary Adams has accepted your offer to help transition the BZ over to the government of the New United States of America."

"You know, I heard that Henry was behind the riot in the stadium that started the uprising," I told Vanessa.

"Really? Why would he do that?" she asked me, puzzled as to why Peloski's right-hand man would have aided the resistance.

"Secretary Adams was a longtime friend of Kayla's father," I told Vanessa. "Adams never cared much for Peloski, but he's always liked Kayla, and he had great respect for the cause. He just never was completely comfortable with the idea of *joining* the resistance, so he would often help when and wherever he could.

"Anyway, Abraham, one of the fighters who came over from The Creed, told me that Kayla asked him to contact Secretary Adams the day before she died to give him a message."

"What message?" asked Vanessa.

"She asked Abraham to go tell Adams what was happening, to ask him to come to see her off," I told her, fighting off the overwhelming sadness I still felt over the loss of my two dear friends. "She also requested that he bring as many of his 'friends' as possible, so they could all make plenty of noise once she was gone."

"Well, I guess it worked!"

"Hmmph. Yeah, I guess it did," I laughed, realizing how

even in her death, Kayla had struck the final blow that had ended the Gentry, Peloski, Romano, and won the revolution.

"See? You've got good news pouring in every day! Now all you have to do is just go out there and let everyone know that law and order will be maintained, and that *you* will be acting president in accordance with the wishes of Daniel and Kayla Washington. You'll then let everyone know that a formal election will be held within six months to elect a new congress and a new president, and that the Revolutionary Leadership team will be assisting you as needed. You know, honey, everyone will be standing with you, including General Hawkins, Marcel, myself, and all the others. We'll get through this just fine, okay?"

I stopped fussing over my appearance and took her in my arms. "Vanessa, let's get married tomorrow. We'll get the pastor, invite the others, and make it official; what do you say? Oops, wait a second...." Having come to my senses, I stooped down to one knee, took her hand in mine—since I didn't have a ring—and asked her, "Vanessa Susan Brooks, my soulmate, my one and only, will you marry me?"

"Ooohhh...Chris! Yes! Yes, I will...I'll marry you. I love you so much!" She leaned down and kissed me with such force she knocked me down and we both fell onto the floor. We were soon interrupted when General Hawkins stepped in.

"Um, excuse me, sir. I'm told it's time, Mr. President."

"You know, General Hawkins, I don't think I'll ever get used to that."

"You've been appointed, sir, elected by a small group, if you will, to the office until the rest of the country has a chance to make it official, which I'm sure they will."

"Thank you for your vote of confidence, General Hawkins. It's just so hard for me to believe we made it here."

"I know, sir; me too." General Hawkins smiled. I believe that was only the second time I'd ever seen him smile.

I then turned back to Vanessa and said, "Okay sweetie, we'll pick this up later, okay?"

"Okay!"

I then turned and took one more look in the mirror before proceeding toward the Press Room. Less than five minutes later I stood before a plethora of holocams representing various news organizations from all over the world. My message would affect them all, but it was directed toward the New American people.

"My fellow *Americans*; good evening."

I paused, allowing the roar of applause I knew would come from within the building to make its way through, and I made no efforts to rush them. The moment had been waiting for well over a hundred years to come, so it deserved its moment in the sun. Eventually, it did wane and quiet back down.

"Just over one month ago, two incredible, amazing patriots named Daniel and Kayla Washington, who also happened to be two wonderful, caring, and loving human beings and my best friends, were brutally executed by the former leaders of the Blue and Red Zones, in an attempt to stop the Second American Revolution and its stated goal to Reunite America. The massive and powerful riots and uprising that followed as a result of said execution, however, served only to add fuel to the massive fire of unrest and revolt that was already sweeping the country.

"This began a period of tremendous social upheaval and anarchy, with the masses of humanity in our country rising up and overthrowing the tyrannical governments of the Red and Blue Zones...governments that had oppressed them, brutalized them, and enslaved them for nearly a century. The people had been robbed of nearly everything promised to them by the people who had founded this great country, the United States of America, nearly four-hundred-years ago.

"One day, just over two years ago, the vile wrongs against one man's family, which led to the deaths of some and slavery for others in the Red Zone, and the selfish unjust death of a sweet little seven-year-old girl named Sam in the Blue Zone, united to touch off a spark of revolution that would reunite a country that had long-since forgotten who and what it really was. That spark soon turned into a raging fire that spread throughout the entire country from coast to coast, inspiring young and old alike to rise up and join the cause. I joined the Blue Zone Militiamen when my best friend since childhood, Kayla Ross, decided she could no longer live with the suffering and misery she saw all around her and decided to act.

"When I first met Daniel Washington, I had my doubts about him. He seemed somewhat brash and short-tempered to me; after all, he'd been raised quite differently than I had, and we were quite different in many respects. But when I saw how Kayla fell so deeply in love with him, very nearly from the day they first met, and once I had the opportunity to get to really get to know Daniel, I discovered for myself what a truly sincere, wonderful, courageous, and selfless man he truly was, and I learned how much and how deeply he cared for this country, and for her people. It was *his* vision, Daniel's vision, which brought us where we are today. So Daniel…and my precious Kay…this is for you." I had to stop for a moment, as a single tear streamed down my face. It took a few moments until I was able to get myself back under control.

"I want every one of you out there watching or listening throughout this great country, throughout the New United States of America, in what was once known as the People's Liberal Socialist Democratic State in the Blue Zone, and what was once known as the Free Market Republic of Conservatism in the Red Zone, to know that you can rest easy in knowing that your country is safe and that order has been restored. Even before General and Commander Washington were *murdered*, much of the military from both zones had already come over to us, and they have already been dispatched to help keep the peace during this critical time.

"You should also know that the Revolutionary Council has elected me as interim president in accordance with General Washington's wishes. Let me assure you, however, that we will be working as quickly as possible to set up special elections for a new, *elected* president, as well as a new American Congress, a judicial system, and state and city governments all across the country. It is my solemn promise to you here and now that these elections will begin no later than six months from today. It will take no small amount of effort to accomplish, and I promise you it will be far from a shining example of what will be to come, but I intend for us to start this fledgling democracy off on the right foot, and if that means my term ends six months from now, then so be it. You know, though, that's perfectly fine with me, and I'll tell you why. Because even if I'm replaced as your president six months from now, I'm still a winner; in fact, *we are all winners*, because this country is once again, for the first time in one hundred years, a democracy!

"In the meantime, we will be working to create and fill leadership positions all over the country, so we can start on rebuilding this great country immediately. I realize that many of you may not be familiar with the structure of government in the former United States, so we will also be working diligently on quickly developing educational material and getting it distributed to your local areas all over the country so you'll be ready when the elections roll around. Just know that democracies, as wonderful as they are, can be messy at times, so I'll ask for your patience as we transition during these challenging times. And I ask you to please, help spread the word about everything you've heard today to those who were unable to watch or listen.

"I have tasked Major General Hawkins with organizing a mobile military presence throughout the country as we work to establish and/or rebuild local, state, and federal governments. Rebuilding the government after a hundred years sounds like a like a monumental task, doesn't it? And it is. But I ask you to just stop for a moment, and consider how far we've *already* come! We've overthrown tyrants, we've abolished slavery, and oppression, and we now have the opportunity to embrace freedom, opportunity, and self-fulfillment. If we can do all of that, I believe we can do just about anything! There will be much, much more for us to discuss in the weeks and months to come.

"Once these special inaugural elections are over with six-months from today, elections will afterwards be held on a regular basis every two to six years depending on the office, giving you, the New American people, the ability to determine *who* will represent your will, because from now on, my friends, my brothers, and my sisters, *you are* the government, so govern wisely. If you don't like your leaders, get rid of them by voting for the other person, it's that simple! Just imagine how much better off we all would have been if we'd only been able to give Peloski and Romano the boot once we decided we weren't happy with the job *they'd* been doing!!

"Lastly, my dear friend and brother in arms, Daniel Washington, shared something very, very important with me, something that he made me swear I'd share with you once we achieved this victory. Daniel believed our ancestors who lived in the times before and during the Great Schism had been foolish, reckless even, in how they governed this great nation. He believed The United States came apart because they had completely and miserably failed in their obligations to themselves, to their families, and to their nation. They failed to hold the country together because they were selfish, egotistical, and close-minded, trying to make the entire nation fit into a single ideology.

"The country's leaders of that time completely overlooked or ignored the elasticity that the founding fathers had built into that magnificent document, the Constitution of the United States, the very document upon which the framework for our government was built. The founding fathers had believed that individual states, which would function a little like zones, would have significant autonomy from the central or federal government, placing far more discretion in the hands of local and state governments. Which meant that the people living in those cities and states decided how they wanted to live, not politicians and bureaucrats who were part of a bloated, centralized government. Our forefathers, however, had gradually ceded far, far too much authority to the central government, gradually *stealing* from the local and state, and thus, *from the individual*, and giving that power to the central government. This is what Daniel believed led to the Great Schism, the Second Civil War, and the Red and Blue Zones.

"Daniel didn't want to see us succeed in this revolution

only to fall back into the same mistakes our ancestors made. So, after considering what happened before the Great Schism, he developed a very basic set of principles, which he believed, if expanded and developed properly, could help us avoid the same mistakes made by our ancestors. He believed that these principles embodied the 'spirit' of what the founding fathers had already built into the Constitution, by limiting the powers of the central or federal government and ceding the rest to the states. His hope was that these principles, if applied when we reconstitute our government, could provide a means for Americans to avoid repeating the mistakes of our ancestors. Please listen carefully, and I will share with you Daniel Washington's Seven Principles of Peace....

The Seven Principles of Peace

The two provinces or zones will be divided back into states according to pre-Schism borders.

The Seven Principles

First Principle — *Keep most laws local.*

Laws, regulations, and decisions impacting the lives of everyday Americans should, to the greatest extent reasonable and practical, be implemented at the state or local level, and *not* the Central, or Federal level.

Over time each state should endeavor to develop and promote a lifestyle and way of living that will appeal to a common group of people.

Every incentive and accommodation should be made for relocation to a more suitable state when a citizen decides they are no longer content to abide in the state in which they have been living.

Second Principle — *Limit the Role of Central Government.*

The role of the Central Government should be considerably more limited than it was before the Great Schism, with each American forever remembering the great cost that was paid when it grew too large.

The Central Government:

Much of what the Central Government did before the Great

Schism will be pushed down to the states when reasonable and practical to do so. Otherwise, it will remain with the Central Government.

Any national law that impacts the states requires a 2/3 approval by the states, and can be overridden at any time by a clear majority of 2/3 of the state governments.

Most laws will be passed and enforced at the state level.

Third Principle—*Citizens should be free to choose the state they wish to reside in based on their beliefs and values.*

Fourth Principle—*Citizens should be free to travel between the states, provided they understand and abide by laws and regulations of the state they are traveling through.*

Fifth Principle—*States and/or citizens may appeal to the Central Government when arbitration is necessary.*

The Sixth Principle—*Each state must do everything possible to resolve disputes peacefully and amicably with other states.*

The Seventh Principle—*States that fail to abide by the Sixth Principle will be subject to penalties, including but not limited to economic boycotts and in extreme cases, the dissolution of the state government and the immediate election of a new state government in each of the disputing states.*

The dissolution of a specific state government requires eighty-percent of all other state governments to concur.

"My friends, the path to a brighter tomorrow lies before us. For the first time in a hundred years we are free. While there is no guarantee that we will be any more successful than our ancestors this time around, we have at least two advantages that they didn't have; history, and the seven principles.

"We *know* the mistakes they made that led us into a second civil war and down a path that literally divided our country into two parts, and we've suffered for their mistakes for generations. These mistakes cost our country dearly—they cost each and every one of us dearly—and we will not...I say again, we *will not repeat* those mistakes. This time, all of our focus must be on what *unites* us as New Americans, and not on what separates or divides us. No longer will we argue over our differences but rather, we will collaborate on what we agree on, and we will build from there. We must begin *and* end with the premise that each and every one of us are New Americans, and that must always be something that *all citizens* hold dear. People immigrating here must leave their old country and culture behind them, or they *cannot* seek citizenship here.

"Furthermore, any citizen charged by the government of working against the best interests of New America risks losing his or her citizenship, whether natural born or naturalized, if found guilty. We must once again be one nation and one people, united, under God, if we are to endure.

"I promise that as we move forward with rebuilding this *New* United States of America, we will also review and implement as much of General Washington's *'Seven Principles of Peace'* as possible, and we will do everything we can to build a better, brighter, safer, and more prosperous future for all New Americans.

"I close by repeating something Daniel quoted once in one of his early broadcasts, with *one* modest change. It was important then, and it's even more important now. It was from the preamble of the Constitution of the United States of America.

"*'We the People of the **New** United States, in Order to form a more perfect Union, establish Justice, insure domestic Tranquility, provide for the common defense, promote the general Welfare, and secure the Blessings of Liberty to ourselves and our Posterity, do ordain and establish this Constitution for the **New** United States of America.'*

"Good night, may God bless you, and may God bless the New United States of America."

EPILOGUE

We called it the Re-Unification Doctrine, and it worked beautifully. The Seven Principles of Peace were implemented much as Daniel had envisioned, in order to give people the opportunity to live as close as possible to the way they saw as good and right to live, with the power of the national government considerably more restrained, filling those critical and vital roles so necessary to the success of any thriving nation.

We were able to rebuild the country far more rapidly than I'd ever thought possible, with significant progress made within the first three years. Whether it was the pent-up energy, the exhilaration of freedom after so many years of oppression, the unleashing of capitalism and opportunity for people to achieve and become whatever they wanted, the highly advanced technology, or the assistance from some of the genetically-engineered intellects we still had floating around, it's hard to say for sure. But man, did the country grow like gangbusters.

I *was* re-elected president six months later, during the first open election in the country for over a hundred years. A beautiful new Capital Building was soon rebuilt for Congress, and by the time that first open election rolled around Puerto Rico became America's 51st state, yet another first in a long and growing list of firsts. Soon, all fifty-one states had governors, and most states had many of the mayors and city councils they needed elected. New Americans were flocking to churches, *real* churches, all over New America again, as people were free to once more worship the same Judeo-Christian God the founding fathers had worshipped.

No one knew, of course, how long this newfound democracy might flourish this time around. I could only tell our friends and family, when asked, that Vanessa and I, along with our four children (including little Sebastian, of course) were having a great time, and that we were especially enjoying our brand new White House.

It became tradition in our home to pray for New America every day with our children. Sometimes, as we prayed together, Vanessa and I might peek open our eyes just long enough to sneak a glimpse of Sebastian for a moment, and the comforting feeling that our dear friends Daniel and Kayla were finally at peace.

About the author:

Jeff W. Horton was an Information technology professional for twenty-five years before deciding to pursue his lifelong dream of being a writer. Since becoming an author and screenwriter blending Christian Fiction and Contemporary Fiction, Jeff has written two screenplays and eight published novels in several genres including apocalyptic-fiction, science-fiction, religious fantasy, and romance thrillers.

His current list of works includes:

-Heaven's Oasis
-New Beginnings
-Frontiers
-Cybersp@ce
-The Last Prophet
-The Way of Nacor
-The Dark Age
-The Great Collapse

When he's not penning his next novel, Jeff enjoys spending time with his family, going to church, and reading. Among his favorite authors are many immediately recognizable names including Sir Arthur Conan Doyle, H.G. Wells, Jules Verne, Edgar Rice Burroughs, Michael Crichton, Tom Clancy, C.S. Lewis, Ted Dekker, and J.R.R. Tolkien. Jeff Horton is a member of the North Carolina Writers Network.